GALATIA ROAD

by

Henrietta F. Ford

Henrietta F. Ford

However, Seaboard, North Carolina is real. It is my hometown.

ISBN Number: 9781475148183

Henrietta F. Ford's North Carolina Mysteries

Galatia Road

The Grave House Guest

Murder on the OBX

Other Books by Henrietta F. Ford

Angels in the Snow

When Sleeping Dogs Lie

The Hessian Link

Acknowledgements

I would like to extend my deepest appreciation to:

Jim Maus, my husband. I thank you for your help and encouragement without which I could never write mysteries.

Linda Eccleston, friend and fellow author. I extend my sincerest gratitude for your time spent in reading and making suggestions for this book.

Trust no Future, howe'er pleasant!
Let the dead Past bury its dead!
Act---act in the living Present!
Heart within, and God o'erhead!

Excerpt "A Psalm of Life"

Henry Wadsworth Longfellow (1807-1882)

To My Son:

Reginald Scott Maus

"Scott"

Prologue

A bald, well-dressed man looked down from the window of the high-rise office building. He found the view exhilarating. Cars, taxis, buses, police cars looked like mechanical toys as they raced about on the streets below. An enormous billboard that declared the city *Home of the 2008 MLB Champions* appeared minuscule from his vantage point. He watched a young man dressed in a long sleeve shirt and flashy tie dart across the lane of oncoming traffic. An angry taxi driver thrust his fist out the window and shook it menacingly at the guy's recklessness. The jaywalker ignored the gesture and rushed to join the lunch crowd milling around in front of a deli that boasted '*The best Philly Cheese Steak Sandwiches in the City*'. Beyond the busy streets flowed the Delaware River where sailboats and fishing boats vied with tug boats and barges for the waterways.

The watcher was mesmerized by the silent activity below. He drew energy from the electricity and human dynamics of the frenzied scene. He was a tall slender man of about fifty. His head was as bald as a bowling ball, and his wardrobe bore witness to money and power. He wore a finely tailored navy blue suit, crisp white shirt, and platinum Rolex. His hand-painted tie was a blend of reds and oranges and his hand-sewn leather belt matched perfectly his Italian shoes.

His office was fashioned of shiny chrome, ebony wood, and black leather. A chrome wet bar stretched across one wall of the room, and a large stuffed black couch and matching chairs stood in front of it. At the opposite end of the room was a glass-top ebony executive desk with a high-back black leather chair. Four black leather straight-back chairs faced the desk.

After a while the bald man turned away from the window, walked to his desk, and sat down. Two men sat silently in the straight back chairs and waited for him to speak. One man looked to be about forty-five or fifty years old. He had a thin greasy comb-over and wore a badly fitted off-the-rack, tan suit. He was nervous and jiggled his leg so vigorously that it was almost audible. His eyes were fixed anxiously on the man behind the desk.

The other man was younger. He wore faded jeans, a leather jacket, and badly scarred motorcycle boots with run-over heels. He was a dour-looking young man and slouched quietly in his chair casually cleaning his nails with a pocket knife.

The man behind the desk cleared his throat. Immediately Comb-Over anxiously leaned forward. Faded Jeans simply snapped his pocket knife closed and stared unblinkingly at Bald Man.

Finally Bald Man spoke, "Okay. Let's talk about what we've got here." He looked from man to man. "So you're telling me that our guy over at *Confidential Observer* thinks one of them smut reporters is snooping around in our business. Planning to make a name for herself writing an article about the…ah…ah… *real* nature of our business. Just how much she got?"

Comb-Over leaned forward in his chair, cleared his throat, and said in a shaky voice, "Our source doesn't know. He just said she's been given the go-ahead to write an exposé…"

"An exposé? Damn!!! Where's she getting her information?" demanded the man behind the desk.

Comb-Over cringed. Then speaking softly he said, "It's thought that she has a contact here…in the business."

"What the ..?" shrieked Bald Man. "I thought we covered that. Thought we had protection against this kind of crap when we put a man *over there*. Now you're telling me *they're* playing the same game. They have their own stoolie *here*. Who does our guy think the snitch is?"

"He doesn't know," groaned Comb-Over.

"Doesn't know. Doesn't know. What *does* he know?" Bald Man shouted. He threw down his pen and it bounced across the desk. Comb-Over shrank back in his chair. Then Bald Man leaned across the desk and said threateningly, "What does he think we're paying him for? Doesn't sound to me like the man's very reliable."

"He's never let me down yet," Comb-Over said cautiously.

"Well, hasn't let you down *yet* doesn't translate into reliable. How long's he been sitting on this?"

"Oh, he wasn't holding anything back," Comb-Over stammered. "He just found out about it today...through office gossip."

"Office gossip!" shouted Bald Man. "Christ! What's going on here... teen age tittle-tattle?"

Bald Man rocked back in his chair and rubbed his eyes with the heel of his hands. Finally he sat up, leaned forward again, and looked Comb-Over straight in the eye. "Okay. Here's what you gotta do. First, find out who the hell *her* contact is in our company. Then take care of him...or her. Make it messy, conspicuous. Want lots of news coverage. I want it to be done in a way that it sends a clear message to everybody that we aren't gonna tolerate snitches in our business!"

He paused a long time and drummed his fingers on the desktop. His audience said nothing. Then Bald Man eyed Faded Jeans.

"The other thing we gotta do is get rid of this smut reporter, and that's your job." And he pointed a finger at Faded Jeans. Faded Jeans' expression still didn't change. While Comb-Over was getting his marching orders, Faded Jeans had focused on a piece of spinach stuck between Bald Man's front teeth.

Bald Man continued, "Now here you're gonna have to be more cautious. I don't want the cops digging around in our backyard. I don't care about your method...accident, mugging, burglary gone bad. But I want it to be done

14

someplace else.   Someplace way away from here. Someplace where she won't be connected to our business or to her...er...current assignment."

Comb-over cleared his throat. "Ah-h-h. I might be able to help out here. She does a lot of traveling...tracking down stories and such." He reached into his shirt pocket, took out a small notebook, and flipped to a certain page. "Ah...our source says that she's flying down to North Carolina soon.   To...ah...Raleigh-Durham Airport.   He gave me the date and flight info."

Bald Man tapped his finger tips together and looked thoughtful. "North Carolina, huh? Well that certainly takes her out of our backyard for sure." Then he looked at Faded Jeans. "What do you think?"

Faded Jeans nodded and spoke for the first time. "It's doable," he said.

A look of satisfaction crossed Bald Man's face. He leaned back in his chair, touched his fingertips together, and looked at Comb-Over.   Then he said with satisfaction, "Now *that's* what I mean by reliable."

Chapter 1

The red Sebring Convertible clattered across the railroad tracks, bounced through a few potholes in the road, and finally screeched to a halt at a stop sign. The driver concluded miles ago that all the roads in Northhampton County, North Carolina were alike...narrow two-lane stretches running parallel to dusty fields of corn, soy bean, and tobacco fields.

The driver of the flashy car was an attractive woman who looked to be about thirty. Her short dark hair was stylishly cut in a sleek page, and her teal blue dress complimented perfectly her dark tan. Pink toe nails peeped out of sling-back sandals and several times the shoes had caused her foot to slip precariously off the accelerator or brake.

She glared across the way at a white and black sign that identified the road in front of her as US Highway 301. Now the question was should she turn left or right. She reached for a crumpled map lying on the seat beside her. She snapped it open and laid it across the steering wheel. She spotted the red X pinpointing her destination, Seaboard, North Carolina, but just where was she now? She placed her finger on the X then began to backtrack toward US Highway 301. After close scrutiny she decided she should turn left on 301 and then make a quick zigzag to the right onto 186. That should take her straight to Seaboard.

She was so intent on examining the map that she hadn't noticed a dusty red Toyota pickup barreling down on her from behind. The driver of the truck came up fast, screeched on his brakes, and laid on the horn. The woman shrieked, and her map sailed into the air. Before she could gather her wits, the truck whipped around her car and pulled up beside her. Both occupants of the truck wore dark blue tee shirts with Northampton County High School stamped on it in gold letters. The driver had unruly red hair and looked barely a teenager. His companion, a young man with long blonde hair and just a thin patch of peach fuzz above his lip, was apparently the designated spokesman. He leaned across the driver, poked his head out the window, and shouted, "Hey lady, next time get a car with a GPS." Then the driver, apparently a man of few words, simply flipped her a finger sign, burned rubber, and sped away down US 301.

When her heart stopped racing, the woman clicked on the left turn signal and cautiously pulled onto US 301. After going only a few yards, she signaled right onto

Highway 186 and settled back to relax on the last leg of her trip to Seaboard. She drove into the late afternoon sun, and tall pines cast uncanny shadows on the road.

To her left she noticed a white, wooden building with a cross set on a small bell tower. She pulled onto the side of the road directly in front of the building and began to double check her right turn onto Highway186. A quick look at the map assured her that she had indeed made the correct turn. As she started to pull back onto the road she heard singing, shouting, and wailing from inside the white building. Then she noticed a sign that identified the building as New Jerusalem Church. Apparently a funeral was taking place inside. A matronly-looking black woman dressed in a white nurse's uniform, white shoes, and white stockings stood talking with a group of men under the shade of a sprawling oak tree. The churchyard was filled with large highly polished cars as well as clunkers and battered pickup trucks. A glossy black hearse with a wreath of red flowers fastened to its hood was parked beside the front door. The driver of the red convertible sat briefly in silence in reverence to the funeral taking place inside New Jerusalem Church. She tried to identify the hymn being sung so exuberantly but couldn't place it. After a few moments she pulled back onto the road and sped away impatiently.

She drove pass uncultivated fields, deserted farm houses, and dilapidated buildings. Shattered display windows and billboards advertising products that had not been around for years identified some of the old buildings as abandoned stores. A rusty gas pump missing a hose and nozzle stood in front of a ramshackle gas station, and a corroded metal sign above the entrance to the station recommended that you *Trust Your Car to the Man Who Wears the Star.*

The driver began to have an unsettled feeling at being alone on such a desolate stretch of road. Reluctantly she pushed ahead. Then with great relief, she spotted a sign indicating that Seaboard was only three miles down the road. She breathed a sigh of relief and swore she'd never drive this stretch of road after dark.

Soon a sign welcomed her to Seaboard. She didn't have a map of Seaboard, so she'd have to rely on 'ask and tell'...that is if she ever spotted a living person. She'd passed no cars and seen no people as she drove pass the city limits sign. She smiled when she saw a road sign that demanded a 25 mph speed limit.

Then she saw a traffic light ahead. "I can't believe they'd need a traffic light here," she said. She reached the light just at it turned red. She stopped and used the wait time to study her surroundings. There was one gas station/quick market on the corner. Other than that there were just more deserted houses and a couple of dilapidated warehouses. She looked to the right and spotted buildings just over the railroad tracks. She flipped on the right turn signal.

Just as the light turned green, she heard the warning whistle of an approaching train. She took a right but was abruptly stopped when a railroad crossing arm dropped across the road. The looming locomotive was pulling a long cargo train. It moved at a snail's pace through the town, and the red convertible shook under its vibrations. The driver mindlessly counted the cars.

When the train finally cleared the crossing, it was as if someone pulled the curtain on a nineteen fifties' sci-fi movie. The town ahead appeared to be deserted. A gentle breeze lifted a white plastic bag and tumbled it down the empty street. Small puffs of dust spun above the road like swirling dervishes. There was no one on the sidewalks and there were no cars parked along the curb. On the left side of the road was a small brick building. A sign identified the building as Farmer's Bank of Seaboard. The building beside it was vacant. Faded print on the window read Vick's Drugstore. Next to the empty drugstore was another small brick structure. The letters US Post Office were clearly marked on its glass front. Beyond the post office there was another empty building and then a mom and pop market. The sign outside simply read, *Mom & Pop's Grocery.* A torn green and white awning reached across the front of the store providing shade to several baskets of fruits and vegetables. Hand-written cardboard signs identified the contents of the baskets...*Late Season Green Beans, Fresh-Picked Tomatoes, Juicy Peaches, Just Dug Potatoes, White Corn, Picklin' Cukes.*

On the right side of Main Street was a large two-story brick store. A green and yellow John Deere sign hung in front of the store. On a side lot farm implements set waiting to be purchased and put in motion. Beside the John Deere store was another brick building, and the sign painted in the window read Seaboard, North Carolina Town Hall. Also facing the right side of Main Street was a brick store that had once been a gas station. The words Sudsy Laundromat was sprawled in childlike fashion across its window announced the building now had a new function.

Before making the trip the driver learned as much about Seaboard as she could. She'd learned that it was a small town surrounded by fertile farm land in Northampton County, North Carolina. It was an old town dating back to 1751. Settlers from Virginia were attracted by the fertile farm land. They came down, built a small village, and called it Concord. Then in 1832 Seaboard Road (later known as the Seaboard Railroad) was built through their town to connect Portsmouth, VA to Weldon, NC. Townsfolk believed it might be advantageous to change the town's name from Concord to Seaboard to honor the new technology. Unfortunately, the town realized few benefits from this name change, and when trains outlived their hay-day, Seaboard like many other small towns along rail lines declined with the railroad.

The driver parked the red convertible in front of the post office, unbuckled her seatbelt, and threw open the door. As she stepped out of her car she heard a screen door slam. Looking up the street she saw a young woman precariously balancing two large drink cups and two bags of snacks. She wore white walking shoes, light weight gray slacks, a white blouse, and a bright smile.

The driver stepped onto the sidewalk and turned toward the approaching woman. She returned her smile, and waited.

"Hey," the young woman said as she approached the driver.

"Hello," said the driver. "Wonder if you can help me?'

"Why sure will if I can," she said as she steadied the drinks.

21

"I'm looking for the old Blankenship farm. Do you know where that is?

"Why sure. Everybody knows where the Blankenship farm is," she said. Then she turned and looked down the street. "See this street here running pass the John Deere place? This here is Main Street. You go to the end of this street…where the sidewalk ends. Take a left on Elm Street. Go a mile or so. Then just as you're about to pass the city limits sign, you look to the right. That old run-down house and dilapidated barn is what's left of the Blankenship farm. It's so covered with weeds and kudzu you can't hardly see neither one."

The driver looked confused. "I thought the farm was on a road called Galatia Road," she said.

"Was…is," said the girl who was beginning to have trouble holding the drinks. "A while back they changed the names of all the streets and roads in town. Don't know why. Guess they thought it would make things classier."

The driver of the red convertible smiled at the attempt to *make things classier.* "Well thanks," she said and turned toward her car.

"You a Blankenship?" asked the girl as she shifted the bags of snacks.

The driver paused and said, "No, I'm not." Then she quickly slid into her car, backed out, and drove down Main Street.

* * *

The young woman holding the drinks shrugged and walked to a side entrance of the post office. She gave the door a couple of kicks and called, "Hey Irma it's Dr. Pepper time."

"Wait up, Frances," said an impatient voice with an eastern North Carolina accent.

Soon there was a click as the door was unlocked. It opened and the woman in the doorway was dressed exactly like her coworker...gray slacks, white blouse, and white walking shoes. She, however, was not wearing a smile. She was an older woman of about fifty, overweight, with gray hair, and a sour expression on her lined face.

Frances walked to the sorting table in the middle of the room. "Here you go, Irma. Fountain Dr. Pepper in crushed ice with three squirts of cherry juice." She set the drinks and snacks on the table. "You know, Irma, Dr. Pepper comes in a bottle now with cherry juice already in it."

"I know that," said Irma as she tore open a bag of Lay's potato chips. "But it's not as good as the fountain kind."

The two women sat silently for a few minutes enjoying their late afternoon break. Finally Irma said, "Frances who was that woman you was talking to out on the sidewalk a few minutes ago?"

"Have no idea," Frances answered through a mouthful of potato chips.

Irma waited a few minutes and said, "Well what was you talking about?"

"She wanted to know how to get to the old Blankenship farm," Frances said.

"What for?" asked Irma determined to drag out every bit of information from Frances she could.

"I don't know. She didn't say"

Irma munched her chips for a few seconds and then supplied the answer to her own question. "Probably a distant cousin or something," she said.

"No, I asked her that. She said she said she wasn't kin," Frances said.

* * *

The driver of the red Sebring turned onto Elm Street, and as she approached the town limits sign the sky suddenly turned yellow with dust almost obscuring the road. She slowed and spotted a green John Deere tractor moving slowly back and forth in a field as it turned up soil and withered corn stalks. Crows, hundreds of them, blanketed the field. As the tractor approached they took flight, and the sky became speckled with birds rising from the fields. Then they circled back behind the tractor, lit again, and continued searching for food in the chaff from the season's harvest. The tractor driver appeared oblivious to the birds and simply lifted a hand to the driver of the red Sebring. The driver waved back.

The driver's visibility was clouded by the dust, and kudzu vines and other weeds were so thick that she almost missed the dirt path leading to the Blankenship shack and barn. The shack was ensconced behind a stand of scraggly trees. She pulled her car in close to the barn, killed the motor, and sat looking at the place incredulously. A plank placed across a ditch connected the road and a path that led to a shack. Rickety steps led up to a porch that had rotten boards and broken windows. Chards of glass lay on the porch. A door frame that hung by one hinge still held pieces of rusty screen. There was no entrance door. Through cracks between the siding boards it was possible to see from one side of the shack to the other. It appeared to have only two rooms and a large rock fireplace.

She wasn't sure how long she sat there, but the sun began to set in the western sky and the glow of the setting sun through the dust created the appearance of a fiery furnace. A gigantic black crow perched on the precipice of the barn like a jet black statue and cawed menacingly at the woman in the open car. There was a definite ghost factor about the place.

"So this is where it all began?" she said aloud. Then a crunching sound caused her to look in the direction of the path. Soon she relaxed as she remembered the crows scratching and cawing in the field. Then she heard it again. It was the crackle of footsteps on dry grass.

Chapter 2

With impending nightfall a serene silence settled on Seaboard. Farmers were home from the fields. Housewives were at last resting in their recliners. And children sat at kitchen tables, homework in front of them and one eye on the television.

Dusk soon turned to dark and lights began to blink on along Main Street. Peace and quiet settled on all the houses...except one. It was a small white frame house with a wrap-around porch and gingerbread trim. There was a detached garage in the back, and both house and garage were in dire need of repair. Steps leading to the porch were missing planks. Dirt dobbers had plastered the corners of the porch with muddy clots. Pieces of gingerbread trim hung precariously from the eaves of the house, and out back the garage roof was propped up by two by fours. Continuous banging of a hammer, occasional buzzing from a power saw, and the sound of country music emanated from the house.

The interior of the house resembled a warehouse more than a home. Large taped boxes and moving barrels stood unopened. A sofa and a few chairs were placed haphazardly about. A metal kitchen table and two kitchen chairs were in the front hall. The table held a pile of carpenter tools and a stack of dirty coffee mugs. Cartons from carry-out meals were strewn about. In a back room were a cluttered desk, a pile of dirty clothes, and an unmade bed.

Dillon, the man responsible for all the racket, was the town policeman. He squatted beside a fireplace hammering a strip of mantle frame securely into place. Beside him was a taped-up box, and on the box were several tools, a cell phone, a radio, and two Smith and Wesson 38 revolvers that fit snuggly into the holsters of a gun belt. As he paused to eye his work he heard the sound of soft footsteps on the porch steps and then the screen door opened.

"Hey Little Sister," he said without turning, and he grasped a chisel from atop the taped box.

"Hey yourself, Dillon," Frances said. "You oughta fix those front steps, Dillon. Nobody wants to come in here and break their neck." Frances, dubbed Little Sister, was sister to Dillon's late wife.

"Maybe that's why I haven't fixed them...so nobody'll come in here," he said still not looking at her.

"Brought you some supper. A mess of ribs and fries," she said as she put a carry-out carton on the table.

Dillon said, "You didn't have to do that, Little Sister," he said and turned a hungry eye toward the carton. Then he stood up, and walked to the table.

"Well somebody has to see to it that you eat," she said and joined him at the cluttered table.

Dillon ate hungrily using the paper napkins she'd brought to wipe his greasy fingers. They sat in comfortable silence until Frances lit a cigarette.

Dillon wrinkled his nose in disgust. "I wish you wouldn't do that," he said.

"You sound like Irma," she said and blew smoke away from Dillon.

"Speaking of Irma, how are things going down at the Post Office?" Dillon said as he reached for another rib.

"Okay, I guess," Frances said. "Irma acts like an old stick in the mud, Dillon. Everything is strictly business with her...lessen she's gulping down that fountain Dr. Pepper with squirts of cherry syrup in it."

Dillon said, "Doesn't she know they make Dr. Pepper with cherry flavoring already in it?"

"She knows. But she says it's not as good," said Frances. "She's got her ways about her I'll say...her way or the highway."

"Well, she's got a responsible job there, you know," said Dillon as he piled the last of the bare ribs in the carton and closed the top. "Post Master job requires a responsible person."

"Knew you'd say that," she said. Suddenly she remembered the most exciting event of her day. "Dillon, today this woman stopped me on the street. She was real stylish-like...a snazzy teal-blue dress, swanky shoes. And I loved her hair style. She drove this red convertible. And guess what she asked me?"

"Don't like to guess," said Dillon. "Tell me or not." And he returned to the mantle and began to chisel away at the many layers of old paint.

"Well, she wanted to know where the old Blankenship farm is," Frances said excitedly.

Dillon stopped chiseling and looked perplexed. "That place is deserted and falling down. Why in the world would she want to go there?" Then as an afterthought he answered his own question. "She's probably a relative."

"No. I asked her if she was kin. She said she wasn't"

"Huh," said Dillon and returned to work.

The cell phone rang and Dillon grabbed it, clicked receive, and said impatiently, "Dillon."

At first he just listened intently. Then his expression slowly took on concern…then alarm. He said, "Where are you now?"

There was a pause and Dillon said, "Alright. You stay right there. Don't move around, don't touch a thing, and don't let anyone on the premises. In fact don't let anyone even *near* the premises. I'm on my way."

"What?" asked Frances.

"Little Sister, turn off lights, radio, everything. Then go home. And *stay there*," Dillon said. He reached for his gun belt and buckled it on. Then he grabbed a baseball cap that was stamped POLICE, flipped a badge out of his shirt pocket, and raced out the door.

Frances shouted, "Dillon what?"

* * *

Dillon didn't turn on the emergency lights or siren. That kind of commotion would wake the town and summon the people. Instead he raced the short distance down Main Street and turned left onto Elm. As he approached the town limits sign he saw the bright headlights of a car pointed directly toward the old Blankenship tobacco barn. A porch light was on at the farm house across the road. Three women stood huddled and peered at the scene across the road. A rusty pick-up and a Camry were parked beside the road next to the path that led to the barn and a dilapidated shack. Several men and a teen-aged couple stood huddled together. The teen-aged girl clasped a cell phone firmly to her ear and as she spoke she waved her hand about animatedly. Dillon knew that the Seaboard grapevine was being activated and soon the curious would begin to congregate.

Dillon's car was spotted and the onlookers walked in its direction. Dillon didn't stop but turn sharply onto the path and parked directly behind a car marked POLICE. Dillon threw open his car door and rushed toward a skinny, loose-limb man wearing a tan shirt, tan pants, and a baseball cap with Police stamped on it. The policeman was pacing nervously back and forth at the entrance to the barn where a red convertible was parked.

A man called from the road, "Hey Dillon, what's going on?"

Dillon yelled back, "Don't know. Just got here."

Dillon rushed to the nervous policeman and said, "What we got here Stewart?"

Stewart was as pale as a ghost. Dillon was afraid he was going to faint. Stewart stammered, "What we got here? What we got here? I'll tell you what we got here. We got murder, Dillon. Murder pure and simple."

"Okay, take it easy," Dillon said. He looked back toward the road where several more people had gathered.

"I'm going in. You just keep those people out of here. We don't want evidence destroyed."

Stewart nodded and began backing away from the scene toward the road. He was thankful to be near the living instead of the dead. Stewart was a part-time police officer. His other part-time job was city maintenance... reading the city's water meters, mowing the grass on the shoulders of the town streets, and caring for the Seaboard Cemetery grounds. He'd never considered that his part-time police job would actually require him to deal with dead people...not in Seaboard.

Dillon walked toward the red convertible that stood in front of the barn entrance. He remembered Frances telling him about the woman who asked directions to the Blankenship farm. He pointed the flashlight beam at the car. There was a rental car sticker on the back bumper. The driver's door was open and the seat was spattered with blood. He moved the light to the ground beside the driver's door where there was a large wet circle on the ground. He directed his flashlight beam along a drag track that led to the barn door. He approached the barn door slowly. Drawing one of his guns, he held it in one hand and the flashlight in the other. He didn't have to go far because just inside the barn lay the bloody, lifeless body of a young woman. She wore a teal-blue dress and a pair of swing-back sandals lay nearby. Both were soaked with blood. Dillon carefully stepped closer. He felt her neck for a pulse although this was a mere technicality. Dillon knew no one could survive those wounds and that much blood loss. It appeared that her throat was cut from ear to ear. Then without touching the body he studied her face...or what had

31

been her face. There were only bloody holes where her eyes had been, and there were deep punctures all over her face. Her nose, fingers, and ears were mutilated.

Dillon felt sick. He tasted the ribs he'd had for supper. Not wanting to contaminate the scene he pushed himself up and backed out of the barn. He took several deep breaths, returned to the red convertible, and looked in again. Beside the driver's seat was a small purse. It was open and its contents spilled on the floor. Dillon pulled out a ballpoint pen from his front shirt pocket. He carefully leaned into the vehicle, flipped open the wallet with the pen, and turned it so he could read the name on the driver's license.

"Good God!" he exclaimed.

Dillon backed away from the car. Amid questions being hurled at him from the road, Dillon removed his cell phone and dialed the number of his friend Arlis Bryant, Assistant Director of U. S. Marshal Services in Raleigh.

After several rings an impatient voice said, "Bryant"

Dillon said, "Bryant, I got a problem."

"That can't wait till morning?" said a petulant voice.

"Don't think so, Bryant. Not this one. You see, today a good-looking, expensively dressed young woman driving a red convertible showed up in Seaboard..." Dillon began.

"Well now, Dillon," interrupted Bryant, "I can see why you are so baffled. That *would be* unusual for such a woman as you describe to visit Seaboard of all the places." Bryant snickered at his attempt to make a joke.

Dillon ignored the dig. "This is serious, Bryant. Real serious."

"Sorry, Dillon. Go on," said Bryant.

"The woman was looking for an abandoned farm. Little Sister…"

"Little Sister? Dillon if you want me to take this seriously, stop being flippant."

"Little Sister is my sister-in-law. Hell Bryant, I got a murder here," Dillon shouted. Then he turned to see if the onlookers overheard his outburst.

Bryant's tenor quickly changed. "Again, sorry. Go on," Bryant said.

"Little Sister who works downtown gave the woman directions to a farm. Then tonight I got a call from my part-time officer saying that a red convertible had been parked at the abandoned farm since late afternoon."

"Go on," said Bryant.

"Well Stewart, my officer, investigated and discovered the woman's body in a tobacco barn. She's dead. She's been *mutilated*, Bryant," said Dillon.

When Dillon finished Bryant remained silent finally he repeated, "So how can *I* help you Dillon?"

"Bryant, that's not all of it. I managed to get a look at her driver's license and it's issued to one Nicey Parsons, Investigative Reporter for the *Confidential Observer*."

"Jesus!" exclaimed Bryant. There a long silence. Then Bryant said, "Okay Dillon, just exactly where is this farm located?"

"On Elm Street. It's setting right on the Seaboard city limits. Part of the farm is in my jurisdiction, Seaboard, and part of it's in Northampton County's," he said.

"Have you called the county Sheriff yet?" asked Bryant.

"No. You're the first one I've called. Bryant, can you imagine the publicity this could draw? A national investigative reporter brutally murdered in a little country town in North Carolina. All I've got is me, a part-time policeman, and whatever help the Sheriff can give me."

More silence. Then Bryant said, "Alright here's what you do. First, call the Northampton County Sheriff. He's a real co-operative fellow. Tell him you need help right away to secure the scene before some of your curious citizens compromise it. Don't tell him you've called me until after he gets there. You don't want him to think you called me first. Turf thing, you know. Don't touch or move a thing. Just protect that crime scene from the citizens and from other law enforcement. You're in charge. Hear?"

"Got cha'," said Dillon. Dillon had worked with the Northampton County Sheriff when he first came on the job as policeman in Seaboard. They responded to a disturbing the peace in the projects and ended up breaking up a dog fight. They also found crystal meth, pot, and ecstasy.

Bryant continued, "Now I'm going to send a state crime scene team down as soon as I get off the phone. You can tell the Sheriff that when he arrives at the scene. The team will be there in a couple of hours. Nobody touches that body or anything till they get there. Next I'm going to send two Marshals down. They've been on the road for a while and they're exhausted, but at their worst they're the best. They'll get there right behind the scene guys. We got to try to keep this under wraps till we get a handle on it."

"Yeah, that's what I'm thinking. Thanks Bryant. Maybe when you move the body to Raleigh it'll take the focus away from Seaboard," said Dillon

"I wouldn't count on it," said Bryant.

Chapter 3

A harvest moon shone full and dazzlingly bright. In fact, the moon was so bright it made headlights almost unnecessary. The moonlight penetrated the autumn leaves and tinges of red and yellow dangled from the tree branches. Tall long-leaf pines were silhouetted against the sky.

The only car on this road at one o'clock in the morning was driven by Jeff Sands, U. S. Marshal. Jeff fought to stay awake on the last few miles of his trip home. He drove pass Garner High School, and finally saw the two story farm house in the distance. He turned right off of US 70 and drove up the dusty road to the house where he lived with several other law enforcement officers. There were four vehicles parked under the trees in front of the house, and he recognized all of them. One belonged to Wake County Sheriff's Department, one was a NC State Trooper vehicle, and two were unmarked.

Jeff Sands pulled up beside one of the unmarked cars. He got out of the car and stretched widely. His clothes were crumpled and soiled with greasy stains. His shirttail hung over his belt in several places. His tie was unknotted and hung loosely, and his shirt sleeves were rolled up to his elbows. He reached into the car and grabbed his briefcase, jacket, and canvas bag. He was exhausted after having driven for hours.

After slowly climbing the steps up to the porch he pulled out a key and unlocked the door. The house was cool and quiet. The only sound was the ticking of a mantle clock and the hum of the refrigerator in the kitchen down the hall. He spied his next test...the stairs to his room on the second floor. Slowly, wearily he climbed the steps. He knew he'd made it when he reached the upstairs hall and grasped the first door handle on the left...his room.

He pitched his briefcase and luggage on the chair, stripped off his clothes, and let them drop in a pile on the floor. Then he threw himself onto the bed and immediately fell into a deep deathlike sleep.

* * *

When the alarm went off he couldn't believe it was already morning. He felt like he just fell asleep. He slapped the clock knob and pushed a button for snooze time. Almost immediately the alarm went off again. He hit the knob again. It rang again, and he cursed, sat up in bed, and grabbed the clock. It rang again and again. He shook it until finally reality clicked in. It wasn't the alarm ringing, it was the phone.

He dropped the clock and jerked up the cell phone. "Yeah," he growled.

"Jeff?"

"Um huh."

"Jeff...Bryant. I want you down here as soon as possible," a brusque voice commanded.

Jeff replied tersely, "I just got back from Kentucky at one o'clock. Don't you want to call someone who hasn't been on the road for three days?"

"Jeff, if I'd wanted someone else, I'd have called someone else. So how soon can you get here?'

Jeff looked at the clock. It was six am. He swore silently. "I can make it in...oh forty-five minutes."

"Get here in thirty. Oh, and bring along your sidekick," Bryant said. "And Jeff...pack."

Jeff sat on his bed for a few minutes rubbing his eyes and shaking his head. Then he stood up and headed for the bathroom. He took a cold shower hoping to wake up, and then shaved cutting himself twice. He walked back into the bedroom, kicked the pile of dirty clothes aside, and put the canvas bag on the bed. He threw in socks, underwear, several sweat shirts, toilette articles, a pair of jeans, and a pair of khaki pants. He also took along an extra pair of athletic shoes. He put on jeans, boat shoes, and a gray knit shirt. He strapped on his 357 magnum revolver and pulled on a dark blue zipper jacket with U.S. Marshal printed on the back.

He grabbed his briefcase and bag, quietly slipped out of the room, and down the stairs. When he got to the bottom of the steps he smelled coffee. His stomach growled reminding him that he hadn't eaten since lunch the previous day. He walked to the kitchen. Standing there with a mug of coffee in her outstretched hand was a plump, white haired lady of about sixty five or seventy.

Mrs. Smiley was the widow of a Raleigh, North Carolina city cop. After his death the big farm house they'd lived in for years was suddenly lonely and even intimidating. Then one day a young policeman dropped by to offer his condolences. During his visit Mrs. Smiley learned that the young policeman was recently divorced, very lonely, and needed a place to live. So naturally Mrs. Smiley did what any widow of a law enforcement man would do...she rented him a room with breakfast included. Mrs. Smiley was accustomed to the comings and goings of men in law enforcement and welcomed the return of the hectic, unpredictable lifestyle reminiscent of the happy years with her policeman husband. News of Mrs. Smiley's farm house spread and soon men from various branches of law enforcement inquired of vacancies. Jeff Sands was one of the lucky ones. He got a small, sparsely furnished bedroom with a postage-stamp sized bathroom. In fact, the toilet, sink, and stand-up shower were installed in what had once been a closet. The closet was replaced with a huge old wardrobe.

"Here," Mrs. Smiley said as she held out a cup of coffee. "You'll be needing this." She didn't inquire about how late he'd gotten home or how much sleep he'd missed, or even where he'd been. She'd just said that he needed that cup of coffee.

Jeff took the cup gratefully. "Thanks, Mrs. Smiley."

"Now sit yourself down, Jeff. Your eggs and biscuits are ready."

Jeff sat and practically inhaled the breakfast placed in front of him. After a few minutes, he took out his phone, punched a familiar speed dial, and waited for a pickup.

Soon a gravelly voice said, "What?"

"Buddy...Jeff. Roll out. He wants us in his office fifteen minutes ago," said Jeff.

"What? Didn't he check the assignment roster? Doesn't he know we just got back from transporting a nut-case fugitive who did rap non-stop all the way from Kentucky?"

"He knows, Buddy, and he doesn't care. Now get up and dress. See you at the office ASAP. And Buddy... pack." As he clicked off, Jeff heard Buddy swear.

Buddy lived in a small apartment in Raleigh, on Hillsborough Street across from St. Mary's School for young women. His place was not far from the offices of U.S. Marshals on New Bern Avenue. Buddy Turner was single and still very new to the job. At first Jeff had doubts about the young Marshal. Buddy was at times unsure of himself and impulsive. But Buddy was bright, dependable and enthusiastic, and he had an intuition that was valuable for anyone in law enforcement. He also admired Jeff so much that Jeff found it embarrassing. So Jeff took him on as partner.

* * *

A short time later Jeff Sands and Buddy Turner pulled simultaneously into the parking lot of the Terry Sanford Federal Building and Courthouse on New Bern Avenue in downtown Raleigh. The building was a modern design, low-rise building constructed of steel and concrete. It housed several government offices, a Federal Courtroom, and was headquarters for the United States Marshal Offices for the Eastern North Carolina District.

Theirs were the only cars in the lot at 7:30. They grunted at each other as they fell into step and walked toward the entrance.

"What's he thinking about, Jeff...calling us when we got only a few hours sleep?"

"I don't know, Buddy," said Jeff.

"Where does he want us to go?"

"I don't know, Buddy."

They reached the entrance and Jeff opened the door allowing it to almost slam on Buddy who was still throwing out questions Jeff had no answer to. They reached the elevator, entered, and pushed the button to fifth floor.

On the ride up, Buddy said, "Not a soul around. Just look at this. We're the only ones around."

"I know, Buddy," said Jeff, and the elevator door opened.

They walked down the hall toward the only office that had lights on. Jeff opened the office door, and they were not surprised to see Ms. Cathy Roberson. Cathy always seemed to be there regardless of the time...day or night. She was a striking woman somewhere between thirty and forty years old who had risen quickly from a job in the steno pool to the position of private secretary to Arlis Bryant, one of the Assistant Directors of U.S. Marshal Services at the Federal Building. Cathy had blue eyes and shoulder length natural blonde hair. She was slim and her skin looked like porcelain. Her makeup was always impeccably applied. She dressed tastefully usually in two piece suits. Her skirts were slightly above her knees and usually had a sizable slit in the back that widened as she took long strides across the office. Underneath her jacket her blouses were unbuttoned at just the right spot to show a hint of cleavage. She always wore heels with stockings...summer and winter. And her stockings hugged remarkably shaped legs.

Cathy looked at Jeff and Buddy indifferently as if their early morning arrival was their idea. Then in an impatient voice said, "He's waiting for you."

Cathy walked around her desk and passed the Marshals. "This way," she said, as if Jeff and Buddy had never been in Arlis Bryant's office.

She opened the door and announced, "Jeff Sands and Buddy Turner to see you Mr. Bryant." Then she stepped aside and allowed them to enter. "Will there be anything else Mr. Bryant?"

"Yes, Ms. Roberson. How about making us some coffee and run down some of those pastries...you know the kind that has apple in the middle and a white sugary glaze squirted across the top."

"Right away, sir," she smiled and slipped quickly through the door.

Bryant grinned and looked at Jeff. "Lady takes real good care of me."

"I can see that," Jeff said returning the grin.

Bryant sat behind an enormous mahogany desk in an enormous built-to-order chair. To say that Bryant was fat was a gross understatement. He had a humongous round face, practically no neck, and a shiny balding head with a bad case of dry scalp. He had pink cheeks and tiny red veins showed through the thin flesh on his nose. His ears were red and pinned so tightly against his head that he appeared to have no ears at all. His hands and fingers were so fat that the flesh seemed to be growing over his University of North Carolina class ring. His height measured about six two and the first number of his three-digit weight had to be a three. When he walked he wobbled in such a way that he'd been dubbed *Walrus*.

"We got ourselves a real celebrity this time, guys," he said. "Ever here of Nicey Parsons?"

Jeff looked thoughtful and after a few seconds said, "Nicey Parsons. Nicey Parsons. Why does that sound familiar?"

Bryant picked up a newspaper and tossed it across the desk. "Because she's a so-called investigative reporter for a smut-rag called the..."

Buddy almost sprang from his chair. "*Confidential Observer?* Sure. I remember her. Nicey Parsons covered that story on the walking fish," he said. Now he was on the edge of his chair. "You see there were all these rumors about a fish that could come right up out of the swamp, walk across the road, and jump back in the swamp on the other side. Nobody believed the story until Nicey Parsons went down to Florida and actually took pictures of the thing walking across the road." Buddy paused to allow for the full impact of what he'd said. Then he nodded and continued, "Yeah, she did. The picture was right there on the front of the *Confidential Observer*...big as life...a walking fish." Bryant and Jeff gawked at Buddy as if there were a fish walking out of his ears.

At that point Cathy Roberson entered carrying a large tray with three steaming mugs of coffee and three apple streusel pastries on small plates. She set mugs, plates, napkins, and a fork in front of each man. Bryant's eyes opened wide, as he looked hungrily at the pastries.

Cathy cooed, "Do you need anything else Mr. Bryant?"

"Huh? Oh...not right now, Ms. Roberson," he said and grinned widely. She grinned back and glided out the door.

Bryant ignored the fork, picked up the pastry with his fingers, and got half of it in one bite. Buddy and Jeff ate slowly and waited for Arlis Bryant to finish eating and brief them on just why they were there.

They didn't have to wait long. Arlis Bryant brushed his hands together and through a mouthful of pastry said, "Nicey Parsons was found dead in a deserted barn. Her throat was cut ear to ear. Bleed to death."

"Sounds like it could be a professional," said Jeff.

"That's my thoughts," mumbled Bryant spraying pastry crumbs onto his desk. "And Jeff, this brings me to why I called you two in for this particular job."

"I was wondering when you'd get around to telling us why we're lucky enough to get this one after driving in from a three day non-stop trip to Kentucky and back."

"Well, I got a good reason for that," said Bryant. "You know the territory, Jeff. Nicey got herself killed in your stomping grounds...Northampton County."

Suddenly Jeff was wide awake. "Where?"

"Right there in your old hometown, Seaboard," Bryant reached for a yellow legal pad, "on a street called Elm Street. Say...wasn't there a horror movie about murder on Elm Street,"

"Yeah. I know the street...the one in Seaboard that is," said Jeff. "Used to be called Galatia Road. When I was a kid I drove down that road many times on the way to Bullock's Pond, a favorite party place for teenagers."

Bryant was flipping through his yellow pad. "Body was discovered about ten-thirty tonight...or last night. As soon as Dillon identified the body and realized that it might be a professional hit I got a call. He knew this would be too explosive for him to handle alone. I've already sent down a crime scene team. "

"So what do you want us to do?" Jeff asked.

"Go down. Check out the scene. Talk to folks, and evaluate the situation," said Bryant. "When you get a read on things... call me. We'll go from there."

"Good," said Jeff and he stood up. "Well, Buddy, let's hit the road...again." And they walked toward the door.

"Oh, and ask Ms. Roberson to step in here," Bryant said.

"Sure," Jeff said as he closed the door.

Cathy Roberson was leaning against an open drawer of a file cabinet. She gave the men a disinterested look as they walked out of Arlis Bryant's office and did not acknowledge them.

Jeff grinned, looked at Cathy, and said simply, "He wants you."

Cathy Roberson lifted her chin, turned abruptly, and walked into Bryant's office.

"What do you suppose she sees in him?" Buddy whispered as they walked into the hall.

"I don't know Buddy," said Jeff.

"Do they think nobody knows?" asked Buddy.

"I don't know Buddy," said Jeff

They reached the elevator, pushed the down button, and waited. "She's so pretty and slim, and he's so...so...," Budd persisted.

"Don't go there, Buddy," Jeff said as the elevator door opened. They stepped into the empty elevator and pushed the button for ground floor.

"But how do you suppose they..."

Jeff held up a hand in the stop position. "Whoa. Don't even *think* about going there, Buddy."

The door closed and the indicator light moved steadily down.

Chapter 4

Buddy took his turn at the wheel. He pulled out of the parking lot, turned right onto New Bern Avenue and made their way toward Highway 64. Soon he accessed I-95 and they settled in for a long boring drive that would eventually get them to Seaboard.

Jeff laid his head back on the seat, closed his eyes, and decided to get some sleep. It had always been hard for Jeff to sleep while riding in a car. That's why he usually ended up driving. Then Buddy roused him just as he started to doze off.

"Say Jeff, have you ever noticed that Bryant is all times doing for Dillon? Like special favors or something," said Buddy.

Jeff didn't open his eyes but answered, "Bryant thinks he owes Dillon."

"*He* owes *Dillon*?" said Buddy with surprise.

"Yeah," Jeff said. His eyes still closed.

Buddy waited a while and then said, "What for? I mean what did Dillon ever do for Bryant?"

"He saved his life," said Jeff.

"Really? How did that happen?" said Buddy.

Jeff stirred and opened his eyes. It appeared that he wasn't going to get any rest even with Buddy driving. Jeff rubbed his tired eyes and said, "They were just a couple of kids. Bryant and Dillon joined the army in 1989 just in time for the Invasion of Panama. They both admit they were reckless and headstrong. One day Bryant, Dillon, and two other men were trying to take a building. Bryant got hit real bad. The other two men were killed. Dillon risked him own life to pull Bryant to safety. Bryant was losing blood bad. Dillon did a tourniquet and stayed with him till help arrived. Dillon received an award for bravery and undying appreciation from Bryant."

"Holy cannoli," said Buddy. "I can't believe it! The Walrus saw combat?"

"That was years ago. I doubt he was a walrus then," Jeff said.

"So by coincidence Bryant and Dillon ended up right here, in all places, Raleigh, North Carolina?" asked Buddy.

"Not strictly by coincidence," said Jeff. "After they got out of the army, they didn't see each other for awhile. Dillon went home to Okalahoma. He got a job chasing bail skips for a bond office, and Bryant went to work here as a U.S. Marshal out of Raleigh. Then Dillon fell on real hard times. Lost his job and couldn't find another one. Meantime Bryant moved up in the U.S. Marshall Services. He heard about Dillon's trouble, contacted him, and urged him to come to Raleigh. Bryant remembered Dillon had talked about wanting to be a State Trooper, so Bryant got him in the program. Later he helped him get assigned in the Raleigh area."

Buddy didn't say anything for a long time. Jeff thought he'd finally satisfied his curiosity so he laid his head back again to sleep.

But Buddy wouldn't let it go. He said, "You know, Jeff, this gives me a whole new take on Bryant. I never thought he had a sympathetic side to him."

"We all got sides people don't know about," said Jeff.

"Yeah, I guess so," said Buddy.

Jeff closed his eyes again, but Buddy pushed on. "Jeff," he said, "how'd Dillon end up in a place like Seaboard?"

"Alright, Buddy," said Jeff who was irked at not being allowed to rest. "Now listen. I'll answer this one question and then no more.   OK?"

"Yeah sure. Don't have to get all riled up about it," Buddy said obviously offended.

This time Jeff spoke rapidly and not so abrasively, "Okay, here's how it was. While Dillon was a trooper in Raleigh he met a woman, Janet. The woman was from Seaboard but working in Raleigh. They fell in love and got married. Shortly afterward she was diagnosed with cancer, and eighteen months later she died. Janet always dreamed of going home...back to Seaboard. She wanted to buy her old home place, and renovate it. I suppose out of grief and as a tribute to Janet, Dillon decided to fulfill her dream. He quit his job as Trooper, moved to Seaboard, and bought her old home place. He's fixing it up. Bryant also helped him get the job as Seaboard policeman and that's the end of the story of Dillon and Bryant. Satisfied?"

"Yeah. Was that so hard?" said Buddy. He paused briefly than muttered, "Still can't see moving back to Seaboard. That town seems like it was trapped in a time warp. It is one *boring* place."

Jeff had had it. He sputtered heatedly, "Ever occur to you, Buddy, that what's boring to one person might be just...just peaceful-like to another? Now shut up so I can sleep."

But sleep didn't come that easily. Now Jeff's mind traveled back to a time when his world barely extended beyond Seaboard.

Seaboard was a small town where everybody knew everybody else. People went to bed early and got up early to work from dawn to dust on the farms, in the filling stations, and in the small grocery stores. Then at night old men sat on their porches, watched cars drive pass, and sipped bourbon with thin slices of orange in it. Women talked endlessly on the phone about their day which was always like the one before. Adults felt a responsibility to scold any child who didn't 'behave themselves'.

Then one summer Jeff's whole young existence was turned upside down. Something amazing happened. He noticed that a scrawny little girl who lived in a big yellow Victorian house, across from the Methodist Church, on Main Street suddenly developed into a budding beauty. Her name was Sophie Singletary. Ah Sophie...even her name sounded mysterious. For the rest of the summer Sophie and Jeff went everywhere together. They giggled and he kissed her and told her she was the only girl he'd ever loved. She'd say she'd always love him too. But sadly their summer romance ended bitterly, and Jeff suffered the attrition of an unfortunate teen-age love affair.

After graduation Jeff didn't see Sophie for many years later. Then U.S. Marshal Jeff Sands was given an assignment to protect a witness in one of his most treacherous investigations. That witness turned out to be Sophie Singletary. And where did Sophie live at that time? Seaboard of course.

"We're back in Seaboard together again," she'd said simply. "It was meant to be."

"Hey Jeff, Jeff," a faraway voice intruded on Jeff's thoughts. It was Buddy. "We're almost in Seaboard."

* * *

It was early afternoon when they arrived in Seaboard. As they drove through town, they noted small groups of people huddled together talking excitedly. Then the car with U.S. Marshall on the door was spotted.

"It's Jeff," someone shouted and all heads turned and watched the U.S. Marshal car drive by. Jeff was well known in Seaboard and was still thought of as one of their own.

Buddy drove down Main Street, up the hill, pass the Baptist Church, and then the Methodist Church. As they reached the Methodist Church Jeff turned to look at the big yellow Victorian house across the street. There was no one outside but two cars were parked in the driveway. They drove to where the sidewalk ended and turned left on Elm Street. Then Buddy stopped abruptly. The number of curious onlookers had increased exponentially as law enforcement vehicles arrived.

Jeff said, "Use your horn. Dillon needs to clear this road before somebody gets killed."

Buddy tapped the horn. People turned angry faces toward him until they realized it was a U.S. Marshal Vehicle. Then they cleared a path. Several people slapped the car in greeting to Jeff.

"Good to see you, Jeff."

"We got ourselves a mess this time, Boy."

"This here's a bad one"

Jeff nodded in acknowledgement of their assessments of the situation.

Buddy finally reached the path that led up to the barn. Several Sheriff's Deputies had cordoned off the entrance to the crime scene. They waved Jeff and Buddy through, and Buddy drove to the barn. Jeff saw Dillon and Northampton County Sheriff White talking while Stewart paced nervously outside the yellow tape that circled the red convertible. The State Crime Scene Team was still hard at work.

When Dillon and the Sheriff saw Jeff they hurried to the car. As Buddy cut the car engine Dillon extended his hand. "Jeff Sands. I didn't know Bryant was sending you. You don't know how glad I am to see you."

Jeff stepped out of the car and shook Dillon's outstretched hand. "Got a lot going on here, Dillon. Looks like you're on top of it though."

"Don't know about that," said Dillon. "We're just keeping people back and letting the scene guys do their job."

Sheriff White stepped up and held out his hand. "Hey, Jeff," he said. "Good to see you again. Always relieved to see you come on the scene. You don't treat us down here like a bunch of ignoramuses."

Jeff took the Sheriff's hand and smiled. "Good to see you again Sheriff. When do you think they'll let me in?" he said nodding toward the scene team.

"Don't know exactly," said Dillon. "I know they plan to take everything back to Raleigh...the body and the vehicle. I'm glad too. Maybe that'll take some of the heat off us." Sheriff White slapped Dillon on the back. "Ain't gonna happen, Dillon. News folks gonna want to know what she was doing here in the first place. No, I'd say this is just the beginning."

"Do you *know* why she was in Seaboard, Dillon?" asked Jeff.

"Not the faintest idea. Haven't had time to question anybody yet, Jeff.," he jerked a finger in the direction of the increasingly restless crowd.

"Well, I expect most people will go home when they take the body out. Don't worry about it. We'll get started then," said Jeff.

"You're going to help me with the interrogations?" asked Dillon.

"Sure am," said Jeff watching a member of the crime scene put away his equipment.

"That's a relief," said Dillon. "Ah Jeff, this is my first murder case."

"We all had a first, Dillon," Jeff said.

Jeff began walking towards the yellow tape. Then he spotted Stewart, the part-time policeman, still pacing back and forth just outside the cordoned-off area. Stewart was literally wringing his hands.

"Just a minute," said Jeff and he walked over to Stewart. "How you making it, Stewart?"

Stewart jumped like he'd been popped by a rattle snake. "Oh, Jeff," he sputtered. "Didn't hear you come up. I'm doing as best I can. This here's been a nightmare. I don't know what I expected when I signed on to be part-time policeman, but it certainly wasn't nothing like this. Jeff, you should see her face…what's left of it. And her neck. How come anyone would do something like that? You should just see it."

"I'll see it just as soon as the scene guys finish up. Look Stewart, I know this was a shock. I was horrified the first time I saw a murder victim," said Jeff.

"You were?" asked Stewart.

"Sure," said Jeff.

"You always seem to be so calm and cool. I guess I thought you'd always been able to handle this kind of thing," said Stewart.

"No way," said Jeff. "You'll feel differently when we really get into the investigation and catch the bastard."

"Then you think we'll really catch the guy?" asked Stewart.

"I don't think so…I know so," Jeff winked and nodded.

At that moment a member of the crime scene team took down the yellow tape, spotted Jeff, and said casually, "Jeff Sands, come on down."

Jeff slapped Stewart on the back and walked toward the scene. Buddy fell in step. They stepped around the yellow tape and went to the red convertible first. They examined the large dark area where blood had soaked into the ground.

"She must have bled out here," said Buddy.

"Maybe," said Jeff.

Next they searched the driver's side of the front seat.

"Probably cut her in here and then pulled her out," Jeff said.

Buddy pointed to the purse on the passenger's side of the car. "Her bag," he said stating the obvious.

"Yeah," said Jeff. "And there's the billfold containing her driver's license. That's how Dillon identified her."

Jeff popped the glove compartment open and using a pen lifted the documents inside. There were the car rental papers, insurance papers, and registration made out to the rental company. "We need to check with this rental company. See if they can give us any additional information."

They stepped away from the car and Jeff pointed to the sand.

"Sure 'nuff looks like drag marks," said Buddy.

"Yeah, and they lead in there," said Jeff pointing in the direction of the barn.

The men slowly followed the trail toward the barn. Inside smelled stale and musty. And there was the distinct scent of death. As they entered they heard the flutter of wings and angry cawing sounds. Jeff looked up toward the dark loft. He played his flashlight around the rafters. Long poles stretched from one rafter to another. The poles had been used to hang and dry bunches of tobacco leaves.

Perched on the poles were crows. Many big, shiny black crows that squawked noisily in protest of yet another intrusion into their roosting place.

"A murder of crows," Jeff said.

"What?" said Buddy. "You saying that the *crows* are the murderers? Why that's ..."

"No, Buddy. A large flock of crows like that is called a *murder of crows*. Term seems real appropriate here," Jeff said

There near the entrance to the barn was the body of a young woman. Her head was lying in an enormous wet, dark circle of earth. Her dress was saturated in blood and one shoe lay near the body. Her skin was a grayish tone, and her face was a mass of cuts and punctures. In several places the skin was actually torn off. Sockets that had once held her eyeballs were now empty holes. Her earlobes and fingers were mutilated.

"*This* is where she bled out," said Jeff kneeling on one knee as if in reverence to the maltreated body.

"Yeah," said Buddy following Jeff's lead and kneeling to look squarely at her brutally desecrated face. "Good God look at her face. What kind of person would do that to anybody?"

Jeff stood and said, "It wasn't a person who did that to her face, Buddy," said Jeff and he pointed upward, and as he did there was a stark fluttering of wings overhead. "It was them."

"What? You mean..." Buddy looked up at the rafters in horror. "You sure..."

"Yeah. In this case the crows are guilty in the mutilation," said Jeff. "Crows are scavengers. Dead meat of any kind is just another meal to then. They found a body in their roost and just did what comes naturally for them."

"I can't believe it," said Buddy.

"Believe it," said Jeff. "Ask the crime scene guys what they think happened." And he turned and walked away. Buddy hurried after him.

As they exited the barn they blinked into the sunlight, spotted two of the crime scene men, and walked toward them.

"We're gonna pack up now, Jeff," one of the men said. "A tow truck will be here directly to move the car and a van's gonna move the body. We're taking everything to Raleigh. We'll know a lot more once we get 'em there. How about the job the crows did on her face? That's a first for me."

"Then it was the crows?" asked Buddy.

"Yeah, the crows pecked out her eyes, dug at her wounds, and perforated her face but that neck injury was man-made," said the crime scene member.

"Weapon…find any weapon?" Jeff asked the crime scene man.

"Nope no weapon," he said.

"Could she have been garroted?"

"Nope."

"Any guess what was used?" asked Jeff.

"Guess is all I have right now," he said. "Looks like a knife…something like a hunting knife….big with a thick blade. Can't really tell yet. Jeff, we can be more specific when we get her to the lab."

"Yeah, sure. How long had she been dead when you got here?" Jeff asked.

"Oh, when we got here, I'd say about ten-twelve hours. I understand there might be a witness to when she arrived on the scene. Of course she might not have been killed right away, but it could help with a timeline."

"I know," said Jeff. "We haven't had a chance to talk with anyone yet. Find many fingerprints on the car ?

"Lots and lots of fingerprints. The car's a rental. So you'll have lots and lots to work through."

"Great. By the way, I'll need copies of her driver's license picture," said Jeff.

"Sure."

"Thanks," said Jeff.

"Any time." He turned toward van. "We'll give her a smooth, fast ride back to the lab."

"See you back in Raleigh. Maybe you'll know more then."

"I'm sure we will." The crime scene guy turned and walked toward a tow truck that was backing down the path that led to the barn.

Jeff and Buddy walked over to Dillon and Sheriff White. He noticed that Stewart had joined them and appeared calmer.

"Pretty bad, huh?" said Sheriff White.

"You're right there," said Jeff.

They turned and watched as the tow truck loaded the car onto a bed, chained it securely, and slowly drove up the path and onto the road. Then the van that would transport the body to Raleigh took its place. It backed onto the path and down to the barn entrance. Soon a stretcher carrying a black body bag appeared. There was a gasp from the road and then a hush fell over the crowd. The attendants carried the stretcher to the van, lifted the body bag, and placed it inside the vehicle. Then the van slowly made its way up the path to the road and turned left. The crowd parted silently as it passed. When the van reached Main Street and turned right, an audible sigh could be heard as the onlookers returned to their cars relieved to get back to their work.

"What about footprints?" asked Jeff as he knelt on one knee examining the hodgepodge of footprints that covered the scene area.

Dillon knelt beside Jeff and they both stared at the jumble of prints in the sand. "Most of these belong to the scene guys. But they got lots of shots before they came in to work the scene. Mostly they were mine, Stewart's, and kids. Kids come round to play in the barn." Dillon looked up at the rickety old structure and shook his head. "Ain't safe. Ought to be torn down."

"Where did the prints lead?" asked Buddy who stood watching Jeff and Dillon.

"Oh, out to the road, of course, and then some out into the fields," said Dillon.

Jeff and Dillon stood. "I understand a woman phoned this in," he said.

"Yeah, Stewart was on duty then and he took the call," said Dillon nodding toward Stewart.

Stewart stiffened. "Sure did," he said. "I was just doing my nightly rounds when I got a call from Miss Sara Wood. She lives directly across the road there," Now Stewart was more relaxed and became excited. "Anyway, she says that a red car with no top on it turned into the old Blankenship farm road. I says you mean a red convertible and she got real testy and said 'who's telling this?' So I shut up. Miss Sara is like that you know. Real testy."

The men waited patiently. Stewart cleared his throat and continued, "Then she says it's still setting over there. I says 'is it hurting anything?' And she says, 'no but it's been there for hours and the place is deserted'. Well, everybody knows the place is deserted but I says 'how long it's been setting there?" and she says 'since about four thirty'

Now the men were beginning to become a little impatient. "Get to it, Stewart," said Dillon.

Stewart enjoyed having an audience. He knew he had their attention and wouldn't be rushed. He was on a roll and intended to tell it his way. "So," Stewart said "I knew Dillon was busy working on his house and besides it was my time, so I drove on over here to check out Miss Sara's complaint."

Now Stewart's report took on a dramatic bent. He spoke in a whisper, "It was pitch dark when I got here. I didn't have nothing but my headlights and a small flashlight...Dillon we got to get some of those big flashlights. You know the kind I mean?"

Dillon nodded, "Yeah, yeah. Get to it Stewart," he said impatiently.

"Right," Stewart said resuming his dramatic dialogue, "Well, in spite of the darkness I spotted the car right away. I went in to check it out it and saw... *blood*. So much blood." Now his voice was getting shrill and louder. "I never thought I'd ever see that much blood. Then I turn the flashlight on the barn door and...and...saw...saw a...saw something just lying there real still." Now Stewart's voice was beginning to crack.

"Take it easy son," said Sheriff White .

"I walked over to the door and shined my light down and...and..."

"What did you do after you realized it was a body?" asked Jeff.

"I didn't do nothing, Jeff. I mean I didn't touch nothing. I swear. I just ran out of there, called Dillon on my cell, and waited for him to show up. I didn't think he'd ever get here...Don't mean nothing by it, Dillon. I know you got here as best you could but... but..." Now Stewart began to shake again. His newly found confidence was short lived.

"Seems to me like you went by the book," Buddy said reassuringly. "That's exactly the way I'd have handled."

Still shaking Stewart looked at Buddy, nodded, and smiled. "Really? Thanks, Buddy. Thanks."

Realizing they'd gotten all they'd get from Stewart, Jeff said, "Okay, guess it's time to talk to Miss Sara. What did you say her last name is?"

Stewart said, "Wood. Miss Sara Wood. She ain't never been married. Just lives there with her two old maid sisters." He nodded toward a farm house across the road. "She's a crusty old lady, Jeff. Even on her best day she's rude and such."

"Guess I'll take my men and go home," said the Sheriff. "Keep me posted, and if you need us, Dillon, give me a call."

"Thanks, Sheriff," Dillon said. "Okay, Stewart, lead the way. Let's go talk to Miss Sara."

* * *

The four men piled into the Marshals' car thinking that Miss Sara might be alarmed if three vehicles pulled into her driveway at the same time. However, they would quickly realize their fears were unfounded. Miss Sara feared nothing.

Miss Sara Wood's farm house was set back farther from the road than the Blankenship shack. There was a soy bean field on one side of the property and a corn field on the other. There was a small back yard with a kitchen garden and hardly any front yard at all. It was a modest one story farm house that badly needed a coat of paint and repairs. The unpainted front porch floor showed signs of rot and ground could be seen between the planks. There were three straight-back unpainted chairs. Shades were drawn covering the two windows that looked onto the porch. Two large pecan trees were in the front yard and there was not a blade of grass to be seen.

They spotted Miss Sara in the back yard. They watched as she ripped down twine and dead vines that clung to tall poles. Then she gathered the trash into bunches and tossed it into a steel barrel where flames immediately ignited the dry debris. Black smoke billowed from the barrel and a stiff wind blew it across the backyard. Nearby, frightened chickens squawked and fluttered as smoke engulfed their pen. Sara was a big Amazon-type woman. Single-handedly she pulled up a heavy pole that had been driven deep into the ground. Then she effortlessly tossed it onto a tall stack. She was tall and muscular weighing in at about two hundred pounds if an ounce. She had a field hand's suntan, and her arms were covered with deep, large brown sun spots. Her hair was cut short and beads of perspiration glistened on her head She wore bib overalls with a T-shirt, and her biceps were as large as a burly person's thigh. She stopped what she was doing when the car pulled into the back yard.

She pulled a red bandana from her hip pocket, wiped her face, and said, "Well, y'all come on in. 'Bout time you got back to me." She dropped her rake against the tall stack of poles.

The men got out of the car and walked toward Miss Sara.

"Hey Miss Sara," said Dillon. "This is Jeff Sands and his partner Buddy Turner. They're U.S. Marshals. They're going to help us out on this case. We've got a puzzler on our hands."

Miss Sara eyed Jeff. "Jeff Sands," she said. "I remember you from back when you wuz a young 'un. Later you used to speed up and down dis here road. Trying to see how fast you could take Devil's Racetrack weren't you?"

"Yes, ma'am," Jeff said through a wide grin. "Guess I was just lucky not to get hurt." Devil's Racetrack was a treacherous curve on what was then called Galatia Road. Sand often collected in smalls piles on the road and kids took the curve at a high speed hoping the sand would make their car spin out.

"Lucky not to get killed," Miss Sara corrected. "Well I told your mama. Reckon she gave you a whupping, huh?"

"Yes, ma'am," Jeff lied. "Miss Sara, We'd like you to tell us exactly what happened yesterday…starting with the first time you saw the red car."

Miss Sara shrugged. "Ain't that much to tell," she said. "Like I told Stewart here I seen that red car with no top turn into the path to the Blankenship shack. I wondered why anyone would go to that rundown deserted place…expecially a woman by herself."

"Excuse me Miss Sara," said Dillon. "Do you remember about what time that was?"

"Of course, I remember. Ain't nothing wrong with my memory," said Miss Sara.

"Sorry," Dillon said apologetically.

Miss Sara continued, "It was 'bout four or four-thirty."

"And you're sure she was alone?" Buddy asked.

"Sure, I'm sure," said Miss Sara. "If'n somebody had been in there with her I'd a seen them that car not having a top and all."

"Did you see anyone go over there later…after she pulled in?" asked Jeff.

"Not a soul," said Miss Sara.

Dillon said, "How was it that you noticed the car was still over there last night?"

Miss Sara thought for a few seconds and then said, "Me and my sisters wuz a-settin' out there on the porch after supper. Well you know how the moon was as bright as day last night, so I caught myself a-lookin' over thata way, and I saw the car still there. I said to my sisters, 'look that car is still over there'."

"And what did they say," asked Stewart.

"They said 'yes, it sure is'. They don't talk much you know," said Miss Sara.

Jeff cleared his throat, "Then what did you do?"

"Why I called the law," said Miss Sara. She raised her eyebrow and gave Stewart a cross look.

"What time was that Miss Sara?" asked Jeff.

She nodded at Stewart, "Don't you know?" she said impatiently.

Before Stewart could answer Jeff said, "I'm sure he does, but we'd like to hear it straight from you."

Miss Sara huffed. "Well, lemme see. It was 'bout ten o'clock...maybe a little after, I'd say."

Buddy said, "Have you ever seen the driver of the car before?"

"No," said Miss Sara.

"Are you sure, Miss Sara?" asked Dillon.

Miss Sara replied heatedly, "Listen up Dillon, if'n I'd seen her before, I'd remember it."

Jeff said, "Thank you for your cooperation, Miss Sara. If you remember anything else, please give either Dillon or Stewart a call." The men turned toward the car.

"Ain't likely I'll remember nothing else. I've remembered it all," Miss Sara said.

Jeff turned back and said, "Probably you have, but sometimes a witness recalls something that she forgot or thought was unimportant at the first interview. By the way Miss Sara, where are your sisters now?"

"They walked into town. It's just a short piece down the road. They'll be back directly," she said.

Chapter 5

Jeff drove to the end of Miss Sara's drive. Remembering that Dillon and Stewart had cars across the road, he zig-zagged to the Blankenship farm path and cut the motor.

"Miss Sara is one bi-i-i---g woman," said Buddy. "I'd hate to meet her in an alley on a dark night."

"Yeah and cantankerous as a wet hen. But Jeff here he stayed cool just like he wuz a-havin' a nice chat with a fine lady," said Stewart. "How on earth do you keep your cool, Jeff?"

Buddy laughed. "Jeff has that Clint Eastwood thing going for him. Almost never loses it, but when he does...well look out. He's a force to reckon with."

Then Dillon continued the banter, "Jeff you ever say *make my day?*" They all laughed.

After they'd had their fun, Jeff said seriously, "She's gonna be hard to deal with. Never saw anyone so defensive. The question is *why?*"

"She's intimidating alright," said Dillon.

"I still want to talk to those sisters," said Jeff.

"Won't do no good," said Stewart. "Miss Sara does all the talking in that family. Miss Mary and Miss Rebecca just go along with whatever she wants."

"I can understand why," said Buddy.

There was a long silence. Each man was lost in his thoughts. Finally Dillon said, "Jeff, so what do we do next?"

Dillon was exhausted, perplexed, and quite willing to turn over the lead to Jeff.

"Well, since we got nothing from Miss Sara, and it's doubtful we'll get anything from her sisters, I say we look for another witness. Surely someone else saw Nicey Parsons."

"Damn," exclaimed Dillon. "How could I forget? We do have another witness. Little Sister."

"Little who?" asked Buddy.

"Frances. Frances Powell. She's my sister-in-law. My wife always called her Little Sister when they were growing up. It stuck and pretty soon the whole family called Frances Little Sister. How could I forget? How could…"

"Because you've had urgent things to 'tend to, Dillon. You had to think in the moment. Now what about Little Sister?" Jeff said.

"I was working on the house and Little Sister came over to bring me supper. While I was eating, she told me that earlier that day she met a young woman driving a red convertible. She's met the victim, Jeff," Dillon said excitedly.

"Good! Where can we find her…Little Sister?" Jeff said.

"She works at the Post Office in town. She oughta be taking her afternoon break about now," Dillon said looking at his watch.

"Okay," said Jeff. "Let's find Little Sister.

Dillon and Stewart threw open the doors and rushed to their cars. Soon all three cars turned onto Main Street and headed downtown. Jeff looked closely at the big yellow Victorian house across from the Methodist Church. He thought he saw movement in the backyard but accepted it was probably just wishful thinking.

The three law enforcement vehicles pulled up in front of the Post Office simultaneously. Heads turned as Jeff and Dillon hurried inside. Buddy said he'd sit this one out and try to catch a couple of winks.

Irma, the Post Mistress, was standing behind the counter. An elderly lady leaned against the counter on the customer side. She had blue-gray hair, wore an outrageous-looking floral garb, and carried an enormous black pocketbook. Both women were startled when the two men rushed in.

Dillon said, "Hey Irma...Mrs. Bernice. We need to talk to Little ah...to Frances."

Irma soon found her voice and said, "She's gone to get snacks at Mom & Pops. Hope nothing's wrong." Her face took on a worried expression.

Dillon wanted to say *'Nothing wrong. Just the murder of a national investigative reporter right here in Seaboard that's all'*, but instead he simply asked, "She's coming back here, right?"

"Ah, yes," she said and looked at Jeff. "How you doing Jeff? Good to see you again."

"Hey, Irma," said Jeff. "Will you tell Frances we want to talk with her. Outside if that's okay with you."

"Sure. That's fine with me, Jeff," she said. "I'll bet you want to talk to her about that woman in the red convertible. Don't you? I said to Harold last night I'll bet that woman is trouble strutting 'round here like she did. She wouldn't hardly tell Frances nothing. If'n you ask me she's plain stuck-up." Now being stuck-up was an unforgivable breach of Seaboard etiquette. Obviously the woman in the red convertible had not made a good impression on Irma.

"Well, we'll just wait for Frances outside then," said Jeff and smiled as they walked out.

"Ain't that Jeff something?" said Irma.

"Sure is. Sophie Singletary got herself quit a catch. Jeff's a real hottie," the blue haired lady chirped.

"Mrs. Bernice! A hottie? Where'd you get that? Why that's awful," Irma quipped.

"Heh, heh, heh" giggled Mrs. Bernice. "I just call 'em like I see 'em.

* * *

Jeff and Dillon waited patiently in front of the Post Office for Little Sister to come out of Mom & Pop's Grocery with afternoon snacks.

"It really hasn't changed that much...Seaboard that is," said Jeff as he glanced up and down Main Street.

"Really?" said Dillon. "Janet used to say that every time we came here to see her folks. She loved it, you know."

"Yes, I know. I knew Janet and her whole family well. Of course, everybody knows everybody else in Seaboard," said Jeff. "Sometimes that's a problem, but other times...well, it's reassuring."

69

Their reminiscences were interrupted when they heard a screen door slam. They looked in the direction of Mom & Pop's Grocery, and the young woman walking toward them was not the Frances Jeff remembered. The transformation was amazing. Underneath that simple white blouse and baggy gray slacks lurked the body of a full-grown, authentic, desirable woman. She saw Dillon, smiled broadly, and quickened her step. Then she recognized Jeff. The smile disappeared and her step slowed considerably.

"Hey Little Sister," said Dillon. "We've been waiting for you. Irma said you'd be right back."

She reached the two men but her eyes avoided Jeff. "Hey Dillon. What's up?"

"We'd like to talk to you," said Dillon.

Frances shifted the drinks and snacks splashing some of Irma's Dr. Pepper with cherry juice on her white blouse. "Damn," she said and looked down at the liquid that was already being absorbed into her blouse and bra.

"Here let me help you," said Jeff and he drew out a handkerchief, leaned toward Frances' blouse, and then realized the awkwardness of the situation. He immediately withdrew his hand.

"No thanks," Little Sister said without looking at Jeff. "I got to go inside. Irma will pitch a conniption fit if I'm gone too long."

As she turned toward the Post Office the door on the Marshal's car opened and Buddy bounced out. He quickly joined them, and he was grinning ear to ear.

Jeff still felt embarrassed. He said, "Little…ah…Frances this is my partner Buddy Turner. Buddy… Frances Powell."

Buddy shifted from one foot to the other. "How you doing?" he said.

Frances blushed and grinned. "Fine. Just fine. Well, I best be getting on…"

Jeff stopped her. "Frances, we need to question you as a witness in a murder case. The murder of Nicey Parsons who died last night at the Blankenship farm. Would you come with us please?" He sounded official and looked dead serious.

"Frances' mouth dropped, and she looked at Dillon. "Is he serious?"

"As serious as a heart attack," said Dillon.

Next she looked at Buddy. Buddy simply nodded his head.

"Well, I best take these snacks inside and tell Irma what's going on," she said and started to the side door of the Post Office. Then as an after thought she turned and said, "Where 'bouts you gonna question me?"

"Just over to the office," said Dillon.

"Okay," she said and kicked the side door. "Hey Irma, open up I'm back."

Irma and Mrs. Bernice had watched Dillon and Jeff as they talked with Frances but couldn't hear what was being said.

"Well, Frances," said Irma as she opened the door. "What do they want? What did they say?"

"And don't leave a thing out," said Mrs. Bernice leaning over the counter so far that Frances thought she'd tumble into the sorting room.

Frances walked to the sorting table and set down the drinks and snacks. Then she turned and said in an imposing voice, "Well, they want to question me as a witness in the murder of Nicey Parson out at the Blankenship farm. I have to give an official statement."

"*Official statement?*" Irma repeated with alarm.

"Yes," Frances said nonchalantly.

"*Nicey Parsons?*" Mrs. Bernice reiterated. "Frances, do you know who that woman is? Why she writes trash for that tell-all newspaper, the *Confidential Observer*.

"Yes, I know," Frances said unaffectedly. Then she looked at Irma and said, "I'm supposed to meet up with them in Dillon's office over at Town Hall. Okay?"

Irma was still digesting what Frances told them. "What...what...oh yes, Frances you go 'head. After all it's you civic duty. Here—take your drink and chips with you. They might not give you food."

Frances reached for her snacks, smiled, and said, "I'm not going to jail, Irma. I'm just going cross the street to give a statement." Then Frances was gone leaving both women with their own thoughts.

"Oh Lord," said Irma. "This kind of thing don't suppose to happen in a town like Seaboard."

Mrs. Bernice muttered, "How in the world did Frances get herself mixed up in this? And with the likes of Nicey Parsons? Frances's got no business talking to strangers on the street."

* * *

The Seaboard, North Carolina Town Hall was an old two-story brick building that had once been a grocery store. The second floor was used for storage and the first floor was used for city government business. It was one large open space divided into sections by wooden rails that gave only the illusion of privacy. The front section of the room was largest. Portraits of former mayors stared judiciously from the walls of the front section. Several metal chairs had been dragged into the middle of the area and were occupied by some citizens who had come into town to discuss church, politics, and the gruesome crime out at the old Blankenship Farm. Extra metal chairs were still folded and rested against the wall. The rest of the room was partitioned into specific spaces. These spaces accommodated people who took care of the town's business. There was a space for Harvey Clinton, the town clerk who handled tax collection, sale of cemetery plots, water bills and other money matters. Then there was a space for the Mayor who showed up every day to rub elbows with the citizenry. And there was the space for the town policeman, Dillon. It consisted of a cluttered desk, a chair, a battered four-draw metal file cabinet, and a telephone.

Dillon parked in front of the Town Hall in a space that was posted *City Police.* Stewart took the spot next to Dillon that was also posted *City Police.* Jeff took the next place. It wasn't posted. The men got out of their cars, walked up to the Town Hall entrance, and went in.

73

Dillon looked at the men in metal chairs in the front section of the room. "How you doing gentlemen? This here is Jeff Sands and Buddy Turner. They're U.S. Marshals so watch your language."

"Hell, we know Jeff," said a crusty old man wearing overalls and work boots. "We wuz wonderin' when they'd be a-bringin' in the cavalry. Hee, hee,"

"Not that we think Dillon and Stewart cain't handle the job," a clean-shaven man wearing a short-sleeve shirt and a straw fedora explained. "But we figured that the more men they put on the job the quicker you'll get to the bottom of this thing."

"Ain't like this sorta thing happens 'round here every day you know," said a big black man also wearing overalls and work boots, "Dillon and Stewart here don't get a lot of practice like you Marshals does."

Dillon, Jeff, Buddy, and Stewart had only been listening with one ear. Their thoughts were on the murder at Blankenship Farm and what to do next. Dillon dragged two more chairs into his workspace and said, "Jeff, how 'bout you and Little Sister sit here, and Stewart drag a couple more chairs in real close to the rail. You and Buddy can sit there. It's not like there's a wall to keep you from hearing what's being said." Then he looked at the three men sitting in the front section of the room. "Excuse me fellas, but we need to question a witness and we need a little privacy. Would you mind…"

Before he could finish the man in the fedora stood and said, "Why sure, Dillon. We wouldn't want to interfere with the law at work. Would we fellas?" The other two men stood, laughed, and they walked out.

"Thanks," Dillon called after them. He glanced out the window and saw Frances bouncing across the street carrying a bag of potato chips and a large fountain drink. When she reached the door to the Hall she was stopped by the three men. Dillon couldn't hear what was being said but he saw the men say something, bend over with laughter, and slap each other on the back. Frances rolled her eyes, looked disgusted, and walked in.

"Give you a hard time, Little Sister?" asked Dillon.

"Nothing I cain't handle," she said. "Brought my afternoon snack. Irma was afraid you wouldn't feed me."

"You're not going to jail. We just want to ask you some questions." It was Buddy who spoke.

Frances rolled her eyes again and said, "I knew that."

"Okay Little Sister, you come in and sit here. Jeff's gonna sit there next to you." Frances moved her chair as far away from Jeff's as possible, turned up her nose, and sat with her back to him. Dillon didn't seem to notice the slight. Jeff smiled wryly. "Stewart and Buddy are in on this interview too. We just didn't have room for two more chairs inside the rail."

Frances nodded and took a long sip of her drink. She glanced shyly at Buddy who was sitting just outside the partition but very close behind her. Buddy flashed her a giddy smile. Frances blushed. Jeff cleared his throat.

Dillon said, "Little Sister I'm going to tape this. When four people are involved in an interview, we sometimes remember four versions of what was said. Is it okay if we tape?"

"Sure," said Frances. "But I'll warn you right now, I sound funny on tape."

"I bet you'll sound fine," said Buddy. Frances looked back at Buddy and blushed again.

Dillon turned on the tape recorder, spoke into the microphone, and stated the day, date, time, and names of those present at the interview with Frances Powell.

After Dillon finished with the preliminaries he turned to Jeff and said, "Jeff?" indicating that Jeff should take over the interview. Frances frowned.

Jeff began, "Frances, why don't you just tell us in your own words about your meeting Nicey Parsons.

Frances sighed and said, "At the time I was talking to her I didn't know she was Nicey Parsons."

"I know," said Jeff. "Just tell us what happened."

Frances' face took on an exaggerated thoughtful expression. After a few seconds she said, "Well, I was just a-comin' out of Mom & Pop's when I saw this strange woman a-gettin' out of a red convertible....."

First she gave an elaborate description of the stranger's dress, her hair style, even her manicure. The men waited patiently. Then Frances related in great detail her conversation with Nicey Parsons. When she finished her statement, she looked expectantly from one man to the other.

Jeff said, "Frances, good statement. Very detailed. Now did you see or hear anything that might make you think someone had been traveling with her?

"Not a thing," Frances said quickly

"Think Little Sister. Did you see a cap or two drink cups or anything that might have been used by a second person," said Dillon.

Frances thought. "I couldn't see inside the car real good. But as far as I could see there wasn't nothing like that."

"Do you have any reason to think that she might have asked someone else for directions to the Blankenship Farm?" asked Buddy.

"Don't see why she'd need to. Directions I gave her to the Blankenship Farm was plain and simple," said Frances avoiding Buddy's admiring gaze.

"What did the car look like?" Stewart asked hesitatingly.

"What do you mean 'what did the car look like'? I done told you it was a red convertible," Frances said impatiently.

"A...ah, I meant was it clean, muddy or what," Stewart said. Then he turned to Jeff and as an explanation added, "Just wondering where all she'd driven that car."

"Good question, Stewart," Jeff said. "Frances, was the car scratched, dusty, muddy? Was there anything to suggest she'd driven off the main roads into woods or fields?"

Frances replied, "Not a scratch or a speck of mud or dust. That car was as clean as a whistle...as far as I could see. Of course, I didn't examine it."

The men finally exhausted their questioning. Dillon spoke into the recorder. He repeated the day, date, and the time the interview was terminated. He reached over to click off the machine when Frances stopped him.

"Wait a minute, Dillon," she said. "I just happened to think of something. When she first asked for directions to Blankenship Farm I told her the farm was on Elm Street."

"Yeah, it is," said Dillon.

"But that's not what she thought," said Frances.

"What do you mean?" asked Dillon.

"She told me she thought the farm was on Galatia Road," said Frances.

"So what does that tell us?" Buddy asked.

"That, Buddy, tells us that Nicey Parsons got her initial information about the location of the Blankenship Farm from someone who may not have known the street name had been changed. Or she got her information from someone who still thought of the road as Galatia Road not Elm Street," said Stewart.

"And that means her source could be someone living here or someone who's not living here now," added Dillon.

Stewart nodded his head with great satisfaction.

"Way to go, Stewart. You deduced that all by yourself," Buddy said and smacked Stewart's back.

"Okay guys, this gives us a whole new dimension to the case," Jeff aid. He stood, rubbed his hands together, and began to pace as much as the small partition allowed. Buddy had seen this expression on Jeff's face many times before. It was the excitement over the discovery of a clue.

"So how does this change things?" asked Dillon who was so tired he felt punch drunk.

Jeff stopped pacing, thought for a moment and said, "Granted we've only been on this a few hours, but at first glance it looked like someone right here in Seaboard was our best bet. Now with what Frances gave us, it appears that Nicey might have gotten her information about the location of the Blankenship Farm from someone who used to live in Seaboard but doesn't live here now. We need to expand our investigation to include witnesses beyond Seaboard."

"Got a plan?" asked Buddy knowing full well that Jeff did.

Jeff sat down and singularly eyed each member of the team...including Frances. Then he said, "Dillon why don't you and Stewart keep digging here in Seaboard. Spread the word that you want to talk to anyone who knows anything about Nicey Parsons....anyone that talked with her or even saw her yesterday. Use the newspaper. Use the radio...what's that morning talk show out of Roanoke Rapids?"

"Good morning Lake Country," said Stewart.

"Right," said Jeff. "Talk with Sara Wood again. And especially talk to her sisters. It was just too convenient for those two to be gone when we interviewed Miss Sara." Then Jeff turned to Frances. "Frances, you work in the perfect place to uncover information. Listen closely. Ask around about who remembers the Blankenships or knew Nicey Parsons."

Frances beamed and said, "So I'm gonna be working *closely* with your team, Jeff?"

"Sure are, Frances," said Jeff. "You just gave us a key piece of information."

Frances turned completely around and smiled broadly at Buddy. "This could be exciting."

"And you and Buddy, Jeff?" asked Dillon.

Jeff rubbed his hands together again. "Buddy, how would you like to take a trip to Philadelphia?"

Buddy smiled and said, "Now that's one place I've always wanted to visit...the Liberty Bell and all you know."

"Philadelphia…why Philadelphia?" said Frances.

Buddy said, "Because that's where Nicey Parsons worked. That's where the *Confidential Observer* is located."

Jeff took out his phone and clicked on a familiar number. Two rings and a pick-up. "Cathy. Jeff. I'm gonna need a couple of tickets to Philadelphia."

"Pennsylvania?"

"Yes, Pennsylvania," Jeff said. He rolled his eyes and shook his head. Buddy laughed.

"When do you need to leave?" Cathy asked tersely.

"As soon as we can get back to Raleigh. We'll be leaving in an hour or so. Now lemme speak to the big guy."

"You mean *Mr. Bryant*?"

Jeff laughed. "Yes. I mean *Mr. Bryant.*"

Jeff walked outside to talk with Bryant. He described the crime scene and gave him a report of their investigation to date. He then explained the need for a trip to Philadelphia.

"Good idea. Keep me posted," said Bryant.

"One other thing," said Jeff. "We need to check with the airline and make sure that Nicey Parsons *flew* into Raleigh Durham International."

"I'll have that checked out," said Bryant. "What else?"

"When we get to the terminal, I'm going by the car rental booth to get a make on the person who actually rented the car. I've asked the lab to make a copy of the victim's driver's license photo. A picture is more conclusive than a name."

"Okay," said Bryant. And he hung up.

Jeff clicked off and stuck his head in the door and said, "Be back in a little bit." And he turned, walked to his car, and drove right on Main Street.

"Where's he off to?" asked Stewart.

"I know," Frances said slyly. "I know exactly where he's off to."

Chapter 6

Jeff turned right onto Main Street, drove up the hill, and passed the Baptist Church. He pulled into the driveway of the big yellow Victorian house across the street from the Methodist Church. He didn't see a soul. Then he heard scratching noises from the side of the house. He got out of the car, closed the door softly, and quietly walked in the direction of the noise. On the far side of the house a young woman knelt in a flower bed. Beside her was a flat of yellow chrysanthemums. She carefully pushed a flower from the flat, placed it in a hole, and tamped dirt securely around it.

Jeff approached and using an overstated Southern accent said, "Pardon me Miss, but is this whar Miss Sophie Singleton lives?"

She was slim and wore faded jeans and a red checked blouse. Her auburn hair was sprinkled with silver and pinned up in a twist. She lifted a gloved hand, brushed a wisp of hair from her forehead, and pushed herself up. She said "Why yes, it is. I'm...."

She turned and recognized Jeff. She ran to him almost knocking him down. "Jeff, Jeff. We knew you were here and wondered when you'd get by."

They held each other desperately and kissed eagerly. Suddenly there was the deafening blast of a car horn, and a male voice shouted, "Hey Jeff, get a room."

They moved away from each other, and Sophie called back, "He already has a room thank you very much." Then the horn blared several more times, and the pickup truck sped down Main Street.

Jeff smiled and looked into Sophie's eyes. He reached up, brushed a smug of dirt off Sophie's forehead, and said, "Been busy, Sophie. Got here quick as I could."

They put their arms around each other and began walking toward the front porch.

"Is Buddy Turner with you this trip?"

"Yeah, he's sleeping over at Dillon's place...that is if he can find a spot clear enough to bed down in." Sophie laughed. She'd heard rumors about Dillon's messy house.

Sophie said, "Gladys has been cooking ever since we heard you were assigned to this investigation. She's got a lemon pie in the refrigerator and Lord only knows what else. She says you're the only one who appreciates her cooking."

They walked up the steps to the front door. The door was barely opened when a commanding voice said, "Well, it's about time, Jeff Sands."

The voice belonged to Gladys Spencer. Gladys had cared for Sophie when she was a child. Consequently she was a strong mother figure to Sophie and she ruled the house. Gladys had almond-colored skin, was pleasingly plump, and wore her hair in tightly braided rows. Gladys was ageless. She always wore black comfort shoes and cotton house dresses and smelled like freshly baked bread or cookies.

"Got here quick as I could, Gladys," Jeff said. "You know I wouldn't miss your supper for anything." And as he spoke he and Sophie darted for the stairs.

"Well, I best be getting in the kitchen then," Gladys said. "Come on here Melvin. As usual I'm expected to have it ready any time of the day."

Melvin was a short, thin, dark skinned man. Although he was quiet and passive he considered himself second in command only to Gladys when it came to managing things around the Singletary house. Although they'd been together for years, they weren't married, and Gladys referred to Melvin as her *matrimonial possibility.*

Melvin peeled potatoes, onions, and carrots and added them to the pot roast. Gladys set the dining room table with Grandmother Singletary's best Haviland china reserved for only the most special occasions. At six thirty sharp she and Melvin began bringing in the platters of food…roast, vegetables, salads, and bread. They did not need to announce that dinner was ready. Sixty thirty was Gladys' dinnertime and everyone who knew her knew dinner went on the table at **exactly** six thirty. As the last serving dish was set on the table, Sophia and Jeff appeared in the dining room, sat in their usual places, and began to eat. Jeff noticed that the kitchen door was slightly ajar.

Jeff asked, "So how are the wedding plans coming?"

"I have no idea," Sophie said simply.

"What do you mean?" Jeff asked.

"I mean I don't have to do any planning. Gladys and Julie are the self-appointed caterers, and Jan has taken over everything else. Jan and Julie are on a three-week cruise to Alaska. They left me with instructions to do nothing...they'd have the entire wedding planned by the time they get home." Jan and Julie were childhood friends who felt it their duty to help Sophie even if she didn't want their help.

"So what are *you* doing?" Jeff persisted.

"I'm planning the most important part of all," Sophie said with a wicked smile.

Jeff knew that smile. "And what would that be?" he asked cagily.

Sophie leaned close and whispered, "Our honeymoon."

"You hear that Gladys?" called Jeff.

"Yeah, I heard it," said Gladys. "She better be a-payin' 'ttention to other things. December ain't that far off."

Eventually the conversation turned to the Blankenship farm murder. Jeff reported what information they'd learned so far which was very little. He explained to Sophia he'd be flying to Philadelphia to see what he could learn from Nicey Parsons' friends and co-workers, and he should be back in a couple of days. Since, the murder was committed in Seaboard, it stood to reason that the investigation would stem from there. And yes, he would be staying with Sophie.

After a dessert of Gladys' incomparable lemon pie, Jeff reached across the table, took Sophia's hand, and said hoarsely, "Be nice to spend more than one night at a time with you....," then he added in a loud voice, **"and with you too Gladys."**

"Huh," was the brusque comeback, "Not with me you ain't. I got my own beau."

* * *

When Jeff returned to Dillon's office he found Stewart, Frances, and Buddy surrounded by a jumble of drink cans, dirty napkins, greasy paper plates, and plastic utensils.

"Where's Dillon?" asked Jeff.

"He's back at his house," said Buddy.

"Yeah, he's all tuckered out," said Stewart. "We ain't used to this much goin's-on round here"

"What about you?" Jeff asked Stewart.

"I reckon I got my second wind."

"You're still going on adrenalin overload," said Buddy. "By the way Jeff, we got a flight out of Raleigh-Durham tonight at twelve-thirty."

"Well, we better get going then. I want to pick up some photos of Nicey Parsons at the lab," said Jeff. Then he turned to Stewart, "We're going to Philadelphia to talk with Nicey Parsons' friends and co-workers. Then we'll stop by the office in Raleigh before coming back here."

Jeff took out a pen, a small tablet, and wrote something on a piece of paper and handed it to Stewart. "This is my cell number. Dillon has the Raleigh office number already. Let me know if anything comes up we should know about while we're still in Pennsylvania or Raleigh."

86

Then he looked at Frances. "Keep your ears open, Frances. Never know what's important...like that road name change you picked up on. You don't have to be pushy. Just keep your ears open."

Frances looked peeved, "I ain't never *pushy*, Jeff."

Jeff smiled. "We better hit it, Buddy." And he started toward the door. He glanced back in time to see Buddy lean forward and whisper something to Frances. Jeff smiled again.

This time Jeff took the wheel. As they drove over the railroad tracks Buddy said, "Well do you think we accomplished anything here, Jeff?

Jeff said, "I don't know how much *we* accomplished, but it looked like you accomplished a lot." And he jerked his head back toward the Town Hall.

Buddy groaned, "Ohhhh no." Then he pulled his jacket collar over his ears, shrank down in his seat, and scrunched his eyes closed.

Chapter 7

Stopping by the lab to pick up photos of Nicey Parsons cost Jeff and Buddy precious time. To add yet another delay, just as Jeff pulled into the Raleigh-Durham Airport long-term parking lot, it began to rain. At first it was just a steady drizzle. Then suddenly drops the size of quarters whacked the hood so hard that it sounded like someone was throwing rocks at the car. It was exactly quarter to twelve.

"You wanta make a run for it or wait for the shuttle?" Buddy said.

"Shuttle," said Jeff and pointed ahead just as the bus turned the curve and headed in their direction.

"Okay let's do it," said Buddy. He grabbed his bag, opened the car door, and sped toward the oncoming shuttle. Jeff followed.

They settled into the plastic seats glad to have someone else do the driving. The car smelled of wet clothing and sweat. Luggage jostled about. The floors were wet, and a man who stood clutching a leather strap slipped and fell hard against Jeff. The man grunted an apology. Jeff nodded.

The National Car Rental booth was to the right of the entrance to the main terminal. Fortunately there was no line. Jeff approached a bleary-eyed, disheveled attendant who managed a forced smile.

"May I help you, sir?" said the weary attendant.

Jeff reached for his identification. "I'm Jeff Sands with the United States Marshal Service. I'd like to speak to someone about a car that was rented here and later connected to a crime."

The attendant said, "Yes sir. I'm the attendant who rented the red Sebring convertible to a young woman. I already got a call from the CSI people saying they'd have it for awhile…running tests and all. Hey, was there really a lot of blood?"

Jeff sidestepped the question. "Glad they already got in touch with you. But I'm not here about the car. I'd like you to take a look at a photograph and tell me if this is the woman who rented the car from you. Take a good look now." Jeff reached into his pocket, took out a copy of Nicey Parson's driver's license photograph, and handed it to the attendant.

The attendant perked up immediately. He took the photograph, squinted, and studied the picture intently. After a few seconds he handed the picture back to Jeff and said. "That's her alright. Sure as shooting."

"No doubt?" asked Jeff.

"None whatsoever," said the attendant. "Say, about that Sebring convertible, y'all gonna get all the blood off of it aren't you?"

Jeff pocketed his ID and the photograph, turned, and he and Buddy sprinted for the U.S. Airways Terminal.

When they finally reached the terminal not surprisingly they discovered their flight was delayed. They would soon realize why. Suddenly sheets of rain fell so heavily that visibility was almost zero. Rain water cascaded from the roof of the building. Winds howled and outside tarps that covered carts and luggage were ripped up and sent sailing across the tarmac.   Suddenly a deafening crash reverberated through the waiting room shaking the very foundation of the building, and streaks of lightening flashed across the sky like a colossal fireworks display.   An audible gasp rose from the waiting passengers.   Then the lights flickered, went out, and quickly came back on.   There was a collective sigh of relief.

Jeff said, "Looks like we're going to be here awhile."

They sat in hard seats, faced the window, and watched the lightning dance across the dark sky.   The display was mesmerizing.   There was something primeval about lightening…the unpredictability, the vulnerability that accompanied the phenomenon. Several streaks exploded across the sky simultaneously and when the jolting bolts appeared they lighted the sky behind them exposing black clouds that rolled across the horizon like billows of black smoke.

Jeff was so fascinated by nature's brilliant performance that he almost failed to realize his cell phone was vibrating.   He wrested his cell from his inside pocket, clicked on receive, and stood to walk toward a more private spot.

"Sands," he said.

"Jeff, I was worried."   It was Sophie.

"Sophie.   Now why would you be worried?"   Jeff said.

"I was watching the late news on WRAL and they interrupted the program to report a terrible storm moving over Raleigh…heavy rain, lightening, high winds, the works. Jeff, you don't think they'll try to fly in this do you?"

"Couldn't if they wanted to," said Jeff.

"That's a relief," Sophie said. There was a long pause. "Jeff, how long will you be away?"

"I don't know, Sophie," Jeff said.

"Any idea how long you'll be in Philadelphia?" she said.

"Not a clue," said Jeff.

"Still going to stop by the office in Raleigh when you get back?"

"Yes, I am," said Jeff.

"How long will you be there?" she asked.

Jeff became impatient. "Listen Sophie, we've been through this before. I almost never know how long I'll be on one of these trips. I just stay as long as I have to."

There was a long silence. "Jeff, I'm sorry. I know you have to stay as long as you're needed. It's just that I miss you already."

"I miss you too, Sophie," said Jeff. "But that doesn't change the nature of my job."

"I love you, Jeff."

"I love you, too, Sophie," Jeff said. "Look I'll call from Pennsylvania."

"Okay. Good night." And she was gone.

Jeff returned to his seat. The lightening show tapered slowly. Buddy was sound asleep. Finally a tired voice announced they would be delayed for at least another hour. It appeared that the storm was taking the same path their pilot would fly to Philadelphia. Jeff closed his eyes and thought of Sophie. Would she ever stop thinking of his job as a rival?

He must have drifted off because the next thing he knew a flight attendant was bending over him. "Mr. Sands. Mr. Sands. We're loading your flight to Philadelphia," a lovely young woman of Asian extraction said softly.

"Huh..huh. Oh thanks," Jeff said and he stretched his arms widely. Then he looked at Buddy who was sleeping the sleep of a man with a clear conscience. "Hey Buddy. We're loading."

They trudged slowly on board the 145 ER commuter plane. It was eerily quiet inside although all fifty seats were taken. Passengers seemingly fell asleep as soon as they dropped into their seats.

Buddy whispered, "How long does this flight take?"

"Suppose to be there in about an hour and a half," Jeff said sleepily.

"I can't remember the last time I had eight hours of uninterrupted sleep," said Buddy.

"Goes with the job," said Jeff, and he thought of his conversation with Sophie. "Goes with the job," he repeated

But they didn't arrive in an hour and a half. The plane set on the runway at Raleigh-Durham International Airport for another forty five minutes before being cleared for take-off. But Jeff and Buddy were oblivious to the latest delay. They both had fallen into a deep sleep.

"Mr. Sands. Mr. Turner." It was the lovely young Asian woman with the soft voice again. "We're preparing to land."

Jeff looked at his watch. Almost six o'clock. A trip that was supposed to take an hour and a half had stretched into five and a half hours. They grabbed their bags, and along with the other forty eight passengers were herded off the plane. As he passed the lovely Asian woman she said softly, "Thank you for flying U.S. Airways."

Even at six o'clock in the morning they found the U.S. Airways terminal alive with activity.

"After I find a John, we need to locate the U.S. Marshal Service, for the Eastern District of Pennsylvania. Got the number...." Jeff was fumbling through his pocket.

Suddenly Jeff and Buddy were quietly approached by two heavily built, brusque, unyielding men.

The heavier man spoke with a Latino accent, "Jeff Sand, Buddy Turner?"

"Who wants to know?" Jeff said.

"I am Ernesto Salas. This is Miguel Moretti," he said gesturing to the other man. "I believe you are looking for the U.S. Marshals Services for the Eastern District of Pennsylvania. Yes?"

"And what makes you think that?" asked Jeff.

"Because we, too, are U.S. Marshals. We are here to be of assistance to you while you are in our District," Ernesto said. He reached inside his coat, removed identification, and passed it to Jeff and Buddy.

"Thanks," Jeff said returning the ID to Ernesto.

"We have taken the liberty of reserving you rooms at the Airport Inn. Shall we get you checked in? Then perhaps over breakfast we can discuss what it is that you hope to accomplish while you are here in Philadelphia and how we might be of assistance."

"Good plan," said Buddy. "I need a shower and a change of clothes. I think I'll just burn the ones I have on."

* * *

Later Jeff and Buddy entered the restaurant showered, shaved, and very hungry. They found Ernesto and Miguel sitting in a booth in the back of the Inn's restaurant. They all ordered steak, eggs, hash browns and cheese biscuits. There was little conversation as Jeff and Buddy ate hungrily.

After refilling their cups with hot, black coffee, Eresto said, "Although we are anxious to help you with your investigation into the murder of Nicey Parsons, please remember that Miss Parsons was a resident of Philadelphia so we too have a vested interest in identifying the perpetrator and bringing him or her to justice."

"We understand," said Jeff. "And we do appreciate your help. We haven't found much to work with in North Carolina yet, but you have to realize we've only been on the case for less than forty eight hours. What we'd like to do here is visit Nicey's work place and talk with her friends and co-workers. Then we'd like to go to her home, look around, and talk to her neighbors."

"This is certainly possible," said Miguel. "How about telling us about the case so far?"

During the next thirty minutes Jeff and Buddy briefed the Pennsylvania Marshals on the murder of Nicey Parsons in Seaboard, North Carolina and their short investigation.

"This is a very strange case," said Ernesto. "Some of the information you have disclosed does not agree with what we have learned of Nicey Parsons."

"Like what?" asked Buddy.

"For starter," said Miguel, "Nicey Parsons lived frugally. The manner of dress you described is not consistent with her lifestyle."

Jeff and Buddy looked surprised. "But Nicey was a famous reporter," said Buddy.

Ernesto said, "Although *Confidential Observer* considered Nicey Parsons a top reporter this is not a highly rated magazine. It ain't no *G.Q.* or *Vanity Fair*. Compared to magazines like that their salaries are peanuts. You will see when we visit the places you mentioned." Then he stood signaling that it was time to get on with it. "We'll pay a visit to the offices of the *Confidential Observer* first."

Philadelphia was like so many old cities in the Northeast. There were blocks of abandoned buildings with wretched people milling about and sitting on the curbs. Drivers avoided stopping. A stopped vehicle was immediately set upon by beggars, prostitutes, or drug dealers. Yet not far away, smart stores and shops displayed expensive clothing and jewelry in polished glass show windows, and in the very next block skyscrapers of polished marble and steel spiraled upward as if trying to escape the blight that might spread and taint them.

They finally arrived in a district of old brownstone buildings that had been converted into offices. Some of the buildings were well maintained, but just as many showed signs of neglect. A sign in front of one the neglected building read *Confidential Observer—We Tell It All.*

"Well, here we are," announced Miguel as he pulled into a parking space posted *For Deliveries Only.*

They walked up the steps and into the reception room of the *Confidential Observer.* It was a small room. Metal chairs with ripped plastic seat covers were pushed against the wall. A table covered with cigarette burns held several old issues of the *Confidential Observer* and a chipped ashtray filled with butts. There was a prominently displayed sign that read, "We Pay Money for Secrets". A nervous man wearing a wrinkled tan shirt and black pants sat in one of the chairs clutching a large manila envelope to his chest. The room reeked of cigarette smoke and the origin of the stench was sitting behind a metal desk working a crossword puzzle. She looked like she'd just stepped out of a pulp-fiction novel...bleached blonde hair, bright red acrylic nails, matching red lip gloss, and a sweater that left nothing to the imagination. She brightened as the men walked toward her desk. Her eyes danced and when she smiled her teeth were so white that they looked ersatz.

"Well, hello," she cooed. "What can I do for you gentlemen?" And she actually fluttered her eye lashes.

Miguel took out his identification and held it across the desk. "U.S. Marshals. We'd liked to talk to whoever is in charge."

"Ohhhhhh," she said and her eyes widened with excitement. "I'll bet you're here about the Nicey Parsons story. "

Jeff stepped forward. "Story? What story?"

"Mr. Grant picked it up on the wire this morning. Imagine, someone I know right here in the office, and she's actually murdered," she said eagerly. "Mr. Grant's on it now trying to find somebody down in North Carolina to do some digging. Why this is the most exciting thing that's happened since I came to work here. One of our very own reporters killed 'in the line of duty'. Isn't that exciting?"

For a few seconds the men were speechless. Then Ernesto said, "If Mr. Grant wants to talk to someone from North Carolina perhaps he would consider talking to Jeff Sands and Buddy Turner here. They are the two U.S. Marshals from North Carolina who are investigating Nicey Parsons' murder."

"Ohhhhhh," she squealed again and jumped up. "Wait here. Wait right here." And she rushed toward the back offices. "Mr. Grant! Mr. Grant! You'll never guess...."

Almost immediately a short fat, man with a receding hairline burst through the door. He was breathing so heavily he could hardly speak. After a few deep gasps he extended his hand and said, "I'm Hugo Grant. Welcome, welcome to *Confidential Observer*. I can't believe my luck. I've just been talking to some people in North Carolina trying to get some inside information, and right into my office walk the very Marshals who know it all."

The Marshals were dumbstruck that Grant would think they'd provide him with information. Jeff said, "Mr. Grant, you don't seem to understand. We are here to question *you* about Nicey Parsons. Where can we talk?"

"Oh yes, of course. Of course you want to ask me questions. Please, please, come on back." And he led them into the inner sanctum of *Confidential Observer*.

In spite of being widely read nationally, the tabloid was a bare bones operation. It consisted of Mr. Grant's glass front office and several work cubicles. In the back of the room there was a sign beside a stairwell that read PRINTERS and an arrow pointed downward.

"Come in gentlemen," Grant said, and he motioned them into his office. "How can I help you? Maybe if I help you—you will help me." And he laughed nervously.

"Mr. Grant, this is not a trade-off. This is a murder case. Now we have questions. Questions about Nicey Parsons. For your sake I hope you cooperate."

"Of course, I'll cooperate," Grant said quickly. "But just remember I am—was only her employer. I know very little of her personal life."

"Seems strange. Don't you have a personnel file on your employers?"

"Why of course," said Mr. Grant. "But I am not as particular as some editors. I look for a different kind of reporter."

"Explain," said Ernesto.

"I mainly look for someone with a nose for news. News that is often—well, often overlooked by mainstream media. We report the unusual...the unexplained, secrets and such."

"I get your drift," said Jeff impatiently. "Just what kind of unusual secrets was Nicey Parsons on when she went to Seaboard, North Carolina?"

Mr. Grant looked exasperated. "I don't know," he said.

"What?"

"I don't know," he reiterated. "Nicey was like that. She'd come in and say she had a story in mind. I'd give her the go-ahead, she'd take a few weeks, and come back with a doozy of a story. Take that walking fish story out of Florida…"

"I know that story," said Buddy nodding his head in agreement. "That *was* a doozy of a story." Jeff shot Buddy a look to kill.

"Yeah…see," said Grant. "She was like that. Lots of people had heard the legend of the walking fish. But when Nicey came back from Florida she not only had a class act story and pictures, she had a video of that little sucker walking across the road. That's the way Nicey was. She didn't need to have anyone looking over her shoulder. When she promised a bombshell, she delivered…plain and simple."

"Sounds to me like Parsons was a freelance writer," said Ernesto.

"Well, in a sense," said Mr. Grant. "But I gave her expense money and she always gave me first dibs. Actually I'm the only one who has published her. The nature of her stories being…well, shall we say…unusual. The unexplained."

Jeff reached into his briefcase and removed a manila envelope. "If you can't tell us why Nicey Parsons was in North Carolina, perhaps you can verify that it is actually Nicey Parsons' body we found." Jeff reached into the envelope, withdrew an eight by ten photograph and handed it to Hugo Grant. "Mr. Grant, is this a photograph of Nicey Parsons?"

Grant reached for the picture. He gawked at it, blanched, and quickly shoved it back to Jeff. "My God!," he said. "What happened to her?"

"She was murdered and crows got at her," Jeff said.

For all of the horror Mr. Grant experienced, he quickly recovered as he realized the commercial value of the pictures. "Those pictures…do you have any idea how valuable they are in my news business? Why they're as sensational as anything that came out of New Orleans after Katrina. How much do you want for them? Just name your price…"

The men were stunned. Finally Jeff found his voice and said, "Mr. Grant, we'd like to see Nicey Parson's workspace."

Hugo Grant reacted as if someone had slapped him in the face, but he soon recovered and said, "Ah..ah..yes, of course." And he motioned to a cubicle. "But you'll see there's almost nothing there."

Nicey Parsons' office looked as if it had never been occupied. There were no personal effects, no computer, pictures, pens or pencils. Jeff opened the drawers of a two-drawer filing cabinet. Empty. Jeff stared at the only thing on her desk, a telephone.

"She never used it," said Grant. "Always used her cell. Nicey was secretive. That's why she was such a good match for *Confidential Observer.*"

"Who did this, Grant? Who cleaned out Nicey Parsons office?" growled Miguel and he took a menacing step toward Hugo Grant.

Hugo Grant retreated until he backed into the desk. "No one. No one has touched her office. This is what I've been trying to explain. Nicey Parsons worked alone. She didn't trust anyone. She kept everything…notes, emails, addresses, contact numbers…everything on her laptop. And she never let it out of her sight. She was like that. She latched on to a story, and sometimes I wouldn't see her for days. Nicey Parsons didn't trust anyone. Not anyone at all."

"Sounds paranoid," said Buddy.

"Yeah," said Jeff slamming the file drawers shut. "But just because she's paranoid doesn't mean no one was after her."

"We should now speak with the other peoples in the office," said Ernesto.

"Might as well," said Jeff. "We got nothing here."

For the next forty five minutes, the four Marshals questioned the other people in the office. Miguel volunteered to question the receptionist and Jeff chose the guy whose desk was in the work space next to Nicey. He was a skinny dark skinned young man with spiked hair and an ear for ease-dropping. He made no secret of the fact that he was listening while the Marshals questioned Hugo Grant. Jeff reckoned that if he ease-dropped on the Marshal's interview with Grant, perhaps he'd listened in on Nicey Parson. Jeff had high hopes of getting information from him. Unfortunately he corroborated Hugo Grant's secretive portrayal of Nicey Parsons. The other Marshals had no better luck…except perhaps Miguel who walked away with a smile and the phone number of the light-hearted receptionist.

Ernesto said, "Mr. Grant, there will be some men form our crime scene investigation unit to take some fingerprints from Nicey Parsons' office…"

"Really? How exciting. Pictures. We must get pictures of the CSI at work. Right here at *Confidential Observer.*"

"This you will have to take up with the investigators when they arrive," said Ernesto. And he walked away.

As the Marshals reached the door they heard footsteps pounding behind them. "Wait, wait." It was Hugo Grant. He said breathlessly, "I…I was serious back there about the pictures. I can make it worth your while if you give me copies of those pictures."

The men said nothing but just looked at him in disbelief.

"Listen. You don't understand," he said this time in a whisper. "I can *really* make it worth your while. I can pay *you* money…lots of money. You can divide it among yourselves and no one would ever have to know where the pictures came from." He looked from one man to the other expectantly.

"Is this how you do it, Grant? Is this how you get your pictures and your stories," asked Miguel.

"Yes, yes, it is. This is the way it's played. So what do you say?" Grant said as his eyes moved expectantly from one Marshal to another.

"I say, Mr. Grant," said Ernesto stepping in menacingly, "how would you like to be slapped with a charge of trying to bribe United States Marshals?"

Then the four Marshals turned abruptly, piled into the car, and left as a disappointed Grant shouted after them, "It wasn't a bribe. It was business!"

* * *

They drove to the address Grant gave them. It was in another old section of Philadelphia. This old neighborhood,

102

however, appeared to be well maintained and had been modernized. Neon signs flashed in storefront windows. There were pawn shops, dress shops, insurance companies, and clinics. A large fresh food market spilled onto the sidewalk, and women moved through the baskets of vegetables and fruits as they made choices for their evening meal. Children chased about noisily on the sidewalks and up and down the steps of the apartment buildings.

Ernesto again pulled the car into a delivery parking space and pointed toward a three-story apartment building. The four Marshals got out of the car and walked toward the building. They really stood out as strangers in this busy, noisy neighborhood where everyone recognized neighbors even if they did not know their names. They walked up the steps and Miguel found the button that was labeled Manager. He pushed the button and they heard a click. He opened the door and the four men stepped into the entrance hall. There was evidence that the place had once been a high-end apartment building. The floor was lovely old ceramic tile. Although it was clean some tiles were grooved and cracked. A dusty crystal chandelier with several burned-out bulbs hung from the high ceiling above a staircase that was covered with worn carpet. The first door on the left held a sign that said Manager. Ernesto knocked on the door. No response. After a few seconds he knocked again.

A disembodied voice snarled, "Keep your shirt on."

Finally the door flew open and the smell of garlic and olive oil wafted into the hall. Then a big, burly man appeared. He was wearing dirty jeans and a sleeveless undershirt made of a gauze-like fabric. He resembled a black bear. His bushy black eyebrows grew together. His arms, chest, neck and back were covered with black hair. His head sported a mass of greasy black curls and his dark face indicated a shave was long overdue. He gaped at the four Marshals and involuntarily stepped back into the shelter of his apartment.

"What's going on?" he snarled through a scowl.

"U.S. Marshals," said Ernesto flipping his ID. "We want to talk to the manager."

"You're talking to him, Stanley Barilla" the man said eyeing each man skeptically. "Ain't nothing going on here that would call for four Marshals."

"Who is it, Stanley?" called a shrill, nasal voice from inside the apartment.

"It's four U.S. Marshals," the Manager barked back.

"Yeah. And I suppose they're escorting the Pope," shrill voice said sarcastically.

"Come see for yourself," the Manager said.

The woman who emerged from the apartment was barely five feet all. She wore a large red apron over a navy blue polyester pants suit. Her hair was beauty shop blond and her makeup was excessive but impeccably applied. She stared at the men, turned to Stanley, and said accusingly, "What have you done, Stanley? What in the world have you done now? I knew I shouldn't have gone back to work at the bail bondman's office."

"Stanley hasn't done anything," Ernesto said. "We are here to ask about one of your tenants."

Stanley ignored his wife. "What tenant?"

"Nicey Parsons," said Ernesto.

The woman's face lit up. She turned to the husband, smacked him on the arm with the heel of her hand, and shrieked, "What did I tell you? What did I say? That girl means trouble."

"Why do you say that ma'am?" asked Jeff.

"I have my reasons," the Manager's wife said slyly. "What's she done?"

"She got herself killed," said Buddy. Jeff shot Buddy a sharp look. Buddy instantly realized that he'd given away information before they'd gotten what they needed.

The Manager and his wife looked stunned. The Manager staggered backwards. After a few seconds, the woman said, "Killed? How? I...I didn't particularly like the girl. But I certainly didn't wish her no harm. Holy...", and she crossed herself.

Jeff said, "Did you know of anyone who would have animosity towards her?"

"Huh?" said the Manger.

"Did you know of anyone who would want to hurt her," said Jeff.

"No. No. I don't know of anyone who would want to hurt Nicey," he said.

The wife regained her composure and said, "Now you don't know that *nobody wanted to hurt her,*" she said. "The truth of the matter is that we don't know anything at all about Nicey Parsons."

"I know..." the Manager began.

Ernesto interrupted. "We want to get into her apartment."

"Her apartment?" repeated the Manager as if he'd forgotten she lived in the building.

"We need the key," said Ernesto.

"Yes, let you in," repeated the Manager as if in shock.

He disappeared into his apartment and returned quickly. "The key," he said.

Jeff took the key and said, "Buddy why don't you talk to the lady."

"And I'll talk with the Manager," said Miguel.

"And we'll both talk to neighbors," said Buddy.

Jeff took the key. "Third floor. Number 301. It's a nice sunny corner apartment," said the Manager. He watched helplessly as Jeff and Ernesto started up the stairs.

Jeff and Ernesto took the steps two at a time as they bounded up the three flights of steps. They stopped at number 301. Jeff inserted the key in the lock, pushed the door open, and they stepped inside.

"Whoa!!!" exclaimed Jeff and the two men retreated into the doorway.

The glare inside the room was so brilliant that it hurt their eyes. Everything was white…not just ordinary white but a shiny, glossy, brilliant, shimmering white…the walls, the ceilings, the woodworks. The apartment was sparsely furnished but tastefully done. The cabinets and kitchen table were painted sparkling white. Draperies were white. Two chairs and a hide-a-bed loveseat were covered in white. On the floor lay a white faux-fur rug. A door was open revealing a dazzling small white bathroom. White, white, white. And as the sun streamed through the large windows, the intensity of light on white was excruciating. Black was the accent color in the studio apartment but it had been used sparingly. Two black pillows were tossed on the white

106

hide-a-bed loveseat. A black single-cup coffee maker set on the white kitchen counter. Black towels hung in the white bathroom. On the white walls black frames held black and white photographs.

As was the case with Nicey's workspace at *Confidential Observer*, everything in the apartment was meticulously clean and orderly. It was as if no one lived there. The floors, countertops, and bathroom were pristine. The men snapped on gloves as they entered the apartment. They found themselves walking gingerly to avoid soiling the place.

"This woman, she must spend hours cleaning, cleaning, cleaning," said Ernesto. "Never have I seen such a clean apartment. What for she has to be so clean?"

Jeff didn't answer. He was looking at the black and white photographs in black frames that hung on the white walls. "Hey, Ernesto. Take a look at this."

Ernesto walked over to where Jeff stood examining the photographs. "What?" he said.

"What do you notice about all of these photographs?" said Jeff.

Ernesto moved slowly along the wall looking closely at each photograph. Finally he said, "Why they are all photographs of her, Nicey Parsons. She hung pictures all of herself." And he gestured at the white wall that featured Nicey Parsons. Nicey on a sand dune by the ocean. Nicey standing beside a Ferris wheel holding cotton candy. Nicey at the Grand Canyon. Nicey making a face at the camera. And they looked at a place Jeff recognized...Nicey standing in front of Biltmore Mansion in Asheville, *North Carolina*.

"Right. And no one else is in any of these pictures," said Jeff.

"What kind of girl takes pictures only of herself?" asked Ernesto rhetorically.

"They may all be of Nicey, but someone else had to take them," said Jeff. "And it would be nice to know who that was."

Ernesto stepped into the hall and called for a crime scene team.

Finally Buddy and Miguel came upstairs. "Good grief," exclaimed Buddy as he entered the apartment. "Where're my sunglasses?"

"Looks like we got ourselves a victim who has a hang-up on cleanliness," said Jeff. "Take a look around...especially the pictures there," said Jeff.

Jeff opened drawers, looked through cabinets, and the two closets. As was the case with Nicey's workspace nothing was out of place. Nothing suggested what Nicey Parsons' had been investigating. Most disappointing of all, there was no laptop and no cell phone.

Ernesto came in. "Crime scene team on their way," he said. "Find anything?"

"Not a thing," said Jeff.

"No laptop, Ipad?"

"Nope," said Jeff. "Buddy what did you find out from the Manager's wife?"

"Not much. She's jealous of Nicey. She complained that her husband spent too much time doing odd jobs, painting and such for Nicey. Complained that he didn't do that for other tenants. She even hinted that she didn't trust him to be here all day alone especially if he were working

108

in her apartment which she said he did a lot. She was afraid that Nicey might come back during the day."

"Hum. Jealous enough to confront Nicey?" Jeff asked.

"I think she has the backbone, but I doubt she'd take it any further...especially if she had to go all the way to Seaboard, North Carolina to do it," said Buddy.

Jeff looked at Miguel. "Anything from the Manager?"

Miguel said, "Well, he's got the hots for Nicey. Whether he ever tried to take it to another level...hard to say without knowing Nicey. Right now I think he's satisfied his infatuation by finding excuses to be around her and in her apartment. Knows his wife is jealous. Denies she has reason to be. Says she'd be jealous of the Holy Mother."

"If Nicey rejected him, do you think he'd turn violent?" asked Jeff.

"Speculation," said Miguel, "but I think like Buddy here. The man's capable but I can't see him traveling all the way to North Carolina to commit the crime. If he killed Nicey, I think it would be impetuous not planned. Looks like you're gonna have to look closer at your jurisdiction for this one, Jeff."

"Think you're right," said Jeff.

The Crime Scene Team arrived so fast that the Marshals joked they must have been waiting around the corner. They went to work immediately.

"Say Ernesto, tell your guys I'd like to take some fingerprints, photographs, hair and toothbrush samples back

109

to our lab in Raleigh. Especially want to take shots of her photograph gallery here."

"Sure," called Ernesto who was standing by the bathroom door watching the crime scene team at work.

It was late afternoon before the crime scene team finished up. After they locked and taped up the place the team and four Marshals trudged downstairs. Simultaneously with the sound of their footsteps the Manager's door opened. The Manager's wife stepped into the hall.

"Did you find anything helpful?" she asked.

"We are not completely finished," said Ernesto. "The apartment has been marked as a crime scene and no one should enter for any reason."

"We'll do our best," said the wife. "Ah…you know all that stuff I said about Nicey being trouble. Well, I didn't mean anything by it. Not really. It's just that…like I said my husband did more for her than the other tenants and I don't think that's right. He's in there right now acting like he lost his best friend. Well, he ain't. If the truth be known I don't think *she* had many friends at all."

The Marshals said nothing. Finally the silence was unbearable. The wife fidgeted nervously. Then she said, "I just don't want you to think I ain't got no feelings for the poor girl. I'm a Christian and a church-going individual. Ain't missed a mass in can't remember when."

The men still said nothing. Buddy bobbed his head a few times in an 'I understand' motion. Still silence.

The wife fidgeted some more and then said, "I'll light a candle for her." She turned toward the door to the apartment.

"You do that, ma'am," said Miguel.

Outside daylight had faded into a soft purple. The neighborhood was calm and still. Muffled television noises could be heard from behind closed windows, and the aroma of evening meals drifted into the street. The dog days of summer had passed, and the dampness in the night air was a portent of cooler days and even cooler nights. The streetlights created a deceptive pocket of peacefulness within the restless city. Somewhere in the distance a baby cried. And up in apartment 301 black and white photographs of Nicey Parsons smiled eerily into the emptiness of the bright white room.

On the drive to the airport the four men complained how they knew little more about Nicey Parsons than they did when they began. They discussed strategy. The Pennsylvania Marshals would check Nicey's phone records, banks records, and bring in some of the *Confidential Observer* staff for more in-depth questioning. Ernesto and Miguel also planned to talk with Nicey's neighbors and co-workers again. They stopped by the lab and picked up copies of photographs of Nicey's apartment, and Jeff and Buddy carried pictures, fingerprints, tooth brush and hair samples back to Raleigh. The four Marshals agreed to share any new information.

"Leave anything in the hotel room?" asked Ernesto.

"Nope," said Jeff. "Got everything right here."

"Shame to have rooms and not stay the night," said Buddy.

"Yeah," said Jeff. "Spending last night at the airport was a bummer. Still anxious to get back to Northampton County to see if anything's turned up."

When they reached the drop-off at the airport Jeff and Buddy made a dash for their terminal only to find that once again their plane was delayed. They settled in for yet another long wait.

Jeff took out his cell phone, walked to a quiet less public spot, and clicked in a number.

After several rings a hoarse whisper said, "Hello."

Jeff said, "Sophie, it's me. Sorry to wake you."

"No," she said. "It's okay. Where are you?"

Jeff could imagine her positioning herself on pillows. "Still in Philadelphia. Plane's delayed again," he said tiredly.

"You sound exhausted," Sophie said. "Are you going to drive to Seaboard tonight?"

"No," said Jeff. "We have to drop some things off at the lab in Raleigh. Then I'm going to my room. I plan to get a few hours rest, clean up, and pack some more clothes. Then we'll drive to Seaboard. I don't suppose you've heard anything from Dillon."

"Not really. He did call earlier this evening to ask if I knew when you were getting in," she said.

"I'll give him a call," said Jeff as he raked his fingers through his disheveled hair.

"Miss you," Sophie said.

"Me too," said Jeff. "See you tomorrow." And he clicked off.

Jeff clicked on Dillon's number. There were several rings and Jeff thought he'd be sent to voice mail, but then Dillon's sleepy voice said, "Dillon."

"Dillon, Jeff. Sorry to wake you up."

"No, it's okay. Where are you?"

112

"Still in Philadelphia. Plane delayed again. We'll drive to Seaboard tomorrow," Jeff said.

"Find anything?" asked Dillon.

"Nothing meaningful at this point," said Jeff. "I'll fill you in tomorrow. What about you?"

"Did like you suggested. We made sure the murder was on the front page of the papers…The Herald as well as News & Observer. We had a lot of chatter on the local talk radio show too. Everyone has a theory. You know how that goes. Anyway, it paid off. We got a lead."

"Tell me," Jeff said excitedly.

"Well Mr. Johnson runs a Seven/Eleven out on Highway 301 right before you turn onto 186 to get to Seaboard. Anyway he said he saw a red convertible stop at the intersection onto 301. The driver was a woman and she sat there for awhile studying a map. Then a couple of boys from Northampton High School came up real fast behind her. He said he thought they were going to rear-end that convertible. They slammed on brakes, pulled up beside her, and shouted at her real angry like. Couldn't understand what they said. Then they tore off down the road in the opposite direction from Johnson's store."

"Did Mr. Johnson recognize the boys?" Jeff asked.

"Sure did. Said they buy gas from him," said Dillon.

"Good. We need to get them in," said Jeff.

"Already taken care of," said Dillon. "I talked to the guidance counselor over at the High School and told her the situation. I suggested that we could come to the school to talk to them and their parents or they could come over here. She called back later and said the boys would rather come here after school tomorrow."

"Great," said Jeff. "I'll be there by then. I don't know what they can tell us but you never know. Maybe they'll give us something."

As Jeff clicked off the boarding announcement was being made. The two Marshals trudged onto the plane, claimed their seat, and settled back to catch a few winks. As Jeff was drifting off Buddy said, "Jeff, how about me dropping off the evidence at the lab. I have to drive right past it anyway."

"Thanks Buddy," he said, and he lay back and let the drone of the plane engine lull him to sleep.

Chapter 8

Jeff awoke early to the smell of bacon and coffee. He pushed himself up, swung his feet off the bed, and trudged to the shower. His stomach grumbled as the aromas from the kitchen reminded him that he hadn't eaten dinner the previous night. He dressed hurriedly, strapped on his revolver, and packed his canvas bag with fresh clothes. Then he started downstairs and headed straight for the kitchen. He entered and stopped abruptly when he saw Buddy sitting at the kitchen table with fried eggs, grits with red eye gravy, and crisp bacon on a very large plate.

"Good morning, Jeff," Mrs. Smiley said sweetly. "Buddy didn't pass on my breakfast, and I hope you won't."

"I won't," said Jeff pulling up a chair to the kitchen table. "How's it going Buddy?"

Buddy nodded and shoved in a huge chunk of bacon. After a few chewing seconds he swallowed and said, "Dropped the evidence off at the lab."

"Good," said Jeff as Mrs. Smiley set his breakfast in front of him.

Silence followed as the two men ate hungrily and accepted generous second servings. Mrs. Smiley said nothing but delighted in having hungry law enforcement men at her kitchen table again.

"You saved our day, Mrs. Smiley" said Buddy as they cleaned their plates and stood to leave.

"You come by whenever you can, Buddy," she said.

As they walked down the steps toward the car Buddy said, "She's a real nice lady, Jeff. You know that?"

"Yeah," said Jeff as he opened the driver's door. "A big breakfast is what I needed today. My stomach was beginning to complain."

"Mine too," said Buddy. "I don't know which is worse sleep deprivation or starvation."

It was a gray, wet day with just a hint of frost in the air. The sun finally rose like a pink balloon out of the mist that covered the fields and woods. As he drove, Jeff was silent. Finally he said, "We need to talk with Miss Sara and her sisters when we get to Seaboard."

* * *

Dillon woke up to the clatter of his alarm clock. He made it a habit to put his alarm clock on the other side of the room forcing him to get out of bed to turn it off. He piled out of bed, stumbled across the room, and slapped it hard. The racket stopped abruptly, and Dillon staggered to the bathroom. After he shaved, showered, and dressed he picked up his guns. Then he walked to his car to begin his morning routine that had been seriously disrupted during the Nicey Parsons' investigation. Even before coffee, Dillon started his day with a drive around town.

He placed his guns inside the glove compartment and locked it. As he started to back out of his driveway, a yellow school bus approached. On the side of the bus were the words *Northampton County Schools.* The bus picked up middle school and high school students and transported them to a consolidated school ten miles away. The driver beeped his horn and lifted a hand to Dillon. Dillon waved back. He followed the bus down Main Street to Church Street where it turned left to pick up a load of kids. Dillon continued down Main, crossed the railroad tracks, and drove up the hill to a complex of government housing apartments. Several mothers held their babies and stood on the sidewalk talking animatedly. He got out of the car and was immediately set upon by about a dozen teenagers of all sizes and color. They greeted Dillon excitedly, and he listened as they chattered on about school. Dillon had worked hard to establish a bond with the kids. He felt strongly if teenagers trusted and respected police that the same respect would continue into adulthood when they had to make the real tough choices.

Then he heard the groan of the school bus engine. The yellow bus turned into the project's driveway, blew its horn, stopped, and the door opened with a whoosh. The bus driver said, "We missed you, Dillon. How's it going? I mean with your investigation and all."

"It's going," said Dillon as he stepped onto the bus. His probing eyes swept the bus targeting certain kids who were tagged as trouble makers. "How's it going on here?"

"So far, so good," said Dillon.

Dillon stepped off, and the bus rolled away. Several students waved, and he waved back. He turned toward the women on the sidewalk, tipped his cap, and turned to leave. Then his eyes fell upon a young man sitting on an apartment stoop. At first Dillon didn't recognize him. He was about twenty-five years old and so thin that he looked emaciated. He had long oily braids that hung out of a do rag tied tightly round his head. He wore ragged jeans and a threadbare tee shirt. His arms were covered with jail art. He was smoking a cigarette and held the filter between his thumb and middle finger. He took the last drag and flipped the filter into the yard. He eyed Dillon in a sinister way and Dillon eyed him back in kind.

Then Dillon slowly, purposely approached the man. "When did you get out?" Dillon asked.

The man's eyes drifted to the ground. Then he mumbled, "Last week. Hey, I don't want no trouble."

"You won't get any trouble from me if you behave yourself," Dillon said.

"I be's clean and 'tend to stay clean," he said looking up at Dillon.

"Good," said Dillon. "That's what I want to hear." And he turned and headed to his car.

The young man had just spent eighteen months in prison on dog fighting and gambling charges. Dillon had arrested him along with two men from Virginia who'd brought the dogs down to fight. The fights were held in the back of the complex and bets were made. Dillon and Stewart got tips about the fights. With the assistance of the Northampton County Sheriff's Department, they raided the fights and made three arrests. One dog was so mangled it was mercifully destroyed. Three others were turned over to the county dog pound.

Dillon left the complex and headed back to town. He drove directly to The Kitchen, a small café in a part of town populated mostly by black citizens of Seaboard. The owner and cook was Miss Sadie, an elderly black lady who knew how to cook *right*. Here you could order such Southern delicacies as fried fish, fried chicken, fried pork chops, barbecue ribs, fried green tomatoes, fresh collard greens and turnip greens, potato salad, 'nana puddin', eggs cooked *every whicha* way, and grits with red eye gravy. Then there were the pies...sweet potato, buttermilk, chess, chocolate, all kinds of fresh fruit pies. The pie of the day depended on what the cook *had an intention for.*

Dillon always ate breakfast at the Kitchen. When Miss Sadie saw him pull up in front of the Kitchen she'd immediately began preparing his plate. He always had three scrambled eggs, half dozen pieces of bacon, grits with red eye gravy and a basket of biscuits so light they virtually melted in Dillon's mouth. Other than the home-cooked meals Dillon had another reason for choosing the Kitchen for breakfast. Miss Sadie understood that Dillon was not a morning person, so no one was allowed to ask him questions. If he said something, customers were instructed to just say, "Um, humm." Consequently, Dillon had a perfect start to his day. After breakfast Dillon tipped his police cap, left a bill on the table, complimented the cook, and headed for the post office.

Everybody in Seaboard knew Dillon's routine. This morning the post office was especially busy so Dillon parked in front of Town Hall. As he crossed the street and walked into the post office patrons elbowed each other and nodded in his direction. A silence fell over the room. When Dillon entered there was an eruption of 'good mornings' and 'how you doin's'.

Dillon stopped and looked around at the customers. "Never seen such a crowd this early in the morning. Irma you running a special on stamps or something?" he said. There was nervous laughter.

Then he spotted Frances. "Hey kiddo," he said.

"Dillon all them just want to know what's going on with the investigation," Frances said. "I told them I couldn't answer any of their questions because I'm helping out as part of you investigation team."

An old farmer in work boots, bib overalls, and a flannel shirt said, "Dillon, if'n she's the best help you can get, you won't be solving your case any time soon...if'n ever." The crowd laughed. Frances scoffed.

Dillon said, "Well now, Frances helped us out some already. She's the only person so far who talked with the victim. Little Sister was able to give us some useful information."

"Good for you, Frances," said Preacher. "Solving this heinous crime should be a community effort." Frances smiled.

Irma said, "Dillon, you got them Marshals a-comin' in again soon?"

"Yeah," said Dillon. "They'll be here early today. Got any mail for me this morning, Irma?" Irma walked to the sorting table and picked up a stack of envelopes held together with a rubber band.

Frances said eagerly, "Are *both* the Marshals coming?"

Dillon grinned, "Yep. Jeff *and Buddy* are coming." He picked up his mail and walked toward the door.

"You keep us posted, hear Dillon?" said one man.

"And y'all stay safe. For heaven's sake y'all stay safe. We don't want no more murders 'round here."

There were murmurs of agreement

When Dillon arrived at Town Hall the Mayor was the only one there. "Good morning Mr. Mayor," Dillon said cheerfully.

The Mayor looked troubled. "Dillon I've gotta talk to you. I'm concerned about this murder case. How's it going? And where is Stewart? We're faced with the murder of a national celebrity and only one of our two policemen is on duty."

Dillon walked into his cubicle, tossed the mail on his desk, and said patiently, "Stewart's on duty from noon to midnight, and I'm on duty from six a.m. to six p.m. We are both on call for emergencies from midnight to six am. Stewart got the call reporting the crime a little after ten p.m. and called me. Right now Stewart is over to the cemetery working his other part-time job...town maintenance. We're doing the best we can. As far as a 'national celebrity' I suppose you could call her that, but some people have less complimentary names for her."

"What about the press? How you gonna deal with that?" the Mayor asked.

Dillon grinned. He noticed that the Mayor had dressed quite fashionably the last couple of days. Dillon said, "You know Mr. Mayor, I been thinking that you oughta handle the press."

"Me?" The Mayor feigned surprise.

"Yes sir," said Dillon. "You are our town leader. Captain of the ship. You need to be our spokesman. Just

121

step right up to those microphones and TV cameras and tell 'em that everything's under control."

The Mayor suppressed a look of excitement. "Well…if you think so.   I suppose it is *my* duty to inform the public about our situation.   By the way, will Jeff and his partner continue to assist?"

"Yes sir," said Dillon.

"And is it okay to tell the press that?"

"Yes sir," said Dillon

"Alright I'll assume the responsibility of informing the press." The Mayor began to act more confidently. "By the way, when will the Marshals be here?"

"Any time now," said Dillon.

The Mayor stood. "In that case I'd better get home and prepare my statement to the press."

He walked to the door, turned and said, "You will give me a heads up when they arrive…I mean the press."

"You'll be the first to know," said Dillon.

"Good," said the Mayor and he scurried out…a man with a mission.

The Town Hall was surprisingly quiet and somehow menacing.   Dillon suddenly felt alone, powerless, inept. He'd not foreseen this type of case when he accepted the job as policeman in the quiet, peaceful village of Seaboard. He thumbed through the stack of mail. He tossed half of it in the trash can and began to read the rest. He kept an eye to the street watching for Jeff and Buddy. And he kept his ear tuned to the telephone hoping someone would call in with information about Nicey Parsons or the Blankenships.

The telephone rang. The sound was especially shrill as it echoed through the room. Dillon snatched up the receiver. "Dillon," he said.

"Dillon they're at it again. They're riling ole' Blue so bad I wouldn't be surprised if'n he dropped dead."

Dillon exhaled loudly. "Mrs. Bertha you sure it's the same boys?"

"Sure, I'm sure. Nothing wrong with my eyesight. I caught myself a-looking out to the backyard this morning. Then I spotted them in the act. Nothing wrong with my eyesight," she repeated.

"I'm sure your eyesight is perfect, Mrs. Bertha, but I talked to D.J. and Bobby Lee the other day. They swore they'd leave your dog alone," Dillon said tiredly.

"You oughta lock 'em up, Dillon. Give 'em a taste of life behind the bars," she snapped.

"Riling a dog is not a lock-up offense, Mrs. Bertha," said Dillon.

"You listen here, Dillon, if'n you can't get them boys to leave my old dog alone, I'm gonna call the law," Mrs. Bertha screamed.

Dillon shook his head in disbelief. "Mrs. Bertha, I *am* the law," Dillon said with a sigh.

There was a pause. Then a much calmer Mrs. Bertha said, "Oh. I forgot." Then her indignation returned. "Well, you gonna do something or you just gonna let my poor ole Blue suffer?"

"If you're sure they're the same boys, I'll talk to them again after school."

"Done told you, I'm sure," she screeched and hung up.

At last Dillon heard the sound of brakes and a car door slam. He looked up eagerly and saw Jeff and Buddy walking up the Town Hall Steps. Dillon stood and walked toward them.

"Am I glad to see you," Dillon said. "Come on in and I'll make us a pot of coffee."

"Sounds good," the Marshals said.

Dillon served mugs of dark, strong coffee, and the men spent most of the morning briefing each other about what they'd learned. Jeff and Buddy detailed to Dillon their trip to Philadelphia. They described Nicey's office with no files, no computer, and no personal items. They explained how co-workers claimed to know little about her personal life and nothing about the story she was working on. Dillon was shocked when told how Hugo Grant tried to buy pictures of Nicey's mutilated body and the crime scene. They explained how he'd persisted until they threatened to charge him with attempting to bribe U.S. Marshals.

"Strange," said Dillon. "Where did she keep the story she was working on?"

"According to co-workers, she worked from her laptop computer. Apparently she kept everything on her laptop...notes, addresses, phone numbers, research notes...everything. And she used her cell phone for contacts. She spent practically no time in that office, and she was given a pretty free reign."

"What about where she lived?" Dillon asked.

"Now that was an interesting experience," said Buddy.

They described the love-struck landlord, and his jealous wife. Then they told how Nicey's bleak apartment reflected her life as a loner and didn't yield a clue about her investigation or why she came to Seaboard. They told Dillon about the evidence they'd dropped off in Raleigh and how the car rental attendant identified Nicey as the person renting the red convertible.

Jeff blew into his coffee mug and said, "So you can see we didn't get many answers in Philadelphia just more questions."

"You've really covered a lot of miles this week," said Dillon.

"That's for sure. So what's going on here?" asked Jeff.

"And where's the rest of your team?" added Buddy.

"If you mean Stewart he'll be in at noon. If you mean Little Sister...well, she'll drop by later when she gets off work," said Dillon. Buddy's face reddened. Jeff and Dillon laughed.

The door opened and a tall, slender, fastidiously-dressed man of about fifty walked in. He smiled and greeted the men who were crowded into Dillon's small cubicle. Then he walked into a workspace at the front of the room. He sat down behind his neat desk, opened a folder, and booted up a computer. He reached for a coffee mug that bore the name Harvey and a picture of a giant white rabbit. He stood and turned toward the coffee pot.

Dillon said, "Harvey, this here is Jeff Sands and his partner, Buddy Turner. You've probably heard me speak of them. They're the Marshals down from Raleigh helping out on this Blankenship farm case. Jeff, Buddy... Harvey Clinton."

Harvey flipped his hand in an 'of course' gesture and said, "For gosh sakes, I already know Jeff. How you doing Jeff? Good to meet you Buddy. Coffee refills for anyone?" And he strutted toward the coffee pot.

Dillon said, "Harvey, I was just about to fill them in on the tax situation out at the Blankenship farm." Then he turned to Jeff and Buddy and said, "Harvey here is town clerk. He collects and keeps records on all the city taxes among other things."

Harvey rolled his eyes. "Such as collect water and sewage bill payments, sell cemetery plots, schedule town maintenance, and take care of payroll...if you can call it payroll," Harvey said with a flip of his hand. "So how can I help you gentlemen?"

Dillon said, "Tell them about the ownership and tax payments since old man Blankenship died."

Harvey pranced back to his desk and set his coffee mug on a coaster. Then he turned to the computer, clicked in several words, and read, "Let me see...tch, tch, tch. I have it here that Mr. Blankenship died seven years ago. He hadn't worked the land in years. Can you imagine good farm land setting idle. Anyhow, the farm was valued at...oh, only twenty-five thousand. Can you imagine? It was willed to his only son, Lawrence Blankenship who lives in...would you believe...Buffalo, New York. U...hhh, how cold!!! Now let me go to taxes...yes, here we are. The first four years I received tax payments from Lawrence. Then nothing. No taxes have been paid on the Blankenship farm in three years. Can you imagine? And us needing all the tax revenue we can come up with." With his little finger extended, he lifted his cup, sipped, and then patted his lips with a neatly pressed handkerchief.

Jeff asked, "Did his son pay by mail or in person?"

"Ah, let me look. By mail," said Harvey.

"So what happens if no one pays the taxes?" Buddy asked.

Harvey replaced his mug on the coaster. "Sadly, it will be auctioned off. We try to give a little leeway around here...small town, neighbors, and such. But chances are it will be auctioned off next year if back taxes are not paid."

"Will it sell easily?" asked Jeff.

Harvey waved his hand in a don't-be-be-foolish fashion. "Why that farm will be gone before I can say 'my granny's bustle'. I've already gotten inquires. Most frequently the lady...and I use the term lightly...across the street."

Jeff exclaimed, "Are you talking about Sara Wood?"

"None other than," Harvey said smugly.

Jeff and Buddy exchanged glances. Jeff said, "Harvey, you're the man!"

"Well, if you insist," said Harvey.

"Dillon, it's imperative that we talk to the Wood sisters."

"I know," said Dillon. "I've been out there two or three times a day since you left. A couple of times Sara was there, but I haven't laid eyes on Rebecca and Mary. Guess we're gonna have to pester the daylights out of her till we get to those two sisters."

"And we'll start pestering today," said Jeff. "I want to go to the crime scene again. Now tell me about the two boys who talked with Nicey Parsons."

127

"Not much more to tell. As I said, I've got them coming in after school. I'd rather talk to them here than at school. Of course I'm not charging them with anything, but they don't know that."

"Right," said Jeff. "What time you think they'll get here?"

"School's out at two-thirty. Takes about a half an hour to drive from Gaston...I'd say they'll get here around three."

"Okay, then let's go out to the Blankenship farm. I want to look around with fresh eyes," said Jeff.

"Okay," said Dillon. "Harvey, I think it's unlikely that those high school boys will show up before we get back, but if they do, keep them here. And when Stewart shows up, tell him to come on over to the Blankenship farm."

"Of course, Dillon. See Jeff yet another one of my duties as town clerk...watch the office," said Harvey.'

Harvey stared approvingly at Jeff as the two men walked by. He sighed and turned back to his computer.

Chapter 9

When they arrived at the farm Jeff said, "Pull over on the side of the road Dillon. If we park in the path it might obstruct our view of the street. I want to check something out."

Dillon did as he was asked and the three men got out of the car and walked down the path toward the barn. They entered the barn and stood staring at the spot where the body of Nicey Parsons was found. There was still a large dark circle where Nicey bled out onto the dirt floor of the barn. They heard the flutter or wings and the caw, caw of crows. They looked up and saw a long row of the crows perched on tobacco poles that extended across the eaves of the barn. Buddy thought they resembled an illustration he once saw on the cover of an Edgar Allen Poe book, *The Raven*. Buddy shivered and said, "Those are some evil-looking suckers."

Jeff looked up and said, "Yeah, probably expecting another meal."

Dillon was still staring at the dark spot on the earth barn floor. "How long do you think it took her to bleed out?"

Jeff said, "I wouldn't think long."

"I hope she wasn't alive when they attacked her," said Buddy nodding toward the crows.

Jeff looked at his partner. "I wouldn't think she was. Crows feed on carrion."

Buddy started toward the barn door. "Gotta get me some air," he said.

Dillon and Jeff followed him outside. "This is where the car was parked," said Dillon pointing to where tire tracks ended.

Jeff hunkered by the spot that would have been on the driver's side of the car. He looked toward the barn. The shadows and darkness in the barn prevented him from seeing anything inside. He looked toward the recently mowed field. Except for a pine woods skirting the back of the field, visibility was unobstructed for acres. Then he looked toward the road. There were patches of tall thick weeds on each side of the path leading to the barn. Jeff focused on the tall weeds for a long time. Then his eyes followed the path up from the barn, to the road, across to another path, and straight onto the yard of the Wood sisters. And there Jeff's eyes locked with the enraged eyes of Sara Wood.

"Look Jeff," said Dillon. "Miss Sara is staring you down."

"Yeah, and she looks hopping mad," added Buddy.

Jeff placed his hands on his knees and pushed himself up into a standing position. "She sure does, Buddy. Let's go ask her what she's so mad about."

Dillon said, "Miss Sara is one ornery woman. Don't take nothing to peeve her. She's just one of them who's not happy lessen they have something to be mad about."

The three men walked slowly up the path toward their car. "Let's give her some cool-down time," suggested Jeff.

As they reached the road, Stewart drove up, parked, and joined the procession. "What's up?" he asked.

"We're going to talk to Sara Wood," said Buddy.

"This oughta be good," said Stewart. "Miss Sara don't like to talk to nobody...specially strangers. She's real ornery."

"So I've heard," said Buddy.

Sara Wood stood her ground as the men came into her yard. And they soon realized that Jeff's plan to give her 'cool-down time' had failed. Her face was red and a stream of spittle oozed from the corner of her mouth. She was holding a rake and as they came closer she shook the handle of the rake threateningly.

"I'm fixin' to smack you up side the head with this here rake handle if'n y'all come any closer," she screeched.

Dillon whispered, "The sisters must be home. She's real protective of them. "

Stewart said in an appeasing voice, "Now Miss Sara, ain't no need to go pitching a conniption fit. You know we got to investigate this murder and you're a witness."

Sara Wood looked pass Stewart to Jeff. "Jeff Sands, I want to report these men. I want to get out papers on them. They's been harassing me for two days just 'cause I'm the one what reported that car being parked over there. Well, I ain't a never gonna report anything again."

131

Jeff took a step closer. "Miss Sara I can understand your irritation. Murder is a horrible thing. But as Stewart said you're a witness and I for one think we are fortunate to have such a responsible citizen as a witness..."

"Jeff Sands, don't you go trying to mollycoddle me. I ain't gotta do everything the law comes in here and tells me to do. I ain't some simple-minded, and I ain't gonna be no witness no more."

Jeff stepped even closer. "Now Miss Sara, that's where you're wrong. You're already a witness to certain events that happened across the road at the murder scene. If you refuse to talk to us, I'll arrest you for being uncooperative and obstructing the investigation of a murder. You *and your sisters* do have to talk to us...either here or down at Town Hall. Take your pick."

Miss Sara raised the rake and shook it threateningly. Jeff said, "Don't do it Miss Sara. Don't add assaulting a law enforcement officer to the offenses that we can already charge you with."

Miss Sara dropped the rake. As it clamored to the ground she said vehemently, "This is a sorry day, Jeff Sands, when a boy raised in a fine Christian home treats his elders with such disrespect. Your mama's prob'ly rolling over in her grave knowing her own flesh and blood's behavin' like po' white trash."

Jeff said, "I don't mean any disrespect, Miss Sara, but right now the investigation of that woman's murder is about all that's on my mind. Now, will you get your sisters out here so we can talk to all three of you."

132

Miss Sara's eyes opened wide in disbelief. "Just how'd ya' know my sisters are at home? Y'all been a spying on me some more?"

"No ma'am. We know because you just told us," said Buddy.

Miss Sara glared at Buddy, "Smart ass, huh?"

Jeff said, "Miss Sara…"

"Alright, alright," she said. "But first you gotta understand some things. Both my sisters are real shy…'specially Mary. She's shy, and she's…well, she's sorta whatcha call dim-witted. Always had to protect Mary. Now Rebecca's different. Rebecca talks. Good lord how she talks but she don't always make no sense or tell the truth. That's why I do most of the talking. I ain't dim-witted and I don't lie."

"I see," said Jeff. Jeff turned and walked to Dillon and whispered, "How about talking to all three together now and later individual interviews when they get to know and trust us?"

"Sounds like a good idea," said Dillon. Buddy and Stewart nodded in agreement.

Jeff walked back to Miss Sara. "Okay, Miss Sara. We don't see any reason why we shouldn't talk to all three of you together today. Where are Rebecca and Mary?"

"I'll fetch 'em," she said as she walked toward the front door. "But don't expect too much."

Minutes ticked by. The men waited and became more and more impatient. "You suppose they've skipped out?" asked Dillon.

"Miss Sara's probably giving them last minute orders," said Buddy.

"Let's give them a few more minutes then we go in," said Jeff.

At that very moment the front door opened slowly, slowly. Miss Sara emerged first. She was holding the wrist of a thin, short waif of a woman wearing a blue striped dress sewn from flour sack cloth. She wore blue flip-flop sandals. Her hair was blonde streaked with gray and she wore it long and straight. There was a haunting look about Mary. She appeared to be wary of the men and stared at them fearfully.

The other sister seemed to be more excited than afraid. She was tall and thin and her figure wasn't bad at all. She wore jeans and a sleeveless cotton shirt. She eyed Buddy, smiled, and began to rock from one foot to the other.

"This here is Mary," Sara said holding up the waif's hand. "And that other one's Rebecca. Rebecca, for God's sake...stand still. See, I told you they ain't good with people... them being so backwards and all."

The four men murmured greetings and Jeff wondered if they'd be able to get anything useful from these two women with Sara leaning on them.

Stewart cleared his throat and said, "Glad to meet you ladies properly. Seen you 'round town and all but never took the time to introduce myself. I'm..." Rebecca's attention immediately shifted from Buddy to Stewart, and she took a step toward him.

Sara growled, "Rebecca, get back here." Then she looked at Jeff heatedly. "Alright Mr. Jeff Sands U.S. Marshal, these here are my sisters. Satisfied? What 'cha want to know?"

The four men looked at each other. Then Jeff said, "Miss Sara, I believe you said you saw the red convertible drive up the path to the barn. Right?"

"Done told you that," Sara said tersely.

"And you didn't pay attention to the driver after she parked?"

"Got better things to do than stand 'round here poking my nose into other folk's business."

Dillon said, "Rebecca, Mary, what about you? Did you see the red convertible drive down beside the barn?"

Mary cringed and her eyes grew big. Rebecca grinned, took a step forward, and opened her mouth to speak.

"They ain't seen nothing," said Sara. "They was packin' pickle jars out in the kitchen. Cain't see the road from the kitchen."

"Then you're saying they didn't see the car pull *into* the barn path?" asked Dillon.

"That's what I just said," Sara said.

"Sara, didn't you say that you and your sisters sat on the porch that night?"

"Yeah."

"And didn't you say y'all talked about how strange it was for the car to still be there?"

"What's the point?"

"Rebecca, Mary, if you didn't see the car drive down to the barn, how did you know it had been setting there a long time?"

Again Rebecca started to speak but Sara interrupted, "Because I told them about it a drivin' up that afternoon."

Dillon shrugged. "I suppose that makes sense," he conceded.

Jeff said, "We were just over at the barn. I crouched down in the spot where the driver would have sat. And there's another interesting thing, Miss Sara. When I looked up the path and across the road, I had a direct shot to where you were standing here in the yard."

"So what? I ain'd got no right to rake up my own yard?"

"Of course you have," said Jeff. "But that's not my point. You see, just as I saw you in the yard as I knelt by the driver's seat spot, you saw me from the yard."

Sara was impatient. "So you saying that murdered woman looked up here at my yard? What if'n she did? Ain't no law 'gainst that. You 'bout done?"

"No I'm not done. There isn't a law against the murdered woman looking up into your yard. But you see, if she could look straight up here that means you could look straight over at her."

"And?"

"And you could have watched her all day if you'd wanted, yet you're telling us that you spotted a fascinating stranger. She pulled her car into the path to a deserted barn, the driver disappeared, the car set there all day, and you didn't give it a second thought?" Jeff said.

"Or better yet," said Buddy, "you never go over to check it out?"

"You waited all day and that night until you and your sisters sat on the porch then you said, 'By the way that car's been setting there all day. Let's call Stewart'. You sure don't have much curiosity if you can wait that long," said Dillon.

Mary, the waif, looked frightened. Rebecca grinned and began to bounce around excitedly. Sara's face was red and she was breathing so hard, they feared she'd have a stroke.

After what seemed like an eternity, Sara sputtered, "Rebecca, get still!!! See what you've done here? You've upset my sisters who ain't never done a wrong thing in their lives. I allowed you on my property in the interest of helping out the law 'cause I'm a law-abiding citizen. But you listen up here, Jeff Sands, hell will freeze over twice before I ever cooperate with the law 'round here again. I done spoke my piece. Now get off my property and don't ever come back." She snatched Rebecca's arm and began dragging her and Mary toward to house.

Jeff called after her. "Miss Sara, it's not as simple as that. I told you we want to talk to your sisters. Alone. So far, we've only heard what you have to say."

Sara turned and glared at Jeff. The words she spat were filled with venom, "You stay away from my sisters...ya' hear? You ain't nothing but a fornicator yourself, Jeff Sands. Yeah that's right. I know. I know all 'bout you a-sleeping with that Singletary woman. Just 'cause she's the richest woman in Seaboard don't give you dibs on other women in town."

Jeff remained unruffled. "Miss Sara, we *will* talk with your sisters outside your presence...if we have to have papers drawn up."

Sara did not look back. "Screw you, Jeff Sands! You know what you can do with you papers."

The men walked silently back to their cars. Finally Buddy said sarcastically, "Well, that went well." The other three men laughed.

"Why she want to act like that anyhow?' asked Stewart.

Jeff said, "She's hiding something. I don't know what but she's hiding something."

Buddy said, "I think Miss Sara has conflicting feeling about her sisters. On the one hand she's protective of them and on the other hand she's embarrassed by them."

Chapter 10

As the three lawmen approached the stop sign at the intersection of Elm and Main Street they encountered a number of cars moving down Main Street toward town. They waited at the stop sign for the traffic to pass.

"What the...," said Dillon.

"I think I know. The press has found Seaboard. Get ready for the glare of the cameras," laughed Jeff.

"Oh, Jeez," said Dillon. "That's all I need."

Finally a driver recognized Dillon and Stewart's cars. The driver stopped and waved them through. When they reached the top of the hill, they looked down into town square at the reporters searching for a story and citizens who just wanted to be in the thick of it all.

"Pull up beside the John Deere lot. We'll sneak in the back door of the Town Hall," said Jeff.

Dillon pulled up beside the lot where John Deere equipment was parked. Stewart did the same. The men jumped out of the cars, weaved through the John Deere implements, and made a dash for the Town Hall back door.

"Damn, the door's locked," said Dillon shaking the knob. He banged on the door with his fist and shouted, "Open up, Harvey. It's me, Dillon."

They heard a scrambling inside. Then there was the sound of a bolt being slid, and the door flew open. Harvey stood in the doorway with a keyed-up look on his face.

"It's a madhouse, Dillon…a veritable madhouse. I locked the doors because those reporters were all over everything. The mayor is holding a press conference out front. He's been at it almost an hour. Of course, now they're asking the same questions over and over."

"There's no telling what he's saying," said Dillon as they walked toward his cubicle. "He likes the sound of his voice."

"No, Dillon," said Harvey. "I've been listening and actually he's doing quite well. He's given them a lot of *just begun our investigation* and *can't say at this time* and *we'll keep you informed* type comments."

"Probably heard all that on television," said Stewart.

"At any rate, he's handled himself quite well," said Harvey.

Jeff stepped closer to the front window and peeped out. "I just hope they clear out before those high school kids get here. I don't want them scared off."

"How did your interview with the *darling sisters* go," Harvey asked with a grin.

"It didn't," said Stewart. "Miss Sara was mad as a wet hen just at our being there."

"I think Miss Sara is ashamed of the sisters," Harvey said.

"That's what I think. The sisters couldn't get a word in. Sara did all the talking. Say maybe the sisters *can't* talk," said Buddy.

"They *can* talk," said Harvey. "When they come in they almost talk my ear off. Of course it's just babble. Makes no sense at all. I never try to say anything…just listen."

"We should have taken you with us," said Dillon.

"I suppose if you live your entire life with only one other person and that person is as overbearing as Sara Wood you'd take any opportunity you get to talk," said Jeff. "That's why I want to talk to those two sisters away from Sara."

"You know what you said isn't exactly right," said Harvey.

"What do you mean...about talking to the sisters away from Sara?"

"No...about the sisters living their entire life with only Sara Wood. Of course they were just babies, but technically they weren't alone with Sara until after the death of their brother, John," said Harvey.

"Brother?" said Jeff, Buddy, and Dillon in unison.

Harvey looked startled...then smug. "Oh so you didn't know that the Wood sisters had a brother?"

Stewart said, "Yeah, I knew that. I just plumb forgot."

They men looked toward Harvey. Harvey raised his hands in a stop position and feigned alarm. "Whoa, whoa. Nobody asked *me* about the Wood sisters," he said.

"Harvey, you sat here for two days knowing there was a brother and you didn't think it was pertinent to our investigation?" Dillon said.

"No. I didn't think it was pertinent under the circumstances," Harvey said.

"Under what circumstances?" Jeff demanded.

"Under the circumstance that John Wood is dead," said Harvey. And he turned his chair to face his computer. He clicked in a few words and stared thoughtfully at the screen that popped up. Then he stopped and said, "Here we are. John W. Wood. Section 5, Plot 143." He read the purchase date of the plot and the birth and death dates of John Woods.

Jeff stepped into Harvey's cubicle, looked over his shoulder, and read the cemetery records of John W. Wood's burial plot. "Only twenty years old," said Jeff. "How did he die?"

Harvey who was enjoying the attention took on a thoughtful look and answered, "Well...if I recall he died with complications from the flu."

"That's right," said Stewart. "It all comes back to me now. It was in the dead of winter and we had one of the worse flu epidemics I ever seen. Nobody was surprised when several old folks and young children died, but it was a shocker when John Wood passed. He was young and strong and as healthy a young man as you'd want to work a farm. It was a real wake-up call. After his death folks took flu real serious like. You'd hear somebody say 'Take care. Remember what happened to John Wood'."

"Who was his doctor?" asked Jeff.

"Old Doc Lowell. But if you're thinking about talking to him, you'll have to have a séance. Old Doc Lowell's died. Gone. Caput," said Harvey.

"Just out of curiosity, how did Dr. Lowell die?" asked Jeff.

"Old age if there is such a diagnosis," said Harvey. "He was in his nineties."

The reporters were beginning to disperse. A reporter pressed his nose to the window of the Town Hall and rattled the door knob. Dillon walked to the door and shook his head. The reporter's mouth moved but Dillon ignored him and walked back to his desk. The clock above the town clerk's work space said two-thirty.

"School's out," Dillon said.

"Yeah," said Buddy. "Maybe when the mayor comes inside the reporters will go away."

"I wouldn't count on it," said Jeff.

"Dillon, you think them reporters might go up to the crime scene?" asked Stewart.

"They might. They shouldn't go beyond the yellow tape. Get on up there and keep them from destroying anything. If this becomes more than we can handle I'll ask the Sheriff for assistance. He already predicted we'd have trouble with the press and volunteered to help if we need it."

"Right," said Stewart and he started to the back door.

"Might take more than one man," said Jeff. "Buddy, go with Stewart. And take our car."

"Right. Wait up, Stewart," said Buddy as he dashed for the back door.

Jeff turned to Dillon. "It might be best if only two of us question the kids. Don't want to overwhelm them."

"Good thinking," said Dillon.

The mayor rattled the front door knob. Dillon walked to the front, opened the door, and the mayor swaggered in. It was apparent that he was pleased with his press conference.

"Mr. Mayor," said Harvey, "you did a fine job. Yes sir, a real fine job. I was able to hear all of your comments and most of the reporters' questions. The viewers will never know this was your first time before the camera."

The mayor puffed up visibly. "Do you think so? I just tried to be natural and answered the questions honestly."

"Spoken like a seasoned politician," said Harvey. Jeff and Dillon voiced their agreement.

"Thank you, gentlemen," said the mayor. "Now if you'll excuse me I'll go home and wait to see myself on the five o'clock news."

The clock said three forty five and Jeff and Dillon began to feel anxious. They walked to the front window and looked down the street to the intersection of Main and Highway 186.

"What do you think?" said Dillon.

"I know that when I was a teenager it didn't take me an hour and fifteen minutes to drive from Gaston to Seaboard," said Jeff.

"I sure don't want to have to take them right out of school," said Dillon. "They'd never live it down. You know how kids are."

Harvey who had been listening to their conversation said, "Do you want me to clear out while you question them?"

Dillon turned to look at him. "No. You can stay put, but don't chime in," he said. "I don't want anything to spook them."

Harvey said, "Don't worry. I won't make a peep. I'll be still as a mouse. I'll be a spider on the wall. I'll…"

At that moment Jeff elbowed Dillon and nodded toward the street. They looked down Main to the railroad tracks where a dusty red Toyota pickup bumped slowly across the tracks. There were two occupants. Jeff and Dillon walked back toward Dillon's cubicle.

"How 'bout you taking the lead while I hang back," said Jeff. Dillon nodded and sat down at his desk. Jeff moved back and leaned against a tall file cabinet.

The red haired driver pulled his truck in front of the Town Hall. The two sat talking for a few minutes.

"They're making sure they have their stories straight," whispered Jeff. Dillon nodded.

Finally the truck doors opened and the two teenagers stepped out. They both wore dark blue tee shirts with Northampton County High School printed on it in gold letters. They walked reluctantly toward the Town Hall door. Jeff thought they looked so young and vulnerable. The door opened and the boys came in. They spotted Harvey.

"Are you Policeman Dillon?" asked the boy with long stringy blonde hair.

True to his word, Harvey said nothing but merely nodded toward Dillon in the back of the room. Dillon pretended to be busy with paper work on his desk. The boys walked toward Dillon's cubicle, stood outside the rail, and the blonde kid said, "You Policeman Dillon?"

Dillon looked up slowly. His eyes scrutinized the boys intently. Without saying a word he nodded toward two metal chairs and said, "Sit down." The boys stepped inside the rail and sat. As Dillon pretended to be absorbed in work, the boys' eyes wandered around the stark room. It was quiet and cold and the red haired kid shivered slightly. Neither boy appeared to notice the tall, quiet man leaning against the file cabinet. Finally Dillon tossed his pen on the desk and pushed his chair back from the desk. The boys jumped. Dillon raised his hands and locked them behind his head.

"Are you boys aware there's been a murder in Seaboard?" Dillon said with authority.

The blonde haired boy bolted, "We don't got nothing to do with that."

"That's not what I asked you," said Dillon. "I asked you if you knew there'd been a murder in Seaboard. Listen to my question."

"Yes sir, we heard about a murder in Seaboard," said the blonde haired boy.

"Have you been listening to the radio?" asked Dillon.

The boys nodded. Blonde haired boy said, "Yes sir."

"Read the papers?" asked Dillon.

"No sir," said blonde haired boy. "Mostly just listen."

"Well when you were *just listening,*" Dillon said, "did you hear an appeal for anyone who had information about the victim to contact me?"

The red haired boy began to scratch vigorously...first his arm then his head. The blonde haired boy swallowed hard but said nothing. Dillon let some time pass. The silence was powerful

Dillon demanded firmly. "I repeat, did you hear an appeal for anyone who had information about the victim to contact me?"

"We don't know nothing," said blonde haired boy.

Dillon pushed his chair to the desk, leaned forward, and spoke slowly, "You're telling me that you have not seen or talked with this victim? Son, you're lying. We're talking murder here, and that's about as serious as it can get."

The red haired boy looked as if he were going to cry. The blonde haired boy sputtered, "What you talking about man? We don't know nothing about no murder. Honest to God, man."

"Man? Man?" Dillon said contemptuously, "How about at least showing some manners here?"

"Sir, I mean. Yes sir," said blonde haired boy.

"Alright then," said Dillon. "First of all you need to know that you are entitled to have your parents here while I talk to you."

The boys exchanged anxious looks. "No. No sir. We don't need no parents," said blonde haired boy.

"Okay then. Now I'm giving you a chance to tell me about your coming across Nicey Parsons, who happens to be the murder victim. If there are no objections, I'm gonna record our interview and if I find out later you're lying...well just don't lie. Tape recorder?"

The boys looked at each other. The red haired boy trembled. The blonde seemed to be gathering his thought. Finally, blonde haired boy said, "Yeah fine. Record. I don't care 'cause we got nothing to hide. I guess you're talking about us seeing that red convertible at the intersection of 301." Dillon nodded. "Well there ain't that much to tell. We was heading home from school and when we got to the intersection there was this lady just a sitting there looking at a map. We pulled up beside her and I said, 'Hey lady, need some help?' She just shook her head and we took off and went on home. That's 'bout all there was to it."

Then Jeff stepped away from the file cabinet in the corner of the room. He walked to Dillon's desk and towered over the boys. "Lying in a murder investigation is just about the worse time to lie to a police officer."

The boys cowered. Dillon said, "Boys, this here is Jeff Sands. *Marshal* Sands, that is. You see he's a U.S. Marshal assigned to this case. Now you might take it lightly lying to a policemen, but lying to a U.S. Marshal...well, I wouldn't do that if I was you."

Jeff said, "Police Officer Dillon has a credible witness who puts you two at the intersection of 301 *talking* with Nicey Parsons. That much of your story fits. However, the rest doesn't. Our witness claims you had a loud confrontation with Nicey Parsons and that you drove away fast and angry. Now I want you to think long and hard before you answer. I want you to tell us exactly what was said at that intersection and why you sped away so fast. And I want the truth."

Jeff moved back and sat on the corner or Dillon's desk. His eyes moved back and forth one boy to the other. Finally Jeff said, "Time's up. Now what happened at that intersection of 301 and exactly what was said."

Red haired boys started to speak. His voice was a mere squeak. He cleared his voice and began, "She was just sitting there looking at some stupid map. Acted like she was in a parking lot or something."

"Glad to hear that you can talk," said Jeff. "Go on."

Blonde haired boy spoke up. "If'n Red hadn't been a good driver, we'd a rear ended her." Red haired boy nodded and looked pleased. Blonde haired boy continued,

"Made me so mad, that…that…Yes, I yelled at her, but I didn't threaten her or nothing."

"Exactly what did you yell?" asked Dillon.

"I told her she oughta get a car with a GPS," he said and leaned back against the metal chair.

"Then what did you do?" asked Jeff.

The boys stared at each other. Then they giggled. Jeff thought the giggle was as much for tension relief as anything. The red haired boy whispered, "I gave her the finger." They both snickered again. Jeff and Dillon looked at each other and shook their heads. From the town clerk's cubicle they heard a stifled chuckle.

Jeff put on his serious face again. "Alright, after you gave her the finger, what did you do?"

"I burned rubber and headed for home," said Red.

"Did you *really* go home?" asked Dillon.

"Yeah…yes sir," said blonde haired boy. "Straight home. Honest to God. Red and me, we live right next door to each other."

"Did she say anything to you? Anything at all?" said Jeff.

"No sir. Nothing," said Red. Blonde hair nodded his head vigorously.

"You didn't circle back around and tail Nicey Parsons to Seaboard?"

"NO!" howled the boys.

"You know if we find another witness who says differently, you're in serious trouble," said Jeff.

"Well, we didn't. We didn't tail her. We went home," said blond haired boy.

"And she didn't say nothing," said red-haired boy.

149

Jeff and Dillon looked at each other jadedly. "Okay boys," said Jeff. "Let's move on. I want you to think real hard now. Close your eyes. Pretend you're in the truck right next to the red convertible. Now think…did you see anything in that convertible…anything at all…that would make you think another person had been in that car with her. Wait! Not yet…think. Think about what you saw inside that convertible. Think about the dash, the front seat, the back seat. Did you see anything that would lead you to believe that someone else had been in that car?"

The boys sat silently their eyes scrunched tightly. Red's eyes were so tightly closed that folds of skin creased his forehead. Although blonde hair's eyes were closed, he moved his head from side to side as if scanning different sections of the car.

Finally Jeff said, "Well? Now this is important…was there anything that made you think someone else had been in that car?"

"I got nothing," said blonde haired boy.

"Me neither," said Red. "Only thing I remember is that map laying across the steering wheel and her pocketbook on the front seat."

"No extra coffee cup, carry-out containers for two people, men's sun glasses, cigarettes package, candy wrappers, or anything like that?" asked Jeff.

"No," the boys said.

Jeff said to Dillon, "Anything else?"

Dillon shrugged and shook his head. "Alright guys," said Jeff. "Guess that's all. If you ever again have information that the police might use, I hope you'll come forward immediately."

Blonde haired boy said, "If you mean you hope we won't try to hide anything...I sure won't"

"Me neither," said Red.

"Drive carefully," said Dillon and the two teenagers almost bolted to the door. Jeff and Dillon watched them as they piled into the truck. This time they didn't dawdle. Red put it in reverse and they moved out fast without so much as a wave.

"So what do you think?" asked Jeff.

"I think we got nothing from them that we didn't already know," said Dillon.

"Yeah, but we always gotta verify," said Jeff.

"Right," agreed Dillon. "They saw the same as Little Sister...nothing that would indicate another person had been in the car."

Then there was a derisive voice from the front of the room. Harvey didn't look up from his computer as he said, "It's so enlightening to actually observe the long arm of the law in action."

The back door opened and Stewart and Buddy walked in. At the same time the front door to the Hall opened and Frances entered.

"Hail, the team has assembled," said Harvey.

Dillon gave him a tired look, turned toward Frances, and said, "Hey Little Sister."

"Hey yourself," she said but she didn't look at Dillon...instead she looked at Buddy. She smiled shyly. He grinned, and walked toward her.

"So what did you get from the kids?" Stewart asked Dillon and Jeff.

"Not much," said Dillon. "They did verify Frances' opinion that there was no evidence that anyone else shared the convertible. We're still no closer to knowing why Nicey Parsons was in Seaboard."

Buddy and Frances joined the men. Buddy said, "I still think Sara Wood is hiding something. And I'd like to know more about the deceased brother. Jeff, do you think it's strange her not mentioning a brother?"

"No...not especially," said Jeff. "At that point she had no reason to mention him. But I still want to find out more about John Wood. Not sure where to go from here."

Frances said, "Well, I just might be able to help you with that. You remember Mrs. Bernice?" Jeff nodded. "She was in the post office this morning. She's one of them what likes to congregate early in the morning. They claim they're there to get their mail which they do, but mostly they just stand 'round gossiping. Well this morning the subject was Miss Sara and her sisters...'bout how she bosses them around and all. Then Mrs. Bernice says she recalls John and what a nice young man he was and what a shame he died. 'Specially being so young and healthy as a horse."

Jeff beamed. "Frances, you've done it again. You opened another channel." He turned to Dillon. "Dillon, let's have a talk with Mrs. Bernice before we talk to the Wood sisters again. She may have something that we need in questioning them."

"Sure," said Dillon. "You want to go to her place or get her over here?"

Jeff said, "I don't know. Frances, what do you think?"

Frances grinned. "I think Mrs. Bernice would just love to come to the Town Hall. Then she'd get to tell her morning chitchat friends that she had to come to the police station to help out in a murder investigation. Your only problem with bringing her here would be getting her to leave."

"You think she's trustworthy?" asked Jeff.

"Trustworthy as a Bible," said Frances.

"Okay," said Jeff. "Let's get Mrs. Bernice in here first thing in the morning. Then depending on what we get from her, we'll have another go at Miss Sara."

Buddy and Frances moved toward the back of the room and spoke in conspiratorial whispers. Jeff looked at the clock. It was six fifteen. "Hey, I gotta get out of here. As we speak Gladys is setting the table."

Then Jeff turned to Buddy. "Want to come along? I can promise whatever Gladys cooks will be to die for."

Buddy looked sheepish. "Ah no thanks, Jeff. Frances is going to show me the best place in town to get broasted chicken. Always been real partial to broasted chicken."

"Oh," Jeff said taken aback. "Well that would be the fast food place up on the highway. Yeah, they do have good chicken. Real good. I gotta go."

Jeff walked quickly to the front door of the Town Hall and then stepped outside. Twilight had fallen heavily this autumn evening and a cool wind caused him to clasp his jacket collar tightly to his neck. Once inside the car he inserted the key and turned it. Then he stopped, sat for a moment, smiled, and wondered aloud, "Is Frances old enough to be going out with men? Especially Buddy."

Chapter 11

Frances pulled her tan Honda into the crowded parking lot of the only fast food restaurant in town. She and Buddy got out and started for the door. Frances reached for the doorknob but Buddy's hand got there first. He smiled and opened the door for her. As the door opened a bell clanked. The sound of voices, the cash register bell, and laughter floated from inside the restaurant. All noise ceased, however, as Frances entered followed closely by a handsome young stranger. Buddy felt like the piercing eyes stripped him bare. Frances walked proudly to the counter and stood under a sign that read *Place Order Here*. Buddy followed her and began reading a menu that was posted on a large board above the grill.

"Hey Frances," said the attractive woman of about forty from behind the counter. "What ya' having this evening?" The table noise in the restaurant resumed and Buddy felt less self conscious.

"Lemme see," said Frances studying the menu intently as if it were the first time she'd seen it. "Ah...I think I'll have the chicken salad plate. And, Mavis, you can leave off that little bunch of grapes."

"Okay," said Mavis. "Willard, one chicken salad plate...hold the grapes. And you sir, what can I get for you?" she said shyly.

Buddy whispered to Frances, "You're not getting the broasted chicken? Thought you said it was to die for." Mavis waited patiently.

"It is," said Frances. "But I had that last night. I want something different tonight."

"Oh," Buddy said simply. Then he turned to Mavis and said, "I'll have the broasted chicken plate."

"Good choice," said Mavis. "Mostly only women order the chicken salad plate." Then she turned toward the grill and said. "One broasted chicken. And what can I get you to drink?"

"Sweet tea," said Frances.

"Make that two," said Buddy.

Mavis tore a small slip of paper off a pad and handed it to Buddy. "Your numbers are 213 and 214. You can find a seat if'n you want to. I'll call your number when it's ready."

Buddy and Frances turned toward the dining area. It was a small room with an asphalt tile floor and vertical blinds hung at the large windows. The tables were metal with formica tops and the seats were covered in turquoise plastic. Large napkins holders, tomato ketchup, salt and pepper, and Tabasco sauce set on each table. A few booths hugged the hospital green walls. Frances spotted a booth where an over-weight, elderly couple were gathering their things to leave. She walked toward the booth and Buddy followed.

"Hey Mrs. Edwards," said Frances. "How you tonight?"

The elderly woman looked at her and stopped trying to extricate herself from the booth that was much too tight for her hefty body. She looked at Frances, smiled, and then noticed Buddy. "Why I'm making it pretty good, Frances. And who are you young man? I know everybody in Seaboard, and I don't recognize you."

Buddy smiled, "I'm Buddy Turner."

"And I'm Lily Mae Edwards. This here is my husband, Earnest." Earnest nodded and held out a rough, sunburned hand. "You from round here Buddy? You kin to the Turners over in Jackson?"

"No ma'am," said Buddy. "I'm from Raleigh."

"Raleigh?" She looked at Frances and then back at Buddy. "Well, now don't you go a taking Frances to Raleigh. You know her sister moved up there...God rest her soul... and we never got her back."

Lily Mae Edwards finally struggled out of her seat, stood, and patted Frances on the arm. Then she turned to Buddy, "It was nice to meet you young man. What's your business?"

"What?" said Buddy.

Frances laughed, "He's a U.S. Marshal here working on that murder out at the Blankenship farm."

Mrs. Edwards gasped. "Well it's doubly good to meet you. I hope y'all can put a stop to that kind of doings." She took her husband's arm and they ambled toward another table. Frances knew that Mrs. Lilly Mae would make the rounds of the tables and tell the diners what she'd learned of the young man with Frances.

Frances and Buddy slid into the booth. A young black man appeared. He removed the Edwards' plates and wiped the table. Buddy leaned across the table and

156

whispered to Frances, "Your Mrs. Edwards is a piece of work."

Frances laughed and watched Mrs. Lily Mae as she began her rounds, table to table, town crier. "Bless her heart. She means well," said Frances.

A loudspeaker announced that numbers 213 and 214 were ready. Buddy pushed himself out of the booth and started to the counter. He reached the table where Mrs. Lily Mae was speaking with another elderly woman who might have been her twin...same hair style, same dowdy dress, same gnarled fingers painted with chipped red nail polish.

"Ah Buddy," said Mrs. Edwards, "I want you to meet Mrs. Clara Taylor. She goes to my church. Clara, this here is Buddy Turner I was speaking of."

"Nice to meet you, young man," she said in such a low voice that Buddy leaned close to hear. "Lily Mae said she told you not to take Frances away from us. I second the motion."

"Yes ma'am," said Buddy. "I can tell Frances is well liked in Seaboard."

"She's our pet," whispered Clara Taylor and patted Buddy's arm.

At that moment the loudspeaker repeated again that 213 and 214 orders were ready for pickup. "It's a getting cold here," the announcer added.

Buddy excused himself and hurried to the counter. The woman behind the counter laughed, "Thought you needed a little help back there."

Buddy took out a bill and placed it on the counter. "Thanks. Thanks a lot. And keep the change."

When Buddy got back to the table, Frances was laughing so hard that tears ran down her cheeks. "I could just imagine what Mrs. Edwards and Mrs. Taylor were saying to you. Then when your order was announced a second time…you should have seen yourself. You near 'bout ran to that counter."

Buddy set the paper plates on the table. "Glad to provide some dinner entertainment," he said. This brought on a hoot of laughter from Frances and heads turned to stare again at the couple.

"Buddy, what about the sweet tea?" asked Frances. Buddy groaned and this brought on another fit of laughter from Frances and more head turning from the diners. Buddy weaved his way through the tables again, skulked to the counter, and picked up the sweet ice teas. The waitress behind the counter grinned slyly.

Buddy returned to the table with the drinks and they dived into their supper. "Good chicken," said Buddy.

"Told you. This supper is every bit as good as you could get if you'd gone with Jeff Sands. Maybe even better," said Frances.

"So…hear anything new today? Anything else that might help in the investigation," asked Buddy.

Frances shook her head and swallowed. "Glad you asked though. Glad you are interested. Jeff sure don't pay much attention to my contributions."

Buddy looked surprised. "Now Frances, Jeff's acknowledged your contributions to the team many times," he said.

"Humph," scoffed Frances.

"Frances, how come you're all times scoffing about my friend Jeff? Most folks think he's a pretty nice guy. He's smart. He works hard. He's considerate. He..."

"And he thinks he's God's gift to women," blurted out Frances.

"What?" said Buddy. For a moment he was dumbstruck. Then he continued, "It's my opinion that Jeff is totally devoted to Sophie Singletary. Why he doesn't seem to think another woman exists."

Frances blushed. She'd said far more than she intended. She'd never revealed her secret crush on Jeff to anyone. Finally Frances said, "Well, regardless, Jeff seems to me to think way too much of himself."

Buddy gave Frances an indulgent look, took a long swallow of sweet tea, and said, "Good sweet tea, too."

When they finished eating, Buddy gathered paper plates, plastic forks and cups, and took them to the trashcan. As they walked through the restaurant Buddy thought Frances was walking a bit too slowly...or perhaps he was just anxious to get away from prying eyes. Outside he opened the driver's door, Frances slid in, and he closed the door. Frances felt the approving looks of the older patrons who watched from inside the restaurant. Then Buddy circled the car and took his place in the front passenger's seat. Frances started the engine but before backing out she said, "Want to see my apartment?"

"Ah...yeah. Sure," said Buddy. "Where do you live?"

"Just round the corner from Dillon," she said.

Frances drove across the railroad tracks, down Main Street, pass Dillon's house, and took the first right. On the

159

left side of the street were one-story bungalow type houses. On the right side of the street was a row of WWII surplus prefab apartments. Frances pulled into the drive of one of the apartments and hopped out of the car. Buddy followed her and waited as she unlocked the door. She threw open the door, stood back, and her hand swept down in an *enter* motion. Buddy stepped into the apartment and stopped short.

It was like stepping out of a time machine. From the pungent odor of incense to the tie-dye throws on the sofa and bean bag chair, the nineteen sixties/seventies were alive and well. Black lights illuminated posters of old sixties and seventies rock stars that papered the walls. A make-shift entertainment center constructed of bricks and boards hugged one wall and against the opposite side of the room was a sagging old sofa with enormous pillows that could be thrown on the floor for extra seats. At one end of the sofa was a wooden table painted metallic orange and setting on it was an amber lava lamp. At the other end of the sofa stacks of Rolling Stone Magazines were dumped into a large straw basket. In the back of the room were a metal table and two matching chairs. The table was littered with newspapers carrying articles about the Blankenship farm murder. Long hanging ropes of multi-colored beads hung from the entrance to a tiny kitchen. Off to the right was another room that Buddy reasoned to be the bedroom. The apartment was a study in 1960 and 70 décor.

"Ahhh…this…this is something!" said Buddy.

Frances stepped into the room and closed the door. "Do you like it?" she asked.

"Whyyy…this is *really* something," he repeated.

"Again with the *it's something,*" she said. "Are you poking fun at my apartment?"

"No, no, no. It's just that it's...it's indescribable," said Buddy.

"It was Janet's," Frances said proudly. "Well, not this particular apartment, but when we were growing up over on Main Street Janet had all this stuff in her room. It originally belonged to mama and daddy. So when Janet moved to Raleigh she passed it down to me. And here I am still using it. Some trends just never go out of style you know."

"Yeah, well. This is something. Just look at that thing-a-ma jig," he said pointing to the lava lamp.

Frances laughed. "I like being different. I like adventure...like this investigation we're working on. It's fun snooping around and trying to figure things out. It's exciting. Can't wait to get up in the morning and get on with it. I've always been a free spirit...a little unusual. I'm restless. I like to experience new things."

Buddy smiled. "I like that in a woman," he said and moved quickly across the room toward Frances.

* * *

Jeff pulled into the driveway of the yellow Victorian house. He took the steps two at a time, crossed the porch, and tried the door knob. The door was locked. He smiled. Sophie finally got it. She'd locked the doors. Sophie felt too safe in Seaboard, and thought locking doors was a nuisance. Jeff took out a key, unlocked the door, and stepped inside. A blizzard of memories struck him. The murmur of soft voices from the kitchen floated into the hall. The smell of baking bread mingled with the faint odor of smoke from the den fireplace where an early autumn fire sent licks of flames up the old brick chimney. On the hall table the glow from the glass globe of the orange Handel lamp cast shadows on the wall and up the stairwell. From upstairs he heard Sophie humming a tune he did not recognize. He listened for a few seconds in an effort to identify the melody. Then he gave up.

"Sophie," Jeff called.

"Is that you, Jeff?" she replied.

"Who were you expecting?" he said.

His quip was followed by footsteps rushing across the upstairs hall and then thumping down the steps.

Sophie flew into Jeff's arms. He grabbed her around her waist and pressed her hard against him. They kissed long and deep and hard. Then Jeff heard the steady approach of footsteps from the dining room and without pushing away he opened one eye and saw Gladys standing in the dining room door hands on her hips.

"Y'all can stand there a messing around and acting like childrun as long as you want to but I'm a-puttin' supper on the table right now." Then impervious to the passionate scene, she turned and walked toward the kitchen.

Sophie pushed away, laughed, and pulled Jeff toward the dining room. "Gladys has been cooking all day. I'm sure she cooked enough for an army."

From the kitchen Gladys said, "Onlyest time you eat is when he's around so I'm a takin' advantage of the situation."

And take advantage she had. Dinner featured exceptional southern cuisine...cherry salad, paper thin slices of country ham, angel biscuits, corn pudding, spinach soufflé, and chocolate cake with Gladys' home-made ice cream for dessert. The meal was served with an exquisite wine from Grandmother Singletary's small wine cellar beneath the kitchen.

"Gladys, you've outdone yourself this time," Jeff said loudly.

"Just a little something I throwed together," she said and they laughed.

As the meal vanished, Sophie said reluctantly, "Jeff, how was your day...I mean the investigation. Did you find out anything helpful?" Sophie was always reluctant to ask about Jeff's work because he usually said, *I can't talk about my work, Sophie.* Then she'd feel shut out.

Jeff sighed, shook his head, and said, "I don't suppose there's any reason not to talk about what happened today. Nothing happened."

Sophie looked disappointed. All went quiet in the kitchen. Then Jeff stopped eating, created a steeple with his fingers, and said, "No really. We're frustrated because for three days we haven't raised a single clue. We went out to the crime scene this morning just to give it a second look. I did discover that the view from where the car was parked was a straight shot to the Wood's front door. Went to talk to the Wood ladies. Sara was hostile for no good reason, and we were not allowed to question the two sisters alone. Nothing accomplished there. Came back to where the Mayor was conducting a press conference. We'd heard it all. Then two boys from Northampton High School came in. They'd seen Nicey Parsons driving toward Seaboard. Nothing new there. I told you...we are frustrated."

Jeff fell silent, took a sip of wine, and looked at Sophie's disappointed face. Apparently the kitchen listeners were disappointed too. Dishes began to clatter again. Then the door opened, Gladys entered, and began to remove plates from the table.

Jeff decided that sharing everything they'd learned today wouldn't put Sophie, Gladys, and Melvin in danger. So Jeff lifted a finger heavenward and said in a loud voice, "*BUT* all was not lost. Our intrepid investigator, Frances, came through. She gave us something to work on tomorrow."

"Frances? Really?" Sophie said.

Sophie leaned forward, Gladys pulled up a chair, and Melvin appeared at the kitchen door.

Jeff grinned and said jokingly, "Sure did. Frances saved an otherwise worthless day. Harvey remembered there were more than three sisters in the Wood family."

"Really? I've only known *three* sisters," said Sophie.

"Ah...*sisters* yes. *BUT* how about brothers...or brother?" said Jeff. He leaned back pompously in his chair, crossed his arms across his chest, and raised his eyebrows quizzically.

"Jeff," said Sophie. "I don't remember a brother."

"I does," said Gladys.

"Me too," said Melvin who moved a few steps closer to the table. "He hulped me once brush some leaves offen the roof."

"Yeah, I 'member that," said Gladys. "That was while you wuz on your first marriage, Sophie. That's how come you don't member him."

"But he ain't gonna hulp you none now," said Melvin. "He's daid."

"I know he's dead. John. John Wood was his name," said Jeff.

"Okay. Harvey told you about John Wood. How did Frances help?" said Sophie.

"Frances heard Mrs. Bernice talking about John Wood at the post office," said Jeff. "Mrs Bernice apparently remembers him well. I'm hoping Mrs. Bernice can give us useful information. I have this feeling there's something there."

"I knows that feeling. It's a gift. Some folks throws it off and don't pay no 'ttention," Gladys said shooting Sophie an accusatory glance. "But I does. Whenever I get that feeling that something's 'bout to happen I prepares for it."

"Well I don't know what it means," said Jeff. "But John Wood was real young when he died with complications from influenza, and Miss Sara took care of him. Sara Wood wouldn't be my choice for a nurse."

Sophie's eyes widened. "Jeff are you saying that Miss Sara…"

"No," said Jeff. "I'm not saying anything except that Harvey told us about Brother John and Frances led us to Mrs. Bernice. Hopefully Mrs. Bernice can give us something to move on."

Sophie leaned back and smiled. "Frances. Can you believe? She's a resourceful, contributing member of a real investigative team. Little Frances."

"Yes, this is the second time she's come through," said Jeff. Then he was silent for a few seconds. "You know, sometimes I think she doesn't like me. It's just the way she acts and things she says. She doesn't want to sit next to me. She throws me disgusted looks. She mocks me. She..."

Sophie laughed. "She has a crush on you, Silly. She has a crush on you and hasn't been able to get your attention the appropriate way so she's goading you."

Jeff looked astonished. "What? How do you know she has a crush on me?"

Sophie and Gladys laughed. "I was once a young woman too or have you forgotten," said Sophie.

* * *

Jeff was totally exhausted and Gladys' fine dinner made him sleepy, relaxed. He lay on Sophie's bed resting his head on his bent arm. The only light in the room was from small flames darting about in the fireplace. As the fire burned low a log dropped from the grate shooting embers up the chimney. Outside a fine rain whispered against the windowpane.

Jeff heard Sophie humming in the bathroom and tried again to identify the tune. He couldn't. Music was not one of Jeff's talents. The shower turned on, the humming was muted, and Jeff fought to stay awake. Finally the bathroom door opened and a sliver of light pierced the dimly lit room.

166

Jeff opened his eyes to see Sophie silhouetted against the bathroom light. She wore a white terry cloth bathrobe and no shoes. Her hair was damp and wet strands were pasted to her forehead.

"Hey," he said in a hoarse voice. He wiggled his fingers at Sophie in a come here motion.

"Hey yourself," she said. And she flipped off the bathroom light and walked across the room to the bed.

Sophie lifted her knee onto the bed, leaned forward, and said, "Tired?"

"Yeah," whispered Jeff.

"TOO tired?" Sophie asked.

Jeff placed his hand on her knee and said, "Never. Never too tired for you."

Sophie untied the terry cloth robe and let it slide to the floor. Jeff reached up, took her arm, and pulled her onto the bed and under the down comforter. Years of being apart had left scars. Now when they made love it was passionate, desperate, as if they would not have another night together.

At last they lay quietly, contentedly. Sophie quickly fell asleep. She slept on her side one leg stretched across Jeff's, her hand curled under her chin. Jeff gently stroked her arm. It was cool and smooth. He pulled the comforter up and snuggled it closely under her chin.

Sleep did not come so easily to Jeff. He always searched for rational explanations. But tonight he tried a new technique. He let his mind roam freely into dimensions he usually checked. Perhaps using this technique would shed some light on the complexities of the Nicey Parsons murder. Why had Nicey Parsons come to Seaboard? What story could she be pursuing in such an unlikely place? What took her to the Blankenship farm of all places? Who knew she was there? Was she really alone? Was the killer a hit man or woman? A local? What was Sara Wood trying to hide? Why wouldn't she let her sisters talk? Questions. Questions. Questions. But no answers.

The gentle rain increased. Now raindrops sounded like small pebbles being tossed against the window glass, and the wind became stronger. A gust swept down the chimney and revived a dying ember just long enough for it to morph into a small flame then quickly die. Jeff lay still as the firelight disappeared and darkness engulfed the room.

* * *

Sophie awoke and touched the bed where Jeff had slept. The sheets were cool. As she sat up she saw her terry cloth bathrobe folded neatly on the foot of the bed. She reached for the robe, slipped it on, and walked into the bathroom. The room was warm and damp and smelled like Jeff. Finding her slippers, she put them on and headed downstairs. When she reached the dining room she heard voices and laughter coming from the kitchen.

"That right?...You don't say?....Go 'way from here!" she heard Melvin say with a hearty chuckle.

Sophie pushed the door open to find Jeff and Melvin sitting at the small kitchen table. A large plate of half eaten breakfast set in front of Jeff, and Melvin held a large mug of coffee.

Jeff looked up, smiled brightly, and said, "Morning Sunshine."

168

Sophie walked to him, took his head, and pressed it to her breast. Jeff placed his hand on her thigh, and smacked her affectionately.

Accustomed to their intimate display of affectionate, Gladys simply said, "You eating this morning or no?"

"Just juice and toast, please," said Sophie taking a seat on Jeff's knee.

"You ask me you gonna be marrying a bunch of bones come December," Gladys said to Jeff. Then turning to Sophie she added, "He ain't gonna want to cozy up to no bunch of cold bones on a winter night, Missy. You just wait and see."

"Is she right, Jeff?" Sophie asked.

"Better listen to the woman, Sophie," said Jeff.

Sophie punched his arm playfully, slipped into a chair, and said, "Give me what Jeff had…just not as much."

For a few minutes they watched the small screen television in silence. "So what's on your agenda today?" Sophie asked.

Jeff swallowed, looked at his watch, and said, "First on the agenda is talk to Mrs. Bernice about John Wood. Don't know what's there but…well we'll see,"

Jeff wiped his mouth, stood, and said, "Gladys, I don't know about Sophie, but I'm gonna be putting on the pounds if you keep feeding me like that. Good. Mighty good."

Gladys beamed, "Good to be 'ppreciated."

"I appreciate you, Gladys," said Sophie as she stood and followed Jeff to the front hall. "Jeff will you come home for lunch?"

Jeff turned and raised a critical eye. "Sophie, how many times...."

"I know, Jeff. I know you don't know how your day will go. Sorry," she said and reached for him. "I'm trying. Have you noticed?"

Jeff laughed. "I've noticed. It's gonna take some doing on both our parts. But it can be done. I'll call you." And he kissed her, turned, and left.

Chapter 12

Frances drove into the parking area behind the post office, and she and Buddy looked around the lot sheepishly. When she turned off the engine they leaned toward each other and their seat belts pinched them. They laughed, unfastened the belts, and kissed hurriedly.

Frances reached for the door handle. "Gotta go. Late. Irma'll pitch another one of her hissy fits."

"Me, too," said Buddy and he exited the car.

Outside they looked at each other over the top of the car. Frances smiled. "See you tonight?"

"If I can," said Buddy.

They rushed down the short alley. Frances reached the side entrance to the post office, kicked the door, and said, "Open up, Irma. It's me." Then she turned to watch Buddy trot across Main Street.

Irma opened the door with a scowl on her face. "You're late, Frances. Real late."

"I know," said Frances hanging her jacket on a rack.

"Well, what do you expect. Irma?" said a cackling voice from the front of the room. "She's been out *investigating.*"

Frances turned and saw Mrs. Bernice leaning over the counter into the sorting room. She wore full makeup and smiled her brightest smile. "We done heard about your *date* last night from about half a dozen sources this morning,

Frances. Now you come on over here and give us the inside poop."

Frances grinned broadly and joined the women at the counter. "Well?" coaxed Mrs. Bernice. "What kinda fella you snared?"

Frances cleared her throat, paused for a few seconds to add drama, and said, "He's *real* nice. He's a gentleman, smart, and good at the conversation. He seems to like me and I really like him, too."

Mrs. Bernice looked disappointed. "That's all you gonna give us...gentleman, smart, talks good...might as well be describing a preacher."

Then Frances leaned in close and whispered, "And he's got this sexy thing going on."

Mrs. Bernice leaned back, slapped the counter, and cackled. Irma looked shocked.

"Frances, I don't want to hear this," she said and walked away.

"I do," shouted Mrs. Bernice. "Tell me everything, Frances."

* * *

Dillon and Jeff turned as Buddy rushed through the front door of Town Hall. He had shaved and his hair was damp. He wore yesterday's jeans and a fresh knit shirt that he hurriedly picked up at Dillon's house. He looked flushed and embarrassed.

Dillon stood and all six foot three inches slowly unfolded. Jeff also stood and a dark frown crossed his face.

172

Dillon looked at Buddy sternly and said in s deep, husky voice, "You with my Little Sister all night?"

A look of panic crossed Buddy's face. His face turned pale and he felt like he was going to be sick. He thought this must be how a raccoon feels when it's treed by hounds. He looked from one man to the other. Dillon approached him with Jeff close behind. Buddy stepped back. He opened his mouth but it was so dry he couldn't speak.

"I...I d...did..." Buddy sputtered. He felt faint.

Then Dillon stepped in close, grabbed Buddy by the shoulders, and pulled him into a bear hug. And in a loud voice Dillon said, "Way to go Buddy!!! Hoped you would hit it off with Little Sister ever since I saw you checking each other out."

The room exploded in laughter as Jeff and Harvey Clinton joined in the teasing. Buddy thought he'd collapse. Then he excused himself and headed toward the restroom. That brought on another round of laughter.

"That was mean. I don't hold with practical jokes myself," said Harvey. Then he added with a snicker, "But I have to admit it was hilarious."

When Buddy came out the restroom, both men apologized and things settled down. Then they looked out the front window just in time to see a silver gray Crown Victoria pull into a space marked *Police Only* and bounce off the curb. Mrs. Bernice had *driven* from the post office that was just across Main Street from Town Hall. The door opened and Mrs. Bernice climbed out of the car, stood, and wrestled her skirt down. She frowned at the two steps she'd have to climb to reach the door of the Hall. Then with a determined look she started to climb. Finally, she threw open the door and walked in with bravado.

"Well, here I am," she said a loud shrill voice. "I understand my input is needed in this *puzzling* case."

"Mrs. Bernice," said Dillon. "Glad you're here. We were gonna call you first thing this morning."

She waddled toward the back of the room, and looked at the rail partition that identified the police office. Then she studied the chairs inside.

"Well, if'n you expect me to sit, you're going to have to find a larger and sturdier chair than that little metal thing," she said.

Buddy scurried to the front of the room and returned pushing the mayor's large rolling leather chair. "Yes, now that will do fine," Mrs. Bernice said. "Only Jeff, you hold on to this thing while I get situated. I don't want to roll out on Main Street."

Jeff held the chair steady while Mrs. Bernice eased herself into the chair. "Frances tells me you want to see me. Now how can I help you gentlemen?" she said.

Jeff nodded to Dillon. Dillon said, "Mrs. Bernice, do you mind if we record our conversation. Sometimes it difficult to remember details later on."

"Not at all. I'd be disappointed if'n you didn't. I want you to do this the way they do on television...record and all."

Dillon put a small tape recorder on the desk. He turned it on, stated the date, time, place, and names of those present at the interview. "Mrs. Bernice, there are two things we're hoping you can help us with. First, we'd like you to tell us what you know about John Wood. And

174

second, we hope you can tell us about Mr. Myron Blankenship."

Mrs. Bernice's eyes were fixed on Dillon as she listened to him. "That's it?" she said.

"Yes ma'am," said Dillon.

"Which first?"

"Which ever one you want to start with," said Dillon.

Mrs. Bernice tapped her lips with her finger and looked up at the ceiling. Finally she said, "Myron Blankenship first. Myron was a true gentleman of the old school, and he was rich. Not just by Northampton standards, but by any standards. At one time the Blankenship family owned a big piece of the county. Back when he was getting started wealth was measured by the amount of land you owned. *You aren't a man if you don't own land* is how the saying went. If you apply that to Myron Blankenship...well then he was quite the man. Mostly he was a farmer...a gentleman farmer. Although I heard that he dabbled in stocks and such on the side. Back then some thought of that as gambling. And he was quite a dandy. You boys don't know what a dandy is do you?"

In unison they said, "No ma'am."

Mrs. Bernice chuckled. "A dandy is a fellow who likes to dress up real smart like. Myron was a real dresser. He always wore a three piece suit with a gold chain and a Masonic fob dangling from his vest pocket. He wore a hat...fedora I believe...and tipped it low to every woman he passed. Heh...heh. Now notice I said woman not lady. I don't want you a-thinkin' that Myron was just polite to *rich* folks...as if'n there were many rich people in Northampton County. Myron had a big heart and loved everybody.

175

Never looked down on anybody because they was poor. Why you were just as apt to catch him a talking to a tenant farmer out on the street as a doctor or judge. He was a kind man. You was likely to see him and his friend Jim Beam a sitting out on his front porch with a bunch of dirt farmers. Why they'd all be a sipping a glass of bourbon with orange slices in it."

Realizing that Mrs. Bernice was wandering a field, Jeff motioned Dillon to speed up the interview. Dillon said, "'Cuse me Mrs. Bernice, but can you tell us anything about the field next to his barn on Elm street?

"Elm Street!," scoffed Mrs. Bernice. "I don't hold with all this here name changing. Galatia Road's what it always was and Galatia Road is what it will always be in my mind."

"Yes ma'am," said Dillon. "But can you…"

Mrs. Bernice interrupted. "Heard you the first time Dillon. Just collecting my thoughts. Lemme see now." There was a brief hesitation. "I don't remember anything note worthy 'bout that particular piece of his land. He built a shack and that great big old tobacco barn you see out there now. He planted tobacco on one side of the land and another crop…maybe peanuts or such…on the other. Then the next year he'd rotate the fields not planting the same crop on the land two years in a row. That's called rotating your crops. You see if'n you just plant the same crop on a field year after year you deplete the nutrients and…"

Jeff gave the speed-up sign again as Mrs. Bernice prepared to launch into an agricultural lesson. Dillon said, "Yes ma'am. Did you know any of the people who lived in that shack?"

It was hard for Mrs. Bernice to change gears abruptly. Again she pressed her fingers to her lips, looked at the ceiling, and then said, "No."

"You don't recall *any* of the workers who stayed in that shack?" asked Dillon.

"I do not," said Mrs. Bernice emphatically. "You see, Myron took on some pitiful folks back then. He'd hire them just when the tobacco started coming in. They'd strip the tobacco leaves, tie them in bunches you know, and hang them cross poles in that big old barn to dry. Then when the leaves were dry and ready for market they'd trail along behind Myron…usually to Durham…to market. After he sold the tobacco he paid them cash money right on the spot. That's how they did things back then you know, you didn't have to keep such good tax records and such."

"What did the workers do after they were paid?" asked Dillon.

Mrs. Bernice shrugged. "I don't know for sure," she said. "I reckon they just took off as soon as they got their money. On occasion they'd come back here for the winter but not often enough for me to remember."

"When they did stay for the winter, how did the folks of Seaboard treat them?" asked Dillon.

"Far as I know, fine," said Mrs. Bernice. Then she suddenly seemed to remember something. She waggled a finger at Dillon and added. "Come to think of it, I do remember one year when a family stayed after harvest. Now they was real pitiful folks. Myron was all times taking food and such to them. Well, Sara Wood…lives 'cross the road you know…pitched one doozy of a fit. She criticized Myron for letting that *poor white trash* stay the

177

winter…that's what she called them. She was a ranting and a raving all over town about it. Sara's got a real short fuse so to speak."

Jeff said, "Yes, ma'am we found that out. Mrs. Bernice you are really a big help and a great storyteller. Would you like something to drink…coffee, water…before we ask you about John Wood?"

"No thank you, Jeff," she said. "Let's get on with it. I got a pot of Brunswick stew on the stove. You taking over the questions now?"

"Yes ma'am, if that's okay," Jeff said with a smile.

"Okay by me. Shoot," she said.

"Mrs. Bernice, did you know John Wood?" asked Jeff.

"Sure did and he was as nice a boy as you could find. Did a lot of yard work for my husband. My husband used to say he was as dependable as a rooster at the crack of dawn."

"How old was John when he worked for your husband?" asked Jeff.

"Oh, he was just a boy. Teenager. Maybe a little older. He was bright. He would have amounted to something if'n he'd lived. Now he and Sara, they was right smart not like the two young sisters. Those two are dim as a burnt out light bulb and just about as useless. I don't understand how those four came out of the same nest." She leaned forward and whispered, "I heard tell that old man Wood and his wife were first cousins. That would count for the last two young uns…but like I said John and Sara were sharp as tacks."

"What can you tell us about the illness that killed John?" said Jeff.

"Not much to tell," said Mrs. Bernice. "Seaboard had a rough year of it. That flu epidemic was the worst I can remember. Old folks died like flies and we lost some babies. But I think everybody was shocked when young John Wood succumbed...him being so strong and young."

"Yes, ma'am," said Jeff. "Did you know Doctor Lowell, John's doctor?"

"Why sure," said Mrs. Bernice. "If'n you lived in Seaboard you knew the Doc. He was the only one in town."

"Did you ever hear Doctor Lowell mention John's illness?"

"No, not really," she said. Then added, "Once he did question Sara a takin' care of John."

Jeff perked up, "What did he say?"

"Not much. Just said that he didn't hold with close kin a takin' care of someone as sick as John was. Said they couldn't be objective."

Jeff said, "Mrs. Bernice, this is a long shot, but do you have any idea where the doctor's records might be?"

Mrs. Bernice shook her head vigorously. "None whatsoever," she said. "Why all his kin came into his house a-tearin' things up. They pitched out everything they didn't want and carted the rest away. Why I'd say those records are liable to be anywhere."

Jeff looked disappointed. "And you can't remember anything else that the doctor said about the illness or death of John Wood?"

Mrs. Bernice shook her head sadly. "Only other time he mentioned it in front of me is when John died. He was

179

talking to my late husband 'cause he knew how fond he was of John. The doc said, *If'n I could have taken him to the hospital in Roanoke Rapids, maybe we could have saved him."*

Jeff perked up again. "He said that?"

"Sure did," said Mrs. Bernice. "I was standing not six feet from them."

"Then why? Why didn't he just move him to the hospital?"

"Sara," Mrs. Bernice said simply. "Sara said sick folks should be taken care of by family. And that was that. She also said she had those two sisters to look after and couldn't be a trotting to the hospital to check on John. Doc couldn't stand up to the likes of Sara Wood. He was too gentle. Of course, I don't know of anyone what can stand up to her."

Jeff exhaled loudly. "Mrs. Bernice, thank you. Thank you so much you've been a great help."

Then he looked toward Dillon and Buddy. "Questions?" Dillon smiled and said no.

For the first time Mrs. Bernice noticed Buddy. She grinned widely and said, "Are you Frances' young man?"

Buddy blushed and looked at Jeff then Dillon. He remembered their ribbing. Both men grinned and nodded. "I...I guess so," Buddy stammered.

Mrs. Bernice positioned her hands on the arms of the rolling chair in preparation to stand. Jeff and Dillon rushed to assist her. She finally got to her feet, walked to Buddy, and looked him squarely in the eyes. Buddy froze. "What's your name?" she demanded.

"Why...why, my name is Buddy," he sputtered.

"No, that's not what I mean," she said. "What's your *real* name. Buddy is not a name."

Buddy's face took on a bitter expression as if he'd just licked a lemon. Dillon and Harvey leaned forward in an effort to hear. "Buford," he said. "My name is Buford Turner."

Mrs. Bernice stepped back and looked at him proudly. "Buford. Now that's a name to be proud of. I don't hold with those nick-names. Buford. Say it proudly, boy."

And she turned and headed toward the front of the Hall. Harvey moved quickly and took her arm to help her to her car. As she reached the door she stopped, turned, and said, "You any kin to the Turners over at Jackson?"

"No ma'am," said Buddy.

"Nice family. Good stock," she said as she exited the Town Hall.

"Buford?" taunted Dillon. "I don't know how I feel about my Little Sister hanging out with a guy named *Buford.*"

Jeff was preparing to join in when his phone vibrated. He looked at the display. "Sands," he said as he walked toward the back door. In a few minutes Jeff returned with a scowl on his face. "Well that's perfect timing," he said sarcastically. Just when I think things are shaking loose in Seaboard we get called back to Raleigh."

"Raleigh?" echoed Buddy and Dillon.

"Yeah, Bryant says the M. E. has new information for us that just can't wait. I just hope he's calling it straight. Now that we've talked with Mrs. Bernice, I'm more anxious than ever to talk with Miss Sara Wood and her sisters. What do you think Dillon?"

Dillon was every bit as disappointed. "I'm ready to tear into her, too, but I'd feel more confident if you were along."

"Me too." said Jeff. He paced for a few seconds then said, "Okay, Bryant said the conference won't take long. Could be back tonight. Of course, we've heard that before."

He looked at Buddy. Buddy nodded in agreement. Jeff continued, "Most importantly I don't want Sara and her brood to disappear. Dillon, keep an eye on her but stay out of sight. Who knows, Bryant might give us something to use when we talk to her...although I don't know what."

Dillon said, "I got to pull these two interviews together...Mrs. Bernice's and the two high school kids. You know I don't have a secretary...I'm it. I'll have Stewart keep an eye on the Woods."

"Good," said Jeff. "I can't see that we'll lose much by waiting a day. Hopefully we'll be back the latest tomorrow. I gotta call Sophie." And he began to walk toward the back door again, paused, and said, "By the way, where is Stewart?"

"Remember he's part-time. One of his jobs is road maintenance. He's over on Harris Street scraping sand off the road. That rain we had last night washed sand onto the pavement. Mrs. Josie's afraid the sand will cause a vehicle to spin out."

Jeff nodded and continued toward the back door. Suddenly Buddy jumped up, "I just remembered. I gotta run to the post office a minute." Dillon smiled.

182

Chapter 13

Jeff pulled into the parking lot of the Terry Sanford Federal Building at 310 New Bern Street in Raleigh at exactly four fifteen. He and Buddy had vented the first fifty miles of the trip then fell into sullen silence the rest of the way. Several early quitters were heading home, and they waved to Jeff and Buddy. Without lifting his hand from the steering Jeff raised two fingers in response to their greeting. Inside the building they took the elevator to the fifth floor and walked to a door marked Arlis Bryant, Assistant Director Eastern District, U.S. Marshal Services.

They walked into the office and saw Cathy Roberson seated behind her desk. She held a pencil poised above a yellow legal pad. She looked at the men impatiently, made a check on the legal pad, and stood.

"Mr. Bryant has been waiting for you," she said.

"We'll go on in," said Jeff and he headed to the closed door.

"Just a minute, Jeff," Cathy said as she scurried pass him. "I must announce you."

Jeff stepped aside to let Cathy enter first then looked back at Buddy and shook his head. Buddy just rolled his eyes.

Cathy tapped softly on the door, opened it, and said, "Mr. Bryant, Jeff Sands and Buddy Turner are here to see you."

"Good. Good," said Bryant in a deep, booming voice. "Show them in."

Cathy stepped aside and made a sweeping gesture indicating that *now* they may enter. As Jeff and Buddy walked in Cathy said, "Can I do anything else for you, Mr. Bryant?" And she smiled slyly.

"No thank you. Not just now," he said and returned the sly smile.

Bryant did not bother to stand. His near three hundred pounds made standing too great an effort. However, Ned Cosden, the Medical Examiner, did stand and walked toward the two Marshals.

"Good to see you Jeff...Buddy," he said hand extended. His handshake was firm but not pretentious.

"Good to see you too, Ned."

"Okay, let's get this show on the road. I've got an evening appointment," said Bryant by way of opening the meeting. "Ned, you start us off...after all this is your party." And Bryant leaned back in his over-sized leather desk chair, crossed his hands across his enormous chest, and closed his eyes.

"Right," said Ned. "Jeff, Buddy, I think I have some information that's gonna help you in your investigation."

"I certainly hope so," said Jeff. "We could use some help about now."

Ned opened a folder and looked at the top sheet. "We did a complete autopsy of the victim. She bled to death of course. Her throat was cut from ear to ear, and the weapon was a very large knife...possibly a hunting knife. Too bad we didn't come up with a weapon."

"That was unfortunate," said Jeff moving about in his chair impatiently.

"She was cut in the car, pulled out, and dragged into the barn where she bled out. It didn't take long for her to bleed out either…we won't go into that right now. The injuries to her face and fingers were done by the crows. They pecked out her eyes, tore off both ear lobes, and did a mess of her fingers."

"I thought crows ate meat that was rot…spoiled," said Buddy.

"That's true for the most part. They're so often seen pecking at road kill." said Ned. "But this young woman was dragged right into their roost and left. I guess it was just too much of a smorgasbord for them to pass up."

Jeff was becoming edgy. "We already figured all this, Ned," he said thinking how their time could be better spent in Seaboard questioning Miss Sara.

"We checked handwriting. The handwriting on the car rental papers matches Nicey Parson's signature on her driver's license," Ned said.

"I already said I thought they were the same," said Jeff.

"I know that, Jeff," said Ned, "but we checked officially. Now hang on, the best is yet to come."

Ned shuffled through his notes. Buddy and Jeff exchanged impatient looks. And Bryant lay back with his eyes still closed. Jeff wondered if he'd fallen asleep or was just resting up for his *evening appointment.*

Finally Ned found the document he'd been looking for. He cleared his throat and began, "We ran a DNA on the victim downstairs, and we ran DNA on the evidence

185

you brought back from Nicey Parson's apartment in Philadelphia...you know the hair from the brush, the toothbrush and all." Jeff and Buddy nodded.

"I thought it took weeks to get DNA results," said Buddy.

"We were just doing a comparison. Comparing the victim's DNA to the DNA from the apartment. That kind of comparison just takes a few hours. Had we been doing another more extensive type of DNA test...such as identifying paternity...well, those kinds of tests take weeks and weeks."

"So what did you find?" Jeff asked.

"Well we found that the DNA from the Philadelphia apartment matched exactly the DNA of the victim downstairs," Ned said simply.

"Isn't that what you expected to find?" asked Buddy. "After all it was Nicey Parsons' apartment."

"Yes that is what we expected to find. But we also checked something else," said Ned. Again he shuffled through the sheets in his folder. Now Jeff's curiosity was peeked. Finally Ned found what he'd been looking for.

"We ran a fingerprint check. We took the victim's fingerprints from fingers that were not so mangled. Then we took prints from items brought back from Philadelphia." Ned paused for effect, "Gentlemen, the prints from the victim do not match any prints from the apartment belonging to Nicey Parsons."

"What? I don't understand," said Buddy. "You just said that the victim's DNA matched the DNA from the apartment. Now..."

Ned held up his hands in a *wait a minute position*. "We did one more check. We ran a *background* check on both sets of fingerprints. We didn't find anything to match the victim's prints. But voila...we found the prints from the apartment and the prints on the car rental papers matched prints in the criminal fingerprint data bank. Nicey Parsons was arrested and held three years ago in Phoenix for disturbing the peace and resisting arrest while covering an environmental demonstration. That's how her fingerprints ended up the data bank. The apartment prints and the prints from the car rental papers definitely belong to Nicey Parsons. Guys, I don't know the name of the woman in the morgue, but she's not Nicey Parsons."

The room fell silent. Even Bryant lifted his head. "So? How you like those apples?" Bryant said. "We've been trying to solve the murder of the wrong person."

"But we got a positive ID from the rental car attendant. And *several* people in Philadelphia identified the pictures," Buddy said.

"Buddy, witness identification is the least reliable of all evidence. Eighty per cent of prisoners later found to be innocent and released from jail were convicted by witness ID," Ned said.

Buddy looked frustrated. "Fingerprints...DNA. How can two people have the exact DNA and have different fingerprints?"

Ned said, "Aha! DNA has come to be thought of as the Holy Grail of identification. But fingerprints...ah, they are the true gold standard. There are *no* two sets of fingerprints in the world that are alike. But there is *one* way that DNA can be the same."

"How?" said Buddy.

Jeff answered this one, "Identical twins."

"Exactly," said Ned pointing a finger at Jeff. "Identical twins have the exact DNA. However, they have different fingerprints."

"So the victim is Nicey's Parsons' identical twin," Buddy stated simply.

"And that means that the identification given by the car rental attendant and the people up in Philly is bogus," said Jeff.

Buddy said, "You know what...I'll bet those pictures on the wall in her Philadelphia apartment were pictures of Nicey Parson's twin sister. And here I was thinking Nicey must really be an egotist to hang so many of her own pictures on the wall."

Ned closed the folder and handed it to Jeff. "These are copies. Keep them," he said. "Thought you might want to read the reports again."

"And share it with Dillon," added Bryant.

"Of course," Jeff said. "And we gotta notify the Pennsylvania Marshals about this turn of events. They've been looking for the murderer of Nicey Parsons, Philadelphia citizen. We all have a lot to think about. And I think the best place to think about it is back in Seaboard. Things are surfacing there, but I don't know how this new information will fit in."

Then for the next twenty minutes Jeff told Bryant and Ned about Miss Sara and her bizarre behavior. They reported their interview with Mrs. Bernice and how they'd hoped to use her information in their next interview with Sara Wood. They also told them about the conference with the high school boys which confirmed that the driver of the convertible was alone shortly before reaching Seaboard.

"So you see," said Jeff, "we've got to factor what you've told us today in with what we've learned in Seaboard."

"Good luck," said Ned. "Let me know if I can do anything else. We'll just hold the body here pending notification of family. We're not releasing the car, of course, because it's part of a crime scene. So it's all here if you need to see it or want me to run any more tests. Take a look at those reports I gave you and let me know."

"Right. In light of the twins connection, I think we'll take a run by the Archives. See if there were twin girls born in the year shown on Nicey's driver's license…that is if anyone is still at the Archives." He looked at his watch.

"I'll call Mert and see if she can meet you there," said Bryant.

"Good," said Jeff.

Bryant slapped his hands on the arms of the desk chair in a dismissive jester. "Okay Jeff, Buddy, keep us informed and we'll do the same. Best to Dillon. By the way, how's that Little Sister of his?"

Jeff grinned and said, "She's doing swell…real *swell*." Buddy's face flushed. The men walked to the door.

"By the way, ask Miss Roberson to step in here please," Bryant called after them.

When they entered the secretary's office, Jeff grinned knowingly at Cathy Roberson and said, "He wants you."

Chapter 14

As they pulled out of the parking lot at the Terry Sanford Federal Building Jeff picked up his cell, scrolled down the menu, selected a number, and clicked it on. Two rings then a pickup.

"Moretti," a voice growled from the cell.

"Moretti, Jeff Sands here," said Jeff .

"Hey Jeff, just packing up to go home. How goes it in Carolina?"

"Well, we just got handed a bombshell that turns our investigation upside down," Jeff said. He gave Moretti a complete rundown of Ned Cosden's autopsy report, DNA results, and fingerprint analysis wherein he'd concluded that the victim was not Nicey Parsons but Nicey's twin sister. Jeff also explained that Ned's findings meant they'd have to take a new look at how to proceed in Seaboard.

Moretti said, "Same here. Now instead of looking for the **murderer of** Nicey Parsons, we're looking for **missing person** Nicey Parsons. Or…how about this one…maybe

190

we're looking for **murder suspect Nicey Parsons** who slashed her twin sister. Geez can this get any more complicated?"

"I sure hope not," said Jeff.

"Listen, Jeff," said Moretti. "I think if you connect Nicey Parsons and her twin to Seaboard, North Carolina you'll go a long way toward solving this thing."

"That's my thinking too," said Jeff. "We're on our way to the Archives now to do some research. Keep you posted."

Jeff drove down Hillsborough Street, turned right on Salisbury, circled the Capitol and zig-zagged over to Jones. He parked in a lot on Jones just a few yards from the Archives Building. The two Marshals rushed to the side door of the building. Jeff banged loudly on the door. A few minutes later they heard a key card being inserted in the door, a loud click, and the door opened.

"Jeff Sands," said a middle aged woman in a gray light weight wool pants suit. "I wouldn't do this for anyone but you two...of course, it helped that Bryant called."

"Thanks Mert," said Jeff.

Mert closed the door and they walked down a long, dimly lit hall. It was empty and they could hear the echo of their voices. "So what can I do for you two?" asked Mert.

"We need to know if twin girls were born in North Carolina in this year...or maybe a couple of years before or after this year," Jeff said and handed her a piece of paper.

"I could have given you this on the phone, Jeff," Mert said.

"I know, but sometimes I spot things if I can look at the original document."

"Okay, follow me," Mert said.

She took them to a room at the far end of the hallway. She took out a key and unlocked the door. She flipped on the light that illuminated a room with several computer stations, about a dozen file cabinets, and shelves that held magazines, books, and journals. She sat down at one computer and turned it on. A few seconds later the screen lit. She typed in several words and a menu came up. She chose one and clicked. Then she typed in the date and selected twins—girls—search She sat back and smiled. In a few seconds information popped up on the screen.

"Hey, we got a hit already," Mert said. Jeff and Buddy leaned in close and looked at the screen.

Using the eraser end of a pencil Mert pointed to the data on the screen as she read, "Twins. Girls. Place of Birth...Northampton County North Carolina. Name of mother...Katie Hollis...Name of attending physician... indistinguishable first name, last name Lowell. See how simple it is."

"No name for the father?" asked Jeff.

"No name was given," said Mert.

"You sure?" asked Jeff. "Maybe it was left off when it was put on the computer."

Mert looked determined. "If it had been on the certificate, it would be in the computer."

Jeff looked apologetic. "Could we look at the original?"

Mert sighed. "Okay. But this will take a while." She pushed herself away from the computer and headed for the door. "You'll have to wait here."

After quite a wait Mert returned. She was holding a document encased in a protective sheath. "Here you go. See for yourself. Father's name not given."

Jeff took the document and he and Buddy studied it for a long while.

"Look at the doctor's signature. No wonder they couldn't figure out his first name. It's barely legible."

"Mrs. Bernice said he practiced until he was quite elderly," said Jeff. Then turning to Mert he said, "Could we have a print-out of this record?"

"Better still how about a copy of the certificate?" said Mert.

"Even better. Thanks," said Jeff.

"Be right back," she said and walked to a copy machine in the back of the room.

Mert returned quickly, handed Jeff the copy, and said, "I'll have to walk you out."

When they left the computer room Mert locked the door and pocketed the key. At the side entrance she used the key card again. When the lock clicked she pushed the door open and the two men stepped out into the chilly, damp evening air. At seven o'clock there was no traffic on these streets that fronted government buildings and creepy museums. The streetlights cast dancing shadows off the austere buildings and the empty streets created a disquieting feeling.

"You okay alone here, Mert?" asked Jeff.

Mert smiled and said, "It's my home away from home. Night." And a metallic clank sounded as she closed the door.

Back in the car Jeff took out his phone and began to scroll down the menu again. He clicked a number and after two rings a pick up.

"Hello," Sophie said.

"Hey, yourself," said Jeff. "We're heading back to Seaboard. What's going on there?"

"Nothing really. Gladys is upset because you missed dinner and she'd baked your favorite lemon pie."

Jeff could hear voices in the background and Gladys grumbled, "Ain't upset. If'n he wants lemon pie he's gonna have to fetch it out of the 'frigerator himself."

Jeff could tell that Sophie was moving to another room. "Jeff, have you had dinner?"

"No, we'll stop on our way out of town. We'll be home before long."

"Was Bryant's big surprise worth the trip?"

"Worth the trip? We'll see. Surprise? Definitely. Here's Denny's. See you later tonight." And he clicked off.

Buddy pulled into Denny's parking lot. "Just one more call," he said to Buddy who had been awfully quiet since leaving the Federal Building. Jeff found Dillon's number and clicked it. After only a single ring there was a pickup.

"Dillon," he said. Jeff could hear voices in the background and knew that Dillon was still at Town Hall.

"Dillon, Jeff. We're stopping to eat and then we're headed back to Seaboard. How are things there?"

"Quiet," Dillon said in a tired, low voice. "Stewart's been keeping a close eye on the place across the street. Nothing. No one's gone anywhere. Like I said…quiet."

"Well that's about to change," said Jeff. "Bryant dropped a bombshell on us. And what it means is that we're gonna have to completely rethink this thing."

"What?" asked Dillon as he suddenly came alive.

"We shouldn't try to talk now," said Jeff. "Think we can get together early tomorrow morning?"

"Sure."

"How about eight thirty?" said Jeff. "Will Stewart be able to be there?"

"So far as I know he doesn't do maintenance tomorrow," said Dillon

"Good. Then let's meet at Town Hall at eight thirty."

Dillon asked, "What about Little Sister? Need her too?"

Jeff grinned and looked at Buddy. Buddy said, "What?"

Jeff said, "Sure Little Sister's needed too."

* * *

It was after midnight when Jeff climbed the front porch steps of the yellow Victorian house on Main Street. A faint light shone through the den window. It was accompanied by a blue flicker from the television screen. Jeff tried the door. Locked. He reached into his pocket and took out the key to the front door. He quietly unlocked the door and slipped into the hall. He walked into the den and found Sophie asleep on the sofa her hand under her cheek. Jeff stared down at her. He marveled that they reconnected after so many, many years. Suppose he hadn't found her.

195

Suppose he'd spent his entire life living alone in Mrs. Smiley's room.

Sophie stirred and opened her eyes. "Jeff," she said sleepily and held her hand out to him.

Jeff took her hand and sat on the sofa beside her. "Sorry to wake you up."

Sophie pushed herself up on her elbow, locked her arm around his neck, and drew him to her. They kissed as they always did…as if it may be their last. When they drew apart Sophie smiled and said, "I have something for you."

"Well I certainly hope so," Jeff said raising a wicked eyebrow.

Sophie smacked his arm. "Silly! I mean there's some lemon pie in the frig. It's left over from supper. Gladys was sure you'd be coming in and made sure you had lemon pie for a snack."

Jeff stood, reached out for Sophie, and pulled her up. "Lemon pie, huh? You know I like other kinds of pie too."

"Yes, but Gladys thinks lemon is your favorite," Sophie said as she led him to the kitchen.

Sophie cut two large wedges of lemon pie, and they ate at the kitchen table. Jeff ate his in three bites. Sophie nibbled at hers and then pushed her plate to Jeff who ate the rest of hers in two bites.

"So tell me what was so important that you had to rush to Raleigh," said Sophie.

"New developments," said Jeff.

Sophie looked hurt. "Jeff, I know there are 'secrets' you can't share about your work, but sometimes I feel you push me away unnecessarily. Can't you tell me generally about your meeting?"

Work had been an issue for a long time between Sophie and Jeff. It wasn't that Jeff's work was so clandestine. It was just that Jeff reasoned that the less Sophie knew the safer she would be.

Jeff said, "Sophie let me tell you again, ninety five per cent of my work is an open book. I'm not trying to keep 'secrets' from you. I just feel that you're safer the less you know about what I'm doing."

Sophie reached for his plate, stood, and walked to the sink. She rinsed the plates and forks and placed them in the sink. Then she turned and said, "To begin with I feel you are exaggerating the danger I would be in. I'll bet you talk to other people about it. Secondly, I fear a danger, too, Jeff. The danger I feel is that if you shut me out your job will drive us apart. You see, Jeff, the more you work, the less we have to talk about. Then in the short time we have together you're thinking about the work you can't talk about."

Jeff was silent for a long time. Sophie held her breath but was determined to wait him out. Finally he said, "That bad, huh?"

"That threatening," she said.

"Come here," Jeff said holding his hand out to her. Sophie went to him and sat down beside him. "I don't want that to happen. I don't want you to ever be threatened again...especially by me. I guess in my determination to protect you, I seem to shut you out. I'm gonna change that, Sophie. Starting right now."

"Jeff, I'm not trying to blackmail you," she said. "I just want to be able to talk with you."

"Okay, to begin with, the State Medical Examiner, Ned Cosden, tossed us a real curve today. I want your reaction to what we learned."

Sophie smiled and said, "Shoot." And she took on an expression of intense concentration.

"Ned found that the DNA we brought from Nicey Parsons' apartment in Philadelphia matched exactly the DNA of the woman murdered on Galatia Road."

"Isn't that what you'd expect?" asked Sophie.

"Yes, it is," said Jeff. "But Ned also discovered that the fingerprints of the victim did not match Nicey Parsons' fingerprints that were in the fingerprint data bank."

"What?" said Sophie. "The DNA matched, but the fingerprints didn't? How could that be?"

"Smart girl," said Jeff. "Twins. Identical twins have the same DNA but everyone's fingerprints are different."

"So this means Nicey Parsons had an identical twin."

"Yes," Jeff said. "And *I think* the wrong woman was killed. The hit was intended for Nicey, but her twin was murdered instead."

Sophie looked astonished. "So where is Nicey?"

"That, my dear, is the question," said Jeff. "We have no idea, but wherever she is she's a target."

Later that night after they made love, Jeff drifted off to sleep immediately. It seemed that only a few seconds had passed when he forced his eyes open. He saw it was one o'clock. He looked over at Sophie. Sophie was lying on her back, arm under her neck, and staring wide-eyed at the ceiling.

Jeff pushed himself up on his elbow. "Sophie, what's wrong?"

"I've been thinking about your case," she said.

"What?" Jeff laughed.

"I think the key is Seaboard. Find out why she was here, and we'll find the key to the whole murder," she said.

Jeff guffawed. "Sophie, Sophie, you little gum-shoe. Now neither of us will be able to sleep."

"But isn't it exciting?" she said. Jeff flipped her over and pulled her toward him.

Chapter 15

Dillon stood on the top step of the yellow school bus. He wore his badge and his cap with Police printed on it.

He spoke in an authoritative voice. "Mr. Bus Driver, any problems here?"

"No sir. No problems."

Dillon's face took on a stern look and his eyes surveyed the students on the bus. "Alright, Mr. Bus Driver, carry on." And Dillon stepped off and slapped the side of the bus. The door closed and the bus moved up the drive and onto the highway leaving a trail of loud voices in its wake.

Dillon turned and surveyed the project's courtyard. A woman was hanging laundry on a make shift clothes line beside her apartment. Two tall tomato plants bearing their last fruit of the season drooped by the stoop. Several pre-schoolers rode tricycles on the street while others pushed brightly colored plastic toys through the sand. The aroma of oregano and garlic permeated the air. It was from a sauce that would simmer on the stove all day. Three women stood talking on the sidewalk. One jiggled a toddler on her hip. Another was older and appeared to be monopolizing the conversation. The third woman just nodded and occasionally tickled the baby under his chin.

Dillon walked over to the women. He lifted his cap and said, "Good morning ladies. And good morning to you little guy." He pointed his finger toward the baby. The baby ignored his finger and reached for Dillon's shiny badge.

"You like my badge, huh?" Dillon said. "Maybe you'll be a policeman someday."

The women giggled. The baby cooed. Dillon said, "Where's the young man that was sitting on that stoop the other day?" Dillon pointed to the stoop where the man had sat.

"He just got out of the pen," said the oldest woman.

"I know he just got out of prison," said Dillon. "I just wonder where he is now?"

"You could ask his granny," said the woman with the baby. "She lives in that apartment." And she jerked a thumb in the direction of an apartment behind them.

"She ain't there though. She had a 'pointment to the hospital over at Roanoke Rapids for tests early this morning. She won't tell you nothing no how," said the third woman.

"Shur won't," agreed the older woman.

"Why?" asked Dillon.

"Cause she be 'fraid of him."

"He's real mean to her," said the woman with the baby. "Real mean." And she hugged her baby close.

"Well, thanks, ladies," said Dillon. "I'll catch granny later. Y'all have a good one...you too little guy."

Dillon returned to his car, buckled on his guns, and drove out of the projects. He'd completed his early morning rounds and his stomach told him it was time for breakfast. He crossed the tracks and headed for The Kitchen. The Kitchen was the kind of establishment where a man could fill up fast, move on out, and get on with his day. Simultaneously with Dillon pulling into the parking lot Miss Sadie picked up an extra large breakfast plate. "Three eggs over light," she called over her shoulder. She began to fill the plate...grits with gravy, hash browns, tomato slices, three pieces of bacon, and two sausage links. She took three biscuits from the warmer oven and by then the eggs were ready. By the time Dillon sat down, positioned his guns, and removed his cap, Miss Sadie placed his breakfast in front of him.

"Thanks Miss Sadie," said Dillon. And he dived right in. He always gave full attention to his first meal of the day. Dillon had an approach that had earned him lots of attention over the years. He ate one thing on his plate before moving on to another. He'd finished his eggs and grits and was starting on his hash browns when a car pulled up beside his. He looked up and saw Stewart scuttling towards the door.

Dillon heard Miss Sadie call, "Three scrambled." And she picked up another breakfast plate and began to fill it.

"'Morning Dillon," said Stewart.

"'Morning," Dillon said through a mouthful of hash browns.

Stewart leaned forward and whispered, "What's going on with Jeff? Why so mysterious?"

"Don't know," Dillon whispered back. "That's how come it's mysterious."

Stewart ignored the gibe. "They must've got something real important up in Raleigh to call us up for an emergency meeting like this."

Miss Sadie arrived and put Stewart's breakfast plate in front of him. "Thanks, Miss Sadie," said Stewart. Miss Sadie turned and Stewart said, "Ah, could I have some tomato catsup for my scrambled eggs?"

"Tomato slices *and* tomato catsup?" she asked. Stewart didn't answer. Miss Sadie shrugged, grabbed a bottle of catsup from a nearby table, and put it front of Stewart.

"As I was saying," said Stewart, "Jeff must have a real surprise."

"He called it a bombshell," said Dillon playing along.

"Bombshell?" exclaimed Stewart. "That's even more serious."

"Yeah, I always think of *bombshell* as being more serious than *surprise*," said Dillon. He was down to his last biscuit.

Stewart generously poured catsup on his eggs. "Far as I'm concerned, I'm glad to be off the Sara Wood watch. That was one boring assignment, and I kept a wondering what she'd do if'n she realized I was watching her instead of doing some work over at the crime scene."

Dillon picked up all three pieces of bacon and bit them in half. "I'm ready to focus on something else too. Keep feeling like we were spinning our wheels." Another bite and the bacon was gone.

"I'm just glad I don't have to read water meters or something like that today," said Stewart. "After all the hours I've put in on this thing, I want to be in on the kill."

"Don't say *kill*. Somebody'll hear," Dillon said as he downed his last sausage link. Dillon always thought of

203

tomato slices as a kind of a breakfast dessert and saved them for last.

"Well, I'm just glad to be one of four working the case today," Stewart said.

Dillon cut his last tomato slice with his fork and said, "Not four...five. Little Sister's coming in this morning too...that is if they get out of bed in time."

* * *

Jeff was already at Town Hall when Dillon and Stewart arrived...and so was Harvey Clinton. Jeff and Harvey were sipping cups of coffee heads bent over a copy of *The News and Observer*.

"Anything new?" asked Dillon.

"Just a rehash of what's already been reported," said Harvey.

Then Dillon realized that Harvey Clinton was at his computer half an hour early. "You're early Harvey," Dillon said.

Harvey grinned, "When I heard you were having an emergency meeting this morning nothing could keep me away."

"Alright then," Dillon said to Harvey. "Ears...okay. Mouth ...not okay."

"Now when did I ever..." Harvey Clinton seemed offended.

"Forget it," said Dillon. Then turning to Jeff he said, "Let's hear it then."

Dillon suddenly realized that Buddy and Little Sister weren't there. "Where's Little Sister and Buddy?"

Jeff grinned and nodded toward the front window. Buddy and Frances were crossing Main Street. They laughed and talked and seemed to be in no great hurry to get to Town Hall. Frances elbowed Buddy almost causing him to fall. Several farmers stood on the sidewalk outside the Post Office. They stared at the couple, shook their heads, and smiled.

"They're lost in love," said Clinton attempting to create a romantic aphorism.

"Just so they're not so lost they can't help out on this case," said Jeff. "We got a lot to take in here." And he walked toward the back.

Dillon shook his head. "Look like a couple of love sick pups."

Buddy and Frances came in and joined the others in Dillon's office.

Dillon looked at Frances. "Hi kiddo." Then he grinned at Buddy. "You too Buddy."

"Now listen up everybody," Jeff said looking straight at Buddy. "We got a lot to cover. First we'll tell you about Bryant's bombshell. Then we need to talk about what to do with this new information."

For the next thirty minutes Jeff and Buddy reported in detail what Ned Cosden, State Medical Examiner revealed about the autopsy, the DNA comparison, the handwriting analysis, and the fingerprints. They paused to let things sink in and took questions. There were lots.

Dillon said, "I never heard of DNA from two people being identical. "Have you, Jeff?"

"Once," said Jeff, "back when DNA was just coming into its glory days. I was on a case where identical twin brothers were serial killers. One brother would commit the murder while the other brother went out in public to establish an alibi. Then they'd switch roles. It was a long time before we realized there were two of them. Their DNA was the same. But their fingerprints solved it."

"Do the Marshals in Pennsylvania know about this?" asked Dillon.

"Called them right away and talked with Moretti. He believes if we connect the twin girls to Seaboard we'll be one step closer to finding our killer. I believe that too," said Jeff. "So that's what we need to discuss now. Buddy, how 'bout telling them about the Archives?"

Jeff walked toward the coffee machine while Buddy gave a full account of what they found at the Archives...name of the twin's mother, Katie Hollis; name of the doctor; date and place of birth being Northampton County, North Carolina. He also informed them of what they did not find...namely, the name of the twins' father.

"So," said Buddy. "Any ideas?"

The audience was still trying to process what they'd heard. Several moments of silence followed. Then from the front of the Town Hall Clinton said, "Time to call in Mrs. Bernice again."

They looked back at Clinton. Dillon said, "That's a good idea. I'll call her." And he reached for the phone.

As Dillon dialed and waited for a pickup Jeff walked to Clinton's computer. "You don't have a Hollis family in your computer do you?"

"No," said Clinton. "Already checked. And I got my recs going back a long, long time. Way further back than when the twins were born."

Dillon continued to wait for a pickup. He looked at Frances. "You don't suppose she's over at the Post Office?"

Frances said, "No. It's way too early for Mrs. Bernice."

Then there was a pickup. "Hello," a voice shouted into the receiver.

"Mrs. Bernice?"

"That's right. Who is this? Dillon?"

"Yes ma'am," said Dillon.

"Well what can I do for you this early in the morning?" she asked.

"I'm sorry to call so early, Mrs. Bernice, but we've come 'cross some new information and hope you can help us."

"Well I'll be glad to if'n I can," she said. "You want me to come down there again?"

"No ma'am. I don't think that will be necessary. I need to know if you know of a certain family."

"Are they from Seaboard?" She continued to shout.

"I don't know ma'am. I do know they lived in Northampton County at one time," said Dillon.

"I know just about all the folks in the county. Shoot."

"The name is Hollis. Do you recall a family named Hollis? Had a young woman named Katie."

There was a long pause. Then Mrs. Bernice said, "Hollis. Hollis. Noooo. Can't say as I know of a family named Hollis. And they lived in Seaboard?"

Dillon said, "In Northampton County at least."

"Hollis," she repeated. "Seems slightly familiar. Hollis. And a young woman, Katie?"

"Yes ma'am."

"You know what, Dillon, it's commencing to come to me...how long ago?"

Dillon gave her the date on the birth certificate.

"You know that was at the height of that flu epidemic? Hollis. Wait. You 'member I told you 'bout that poor family what stripped tobacco for Myron Blankenship and then stayed pass harvest in that shack on Galatia Road?"

"Yes ma'am."

"Well, I believe they was Hollises. Yeah, sure was. I recollect now. That poor family was called Hollis."

Dillon was so excited he stammered, "Th...th...Thank you, Mrs. Bernice. Thank you so much." Then he added, "You don't happen to know where they went when they left here do you?"

"No," said Mrs. Bernice. "Those kinda people come and go at will. They're hard to pin down."

"Well, thanks again, Mrs. Bernice," exclaimed Dillon. "Thanks again!"

"That all you wanted?" Mrs. Bernice asked. She was obviously disappointed.

"Yes ma'am...for now anyway. And thank you." Dillon leapt from his chair and thrust his fist in the air. "We got it. We've found the Hollis family. And guess where they stayed one winter?"

"What? Where?"

"The Hollis family spent the winter of the flu epidemic in that shack across from Sara Wood."

"Now we're cookin'" said Stewart. They babbled on for a few minutes about the lucky break.

Then Jeff interrupted their excitement. "Okay...Okay. Finding the name of the family is definitely a break. But finding the name is not the same as finding the family."

The *team* fell silent. "Like Mrs. Bernice said," said Dillon. "No telling where they went when they left here. How in the world do you track down people like that?" he asked rhetorically.

Silence. Then Frances said, "Human Services."

"What?" said Dillon.

"Real poor folks often go to the Department of Health and Human Services for help. 'Specially if'n there's babies involved. Maybe they have some records in Jackson. If'n this family asked for their help while they were in Northampton County they'd have records," said Frances.

"She's right," said Jeff. "Human Services is as good a place as any to start. There was a long silence and finally Jeff said, "Okay, here's what we do. Frances, you ask everyone who comes into the post office if they knew a Hollis family. Now that we have a name it might stir a few memories. Remember the date, and the fact that it was the year of the flu epidemic might help. Dillon and Stewart, how about you two talking to some of the old tenant farmers? They might remember a family that helped with the tobacco harvest named Hollis. They might even know where they went when they left here. Buddy, you and I are going to pay a visit to the North Carolina Department of Health and Human Services over in Jackson? Questions?"

There were no questions and everyone seemed anxious to get started. Suddenly Harvey Clinton said, "What about me? I feel left out of the loop."

"Harvey, your suggestion to call Mrs. Bernice again kicked off the day. Just hang in there. There'll be plenty to do when we're wrapping this up," said Jeff.

Chapter 16

Jeff and Buddy parked in front of a white building that was marked North Carolina Department of Health and Human Services. They stepped into a long hall and consulted a board that listed the offices housed in the building. They found the office number for Division of Social Services. They turned right and walked in that direction. The door to the office was open and there in front of a computer sat a very striking middle aged woman wearing a short-sleeve floral design dress with a sweater draped around her shoulders. She looked up from the screen, smiled brightly, and said, "Jeff. Jeff Sands. Come on in here."

"Hello Stella. Good to see you. Didn't know you worked here. Like you to meet my partner, Buddy Turner. Buddy…Stella Denton."

"Not Denton anymore. White. I married again. Bob White," she smiled holding up her left hand to show a large diamond ring.

"Oh. Congratulations. Ah…Bob White did you say?"

Stella laughed. "That's right. I get that same reaction every time I say his name. Glad to meet you Buddy. Are you here on business, Jeff, or just dropping by?"

"Business," said Jeff. "Stella I'm looking for information on a family that was in Northampton County some time back." And he gave her the name and date on the birth certificate.

"Oh. Okay, let me see. Anything specific you're looking for?" she said as she turned toward the computer.

"I know there were babies...twin girls," said Jeff.

"If you're searching for birth information Archives in Raleigh is your best bet."

"Yeah, we've already been there. Right now I'm hoping to find out where they went after leaving Seaboard," said Jeff, and he handed her the copy of the birth certificate they got from Archives.

"We probably wouldn't have information on where they went," Stella said. "Once someone leaves the county we drop them from our system...unless they move back and need our services again. But I'll see what I can find."

Stella busied herself at her computer. Jeff and Buddy waited patiently and a young woman appeared at the door and leaned in. She was impeccably dressed...hair, makeup, nails. The heels of her shoes were so high she appeared to be leaning forward. She wore a royal blue dress with matching jacket, and a soft green scarf was tossed casually around her neck. She could easily leave the office at five and head straight for an upscale restaurant.

"Why hi, Jeff," she said in a husky voice. "You're looking grrr...eat."

"You look great yourself Crystal," said Jeff and grinned.

"What brings you to Jackson?"

"Business. Looking for information on a certain family."

"Nothing so far," Stella said impatiently and she looked at Crystal heatedly.

"Tell *me* about the family. I'm good at coming up with ideas myself," Crystal said and she returned Stella's look with one that said 'kiss off'.

"The family was *real* poor. They were migrant farmers, and there were twins...girls. We have the name of the mother, but need the name of the father. And most importantly we need to know where they are now," said Jeff.

"Oh, in that case, better come with me," she said and hooked her arm around Jeff's arm. "Helping babies is my area of expertise. Have you ever thought foster care?" And she led him out the door.

"I'm not through here," called Stella. Buddy shrugged and lifted his hands as if to say 'what can I do' and followed them out of the room.

Crystal's office was in the basement. It looked like most government offices...computer, file cabinets, and cluttered bookshelves. Crystal gave Buddy a look that let him know she wished he'd stayed upstairs with Stella.

"Welcome to my domain," Crystal cooed to Jeff. "It's not much, but it's mine...and the County Government's."

"Nice," said Jeff as he gave the place a quick look. "Now about this family..."

Crystal sighed and said, "Yes, the family. You see, if a family is as poor as you described, they sometimes turn babies over to foster care or put them up for adoption.

213

Adoption records are of course kept in Raleigh. So if you're thinking adoption Raleigh is the place you'll find those records. But foster care records stay in the office of County Department of Social Services. That's me. (Crystal smiled) Now give me the information you have and I'll take a look into my Crystal ball." She turned to her computer, flexed her fingers gingerly above the key, and laughed at her own joke.

Jeff gave Crystal all the information Mert had given them on the Hollis twins when they were at Archives in Raleigh. After only a few seconds, Crystal said, "My magic fingers have done it again. A match."

Buddy and Jeff stepped behind the desk and leaned over the computer. Crystal lifted her face toward Jeff and smiled seductively. Then she turned back to the screen. "See here," she pointed to data. "This is the name of the mother, Katie Hollis. This is the birth date of the twin girls, place of birth, Northampton County, and the Doctor's name."

"It doesn't say *where* in the county?" asked Jeff.

"No, but if Doctor Lowell delivered, it's gotta be Seaboard or at least close by."

"What else you got?" asked Buddy.

Crystal seemed annoyed by Buddy's intrusion. She said, "*What else I got* is that they were signed over to foster care on this date (she pointed). The girls were placed in a temporary home for three days with an emergency family, and then turned over to full-time foster parents. The names of the foster parents were Jim and Dorie Parsons."

Buddy and Jeff sprung up almost knocking heads. "Parsons! We need to find them. Where do the Parsons live?"

Crystal shrugged. "I haven't the foggiest."

"*What?*"

"According to these records, the Parsons moved to Mecklenburg County, North Carolina when the girls were...ah...lemme see...when the girls were about six years old."

"They took the twins with them? Out of the County jurisdiction?" asked Buddy.

"Yes," Crystal said trying hard to ignore Buddy.

Jeff said, "How could they do that? They were just fosters. Can foster parents do that? Move foster children around like that? Who was going to check on the twins...make sure they were being cared for..."

Crystal said, "Let me explain. Standards for licensing foster care homes are rigid. We do health checks, fire and building safety checks on the home, criminal background checks, check room arrangement provisions, and the fosters undergo rigorous training. Then their application goes to the licensing authority and if the parents are approved we'll place children in that home. The homes are visited frequently and any irregularity or deficiencies are reported to this office. If infractions are grave the children are removed from that home and placed in another foster home. Now I've encapsulated what is required to become a foster parent but you get the gist."

"Right. In other words you don't turn children over to just anybody," said Jeff.

Crystal nodded.

215

"That still doesn't explain how the Parsons got away with taking the twins out of the county."

"They didn't *get away with it.* Let me read something to you," said Crystal. She stood, slowly brushed against Jeff, and walked to one of the cluttered shelves. She pulled a badly wore soft-cover manual from the shelf, brushed against Jeff again, and returned to her chair.

"I hate being read to," said Buddy.

Crystal gave him an indignant look, smiled at Jeff, and began to read. "10A NC AC 70E.0706 states, a foster home licensed and in good standing with licensing authority may transfer to the supervision of another county department of social services...."

After Crystal read the entire rule, she added, "There's a particular procedure for transferring. So the Parsons didn't just get up one morning, decide to move, and vanish with two little foster girls. After they moved to Mecklenburg County, their foster home was duly supervised by *Mecklenburg County Social Services.* "

"So we can find the Parsons in Mecklenburg County?" asked Buddy.

Crystal gave Buddy a look that clearly said 'I'm tired of your interruptions'. Then she said sarcastically, "Buddy, I don't know if you can find the Parsons in Mecklenburg County or not. Why don't you go look?"

Jeff said, "Thanks Crystal. You've been a great help."

"Any time. Any way. Just give me a call. By the way Jeff, are you and Sophie Singletary still on for December?"

"That's what she tells me," Jeff said smiling.

"What a shame. But you know...sometimes plans change. If *unfortunately* that should happen, Jeff, give me a call," Buddy swore her voice dropped a couple of octaves. Jeff laughed.

As they climbed the steps to the main floor Buddy said, "I felt like a third wheel at a senior prom. Is there *any* hottie in Northampton County you *don't* know?"

"Nope," Jeff quipped and kept on climbing.

Chapter 17

Buddy drove back to Seaboard while Jeff worked the phone. First he called Bryant. He reported what they'd learned from Social Services about the twins and the foster parents named Parsons. They discussed the importance of keeping the victim's true identity quiet until they actually found the real Nicey Parsons. Jeff requested Bryant clear any red tape that might impede their use of State resources to gather information on the Parsons family. He pointed out Seaboard's limited resources. Bryant approved the plan, mumbled 'keep me informed', and hung up.

Jeff called Michele Reynolds at U.S. Marshal Service. Michele was a computer technician who had the reputation of 'if it's out there, she will find it'. He told her he needed a complete report on the Parsons in twenty minutes.

"You're joking of course," Michele said.

"Kinda," said Jeff. "What I really need as soon as possible is…where in Mecklenburg County are they?"

"Gotcha," said Michele and rang off.

Next Jeff called Philadelphia and filled in the Pennsylvania Marshals on the Parsons, their relationship to the twins, and that they'd moved to Mecklenburg County, North Carolina.

Ernesto Salas said, "Sounds like you're on a roll now, Jeff. That's just the way it is. You spin your wheels and pull your hair out for days then suddenly the dam bursts."

"Yeah," said Jeff, "seems to be what's happening now."

"We've been thinking," said Salas, "it might be a good idea to keep the true identity of the victim away from the press. Just keep playing it like the vic is Nicey until she's found."

"Already thought of that," said Jeff. "If it gets out, that it was Nicey's twin that was killed and that Nicey is probably alive, she could be in jeopardy."

"*Or* if Nicey is the perpetrator, she'd be warned that we're on her tail. I like the element of surprise," said Salas. "Meantime we're still looking for someone here who might want Nicey Parsons dead."

"Good," said Jeff, and he clicked off.

They were almost to Seaboard and Jeff said, "Drive straight to Town Hall."

When they arrived at the Town Hall, Stewart and Dillon were pulling up.

"Anything from the farmers?" asked Jeff as they walked into the building.

"Not much," said Dillon. "We talked to a couple of old farmers who vaguely remember the Hollis family. Didn't know where they went when they left Seaboard. What about you?"

"Think we hit pay dirt," said Jeff and gave a full report of what they found at Social Services to Dillon and

Stewart…and by virtue of his proximity to the police desk…Harvey Clinton too.

"What next?" asked Dillon.

"Next we find the Parsons…a state technician is tracking them down. She's good at it and fast," said Jeff. At that moment Jeff's cell rang. He looked at the phone and said, "What'd I tell you? Sands here."

"Hi Jeff. This is your friendly U.S. Marshal tracking service calling with search results," said a bubbly, sing-song voice.

"Hi Michele," said Jeff. "You're a fast worker."

"You don't know the half of it, dahlin'," she said.

"What ya' got?" Jeff said and reached for a pad and pencil.

"Okay. The census **twenty** years ago shows James, Dorie, Nicey, and Desiree Parsons living in the Matthews District of Mecklenburg County, North Carolina. James is fifty five. Dorie is fifty four. Desiree and Nicey are both eighteen. Twins…did you know?"

"Yes," said Jeff impatiently.

"Okay, **ten** years later, we got James and Dorie. No twins. Same district…Matthews in Mecklenburg County."

"Got an address?" asked Jeff. Buddy, Stewart, and Dillon waited anxiously.

"Sure 'nuff," she said and gave him the address in Matthews. "You got google earth?"

"No," said Jeff. "We're sorta limited here."

"Well I got directions," she said and rattled off direction to the Parsons house.

"So this is where we'll find Dorie and Jim Parsons," Jeff said as much to himself as to Michele.

"Dorie...yes. Jim...not so. I also checked social security records and found that Jim died last year. Dorie applied for and is receiving his social security."

"Anything else?" asked Jeff.

"No criminal records. Jim belonged to the American Legion, Lions Club, and they attended Matthews Baptist Church. They were a typical middle-class American family."

"Okay Michele," said Jeff. "Thanks. And if you come up with anything else, let us know."

"Sure thing." And Michele was gone.

Jeff turned and looked at the pad and his notes. He filled everybody in. Then he said to Buddy, "Let's take a ride to Matthews down in Mecklenburg County."

* * *

Buddy drove in case Jeff needed to use the phone. Buddy liked to drive especially if they were tracking a lead and this time he felt like they had a breakthrough. The car seemed to be soaring. Matthews was about twelve miles south of Charlotte on Highway 16. Buddy knew he was really flying low, but the car marked U.S. Marshal Service gave them a clear runway all the way to Charlotte. Once in Charlotte, however, things got a little sticky. The rush hour traffic was heavy and the last twelve miles of the drive seemed like slow motion.

Michele gave Jeff good directions and Buddy drove to a neighborhood of clapboard houses painted different colors... white, yellow, birds' egg blue, and even cupcake pink. The houses were small...probably not more than five to six rooms. This was a working class neighborhood probably built around the early nineteen fifties or sixties. Lawns were neatly mowed although the bushes and shrubs needed a trim. Approaching darkness caused the street lights to switch on and inside the little houses lights blinked through shining windows.

Buddy drove slowly down the street and they both looked for number 102. They found the house at the end of a cul-de-sac. It was small and white. Buddy drove onto the leaf-covered driveway. A walk leading to the front door was cracked and covered with patches of moss, and an enormous red pyrocantha bush almost hid the front room window. Buddy and Jeff got out of the car, picked their way carefully down the walkway, and knocked on the front door. They saw the flicker of soft blue light from a television screen and heard movement inside. Moments passed and no one came to the door. They knocked again. A weak voice said, "Just a minute." They waited and heard a sound of thump—shuffle, thump—shuffle, thump-shuffle.

The door fastened to the jamb by a security chain opened just a crack. A blurry eye peeped out at them suspiciously. "Yes?" said the weak voice.

"Mrs. Parsons?" asked Jeff.

"Who wants to know?"

Jeff and Buddy took out identification. Jeff said, "Mrs. Parsons, I'm Jeff Sands and this is Buddy Turner. We're U.S. Marshals. Could we talk to you?"

"What about?"

"This is a little complicated," said Buddy. "Could we come in?"

"Well, I don't usually let strangers into my house. Those badges could be fake. You can buy that kind of stuff at Walmart," she said.

"You're absolutely right to be careful, Mrs. Parsons," said Jeff. "But you see, we want to ask you about your foster children, Nicey and Desiree."

Mrs. Parsons stood quietly for a few seconds. "I knew someone would come. It had to happen. Just a minute." She closed the door, unlatched the chain, stood back, and opened the door.

The woman who stood in the doorway was so thin that flesh hung in folds from her face. She wore polyester slacks that were too large, a bulky knit sweater under a heavy cardigan. She had deep wrinkles on a face that had seen way too much sun. Her hair was singed by too many trips to the beauty parlor, and her gnarled hands were covered with age spots. She clutched the handles of a metal walker.

"Come on in," she said and she went to the television and turned it off. "Sit down. Sit down. Just move that newspaper. Don't know why I have it delivered. Nothing in it that interests me any more. Mainly I take it so as I'll know what the date is." Then she walked to a chair, pushed down a big orange cat that was sleeping there, and settled herself into the chair. She parked the walker next to the chair.

"Don't use that thing all the time," she said, "only when I'm real tired." The cat she'd pushed from the chair would not be put off and immediately jumped back onto her lap. The Marshals sat across from her.

"Okay, say your piece," Mrs. Parsons said.

Jeff said, "Mrs. Parsons, we are sorry to tell you that one of your foster daughters was found dead in a small town called Seaboard, North Carolina."

Mrs. Parsons' hands went to her face and her fingers gently tapped her lips. Tears welled up in her eyes but she made no sound.

"We're sorry Mrs. Parsons. We know this must be a shock," said Buddy.

Mrs. Parsons reached into her pocket disturbing the cat again, and pulled out a man's handkerchief. She wiped her eyes and blew her nose. "Ain't no shock to me," said Mrs. Parsons. "I've known about it for several days. Heard about it on television. Just who in the world would want to hurt a sweet girl like Nicey? She never did nobody no harm."

"We don't know, Mrs. Parsons," said Buddy. "We're hoping that you can help us come up with some answers." Mrs. Parsons shook her head.

"Mrs. Parsons, there is something else we have to tell you," said Jeff. Mrs. Parson looked at him fearfully. "Mrs. Parsons, we have proof that the young woman murdered in the barn in Northampton County was not Nicey. She was her twin, Desiree."

Mrs. Parsons exploded into tears and wails. Buddy moved to comfort her but Jeff continued. "At this time we have no reason to think that Nicey is dead. Or even that she has been harmed. But we need to ask if you've heard from Nicey. Have you seen her?"

Dorie Parsons shook her head vigorously and sobbed, "No. No. I don't know where Nicey is. I haven't heard from her. Why do you think she'd..." And Dorie Parson began to moan. "Oh why? Why did this happen to one of my little angels? Who could be so cruel? Ooooh, Desiree, Nicey."

Suddenly a door burst open, and a young woman rushed into the room and straight to the sobbing woman. She knelt in front of her and put her head on her knee. "No mama. Please don't cry. It's alright. I'm okay, and I'll take care of you. Everything is going to be alright."

Jeff and Buddy were stunned by the sudden appearance of the young woman who was a dead ringer for the victim they'd seen on the barn floor a few days earlier.

Dorie Parsons bent over the young woman and began to stroke her hair and kiss it. "Oh, Nicey, she's gone. Baby, your little sister is gone to heaven with her angel mama."

It took Jeff and Buddy a few seconds to comprehend what was happening. Nicey. Nicey Parsons had just burst in the room. They watched helplessly as the two women grieved and consoled each other. Finally they were cried out.

"Nicey raised her head and spluttered, "How did you find me?"

"Through the Archives, Social Services, and State searches," Jeff said. "Right now I'm asking the questions, and the first question is how did you get here?"

Nicey lifted her head from Dorie's lap and sat cross-legged on the floor. "On the bus. I took a bus from Raleigh. I left that night after I saw the news report of the murder of a young woman in Seaboard. I knew it was Desiree so I checked out of the hotel and headed for the bus station. She wiped her red eyes, and said, "Did she suffer? Please tell me...did my sister feel much pain?"

"I don't think so," said Jeff preferring to spare her additional grief. "I think she died quickly."

"Thank God," said Dorie Parsons.

"Nicey," Jeff said sternly, "we have lots of questions for you. The body that was found in Northampton County was initially identified as you...Nicey Parsons. For the time being we're leaving it that way. Let the press continue to report that *you* died in that barn. You'll be safer that way. In the meantime, we want answers."

Nicey rubbed her eyes some more and said, "Okay. Shoot."

"Do you mind if we tape?" Buddy asked taking out a small tape recorder.

"No. I use recorders in my interviews," said Nicey. Buddy placed the recorder on a nearby table and clicked it on.

"Nicey this is not a formal statement or interview, but I gotta tell you if you want a lawyer...," said Jeff.

"What?" Dorie shouted.

"I don't need a lawyer," said Nicey. Then she put her hand on Dorie's arm. "It's alright, mama. This is typical procedure."

"Procedure...?" repeated Dorie obviously confused.

Then Jeff said, "Nicey Parsons did you kill your twin sister Desiree Parsons?"

"No!" shouted Nicey.

The sound that followed could have been the cry of a wild animal being ripped apart by a starving wolf. The guttural moan erupted from the very core of Dorie Parsons' soul.

"Oooooh dear God!!! Oooooh Lord. Please make this pass. Isn't it enough they got one of my angels. Now they're wanting to persecute the only living being I've got left on this earth. Just take me. Take me right now, Lord. I can't bear any more of this. Oh Nicey!"

Nicey reached for Dorie and held her close. Tears ran down both their faces. Their sobs were agonizing. Jeff and Buddy looked at each other. Jeff shrugged his shoulders and spread his hands as if to say 'it had to be asked'.

Then Jeff saw a side of Buddy he'd never seen before. Buddy went to Dorie and knelt in front of her. He took her hand and in a voice so low that it was hardly audible said, "Mrs. Parsons, that question had to be asked. No one's saying Nicey killed her sister. It's just that in this kind of investigation you ask everyone that question."

Dorie's breathing was irregular and she trembled so hard they feared she'd have a stroke. Her hand clasped her breast. Jeff and Buddy realized they made a mistake by questioning Nicey in Dorie's presence. Nicey rushed to the bathroom and came back with a small tablet.

"Here mama put this under your tongue." Dorie did as she was told, and in a few minutes she was calmer.

Buddy was still kneeling in front of Dorie. "Mrs. Parsons, how do you feel now?"

Dorie nodded her head. "Better," she whimpered. "I just can't stand to hear anything against Nicey. She's all I've got."

"I understand," said Buddy. "But would you feel like talking about something else?"

Dorie looked suspicious. "What?"

"Just tell us in your own words how you came to be their foster mother," said Buddy and he stood, went back to his chair, and sat. Jeff to hide his impatience, and soon Dorie was calm.

Dorie thought for a few seconds and then began. "Me and my late husband...his name was Jim...decided we was getting too old to be foster parents any more. So we told the people down at Social Services in Jackson to take our names off the list. Then...it was the year we had that big influenza epidemic...we got a phone call from the Social Service Office asking us to come in next morning. We didn't know what it was all about, but we went in anyway. We were told there was twin girls who was so frail they didn't know as they'd make it. They said if'n anyone could pull them through Jim and I could. Now we knew they was playing up to us but since we was already down there we thought we might as well take a look. Well, that was all it took. There they was two little girls with a head full of black hair all swaddled in pink blankets. They was so thin. Why their little arms and legs were 'bout the size of chicken bones. Well you can guess what happened. We each held one and they just stole our hearts. We took them home that very day."

"Were you told anything about how the twins got to be at Social Services?" asked Buddy.

"As matter of fact yes," said Dorie. "Dr. Lowell. We was told that Dr. Lowell from over at Seaboard brought them in. He told the social worker that he delivered them and their mother died. The family was so poor and ignorant that they couldn't take care of a baby...especially twins. The grandfather asked him to take them. Dr. Lowell told them he was too old to take care of two babies but he knew of someone in government that could help. But they would have to sign some papers giving permission for them to take care of the twins. They signed and Dr. Lowell brought the little girls to Jackson in a wooden orange crate."

Jeff and Buddy looked at Nicey and wondered how she felt at being given away when she was just a sick helpless baby.

Dorie caught their glances and said, "Don't worry none about Nicey's feelings. She's heard all this a million times before. Haven't you Shugah?"

Nicey smiled through tears and nodded her head.

"What about their mother?" asked Jeff. "Were you told anything about her?"

"We was just told that she died giving birth to the two babies. Her name was Katie Hollis. I remember that. I wanted the babies to know the name of their birth mother. Dr. Lowell said Katie was undernourished and weak as a kitten. She might've had flu too. There weren't hardly a family that didn't lose at least one loved one to flu that year. Jim and me was real lucky. Neither of us got sick."

"What about the twins' father? Do you know anything about him?" asked Jeff.

"Not a thing," said Dorie shaking her head.

"Where was their mother buried?" asked Jeff.

"Now that I can't tell you," said Dorie. "I suppose Dr. Lowell took care of all that. When he brought the twins to Social Services he told the social worker that right after they buried the mother her family handed the twins over to him and disappeared. They was migrants, you know. No roots to speak of. Poor. Dirt poor."

"Desiree and I have always wondered where she's buried," said Nicey.

"Mrs. Parsons why did you and your husband leave Northampton County?" asked Buddy.

Dorie stared up at the ceiling in silence. Finally she said, "Well it was like this. Jim and me was always honest with Nicey and Desiree. They knew we was their foster parents and that their real mother was in heaven. We called her their angel mama and me their earth mama. They was happy, healthy, beautiful little girls. One day I was down at the Piggly Wiggly grocery store shopping and as usual I had them with me. They was dressed alike, and everybody just smiled at them. They was about to turn six and was gonna start school that fall. Well, the town busy-body come up to me and she says, *'How are the little orphans today'?* My heart just sunk. I went home a-bawling and told Jim what she'd said. We got to talking and was so afraid that when they started to school they would be teased and called orphans. I couldn't stand the thought of them being bullied. So we come up with a plan. Jim had a job offer working security at a hardware store here in Matthews. We went to Social Services and asked them if'n we moved was there any way we could take the twins with us. Well, it took some doings, but they said yes. There was a whole bunch of paper work we had to fill out, but finally we got permission to move the girls with us to Matthews. We agreed to be placed under the supervision of Mecklenburg County Social Services. That was fine with us. We'd been doing foster care for so long it didn't make no difference to us who supervised. That's how we come to move to Matthews."

"Nicey and Desiree used the name Parsons. Did you and your husband adopt them?" asked Jeff.

"No, we didn't," said Dorie. "We just used Parsons so as to make things easier for the girls. If'n we'd adopted, money as foster parents would stop. We couldn't of took care of two little girls without financial help."

"Did anyone in Matthews ever bully you?" Buddy asked Nicey.

"No," Nicey said. "We didn't try to keep it a secret that we were foster children but since no one knew the details, there wasn't much fodder for gossip."

"When did you move to Philadelphia?" Jeff asked Nicey.

"I was about twenty-one," said Nicey.

"Nicey took a two-year course in journalism at the Community College. She worked over to the Charlotte Observer doing research before going to work as an investigative reporter for the *Confidential Observer*," Dorie said proudly.

Buddy looked at Nicey admiringly. "I've been meaning to tell you that I liked your article on the walking fish."

"Thank you," Nicely said timidly.

Jeff cleared his throat. "Nicey do you have any idea who would want to kill your sister?"

"No."

"Do you have any idea why someone would want to kill you?"

"Not a clue," she said.

"What about the investigations you've conducted. Have you received threats?" he asked.

"No. Not real threats. I do get letters saying my work is spurious. But I expect that...it's the nature of my job," she said shrugging.

"What are you investigating now?" he said.

"Top secret," she said with a grin. "If I let people know what I'm working on I'll get scooped. There is no way I"m gonna tell you or anybody else what I'm working on!"

Jeff thought about the kind of *news* that was reported in the *Confidential Observer* and wondered who would scoop those kinds of stories. He smiled to himself. "Does anyone at your office know what you're working on?"

"Nope," said Nicey. "I keep it secret from them too. This is a cut-throat business. You can't share information with anyone. You never know who'll steal your stuff. That's why I'm not telling *anyone* about the story I'm working on now."

"Then no one knows what you're working on?" Jeff asked.

"I didn't say that," Nicey said. "I got my sources."

"What sources?" asked Jeff. He felt like she was playing games.

"Can't say. I have to protect my sources at all costs," she said decisively.

Jeff became impatient. "Even if that means the life of your sister."

Nicey turned pale. She whispered, "Desiree didn't have anything to do with my investigation."

"You know that, but maybe someone else doesn't,' said Jeff. "Did you ever think that someone thought they were killing you not your twin sister."

Nicey was silent for a while. Then she said, "That's all I got to say about my source."

Jeff leaned forward and put his arms on his knees. "Alright we'll come back to that later. Nicey, tell us why you flew to Raleigh Durham."

"That's simple enough," said Nicey. "I came to see mama."

"And you flew into to Raleigh/Durham International Airport? Charlotte International in closer to Matthews. Why not there?" Buddy said.

"And what was Desiree doing in Raleigh?" Jeff said.

"And why did Desiree drive to Seaboard?" Buddy asked. "And why did she have your driver's license?"

"Whoa. Too many questions. What do you want me to answer first?" Nicey said.

"Okay," said Jeff. "In your own words tell us what you and Desiree were doing in Raleigh."

"And Seaboard," Buddy added.

"I flew into Raleigh/Durham because I had a job interview in Durham. At a real newspaper. I won't say which one because…,"said Nicey.

"Because you're afraid someone will steal it?" Jeff said testily.

"Hey, laugh if you want to but this is a cut-throat profession," said Nicey. "I gotta keep everything close to the vest. Including job opportunities."

"Alright," snapped Jeff. "Go on."

"Alright then," said Nicey indignantly. "So I told Desiree about my interview and learned that she was going to be in the area at the same time. She had to go to Chapel Hill to help wrap up a documentary on Biltmore Estates."

Dorie interrupted excitedly, "Desiree works over at Biltmore Estates in Asheville. She works in promotions."

"Yes ma'am," said Buddy dismissively.

Nicey smiled. She knew her mother momentarily forgot Desiree was dead. Then Nicey continued, "Desiree and I decided to hook up in Raleigh and spend some time together. Then we'd planned to drive over here to see mama."

"They are always surprising me like that," Dorie said pleasantly.

"Yes ma'am," said Buddy.

"Go on," prompted Jeff. He was becoming impatient with Dorie's interruptions.

"So I flew in and rented a car at the airport...a red convertible. I drove to Raleigh, and rented a room at the Velvet Cloak Inn on Hillsboro Street. Then I just waited for Desiree to show up. After they finished their work, the man she rode to Chapel Hill with dropped her off at Velvet Cloak."

"Do you know his name?" asked Jeff.

"No," said Nicey. Jeff made a note to find the name of Desiree's travel companion.

"What did you do next?" asked Buddy.

"We did a little shopping, went out to eat, and then back to the Inn," said Nicey. "My interview was the next morning so I went to bed early."

"What about Desiree?" asked Jeff.

"What about her?" said Nicey.

"Did Desiree go to bed early?" asked Jeff. He was becoming more and more miffed at Nicey's attitude.

"Yes, Desiree went to bed early," Nicey said in a sing-song voice.

"Again with the games," thought Jeff. Then he said, "Nicey we don't have time for this. You need to tell us right now why Desiree went to Seaboard. We've got a murder here. And the victim is your twin sister. I'd think that you'd want to help. You have information we need and you're playing games. Now we can continue this conversation here, or you can take a trip back to Raleigh where interrogators may not be as patient as we've been." Then Jeff shouted, *"So take your pick—tell us all you know or let's take a ride."*

Nicey looked startled and tears welled up in her eyes, but she did not cry. She looked at Dorie sheepishly. "Desiree and I have been searching for information about our birth mother and father for a long time. We knew we moved here from Northampton County and we knew the name of the doctor that delivered us. We even knew our birth mother's name. We've got a copy of the birth certificate. What we didn't know is where she's buried and who our birth father is." Nicey looked at Dorie. "We didn't tell Mama about our search because we didn't want her to think that we're being disloyal. She's the only mama we ever had. But after daddy Jim died, we got to thinking that maybe we have another daddy out there somewhere."

Dorie said, "Nicey, dahlin, I wouldn't give it a thought. I knowed that one day y'all would want to know where you came from. That's why I told you everything we

235

knew about your birth mama and how we come to take you home with us. That's not being disloyal to us. Why it's human nature to want to know your history."

Nicey smiled at Dorie. "Thanks mama."

The conversation had veered off course again, and Jeff was irritated by all the personal recollections.

"Okay Nicey, I've had it," Jeff smacked his hands on his knees, pushed himself up, and bent over Nicey. Angrily he said, "The question was *'why was **Desiree** in Seaboard?'* I want your answer and I want it ***now***."

Nicey drew back in shock said, "For gosh sakes. It wasn't the first time Desiree ever went to Seaboard. She'd been there once before…to the Seaboard Cemetery. We figured that our birth mother had to be buried there since Dr. Lowell apparently made arrangements. You see, according to mama Doctor Lowell told Social Services he'd come straight from her burial. So Desiree went to Seaboard and checked out the cemetery. She walked through the whole place. She checked every name on every single headstone. She didn't find any grave marked for Katie Hollis."

"So what did she intend to do when she made this last trip to Seaboard?" asked Buddy.

"On her first trip to Seaboard, Desiree was starting to leave the cemetery and an old man walked up to her car. He asked if he could help her find someone. She told him who she was looking for and he said he'd never seen the name Hollis on a grave stone in Seaboard Cemetery. She told him a little of what we knew about Katie Hollis' death and about how poor she was. After he heard her story, the old man claimed he vaguely remembered a family living on the Blankenship farm on Galatia Road."

"Did Desiree look for the farm then?" asked Jeff.

"No," said Nicey. "She was on a job assignment in Chapel Hill then, too, and time ran out. But she called me and told me about it. She said she'd go back down when I came down for a job interview."

"Explains why Desiree asked for directions to Galatia Road," said Buddy. "If the man she talked with at the cemetery was elderly, he probably thought of the street at Galatia Road...not Elm Street."

Jeff shook his head and paced the room. Finally he sat on a stool directly in front of Nicey. He eyed her sternly and said, "Nicey this still smells like day-old fish to me. Are you telling me that the next day you go off to your job interview and Desiree takes off to Seaboard to look for the grave of your birth mother? *You* weren't curious? *You* didn't want to go on the search too?"

"Yes I was curious. Yes I wanted to go on the search. But this job interview is important to me. Do you think I want to spend the rest of my life chasing down stories about walking fish?" Nicey said irritably.

"What about the story you were working on in Philadelphia? The one with the *secret source,*" Jeff said derisively.

"It's still a secret," Nicey said mockingly.

"We'll see about that," Jeff muttered.

Buddy could see the questioning was deteriorating. Jeff's face was somber. Buddy said, "Nicey, there's one thing I don't understand..."

"Just *one* thing?" said Jeff.

237

Buddy ignored Jeff's remark. "When we found the body at the farm we found driver's license and other personal items in a bag that identified the victim as Nicey Parsons. How did that happen? How was it that Desiree had your bag and personal stuff?"

"Yeah, how did that happen?" Jeff sneered.

Nicey said, "When Desiree and I get together, we like to dress similarly."

"And?" asked Buddy. Nicey looked off abstractly.

"Nicey this is like pulling teeth. I want a straight answer. How did Desiree end up with your bag? No yarns. No more walks down memory lane. Just tell us how the hell Desiree ended up with your bag?" Jeff looked angry. Nicey looked innocent.

"I'm trying to tell you if you'll let me. Geez!" said Nicey. "As I was saying before I was so rudely interrupted, that day Desiree and I bought matching shoes and bags. That night we put all our stuff in our new bags. Next morning I was in a hurry and grabbed Desiree's bag, and she obviously took mine."

Jeff shook his head and rolled his eyes in disbelief. "Was that so hard?"

Buddy picked it up. "Did you know Desiree was driving to Seaboard?"

"Yes," said Nicey.

"You were okay with her taking the car you rented?"

"Yes. I didn't need it. I met an assistant editor downstairs in the Inn for breakfast. I spent the entire day with her."

"Were you concerned when Desiree didn't return?" asked Jeff.

Nicey looked at Jeff incredulously. "Of course, I was *concerned.* She is ...was...my sister. She'd only been to Seaboard once and she was scared of getting lost. She thought all the roads down there look alike."

Jeff let out a sigh, looked down at his notes and said, "Okay Nicey. I need the name of the assistant editor you spent the day with?"

"What for?" shrieked Nicey. "You wanta screw up my chances of getting the job in Durham? I told you, competition is tight for investigative reporter positions. You wanta scare her away? Why does she have to know anything about this?"

Jeff and Buddy looked at each other and shook their heads.

"What?" shouted Nicey.

Jeff looked at Nicey in disbelief. He spoke softly and very slowly, "Nicey, hasn't it occurred to you that if the assistant editor watches television or reads the newspaper, that she already *knows about this?"*

Nicey leaned forward and her hands moved quickly to cover her mouth. Tears rolled down her cheeks and splashed in large puddles on top of the coffee table. Jeff and Buddy watched silently. Finally Nicey raised her head and looked at her mother mournfully.

"Mama!" she wailed and buried herself in Dories' outstretched arms.

Dorie held her and gently stroke her hair. She looked up at the Marshals and said, "Nicey is just plumb tuckered out. She's not even thinking straight right now. What she needs more than anything is to sleep. Ain't slept since she got here."

Jeff shuffled impatiently. Buddy stared at the contradictory scene of the young woman spirited enough to pursue the urban legend of a walking fish and now trembled like a child in her mother's arms.

Finally Jeff said, "Mrs. Parsons, we're going to stay until we get some more answers from Nicey. I can see she's exhausted. We can sleep in the car or in here. What would you feel more comfortable with?"

"Oh there's no need for you to sleep outside. I don't have beds, but you're welcome to sleep on the couch and in the recliner. I'll fetch you a couple of blankets and pillows," she struggled to the front of her chair and jostled Nicey. "Come on Sugah. I'm seeing to it that you get in that bed...right now."

Nicey offered no resistance and was led off to bed much as Dorie would have done when Nicey was a child. Dorie quickly returned with bedding and said, "Yonder is the bathroom. There's clean towels and wash clothes in the cupboard." She turned and walked in the direction of her bedroom. Then she turned and her eyes were pleading. "Most people don't understand the special bond between twins. It's...it's spiritual. It's like Nicey's lost part of her soul. I understand you have to investigate, and I want you to. I want Desiree's murderer found same as I would if'n it had been Nicey that was killed. But you got to understand Nicey's all I got now. No husband. No Desiree. And I want Nicey treated right."

"Yes ma'am, we understand that," said Jeff. "But our job is to find Desiree's killer. And believe it or not, we want to protect Nicey."

Dorie looked startled. "Do you think Nicey's in danger?"

"She might well be," said Buddy. "That's another reason we're here tonight. For Nicey's protection."

"Oh no," said Dorie. "Now I got to worry about Nicey." Dories turned and walked slowly toward the door. "Oh Lord, help me."

After the door closed behind Dorie Buddy said, "I can't believe she didn't realize Nicey might be in danger too."

"She's just a simple woman, Buddy," said Jeff. "Just a simple woman."

Chapter 18

Jeff slept fitfully. He awoke feeling disoriented and stiff. The recliner that was a snug fit for Dorie Parsons was about a foot too short for Jeff. His left foot dangled limply off the foot board, and he shook it vigorously in an effort to return feeling. The smell of coffee drifted through the house, and Jeff's empty stomach complained. He stood slowly and headed to the bathroom. The many medicine bottles lining the counter top and the elevated toilet chair over the commode revealed that this bathroom was equipped for an elderly, sick person. Jeff thought of Dorie and the conflicting feelings she must be experiencing…the elation of having Nicey alive offset by the sorrow of Desiree's death.

When Jeff came into the living room he found Buddy still sleeping with a pillow covering his face. Jeff tracked the aroma of coffee to the kitchen. It was an old room…old white appliances, a wooden table with chipped green paint, ruffled curtains featuring fading red roosters, a portable dishwasher, and an unpainted wooden shelf that held an assortment of household cleaning products.

Jeff stopped short when he walked into the kitchen. There on the kitchen table he saw a laptop…the laptop that reportedly held all of Nicey's business secrets. Nicey stared intently at the screen.

She did not acknowledge Jeff as he walked to a percolator, poured a thick dark brew, and joined her at the table.

"So, what's new?" he asked.

Nicey slowly raised her head. Fear emanated from her eyes and she licked her dry lips.

"What?" asked Jeff.

Nicey didn't answer and turned the laptop to face Jeff. The headlines from the front page of The Philadelphia Inquirer jumped out at him. *Mutilated Body of Man Found.* The story revealed that the body of 29 year old Robert Ortiz was found in the Delaware River off a fishing pier in Camden, New Jersey. It reported in detail how the nude man had been tortured and died a slow death. He'd been in the river at least three days. Robert was born and grew up in Philadelphia. He'd worked at Costanza Shipping International for three years. He was survived by father, mother, four brothers, one sister, and two nieces and five nephews. Funeral services would be held the following Saturday at Holy Cross Catholic Church. In lieu of flowers it was requested that contributions be made to the Holy Cross after school basketball program of which Robert had been a member at one time.

"Someone you know?" asked Jeff as he slid the laptop back to Nicey.

Nicey licked her lips again. "My source," she whispered.

"What?" exclaimed Jeff.

"Robert. He was my source for the story I'm working on," Nicey said.

Jeff leapt from the chair sloshing coffee onto the table. "Holy…Why didn't you say so?" said Jeff.

"I just did. You got a hearing problem?" screamed Nicey relieved to be able to vent the fury smoldering inside her.

Suddenly Buddy burst into the room his gun pointed down. Wide eyed he looked from Jeff to Nicey. "Hey, what's going on in here?"

"Nicey's source for the story she won't tell us about has been murdered," Jeff said angrily.

"Are you sure?" said Buddy still trying to force himself awake.

Nicey said irritably, "You don't think I know the name of my source? You don't think he's been murdered? Which is it? Here see for yourself. Robert Ortiz was my source." And she shoved the laptop towards Buddy.

Buddy dropped into a chair and began to read. When he finished he said, "Anyone who'd do this wouldn't think twice about killing Desiree. Jeff…"

Jeff waved Buddy quiet. He had his phone out, scrolled down, and clicked on a number. There were several rings and a pickup. "Pennsylvania U.S. Marshal Service. Brackus here."

"This is Jeff Sands, North Carolina Eastern District, U.S. Marshal. Like to talk with Ernesto Salas."

"Salas's not here."

"How about Miguel Moretti?"

"Gone too. Got called over to Camden, New Jersey in connection to a case they're on. No telling when they'll be back in."

Jeff's heart pounded. "That case might be related to one down here. I'll ring his cell."

"Okay. Sometimes they shut off the cell. If you don't get him, you want he should get in touch?"

"Absolutely. Tell him...just tell him Robert Ortiz was Nicey Parsons source."

"He know this Nicey Parsons?"

"He does."

"Will do," said the Pennsylvania Marshal.

Jeff stood, took his coffee mug and walked outside. He tried Salas' cell. No answer. Then he tried Moretti's cell. No answer. It went to message, and Jeff left a message to return his call. Then he called Bryant. Two rings and a soft sexy voice said, "Arlis Bryant's office. Cathy Roberson speaking."

"Cathy, Jeff. I gotta talk to Bryant immediately," said Jeff.

There was an audible sigh. Then she said impatiently, "Jeff, I'll see if he's available. He's real busy this morning."

Jeff yelled, "Listen here, Cathy. Got no time for your chicken shit games. If you don't get Bryant on this phone right away, I'm gonna come to Raleigh and wrap that telephone cord around your skinny little neck."

There was a gasp and then total silence on the other end. After a few seconds Bryant was on the line.

"Jeff, you insulted my secretary again and scared hell out of her. This better be a life or death situation. So what?"

"Well, Bryant this definitely falls into that category. Life and death. You see this morning the body of a young man was discovered up in Camden, New Jersey. He had been tortured to death."

Jeff then related all they'd learned since arriving in Matthews. Then he reported that this morning Nicey read in the Philadelphia Inquirer that the tortured body of a young man was found in Camden, New Jersey. Nicey claims the young man was her source.

"So you see it was definitely Nicey, not Desiree, who was the intended Galatia Road victim. And now, Nicey is a setting duck," said Jeff.

"So what are you going to do? And what do you need from here?"

"I want Nicey to stay here at her mother's and I need about two or three men for her protection. And we still need to keep a lid on the fact that our victim wasn't Nicey but her twin. We especially need to keep it quiet since this murder in New Jersey. We're dealing with a pro here, Bryant. Seaboard alone wouldn't stand a chance of apprehending a pro."

"Okay. That's three men counting you and Buddy?"

"No. Two or three more in addition to Buddy and me."

"What are you and Buddy going to be doing?"

"Bryant, I want to go back to Seaboard. There's a connection there. I know there is. We can't keep Nicey under wraps forever, but while it's not known that Nicey's alive, I want to do some serious digging."

Bryant was silent. "I don't know, Jeff. You sure that's the right track to be on? Seaboard?"

Bryant seldom disputed Jeff's gut feeling. Jeff argued, "That's where it started Bryant."

"Have you let Pennsylvania know about this?"

"Got a call in to them. Ironically they're unknowningly out investigating the murder of Nicey's source."

More silence. Then Bryant said, "Okay Jeff. Hold on a minute." Jeff waited anxiously. Maybe he shouldn't have come down so hard on Cathy. Then he rationalized she was so pretentious she had it coming.

Bryant came back on. "Okay. Got two men heading to Matthews. Wait for them and tell them what to expect."

"Two? Okay. Fine," said Jeff. "Then Buddy and I will head back to Seaboard when they get here. Keep you informed."

"Oh Jeff," Bryant said. "Don't ever talk to Miss Roberson like that. She's...she's sensitive. You made her cry."

Jeff almost choked. Then he said, "Sorry, Bryant. You're right. Cathy is a very sensitive lady. Don't know what I was thinking. Won't ever happen again."

Jeff clicked off, went back inside the house, and to the kitchen. Buddy was drinking a mug of coffee and Nicey was playing around with her laptop trying to find more information about the murder of Robert Ortiz.

"So what's next?" asked Buddy.

"We're moving out," said Jeff.

Nicey jumped up. "Good I've gotta check in with that assistant editor. Let her know I'm alive and still interested in the job. Just drop me off in Durham." She began gathering her things.

"You're not going anywhere," said Jeff. "We got two Marshals coming here, and they'll be your protection until we come back."

"The hell you say," screamed Nicey.

Jeff noticed that Nicey did a lot of screaming and shouting. "You're a witness in two murders, Nicey. You're not going anywhere."

Suddenly Nicey was in Jeff's face. This time she spoke softer but with anger and loathing. "I haven't witnessed anything. I wasn't in Seaboard when Desiree was murdered, and I certainly wasn't in New Jersey when Robert was killed. I'm not a *witness* to anything, and you can't make me stay here."

"You are a witness, Nicey. You have information....information that pertains to the murder of two people...your sister and Robert. You are the one person who can connect the victims to the perpetrators. You're out of here and your life isn't worth a plug nickel, and our investigation goes down the toilet. Now you can stay here in Matthews with your mother under the protection of two Marshals, or you can come with us to Raleigh where you'll be safe in a cell as material witness."

Nicey seem to calm down. "Don't I need a lawyer? I want a lawyer. You get a lawyer when you're arrested."

"You're not arrested. You're in protective custody. That means we protect you as long as you're in our custody. You're out of here and you're no longer under our protection. And good bye, Nicey," said Jeff.

"I can't go anywhere?" asked Nicey.

"You need something, one of the Marshals will get it," said Jeff.

"I'm a prisoner," said Nicey.

"You're safe," said Buddy who had been listening. "This won't be for long, Nicey. And when it's over you've really got a story for that paper in Durham. That ought to land you the job for sure."

Nicey squinted into the distance thoughtfully, and then she said, "You're right. I hadn't thought of that. I have something to offer them in exchange for the job...*My Ordeal in the Witness Protection Program.* That's just off the top of my head, but it's something I can run with."

"Witness Protection Program? Who said anything about the Witness Protection Program? We're just protect...," Jeff blurted.

Nicey decided to declare détente. "Jeff, I've decided to take you up on your offer. I can work on this story while the Marshals are here." And she turned to her laptop and began to type.

Jeff grumbled, "*Take my offer,* my ass. That laptop is confiscated forthwith." And he snapped the laptop shut and snatched it up.

Nicey squealed. "You can't do that. That's private property..."

"I can and I have. This laptop is evidence. Evidence in two murders. It goes with me. You want to write try doing it the old fashion way." And he stomped out of the room leaving behind an angry, sputtering Nicey. Then he heard her bedroom door slam.

Within an hour a black Crown Victoria pulled up in front of Dorie Parson's house. One man got out and one remained behind the wheel. Jeff walked outside. He immediately recognized the men as Marshals from the Western District, Randolph Pace and Riley Stanford. They shook hands and Jeff briefed them on the situation and warned them that Nicey wasn't too happy about being restricted so extra caution would be necessary to prevent her from skipping out. The man behind the wheel leaned forward and asked, "You want the car out front or in the garage?"

Jeff said, "In the garage for now. You might want to move it out tonight and one of you watch the street."

The driver pulled the car into the garage and closed the door and the Marshals followed Jeff inside. Buddy was gathering things to leave. They spoke, and then Jeff introduced the two Marshals to Nicey. She studied their faces and said, "Did Jeff tell you I'll be working on a story?"

"Sure did. Carry on," said Marshal Pace.

At that moment Dorie Parsons came out of her bedroom. She stopped short surprised by two unfamiliar men. She looked at Jeff questionably.

"Dorie Parsons, these two Marshals will be staying here for your protection until we wrap up this case." Then Jeff introduced each man.

"Oh my," said Dorie. "Well this is nice. Protection? Well thank you. Thank you. I'll just have to make an extra big kettle of stew. Now I'll need to run to the grocery. Have you men had your breakfast? I'll do that first then the grocery..." Dorie was already moving to the kitchen.

"Ma'am...Ma'am," said one Marshal. "You don't have to worry about breakfast for us either. We already ate. And I'll be glad to run to the grocery store for you. Just make a list. We don't want you going outside, please."

"Oh well. Not go outside? Yes, I understand," said Dorie. "Jeff, Buddy you've only had coffee."

Jeff said, "Don't worry about us either. We'll grab a breakfast biscuit at a drive-thru."

Then Nicey's door opened and she sauntered in. Dorie said, "Nicey dear, these Marshals are here to protect us. Did you know that? Nicey?"

"Yes mama. I know," said Nicey.

Chapter 19

Buddy drove to Seaboard so Jeff could talk with the Pennsylvania Marshals when they returned his call. They drove in silence until they were well onto I-40.

Jeff looked at his young companion. He remembered when he volunteered to take Buddy on as partner. He'd recognized something persuasive and intuitive about the young Marshal and realized the value of these qualities in law enforcement. Plus it helped that Buddy viewed Jeff with a kind of hero worship.

Jeff said, "You're really getting good at diversionary tactics."

Buddy was taken aback. Jeff was not one to hand out compliments lightly. "Thanks," said Buddy. "What are you talking about...I mean specifically?"

"Oh how you calmed Dorie when she got hysterical. And the way you planted the idea for Nicey to write a story while we work the investigation. That'll keep her busy and out of our hair. This is good, Buddy. Good strategies. And it comes naturally to you."

"Thanks Jeff," Buddy said modestly. "I never thought anything about it. It's just my way of doing things. By the way, this morning while Dorie and I were alone in the kitchen she told me that Nicey and Desiree have been paying most of her medical bills. Maybe that's why Nicey lives so frugally up in Penn..."

Jeff's cell interrupted Buddy. Jeff grabbed it and clicked on. "Sands here."

"Jeff, Moretti. What's up?"

Jeff spent the next twenty minutes filling Moretti in on everything they'd learned since locating Nicey. Most of their conversation revolved around the discovery that Robert Ortiz was Nicey's source for her story.

"Of course she's still not saying what her story's about, but we'll soon know. We've got the laptop she uses for her work," said Jeff.

There was silence at the other end of the line. Finally Moretti said, "Jeff, this young guy, Ortiz, was working for Costanza Shipping International."

"Yeah, I read," said Jeff.

"It just happens that Costanza Shipping International has been under investigation by us, ATF, FBI, and every agency carrying a badge for the last two years," said Moretti.

"Must be big to draw that much fire power," said Jeff.

"Big as it gets," said Moretti. "Weapons. We have evidence that Costanza Shipping International is shipping illegal weapons to third world countries. Countries with which we do not have good relationships."

"Holy...and Nicey was *investigating* them?" said Jeff.

"If this is true, Jeff...if Nicey and Ortiz were fishing around in Costanza's pond her life ain't worth a tinker's damn. She'll end up the same as Ortiz...and Jeff, that ain't no way to go."

"I'm thinking I better put in a call to the Marshals back at Dorie Parsons' house. They need to know the degree of threat they're dealing with. They need to know it can turn lethal and not just for Nicey."

"And Jeff," said Moretti, "we gotta talk to Nicey sooner rather than later."

"I know," said Jeff. "But we've gotta be careful setting this up. First of all we certainly don't want it to get out that she's alive. Second, I'll update the Marshals in Matthews about the seriousness of the situation so they'll be mighty cautious about who they let in there."

"I understand. We'll work it out," said Moretti. "Where you off to now?"

"Back to Seaboard," said Jeff.

"Good. Like I said before, that's where it started and that's where it'll end," Moretti said.

"Keep us posted, and we'll do the same," said Jeff.

"Will do," said Moretti.

* * *

It was afternoon when they got to Seaboard. The town looked almost deserted as folks headed home to home-cooked meals not recommended for those who are weight watchers. Jeff wondered what gastronomic delights Gladys had prepared for tonight's dinner. Just east of Greensboro he called Sophie to let her know they were on their way in and to alert Gladys.

Buddy parked next to the two police cars in front of the Town Hall. Dillon, Stewart, and Harvey Clinton were there. Jeff and Buddy took the next forty five minutes filling them in on what they learned in Matthews. They again emphasized that as far as the public was to know,

Nicey Parsons was deceased. Then they answered questions for the next fifteen minutes. When everyone was clearly brought up to date on the status of the investigation and the deadly turn of events that the Pennsylvania situation revealed, an ominous silence engulfed the room.

"So what's next?" asked Dillon.

"Just what I wuz thinking," said Stewart. "You ain't a- thinkin' that the murderer is still here 'bouts do you?"

"No...I don't know," said Jeff. "But I've been thinking about the torture and murder of Robert Ortiz up in Pennsylvania. Say it's the same guy that killed Desiree...he does this murder in Pennsylvania but how did he track Desiree to Seaboard? A stranger stands out around here like a sore thumb. Been any strangers around here at the time of her death? Sara Wood said she didn't see anyone. The guys in the pickup who harassed Desiree didn't see any car following her."

Dillon said, "Well, we haven't been setting on our hands while you were gone. We did learn we had a few strangers in town that day. A couple of salesmen dropped in at Mom and Pop Grocery to take orders. And a couple of farmers from Warrenton came over to look at new farm machinery at John Deere. A biker blew through on a black motorcycle...most likely on his way to the beach. And Mrs. Carrie Lewis's cousin from up in Virginia came to visit. Not very likely suspects."

"Yeah. But even if he came to Seaboard from Pennsylvania how did he find Desiree at the Blankenship farm way out on Galatia Road?"

"Elm Street," corrected Stewart.

"Yeah, whatever," Jeff said tiredly. "At any rate I don't think we can simply assume that the Pennsylvania hit man also did Desiree."

"So what's next?" Dillon asked again.

"Nicey's safe in Matthews, and the true identity of the Galatia Road victim has not been made public. So we got some breathing space. I say let's go with the plans we had before. Let's tackle Miss Sara Wood again."

There were murmurs of agreement and dread. Suddenly there was a loud clamor from the front of the building. Loud voices bounced off the walls and the front door burst open. Mrs. Bernice used her ample buttocks to push through the front door while balancing a cake in her hands. She was talking a mile a minute, and following close behind was Frances. Frances spotted Buddy and grinned. Buddy grinned back. And Dillon and Jeff shook their heads and chuckled.

"Well, here you go," Mrs. Bernice said. "My best fresh apple cake. I'm a-makin' it my business to put some meat on your bones. If'n we're going to *crack this case* you have to at least eat fit." Harvey Clinton was out of his chair to offer his assistance. "Thank you Harvey. You're always a very polite gentleman."

Mrs. Bernice walked back to Dillon's office. "Get me that big leather chair, Buford. And Jeff you hold it steady while I sit down." Buddy and Jeff did as they were told. Mrs. Bernice continued, "Saw the Marshals' car and ran right home to get this cake." She looked from one man to the other, slapped her hands on the arms of the chair, and demanded, "Okay, let's have it. Where do we go from here?"

Harvey giggled and busied himself cutting wedges of cake, placing them on paper napkins, and serving them. Stewart looked befuddled. Jeff and Dillon looked at each and grinned, and Frances moved close to Buddy rubbing against his shoulder.

"Well?" said Mrs. Bernice.

Dillon said, "As a matter of fact we were just going out to Miss Sara Wood's place again."

"Maybe she's calmed down and she'll agree to let us talk to her sisters," Jeff said.

"Wouldn't count on it, given how protective she is of those sisters. Strict on them too. That's why those sisters won't talk to you unless Sara says it's alright."

"Mrs. Bernice, remember you were telling us about a brother, John Wood. Was he the oldest child?" Dillon said through a mouthful of cake.

"Sure was," said Mrs. Bernice.

"Sara next, of course?"

"Right again."

"Which sister was next...Mary or Rebecca?" asked Jeff

"Now that I cannot tell you," said Mrs. Bernice, "seeings I wasn't there."

"What do you mean?" Buddy said.

Bernice looked at Buddy and Frances who were standing close to each other. She smiled sweetly and said, "Good looking pair...what I mean Buford, I wasn't there when Mary and Rebecca were born and since they were twins I don't know which one actually popped out first."

"Twins!!!" the men exclaimed. Mrs. Bernice grinned brightly and looked from one man to the other. She didn't

257

understand their reaction to what she'd said but was pleased she'd caused some excitement.

Frances just looked confused. "What?"

Buddy whispered, "Fill you in later."

Stewart said, "Why them two women don't look one speck alike."

"That's because they're fraternal twins not identical." Dillon stood and said, "Mrs. Bernice, now we're definitely going out to talk to Mrs. Sara and her sisters."

Chapter 20

The men rode together hoping Miss Sara would feel less threatened if only one car pulled up. They turned into the road that led to the house and parked in the front yard where grass had once grown. The four men got out of the car and stared at the dilapidated frame farm house. There was an ominous aura about the old place. It appeared to be deserted. Shades were down, and the doors were closed. A light, cold wind lifted small clouds of dust and spun them about the yard and over the empty field like whirling dervishes, and a large crimson ball of setting sun turned the horizon blood red. The place looked like a scene from a gothic novel. For some reason the men felt compelled to move and speak quietly as they approached the house.

Suddenly the stillness was shattered and an earsplitting malicious voice shrieked, "Hold it right there, misters. I done told you to stay off'n my property."

In reaction to the shrill command the men whirled and stared horrified in the direction of the backyard. Miss Sara Wood was positioned in an attack stance. Her face was contorted with rage, spittle dribbled from her chin, and her eyes darted furiously from one man to another. But most alarming was her clothes. They were splattered with blood and Miss Sara brandished a large hunting knife. Instinctively the men hands went to their weapons but stopped short of drawing them.

"Don't you go a pullin' no gun on me. I know my rights. I got a knife and I ain't a scared to use it. You got no

259

cause to keep a-comin round here harassin' me and my sisters," Miss Sara shrieked as she continued to wave the knife savagely.

"Miss Sara...the blood...what have you done?" shouted Dillon.

"Put the knife down, Miss Sara. We need to talk about this," said Jeff.

"I'm through a-talkin' to y'all," Miss Sara screamed. "My mistake was callin' the law in the first place."

"You are a witness, Miss Sara," Jeff said as calmly as possible. "We need your help."

"Good luck in that regard," Miss Sara said. "Helping you means trouble for me. Just look how y'all come a traipsing over here any time it suits you and me just tryin' to take care of my own."

Jeff continued to engage Miss Sara in conversation. Miss Sara continued to swear and wave the hunting knife. And Buddy slowly, quietly crept away from the group and behind Miss Sara.

"You done made nervous wrecks out of my sisters, so as I cain't even get a decent day's work out of them. And now here y'all come again," Miss Sara yelled.

"Miss Sara, where are your sisters now?" said Jeff.

"Are they okay?" demanded Dillon.

"Lordy Miss Sara, you ain't hurt them have you?" asked Stewart.

At that moment Buddy hurled forward, knocked Miss Sara to the ground, and grasped the hand that clutched the knife. Jeff sprang in, foot on Sara's wrist, wrestled the knife from her hand, and bagged it while Buddy held Sara in a hammerlock.

"This knife goes to Raleigh for analysis," Jeff said.

"Help! Help!" wailed Miss Sara. "I'm being assaulted by a bunch of crooked policemen. Help!"

Dillon and Stewart raced to the back yard. Jeff knelt beside Miss Sara while Buddy continued to restrain her.

Jeff shouted, "Okay, Miss Sara. Where are they? Where are your two sisters?"

Miss Sara flailed about in an effort to extricate herself from Buddy. "My sisters? What do you want with my sisters? You want to rough them up too? Or are you after them 'cause they're women."

At that moment Dillon rushed from behind the house and yelled, "Jeff, you better come here."

Jeff grabbed plastic restraints from his hip pocket, flipped Miss Sara onto her stomach, and fastened her hands behind her back.

"Get offen me you charlatan. You ain't got no cause to be a-cuffin' me," Miss Sara yelled and kicked hard at Jeff and Buddy.

Jeff said, "No cause? Try assaulting officers with a deadly weapon, resisting arrest, and..." he stood and ran toward the backyard, "possibly murder."

"Murder???" screamed Miss Sara. "You're insane, Jeff Sands. Yeah...you're ..."

Jeff didn't hear anymore. He rounded the house, stopped abruptly, and gawked at the scene before him. In Miss Sara's backyard two dead chickens dangled from the clothesline, and a small dark puddle of blood was on the ground beneath each chicken.

"Augh," said Jeff and he automatically jerked his head away.

"That explains the blood on Miss Sara," said Dillon.

Jeff said, "It doesn't explain her coming at us with a knife, though," said Jeff. "The sisters?"

Dillon just pointed toward the rickety back porch. Mary and Rebecca sat calmly in straight back kitchen chairs totally unaware of the chaos that took place around them. Newspaper was spread over each sister's lap and stretched out on the newspaper was a dead headless chicken. The women rhythmically plucked feathers from the dead chickens and tossed them into the air pausing occasionally to dip their fingers in a large pan of water that set on the floor between them. The yard was covered with feathers, and chickens in the nearby pen cackled and squawked and fluttered about frantically. Jeff detected mutterings between the two sisters, but was unable to distinguish a single word.

Stewart stood beside the porch and asked repeatedly, "Miss Mary. Miss Rebecca. Are you alright?" The sisters appeared to be oblivious to the presence of anyone else in the yard.

Jeff heard a commotion and turned to see Buddy pushing Miss Sara into the backyard. Miss Sara struggled doggedly and was irate. Buddy was provoked. But the sisters simply continued plucking chicken feathers and tossing them up into the air. When Buddy reached the clothesline he stopped, pointed to the hanging chickens, and shouted, "Wha...wha...what kind of a sick ritual is this?"

Jeff walked back to Buddy, gave Miss Sara a disgusted look, and explained, "It's the way she slaughters chickens. A chicken is caught, held by its legs, and flipped upside down. Then one leg is held on each side of a clothesline and the legs bound together. When the chicken is released, it dangles helplessly from the clothesline by its legs. Then she cuts the chicken's head off and it hangs there until it bleeds out."

"That's savage!" exclaimed Buddy.

Miss Sara chuckled and scoffed, "Well mister, just how do you like *your* chicken? Raw? With a head? Feathers and all?"

Jeff gave Sara a disgusted look. "You're just not acquainted with farm life, Buddy," he said. Sara continued to cackle.

"Not this way," said Buddy and he shoved Sara toward the porch. The sisters still didn't acknowledge the audience that gawked at them. They simply continued to pluck and mutter.

Dillon stepped in close to Jeff. "Want to keep her in restraints? Looks like she' not broke no law."

Jeff walked over to Miss Sara who was still laughing at Buddy's reaction to the hanging chickens. Jeff was furious. He said, "Listen up Miss Sara, I intend to question you…and your sisters. Period. Now I can take you to jail in Jackson, or I can take the restraints off now and question you here. So you just think about those two choices. Then tell me what'll it be."

Miss Sara stopped laughing. She didn't say anything for awhile. She just glared at Jeff angrily. Jeff glared back. Then she glanced at her sisters. "Take 'em off. I'll talk with you…*again.*"

Dillon stepped up and removed the plastic restraints from Miss Sara's wrists, and Stewart continued to stare at the sisters.

Sara sat down on a porch step. The sisters continued to pluck the chicken feathers and throw them into the air. Finally Miss Sara shouted, "Stop throwing them feathers in my face. Put 'em down on the newspaper." Then she looked up at Jeff. "Sometimes pickin' chicken feathers is the onliest thing what soothes them when they get this riled up. Okay, shoot."

Not wanting to miss a word of Miss Sara's interrogation Dillon, Stewart, and Buddy stepped in close.

"First let's go back to the night you called Stewart," said Jeff.

Sara rolled her eyes and breathed a deep sigh. "I done told you everything I know about that night."

"Well, tell me again," said Jeff. And Jeff relentlessly pressed Miss Sara for any detail she may have missed in the previous interview. A half hour later he'd learned nothing new. Jeff was frustrated, and Miss Sara was incensed.

"Now looka here," said Miss Sara. "I done told you everything I know about what happened that night. I don't have nothing else to tell you."

Jeff realized Sara had opportunity and possibly motive. However in an effort to placate Sara, Jeff said, "Okay, I believe you."

Miss Sara said, "'Bout time." And she braced her hands on her knees and started to stand.

"Just a minute," said Jeff, "there's another matter I'd like cleared up."

Miss Sara dropped down onto the step again. "What?" she demanded.

"Do you remember a Hollis family that worked for Mr. Myron Blankenship some years ago?"

Miss Sara didn't answer.

Jeff continued, "They were itinerate workers and harvested his tobacco crop. Then for some reason they stayed through the winter. They lived in the house across the road." Jeff pointed to the house at the murder site.

Miss Sara's face turned pale, and she clutched her chest. Her breathing became forced and erratic. Jeff knew he'd hit a nerve. "Miss Sara. Miss Sara," he said, "Are you okay?"

Sara stood. She raised a trembling hand and wiped the sweat from her upper lip. Then she turned away from Jeff, raked her fingers through her hair, and stared broodingly across the parched field that separated her home from the road and the crime scene.

When she spoke her voice was a hoarse, soft whisper. "What for you a-bringin' that up?"

Jeff and Dillon looked at each other excitement on their faces. "Then you did know them." Jeff said.

"Yes, I knowed them," said Miss Sara.

"Tell us how you knew them...how well you knew them," said Jeff.

Suddenly Miss Sara shook her head forcefully. "I didn't. I didn't know 'em well a'tall. They was just po' white folks." Then she back pedaled. "Don't be a-gittin' me wrong. I don't hold it against abody that's po. They wuz...they wuzn't our kind."

Buddy and Jeff exchanged knowing glances. Buddy asked, "What do you mean *our kind*?"

"I mean they wuzn't....wuz...," Sara stammered, turned, and stared down the men who were, after all, still on her property. "I cain't explain. I don't have to explain. That wuz just the way it wuz back then."

Dillon cautiously asked, "Miss Sara, do you know if John knew the Hollis family well?"

Sara suddenly became agitated again. "What for you go a-bringin' my dead brother into this mess?"

"Do you think there's anything wrong with your brother knowing the Hollis family?" asked Buddy.

Sara was still angry with Buddy for throwing her to the ground and restraining her. She looked him squarely in the eye and said, "My brother wuz an honorable man. A good man. He wuz kind to everybody irregardless of their lot in life."

"I'm sure he was, Miss Sara," said Dillon. "So are you saying that he would have been kind to the Hollis family too?"

Sara looked frustrated. "'Course."

"*How* kind?" Jeff asked.

"What do you mean by that crack?" Miss Sara spat out the question vehemently.

"I understand John was your brother, Miss Sara," said Jeff. "Who was older…you or John?"

The question threw Sara Wood completely off guard. Bewildered she just blinked and stared at Jeff. "What's a goin' on here?" she finally managed to say. "I agreed to answer your questions *again* in return for your leaving us alone. Now you go a-bringin up the dead and he cain't even defend himself."

"Do you think John needs to defend himself," said Dillon. "Please answer the question. *Who was older…you or John?*"

"He wuz," shouted Sara. "John wuz. So there."

"How did he die?" asked Jeff.

"Lord, have mercy on me please," wailed Sara. "What've I ever done to deserve this torture? Ain't it enough that I lived through it once?" And Sara's face collapsed in her hands.

Buddy went and sat beside her. "Miss Sara, we don't mean to torture you. But you don't want somebody who would commit that kind of murder running around free do you? As you'll soon see, these questions are necessary. Real necessary to help find the person who killed that young woman across the road."

"'Course I don't want no murderer a-runnin' round free. 'Cept I don't see what my brother has to do with this," Sara said.

"Miss Sara, what would you say if I told you that a young woman, Katie Hollis, was pregnant the winter her family stayed in the house across the street?"

Sara said defensively, "So what?"

"And what if I told you that Katie Hollis had twins?"

"Twins ain't that unheard-of," said Sara.

Jeff said, "Yes, but there's a genetic tendency for twins to run in families, and you have twin sisters. Miss Sara, what would you say if I told you that the young woman who was murdered across the road from your house has a twin? She has an identical twin...alive today."

Sara did not reply. She raked her fingers through her damp hair again.

Jeff continued, "And what would you say if I told you that we think the murderer killed the wrong twin? And now we're afraid that when he realizes his mistake he'll go for the surviving twin."

Sara turned and began to pace the yard wringing her hands anxiously. Then she turned, walked to Jeff, and stood face to face with her interrogator. "I nursed him you know? Day and night. It was the flu...worse epidemic I ever saw. It'd already killed Daddy in spite of me. But I still thought nobody could take care of my brother like me. And *them twins* wuz jest babies." She jerked a thumb in the direction of her two sisters who were giggling and throwing feathers at each other. Sara screamed, "Cut it out, ya hear?"

Sara was opening up. Jeff said, "So what about your brother?"

"I had my hands full alright a-takin' care of everybody, but I never left my brother's side for more that a few minutes at a time. He talked a lot. Most time wuz outta his head from the fever. Kept a-talkin about Katie and a baby. Guess I had so much on my mind that I couldn't take on another thing. Know what his last word wuz?"

"No."

"Katie. *I'd* been a-takin' care of him night and day and him a-callin' for Katie," said Sara.

"Must have hurt," said Buddy.

"A little bit," said Sara. "After John passed I went over to that shack over there. I was gonna tell Katie that John had passed."

"Did you...tell Katie that John died?" asked Buddy.

"No," said Sara. "They wuz all gone. Place cleaned out. A few days later I saw Dr. Lowell at John's burial and asked him 'bout Katie. He told me she'd passed too. I remember thinking that maybe they wuz together."

"And the twins...or the baby as you thought then?" asked Buddy.

"Dr. Lowell said, *Let it go, Sara. You got 'nough on you what with your sisters.* Well, back then nobody argued with Doc Lowell. Doctors were wise and had authority. So I just let it go."

Sara suddenly became very still and dropped onto the steps. The sisters noticed Sara's mood had changed, and they quietly moved to sit close to her on the steps. A cool breeze wafted across the yard, and a curtain of darkness began to fall turning the tall trees into leafless silhouettes against a fading autumn sky. Having survived another day the caged chickens retreated to their roost and buried their heads under their ruffled wings.

The men shuffled restlessly. Needing Sara's reassurance, the sisters nudged Sara's arm nervously. Sara responded by gently patting their arms.

Finally Sara said, "You said the murderer killed the wrong twin and the other one's alive?"

"Yes," said Jeff. "We're keeping that real secret for now...real quiet. We think she is in great danger."

"Where is it?" Sara asked.

Jeff knelt in front of Sara and said, "In due time, Sara. In due time."

Sara emitted a little groan. "I guess I've waited this long, I can wait a little longer."

Jeff stood and the men began to move toward the front of the house. Sara called after them, "Both girls?"

Jeff turned, "What?"

"Both girls? Was John's twins both girls or what?"

Jeff replied, "Girls."

Sarah looked at her sisters and whispered, "Was they alright? I mean not..." and she gestured toward Rebecca and Mary.

"They were fine. Healthy little girls," said Jeff and he turned and walked away.

When the men settled back in car they sat quietly each lost in his own thoughts. Finally it was Stewart who broke the silence. "I was just thinking...Nicey seems to be a mighty strong-willed person. Maybe she got her grit from her Aunt Sara."

"And her bull-headedness," sneered Jeff.

Chapter 21

On the drive back to Seaboard Jeff said, "Dillon you going to be at Town Hall for a while?"

"I can be. Why?"

"I need to get this knife to the lab and it has to be secure till it's picked up."

"I'll take care of it. I'll stay at Town Hall till it's picked up," then he added, "Little Sister can bring me a broasted chicken for supper. Maybe she'll even eat with me although I don't see that much of her anymore." And he grinned at Buddy.

Jeff pulled out his phone and dialed. "Ned...Jeff here...Got a knife for you.....I don't know if it's the murder weapon. I doubt it, but it fits the description......Yeah, it won't leave our sight till a courier picks it up....Good, it'll be at Town Hall...Dillon."

"Drop me at Sophie's," Jeff said as Buddy turned right toward town. "We can sort this out tomorrow." The others murmured in agreement.

Jeff was tired, hungry, and felt an overwhelming sadness as he stepped out of the car and walked slowly toward the front porch of the yellow Victorian house. Comforting lights glistened from the den and hall windows. His gurgling stomach reminded him it was dinner hour. He inserted his key to unlock the front door, but before he could turn the knob the door flew open and there was Sophie silhouetted against the glow of the hallway lights.

"Jeff!" she exclaimed.

"Good evening ma'am," Jeff said in his contrived Southern drawl "Could this fine eating establishment provide a hearty meal for a weary traveler who has not sat down at a table in hours?" Jeff stepped inside, locked his arms around her waist, and drew her to him.

When they finally drew apart Sophie said, "Oh Jeff. Really? You haven't eaten?"

"Only a slice of Mrs. Bernice's apple cake. You think Gladys has some leftovers in the frig? I'm sure you've already eaten."

"No she ain't," said a stern voice from the dining room. "She don't never eat nothing when she thinks you're a-comin'. *I'll just wait for Jeff,* she says, and if'n *you* miss the meal she does too."

Jeff pushed Sophie away, feigned anger and said, "Is that true? Do you skip meals when I don't show up?"

"Only if you say you're going to be here and *then* don't show up," Sophie said defensively and shot Gladys a phony expression of contempt.

Gladys turned toward the kitchen, "Don't see why I even cook a meal if'n she's just gonna eat half the time."

Then Jeff said jokingly, "Gladys, sorry about the trouble. A sandwich would be fine...if it's not too much trouble." And he grinned.

Gladys stopped, her hand poised on the kitchen door, and turned. "Jeff Sands, the day ain't come when I'm gonna serve sandwiches to anybody for evening dinner. I saved what I cooked in the oven. Be ready in about ten minutes…if'n that suits you," Gladys said. She shot Sophie a look of disdain and disappeared into the kitchen.

"She's peeved!" Jeff whispered to Sophie.

"Oh pooh! Gladys loves to have something to be peeved about. Makes her feel needed. You know that. Let's go in the den and have a glass of wine." And Sophie took Jeff by the hand and led him into the den.

He noticed that Sophie had already poured a glass for herself. She went to the side table, uncorked a carafe, and poured a full glass of red wine for Jeff.

"Whoa," said Jeff. "Remember I haven't eaten."

"Take it. It's good for your heart," said Sophie.

"Looking after my heart, huh?" said Jeff.

"Always," said Sophie and she lifted her glass in a silent toast.

At that moment Melvin walked in. "Gladys says come and git it. You want I should put a fire up in the bedroom?"

"Yes," both Sophie and Jeff said.

"Won't that be nice, Jeff?" said Sophie.

"Almost as nice as Gladys' dinner," said Jeff. Sophie punched his arm with her fist almost causing him to spill his wine.

"Hey careful! Remember this is for my heart," and they carried their wine into the dining room.

Between mouthfuls of Gladys delicious chicken pot pie Jeff told Sophie about the trip to Matthews; how he found Nicey with her foster mother; and that they were now under the protection of two other U.S. Marshals. He told her about the trip to Sara Wood's farm but didn't mention the scuffle. During the entire conversation, Jeff was aware that the kitchen door was wide open and that Gladys and Melvin were taking in every word that was said.

When he finished his report, Jeff called, "Did you get all that, Gladys?"

"I gots it," Gladys said and she walked in carrying a lemon pie with a mile-high meringue. "As I see it, Nicey Parsons' life ain't worth a wooden nickel if'n word gets out that she's alive and the dead girl is her twin. Not a nickel." She plopped the pie down in front of Jeff.

"Hey, don't mess up the meringue," Jeff said as he picked up a pie cutter, cut a slice, and reached for Sophie's plate. Then he addressed Gladys' comment about Nicey. "We're very much aware that Nicey is in jeopardy that's why we're keeping the true identity of the victim *top secret.* So don't go letting the cat out of the bag."

Gladys scoffed. "You don't even have to say that to me...cat outta the bag. Huh!"

"Jeff, Nicey must be devastated by the death of her twin," said Sophie.

Jeff paused, a hefty bite of pie suspended in front of his mouth. "I suppose she's upset but she's already writing another article."

After dinner Sophie and Jeff trudged up the steps to her bedroom. Three candles burned on the mantle above the fireplace. The scent of vanilla permeated the room. The only other light came from a small bedside lamp. The fire in the fireplace cast dancing shadows on the walls and ceiling. A window was slightly opened and the lace curtain fluttered in the gentle autumn air. Jeff sank into an overstuffed chair in front of the fire and laid his head back against the soft headrest.

"I'll be back in a minute," said Sophie and she picked up a gown that lay across the foot of the bed.

Jeff reached for Nicey's laptop and scrolled through the document files. He recognized most file names and made notes of others he'd ask Nicey about. He realized how organized and complete her computer office was. And he also realized how valuable the information in the files was to the investigation.

Jeff looked up to see Sophie standing in front of the fireplace. He snapped the laptop shut. The glow from the fire in the fireplace filtered through her sheer gown exposing her slender silhouette. Jeff shook his head and tried to replace the dreadful images with the beautiful vision of Sophie.

"Sophie," he whispered hoarsely and reached out to her. She took his hand, settled onto the arm of the chair, and rested her head on his shoulder.

"Jeff, you look so tired," she said.

"I know," he said. "It seems like every time I show up I'm exhausted. Sorry." And he kissed her first gently then eagerly. "So sorry," he murmured against her neck.

Sophie pushed him away. "You don't hear me complaining."

"That's because you're a *good* woman," he said. They stood and Jeff lifted Sophie, carried her to the bed, and tossed her onto it. Sophie squealed and bounced several times.

"A *very good* woman." And he threw himself onto the bed beside her.

* * *

Jeff awoke to the sound of gentle rain tapping against the windowpane. He reached for Sophie and found only a cool empty spot where her warm body had lain. He grumbled unhappily. The continuing tapping of rain began to lull him back to sleep...perhaps fifteen minutes longer. Then he smelled coffee. Somewhere in the bowels of the big old house someone was trying to coax him into wakefulness. With resentment he threw back the quilt, swung out of bed, and trudged reluctantly to the bathroom. He stepped into the shower and allowed himself five minutes of the hottest water he could take and then five minutes of cold. He shaved, dressed, and started downstairs.

"Good morning, people," Jeff announced as he threw open the kitchen door. But his cheerful greeting was met by long, somber faces. "What?" asked Jeff. "Who died?"

"Oh Jeff please don't," said Sophie. "Don't say such things."

"Okay. What's wrong with everybody?" Jeff asked.

"Sophie picked up the morning paper and handed it to Jeff.

The headlines read, **Seaboard Murder Victim Misidentified.** The article went on to read that local law enforcement assisted by U.S. Marshals had for days been investigating the death of the wrong person. It reported that the victim was not Nicey Parsons but her twin sister, Desiree. Nicey Parsons was feared to be in grave danger. It reported that U.S. Marshal Service in Raleigh offered only *'no comment'*. Most alarming, however, was the discovery of Nicey's whereabouts. It was reported that she was at the home of her foster mother in Matthews, North Carolina under the protection of U.S. Marshals.

Jeff threw the paper across the room. "God....," and he reached for his cell. Gladys who had never seen Jeff lose his cool did the only thing she could think of to diffuse the situation. She poured him a mug of coffee, slid it across the table, and said, "Here."

Jeff dialed Buddy's cell. He heard the phone at the other end ring once, twice, then a pickup. "Buddy?" said Jeff.

"Yeah. I just saw it," Buddy said.

"Where are you?"

"Just across the street at Frances' apartment," he said.

"Get on over here quick as you can," Jeff said.

"Right. Frances too?" Buddy asked.

"Hell, why not?" said Jeff.

Jeff clicked off his cell, reached for the mug of coffee, took a sip, and burned his tongue. "Damn," he swore. "What else?"

At that very moment his cell rang. Jeff looked at the incoming number and groaned. "Sands here," said Jeff.

"Good morning, Jeff," said a dreaded familiar voice.

"Good morning, Bryant," said Jeff.

"Jeff, I don't suppose you can guess what I'm looking at right now can you?"

Jeff looked at the ceiling and shook his head. Bryant's silly games had always annoyed Jeff, but this morning Jeff was especially in no mood to play twenty questions. "I've seen the paper," Jeff said heatedly.

"Good. Then can you guess how many media calls I've received this morning?"

"Listen Bryant, I don't know how this got out. Right now my immediate concern is for two Marshals and our witness over in Matthews, North Carolina."

Bryant said, "They too are of concern to me. However, being in my position, I have to look at the whole picture," and at this point Bryant yelled, *I have to be concerned about the credibility of this office.*"

"Right," said Jeff.

"Now what have you done about the situation in Matthews?" Bryant asked.

"Was just getting ready to call them when you called," said Jeff.

"Good," said Bryant. "Now tell them they will be getting reinforcements. I've already called it in. When the press finds the address of Nicey Parsons' foster mother...and they will find out … they'll be all over that house."

"Right. I'll tell them reinforcements are on the way," said Jeff. "Anything else?"

"No, just keep me posted. I'd rather get my up-dates from my Marshals than from the newspaper," said Bryant and he rung off.

The door bell rang, and Sophie said, "That'll be Buddy and Frances." And she rushed towards the front hall.

Gladys said, "Well, I best be a-gittin' some breakfast together." And she turned toward the stove, slammed an iron skillet on the burner, and began peeling off bacon strips. "I don't never know when somebody's gonna show up to be fed. I tell you what, not every housekeeper would put up with this."

Having heard Gladys tirade before, Jeff walked out of the kitchen and into the dining room where Buddy and Frances sat at the table talking with Sophie.

"Where do you think the leak came from?" asked Buddy.

"I have no idea. It's next to impossible to keep this kind of thing under wraps for long, but I had hoped for a few more days," said Jeff.

"What's next?" asked Buddy.

"Well first I gotta call Matthews. Tell them reinforcements are on the way," said Jeff.

At that very moment Jeff's cell rang. He lifted it and said, "Jeff Sands."

"Jeff, this is Miguel Moretti."

"Right. Miguel," said Jeff.

"You seen it?" Moretti asked.

Jeff sank into a chair. "I should have known that the Pennsylvania media would pick up on it too."

"Yeah, well we're catching a lot of heat up here. Guess you are too."

"Yeah, and it's only begun I'm afraid," said Jeff.

"Just wanted to give you a heads up. Our office is shifting the blame to North Carolina. That probably means you and your team will catch most of the guff," said Moretti.

"Figures," said Jeff.

"What's next for you?" asked Moretti.

"After I get the situation in Matthews secure, I'll try to find the leak. Can't spend a lot of time on that though. We still have a murderer out there."

"Right," said Moretti. "Might be able to help you on the leak thing. When I talked with a person over at the Philadelphia Inquirer, the only information he gave me was that the story first broke from a newspaper in Durham, North Carolina."

Jeff leaped up. "Durham?"

"Yeah. Don't know North Carolina geography all that well, but ain't that close to Raleigh?" Moretti said

"Yes, yes," said Jeff. "Hey, Moretti, thanks. You've been a big help. Gotta go. Thanks."

Puzzled, Moretti said, "Any time," and he rung off.

Jeff immediately began to click in a number. He turned to Buddy and said, "I could ring her neck."

After only one ring a voice at the other end said, "Pace."

"Pace, guess you've seen the papers," said Jeff.

"Just went out and pick up the morning paper. It's on television too," he said.

"Geez," said Jeff. "Well just want you to know what to expect. Press is gonna track down the address there and you're gonna have your hands full."

"We were just talking about that," said Pace.

"Want you to know you got reinforcements on the way. I don't want any reporters anywhere near Nicey. No questions. No pictures. No nothing by nobody."

"Gottcha," said Pace. "What about the Ipad? She's been using it to write her article."

"*Ipad?* So that's how it got out…Confiscate her damn Ipad as soon as I get through talking to her. If she resists, slap cuffs on her and bring her to Raleigh," Jeff said heatedly.

"Right. Want to talk to her now?" asked Pace

"Yes," said Jeff.

A few seconds passed and then an impatient voice said, "What?"

"Nicey, do you know what you've done?" Jeff demanded.

"What?" she said angrily.

Jeff's voice rose to a crescendo, "What? You've just told a murderer that you are still alive and where you can be found."

"Listen here Sands," screamed Nicey, "I told you how important this job in Durham is to me. There's a story out there. Me. And I intend to be the one who reports it. This is my chance to show that assistant editor in Durham exactly what I can do. I ain't giving this over to anyone else. I got all channels open between me and that Durham newspaper and I intend to use them."

"Oh no you're not," said Jeff. "When I hang up Marshal Pace is instructed to confiscate your Ipad. Finding your twin's murderer might not be important to you, but it is to me and I'm not going to have some little hot dogger interfere with a murder investigation."

"How dare you!" yelled Nicey. "How dare you imply that catching my sister's killer isn't important to me? You don't know squat."

"And your foster mother...don't you care about her? Huh? No, Nicey you've done enough damage," said Jeff. "We take the Ipad with no trouble from you or we take it anyway and you're moved to another location." Jeff clicked off.

"Jeff!" Sophie said, "I've never seen you so angry."

Jeff turned to her. "Well you've seen it now. I get angry. Change anything?"

Sophie stood, walked to him. "Of course not. But it was a side of Jeff Sands I'd never seen before."

"That girl really pushes my buttons," said Jeff. He looked at Buddy. "Should have let you handle this too."

* * *

The bald-headed man sat at his desk in his high-rise office in Philadelphia. Several North Carolina newspapers were spread on his desk. He frowned down at the headlines of the Greensboro News and Record that read *Seaboard Victim Misidentified.*

He lifted his red face and glared across his desk at the young man wearing faded jeans, a leather jacket, and motorcycle boots. "How the hell did this happen? You can't even hit the right target?"

"Nobody ever told me she had a double," Faded-jeans said resentfully.

"You're supposed to find these things out yourself. If I do all the research for you I might as well do the hit myself," Bald-man said.

Faded-jeans squirmed. "What do you want me to do?"

Bald-man shouted, "I want you to go back down to Carolina and do what I hired you to do to before."

Faded-jeans voice quivered with anger as he said, "Where do I find her?"

Bald-head slammed his fist on the desk, pushed himself up, and loomed over the desk toward Faded-jeans.

282

"How do *I* know where to find her? I'm paying *you* to find her and do what I paid you to do in the first place." Bald-man straightened up, pounded his fist on his forehead, and looked heavenward. "What have I got here? What have I got here…a moron? I gotta…"

"Ah…ah…sir," came a meek voice from the other chair. It was occupied by the middle aged man, Greasy Comb-over.

Bald-man stopped his tirade abruptly, looked in the direction of the interruption, and said, "What? What? Spit it out man!"

"Ah…I was…I just wanted to say Sir, I know where she is."

Bald-man looked astonished. He sat down hard in his chair. "How? How do you know where Nicey Parsons is?"

Comb-over felt a rush of relief. He sat up straight, leaned forward, and said in a conspiratorial voice, "Well…let's just say *I* have my sources too."

Bald-man gawked at him for a few seconds and then said, "Alright then, let's hear it. Where the hell is she?"

Comb-over cleared his throat and said, "As the newspaper reports, Nicey Parsons can be found in Matthews, North Carolina at the home of her foster-mother, Dorie Parsons. And I have the address and directions to her house." He rattled off Dorie's address.

"Where the hell is Matthews, North Carolina?" asked Faded-jeans miffed that old Comb-over upstaged him.

"You want we should buy you a map?" barked Bald-man.

Then Comb-over calmly, smugly said, "Matthews, North Carolina is just outside Charlotte, North Carolina."

283

Bald-man said, "There. Just outside Charlotte. You think you can find it?"

Faded-jeans squinted and his pocketed hand moved slowly, inconspicuously to his belt where a knife was sheaved. He focused a savage look at the two men and said in a sinister voice, "I don't like it when people poke fun at me. It makes me angry...very angry."

There was something in Faded-jeans' transformation that made the men's blood run cold. Comb-over sank back in his chair. Bald-man cleared his throat, reached into his desk drawer, and took out an envelope. "Alright then. Travel money," said Bald-man and tossed the envelope across the desk to Faded-jeans. Then he added cautiously, "This time...don't screw-up."

Faded-jeans glared at him, reached for the envelope, and stood. Without saying another word he walked out.

Comb-over let out a sigh of relief. "He carries a knife, you know. And I've seen him pull it. He's fast...fast as greased lightening. That guy is crazy," he said.

"Yeah, and that's why he's good at what he does. Not bright...but good."

* * *

The door bell in the front hall of the yellow Victorian house rang urgently. Sophie walked to the front hall. Jeff heard her say, "Dillon, Stewart. Come in."

Dillon and Stewart stepped into the front hall. They looked in amazement at the grand stairwell, the Oriental

284

rugs, the portraits, and the impressive antique accouterments that set on tables.

Dillon removed his police cap and nudged Stewart to do the same. Then Dillon said, "I'm real sorry to disturb you, Sophie, but I need to see Jeff and Buddy right away. Are they by any chance here?"

"They most certainly are," said Sophie. "They're in the dining room. Come on in." And she walked toward the dining room. Dillon and Stewart followed.

Dillon was surprised to see Frances. "Hey Little Sister," he said. Then he spotted Buddy and put two and two together. "Hey Buddy."

"We've seen it too," said Jeff. "Any repercussions yet?"

"No, not yet," said Dillon. Then he added, "It's on television of course."

"How in tarnation did this get out?" Stewart said.

"Nicey," said Jeff.

"What?" Dillon and Stewart said.

"Doesn't she realize she's putting herself in danger?" said Dillon.

"She does. But she's got the light of the newspaper world gleaming in her eye. She'll take any chance and put anyone at risk for a story."

Melvin walked into the dining room and looked at the group. Then he turned abruptly and marched back into the kitchen. They heard him say, "They's two mo out there, Gladys." They couldn't understand Gladys' response.

Jeff's phone rang. "Jeff Sands."

"You can't do this to me." It was Nicey and she was crying.

Immediately Jeff felt anger swell up inside him. Then he looked at Sophie and decided she shouldn't see him explode twice in one morning. So in a cool, sarcastic voice Jeff said, "Nicey, you did this to yourself. You gotta understand that our job is to apprehend the person or persons who killed your sister and to protect our only witness...*YOU.* We're not letting anything or anybody interfere with that job."

Nicey sobbed, "I promise I won't email anything else to the paper or television or anyone. You don't understand that writing about this is...is...therapeutic. It's my way of dealing with the death of my twin." Then her voice became a whisper, "And my guilt."

Jeff was silent for a long time. "Are you there?" Nicey said.

"Yes," Jeff said. "I'm here. What if we took you off line? You could write anything you want but not be able to send it out?"

Silence from Nicey. Jeff just waited. Then she responded weakly, "Okay. I'll just save everything I write until this is over."

"Good," said Jeff. "It'll still be from the perspective of the witness."

"Yeah," said Nicey.

"Okay, let me speak to Pace again," said Jeff.

Jeff heard Nicey shout, "He wants to talk to you, Pace."

Pace was there immediately. "Pace."

Jeff explained the deal he'd made with Nicey...Ipad, okay...online, not.

"Good," said Pace. "She's been hell since you talked with her."

"I can imagine," said Jeff. "Watch her like a hawk, Pace?"

"Right," Pace said. And they clicked off

Jeff breathed a sigh of relief. "Coffee anyone?" And he started to stand.

But at that moment Gladys and Melvin entered carrying platters of eggs, flapjacks, grits with red-eye gravy, fried apples, several breakfast meats, and Melvin's hot biscuits. The group swooned and dug in.

"Gladys, you didn't have to go to all this trouble," said Dillon.

Gladys said, "Yes I did. If'n I don't feed everybody she won't eat a tall." And she nodded accusatorily at Sophie then went back into the kitchen.

Chapter 22

Conversation turned to how to proceed in the investigation. They all agreed that it was more urgent to pursue the perpetrator than dwell on the leaked information about the misidentified victim.

Gladys was in her element. She complained happily as she made fresh pots of coffee, and Melvin rolled out several more plates of sweet rolls.

Frances was so fully involved that she almost forgot about work at the post office where the patrons had provided reliable information in the investigation. Dillon thought it would be a break-through if they could find the old man who talked to Desiree on her first visit to Seaboard cemetery. Buddy questioned whether Nicey had told them everything or was holding something back for her exposé. After a while Jeff noticed that Stewart was silent during the entire discussion.

Finally Jeff said, "Stewart, what do you think?"

Stewart jumped. "Wha…what?"

"I said where do you think we should go from here?" Jeff said watching him carefully.

Stewart squirmed. Then he said, "Y'all gonna think I'm foolish, but I been real worried 'bout Miss Sara."

They all looked stunned. Dillon said, "Why in the world are you worried about Miss Sara?"

"Well, it's just that she's had it real hard all her life what with her mama and daddy and John a dying like that. There she wuz left alone to tend to those two batty sisters. I think that's why Sara acts so mean all the time. She's bitter. Then she all of a sudden finds out she has a niece…a niece that's right in the head." Stewart tapped his temple with his finger. He looked at Jeff. "Yesterday when you told her she'd have to wait to see the only sane, live relative she has she took it fine. But I'm a wondering how she feels this morning when she sees the paper or watches television. Miss Sara is smart. She's gonna know Nicey's in danger, and she's gonna be real scared for her."

The room fell silent. Finally Buddy said, "I never thought of that. Actually I haven't given Miss Sara a thought since we left her place yesterday."

"Me neither," said Dillon.

Jeff stood and said, "Let's take a ride to Miss Sara's."

"You mean you're gonna take time off the investigation to hold the old lady's hand. Hey Jeff that's not like you," Buddy said in jest

"I think that's very thoughtful," Sophie chimed in.

Jeff rolled his eyes incredulously. "There's still a couple questions I want to ask. Since she turned cooperative yesterday now's a good time to ask them."

"That was yesterday," said Dillon. "That was before the newspapers came out."

"I know," said Jeff. "But let's give it a shot."

They stood and moved toward the door. Jeff walked over to Sophie, bent down, and kissed her. "See you tonight. Don't think we'll leave town unless something goes wrong in Matthews." Then he said, "Thanks Gladys."

Thanks also resonated from the hall. Gladys said, "Ain't no need to be a-thankin' me. If'n I had a day go by without some kinda interruption I'd think I wuz in the wrong house."

* * *

When they arrived at Miss Sara's the place was quiet. "This place is as still as death," said Dillon. The others were taken aback. "Just saying," he said.

"I'm hoping that Miss Sara will be more willing to cooperate now that she knows John's daughter is alive," said Jeff. "Maybe a willingness to protect her will kick in. We know how protective she is of those sisters."

"Even if she's just calmed down," said Buddy, "she's more likely to remember detail."

They walked to the back yard and as they rounded the corner of the house they heard a low droning noise. The two sisters sat in the same spot in the same wooden chairs they'd sat in the evening before. A large dishpan full of late butterbeans was on the floor. Their laps were covered with newspapers that held the bean shells and a bowl full of shelled beans set between them. The noise they made was a combination of humming and nonsensical mutterings. The men couldn't help but stare.

Sara approached from the garden. "They gits like that when they're upset. They start that mumblin' and all. I cain't understand what they're saying. I think it's their way of shuttin' me out...of going into their own world. I don't really care though, gives me some time alone."

"Miss Sara sorry to impose when they are upset."
And Jeff nodded toward the sisters. "But I have just a couple more questions."

"I seen it," Sara said wearily. "I read the newspaper and seen the television. The murderer knows Nicey is alive don't he?"

"Yes," said Jeff.

"Now she's in danger all over again," Sara said simply.

"Yes," said Jeff. "that is if Nicey was the intended victim."

Sara looked puzzled. "You mean he may have intended to kill Nicey's twin?

"Possibly," said Jeff.

"We have to *consider* that her twin might have been the target," said Dillon.

Sara was silent. Then she said, "By the way what was her twin's name?"

"Desiree," said Dillon.

"Desiree," repeated Sara. "Sounds real fancy."

The mumbling and humming from the porch got louder and louder. As it reached a fever pitch Sara turned toward the porch and yelled, "Shut up. For Pete's sake shut up. Cain't hear myself think." The sisters cowered, settled down, and their noise reduced to mere utterances.

Then Sara turned a tired face to Jeff and said, "So what you want to ask me now?"

"Sometime when a person is left to concentrate on something for awhile they start remembering things...details pop up that have been buried in their subconscious. Miss Sara, I want to try something.

291

Something I intended to do yesterday. Buddy, I want you to take notes. Sara, sit down here," Jeff said. And he pointed toward a large stump with an ax embedded in it. Jeff removed the ax, laid it on the ground, and held out his hand inviting Sara to take a seat. Sara hesitated then shrugged and sat on the chopping block.

Suddenly there were screeches and cries from the porch. "Oh hush up," said Sara. "He ain't a-gonna chop off my head." Then as an explanation she added, "Dis here block is whar I chop wood." Sara sat down on the chopping stump and looked at Jeff expectantly.

Jeff knelt on the ground eye level with Sara. "Now Miss Sara, I'm going to ask you to think real hard about the day you saw the red convertible turn into the Blankenship farm." Sara started to protest but Jeff made a stop gesture with his hand an added softly. "I know we've gone through this before, but I want you to try it this way. Okay?"

Sara nodded. "I want you to close your eyes. Good. Now take several deep breaths. Slowly, slowly. Good. Now, Miss Sara I want you to think about where you were and what you were doing when you saw the red car turn into Blankenship farm. No, no don't say anything just think. Think about where were you when the car turned into the Blankenship farm. Remember? Good. Now beginning at that time…when you saw the car turn in…I want you to think about what you heard. Take your time. What was the first thing you recall hearing after the car turned in?"

Sara sat perfectly still eyes closed. Then she said, "Some kinda heavy equipment…like some kind of earth moving equipment."

"Good," said Jeff. "Very good. Now think carefully. Take as long as you want. After the heavy equipment what did you hear?'

This time Sara answered quickly. "That one's easy. I heard Jesse Stephenson's old car. He wuz a gunnin' his engine 'cause the heavy road equipment wuzn't movin' fast 'nough to suit him."

"Good. After Jesse what did you hear?"

Long pause. "Just a couple more cars. Don't know who."

"Take them one at a time. "The first one?"

"That would most likely be Miz Ella Conway. Her car always sounds smooth and she wuz just a creepin' along like always."

"Good. What next?"

"I believe it wuz Buck Casey come along 'bout then in his old rattle trap of a pickup truck. Cain't be sure though."

"You're doing fine. Good. Then what?"

"I declare...I believe it was the motorcycle next. Come a roaring 'bout then. Yeah, I'm sure it was the motorcycle next."

"Okay," said Jeff. "Keep focusing. What next?"

"Nothing for a little bit. The Harris boys come by in that old Ford their daddy give them. Then seems like a couple more cars. Maybe Miz Taylor first and..."

"You're doing great," said Jeff.

"Then I believe Harmon Barnes come by. Not sure 'bout that though."

"Good."

"Then the motorcycle come back a roaring and a-gunnin' its stuff. And another pickup..I believe Buck again."

"Miss Sara, the motorcycle, how long before it came back?"

"Cain't really say for sure. Ohhh…thirty minutes. Forty at most."

"Miss Sara," said Jeff, "that motorcycle, have you ever seen that before?'

Sara opened her eyes and blinked hard at the glare. "No, never seen it before."

"Are you sure?" Jeff sounded excited.

"Sure, I'm sure. Ain't likely I'd forget something like that."

"What do you mean?"

"I ain't seen nothing that fancy around here before what with the shiny chrome and that there orange and red flame a painted down the side"

"What color?

"Black. Shiny black…'cept for the flame and all," Sara said. "I ain't sure I got 'em all in the 'xact order but it's best I can do."

Jeff stood and extended a hand to Sara. "That all? That's the best as I can recollect," said Sara.

"That's all, Miss Sara. And thank you. Thank you for your time. You've been a great help," said Jeff and he turned to leave the back yard. The others followed.

Miss Sara called. "Hey, when do I get my knife back? That's the knife I use for killing chickens."

Jeff didn't reply

* * *

They arrived at Town Hall to find Harvey at his desk and about a half dozen men sitting around discussing how *they* would handle the Galatia Road murder case. As the law enforcement team walked in the room fell silent.

An old farmer wearing faded bib overalls and a day-old beard said in a loud voice, "I'll tell you one thing though, if'n I wuz that killer, I'd hate to have Jeff Sands and Dillon a trackin' me down." There were mutterings of assent and chuckles.

More silence. Finally a black man wearing green work clothes and a John Deere baseball cap stood and announced he had work to do. The other men quickly followed and soon there was only Harvey left.

Dillon spied a newspaper on Harvey's desk. He walked over to Harvey and asked, "Harvey, **you** haven't said anything out of school have you?'

Harvey looked offended. "Me?" he said his hands spread across his chest. "I'm hurt, Dillon. Truly hurt. In all my years in this office I have never...I repeat never...betrayed a confidence. And believe me if I wanted to, I have an entire arsenal of dirt ... enough to bury this town."

"Okay Harvey, okay," said Dillon and he turned toward his desk. "Just asking. What did those men want?"

"Oh, they were just evaluating your handling of this case," said Harvey.

"And what did they say?" asked Stewart.

Harvey didn't have a chance to answer. "It doesn't matter what they said," said Dillon. "This is our case and we handle it as we see fit."

The men pulled up chairs around Dillon's desk. "Shall I leave?" chirped Harvey.

"Get off it, Harvey. We already know who the leaker is," said Dillon.

Harvey said, "Who? Tell. Do tell."

Dillon said, "Nicey Parsons, herself." Then turning to Jeff he said, "How about that interview with Miss Sara, Jeff? Anything useful?"

"I'm not sure," said Jeff. "Buddy did you get the vehicle descriptions and names of the people Miss Sara believes drove by her place?"

Buddy reached into his pocket and took out a notebook. "Right here," he said.

"What was most significant to you guys?" asked Jeff.

They all said, "The motorcycle."

"Me too," said Jeff.

"And what really hit me is that it returned. It passed her house once and then some time later came back," said Dillon. "And remember a couple folks we talked to recalled seeing a motorcycle drive through town earlier that day."

"Yeah, and where did it go?" asked Stewart.

"We need to talk with the drivers of some of those other vehicles. Find out if they saw the motorcycle. If so, as Stewart said, where did it go," said Jeff.

Chapter 23

Buddy read aloud the names of the drivers of the vehicles and the vehicles descriptions. The other men took notes. Dillon and Stewart recognized the drivers and vehicles...except the motorcycle. Since Dillon and Stewart knew the territory, the men paired off. Jeff went with Stewart and Buddy went with Dillon to question the drivers about anything unusual they'd seen the day of the murder. They were especially anxious to talk to anyone who had seen the flashy motorcycle.

Most of the people on the list lived 'out in the country' as opposed to 'town folks'. As Stewart drove, Jeff relaxed and enjoyed the ride. Stewart played travel guide as if Jeff had never been to Northampton County. Jeff leaned back and let his mind wander to times when he knew every curve on Galatia road.

Stewart said, "Up here is where Ella Conway lives. Mrs. Ella's real smart. If'n something strange wuz a-goin' on Mrs. Ella would take notice." Stewart turned onto a pea-gravel driveway lined with tall English boxwoods.

297

Simultaneously with the opening of the car doors, the front screen door to the white farm house opened.

"My word!" said Ella. "Just lookee here. I got myself two handsome visitors and it ain't even noontime. Come on in here. Have a seat right here on the front porch."

The men did as they were told and took seats in the white rockers with soft red cushions. Instinctively they began to rock. Jeff looked around at the freshly painted porch floor, the ceramic pot that held a huge green snake plant, and two hanging baskets of ferns. He thought how life on this farm was different from life on Sara Wood's farm.

"Now let me get you something to drink. I've got a fresh pitcher of sweet ice tea or I can put on a pot of coffee," Ella said.

"Sweet tea's fine," said Jeff.

"Make mine sweet tea, too," said Stewart who continued to rock.

The men were silent as they waited. Ella returned balancing a tray that held three glasses of tea and a plate of cookies. Jeff jumped up and opened the screen door for her.

"Thank you, Jeff," said Ella. "Now have your tea and these here are not store-bought cookies. This is my own recipe. I got so many compliments that I shared the recipe with the Baptist Church cookbook committee."

They sat, sipped the sweet tea, and munched cookies. Finally Ella said, "Now I know you young men didn't come out here just to enjoy my cookies. What can I do for you?"

"Mrs. Ella, do you remember driving into town the day the young woman was murdered at the Blankenship farm?"

Ella set her tea down and said emphatically, "I most certainly do. I remember telling Elwood…I says, *Elwood that could have been me.*"

Stewart leaned forward and said, "And what did Elwood say?"

"He said, *Yes it could have.* You know Elwood. He don't say much," Ella said and reached for her glass of tea.

Jeff cleared his throat, "Mrs. Ella what made you think you might have been in danger?"

"Well you know I'm not a fast driver, and this black motorcycle with a red flame painted on the side zoomed up behind me real fast. Why I though he was gonna run right into the rear of my automobile. He kept on a-makin' this loud noise with his motorcycle engine. Real impatient and rude."

Jeff set his tea on the table and shifted forward in his chair. "Miss Ella, that is exactly why we're here this morning."

Miss Ella's eyes grew big and she clasped a hand to her breast. "You mean because you think I am in danger too?"

"No, no," Jeff said quickly. "Not because we think you are in danger. We want to ask you about the black motorcycle."

Ella breathed a sigh of relief. "Thank goodness. I was scared there for a minute. What is it you want to know about the motorcycle? All I know is that the driver was a rude young man."

"Can you tell us what he looked like?"

Miss Ella rattled the ice in her tea glass and took on a pensive expression. Then she said, "Not really. He had on some sort of helmet and sunglasses. I do know he wuz a-wearin' cowboy boots."

"Yes, ma'am, that's good. Real good" said Jeff. "Now Miss Ella did you see where the motorcycle went? Ah, did you see it turn off Galatia road?"

Ella looked pleased and nodded her head. "I most certainly did. We hadn't traveled a quarter of a mile till that young man turned his motorcycle onto that dirt road...runs side of Phillip Faison's soy bean field. I thought to myself, there wasn't no cause for him to be so rude and impatient back there. He was almost to his turning-off place."

Jeff looked at Stewart. "You know where Phillip Faison's soy bean field is?"

"Sure do," said Stewart.

Then Jeff turned back to Ella. "Mrs. Ella did you notice anything else about the motorcycle? Did it park on that road or turn around or what?"

"Well, I can't really say, Jeff," Ella said tapping her finger on her cheek. "I just kept on driving towards home. He did kick up a lot of dust heading toward the piney woods back of the field."

"Is there anything else you remember? Anything at all that was unusual about the driver or the motorcycle?"

Ella frowned as she thought back to the day of the murder. Finally, "No," she said. "Not really. Aside from him a-bein' so rude, nothing stands out in my mind."

Jeff started to stand. "Thank you Mrs. Ella. You've..."

"Except," she said, "I did notice he had a foreign license plate."

Jeff looked confused, "A *foreign* license plate?"

"Yes," Ella said. "From another state you know."

"Oh," said Jeff. "Do you recall what state?"

"Yes, I do," said Ella. "It was Pennsylvania. I remember a-thinkin' that he just hadn't been brought up right."

"Bingo!" said Jeff.

"We've hit pay dirt," exclaimed Stewart.

At first Ella looked puzzled. Then she broke into a wide smile pleased she'd been helpful to her two guests.

* * *

When Jeff and Stewart were back in the car Jeff dialed Dillon. "Dillon, do you know where Phillip Faison's soy bean field is?"

"Sure do," said Dillon. "I'm standing in it. Buck Casey saw a black motorcycle turn onto the side road by the field."

"Ella Conway saw it too. We're on our way," said Jeff.

When Jeff and Stewart pulled onto the side road they saw Buddy and Dillon crouched down examining the road. They hurried out of the car and joined them.

"Find anything?" asked Jeff.

"Bunch of tracks, but not what we're looking for," said Buddy. "They're from a cultivator. A cultivator's been

301

in here turning up the field. I doubt we'll get anything in the way of motorcycle tracks."

Jeff looked over the newly turned field and then down at the road covered with large tracks left by the heavy machine. Then he looked toward the pine woods behind the field. Dillon walked back to the woods and crouched down again examining the ground."

"Anything back there?" Jeff called.

Without standing Dillon motioned the others to come. Jeff, Stewart, and Buddy walked slowly toward the edge of the wood scrutinizing the path as they went. Dillon was famous for his tracking skills. Growing up in Oklahoma he'd been an avid boar hunter. He hunted Russian and European wild boar as well as free-roaming feral hogs. Unlike some other hunters in that part of the country Dillon didn't use dogs. He saw tracking as part of the sport. Dillon's tracking skills served him all his life. In the military Dillon was called up for any assignment that required tracking. When he left the service and took a job catching skips for Arnie's Bond Company back in Oklahoma he became known as Hogman Tracker. It was rumored that when a skip learned Dillon had his sheet, he'd turn himself in just to save himself the trouble of running.

Jeff, Stewart, and Buddy approached Dillon cautiously. "What'd you find?" asked Jeff.

Dillon pointed to a pockmark in the sandy soil. "This here could be a boot track. It's been disturbed by the dust and debris blown over here by the cultivator, but we might find more prints farther into the woods."

"Doesn't look like much to me," said Buddy, "but I trust your opinion."

"What about motorcycle tracks coming back here?" Jeff asked.

"Nothing," said Dillon. "They were probably obliterated by the activity of the cultivator on the path and the debris it stirred up. But look over there. Those pine needles seem to be scrunched down. No tracks, but that indentation could have been made by a vehicle. We just need to go farther into the woods."

"Be careful. If we find tracks...man or vehicle...we'll want to get pictures and pour casts," said Jeff.

Dillon cautiously led the way into the pine woods. The sunlight filtering through the thick tree limbs cast shadows on the ground making it difficult to distinguish grooves and fissures as man-made or natural. As they walked deeper into the woods, the trees became thicker, light faded, and underbrush grew sparse. Soon Dillon motioned for them to stop and pointed to the ground.

"Look here. That's a footprint."

"We'll mark it," said Jeff. He tore a piece of white paper from his notebook, laid it beside the footprint, and anchored it with a small rock. The dismal woods created such uncanny atmosphere that the men realized they'd been whispering.

Dillon laughed nervously. "What do you want to bet we'll find more up ahead?"

And they did. They not only found footprints but suddenly tire tracks appeared. "There you go," said Dillon stooping down to examine the prints. "We just had to get back far enough into the woods to where the tracks hadn't been disturbed. These are perfect."

"Hey Dillon, lookee here. What you make of this?" said Stewart pointing to crumpled pine needles aside from the footprints.

Dillon hunkered down and examined the collection of crushed needles carefully. "Looks like he could have left his bike here."

Dillon stood and stared straight into the dark woods ahead. "Want to plow ahead?" he asked Jeff.

Jeff didn't hesitate. "Sure. What cha' wanna bet we'll come out at the Blankenship barn?" He pointed straight ahead.

"Won't get any takers here. Looks like a straight shot to me," said Buddy.

Jeff said, "Just be careful. Stay to the side of our guy's trail. Don't disturb anything."

As they walked through the woods they crossed several dry creek beds and the footprints became more discernible.

"Look," said Dillon. "See the way the heel is set apart from the sole of the shoe. This is a boot. I'd say a cowboy boot or a biker's boot. Looks like they've had a lot of wear. When our guy walks he favors the outside of his foot. This print shows the heels are run over on the outside."

"You can tell all that, Dillon?" said Stewart peering hard at the footprints.

"Sure can," said Dillon. "And he walked straight down there." And he pointed to the barn which was now in sight.

"Good work, Dillon," said Jeff. "Now we need to get someone up here to take pictures and pour casts…footprints and tire prints." And he pulled out his phone.

Buddy said, "Jeff, before you do that lemme tell you what else we found out."

Jeff paused, cell in hand. "Shoot."

"We got more information about the motorcycle," said Buddy. "And, Jeff this is not just any old run of the mill type motorcycle."

"Go on," said Jeff.

"This guy was driving a Kawasaki Concours 14," said Buddy.

"That supposed to mean something to me, Buddy?"

Buddy shifted excitedly. "Jeff, a Kawasaki Concours 14 means this guy's got money behind him. Besides being one of the most impressive looking bikes on the road, this cycle is big, powerful, blows everything else away."

"Go on."

"It's what's called a supersport touring bike. That means it's built to do some serious traveling. This isn't just your weekend toy. This bike is built for long distance. That means our guy would think nothing of striking out cross country."

"Like from Pennsylvania," said Jeff.

"Huh?" said Buddy.

"Yeah, Mrs. Ella told us the bike she saw had a *foreign* license plate on it," said Jeff,

"What?" said Buddy.

"Pennsylvania. Mrs. Ella said the license plate was *foreign* …from Pennsylvania," said Jeff.

Buddy hesitated then smiled. Then he said, "I suppose you'd need a bike like a supersport touring bike if you did that kind of traveling."

"Sure would," said Jeff and reached for his phone again. Then he hesitated and said, "How did you find out what kind of bike it is?" asked Jeff.

"The Harris boys. They've been salivating ever since they saw it. They're biker want-to-be's. They know all there is that a couple of teenagers need to know about motorcycles," said Buddy.

"Well, we'll just take the Harris boys' word for it for the time being," said Jeff and he finally clicked on a number.

Two rings and a pick-up. "Ned Cosden."

"Ned...Jeff here. We've...or at least Dillon...has come up with some footprints and tire prints. Got someone who can take some pictures and pour casts? Also be aware that the soil is sandy...may be tricky."

"It can be arranged," Ned said efficiently. "Where are you?"

Jeff told him where and that someone would stay there until his people arrived. "And Ned just to give you a heads up...a couple of kids identified the vehicle as a Kawasaki Concours 14."

"Whoa!" said Ned. "Your guy rides well. Don't see many of them around here."

"You a motorcyclist too?" asked Jeff.

"No, just a dreamer," said Ned and he was gone.

Jeff clicked off and said to Dillon, "How 'bout you and Stewart staying here until the scene guys arrive?"

"Okay by me," said Dillon. "Stewart, hear that?"

Stewart looked apprehensive. "Okay as long as we don't find no more bodies like I did the last time I was out here."

"And we need to inform State Highway Patrol to be on the lookout for the bike," said Jeff.

"I'll take care of that," said Buddy and he took out his cell and walked away from the group.

Jeff dialed another number and waited impatiently for a pickup. Finally a gruff voice at the other end said, "Moretti."

Jeff said, "Sands here. Got some news that might interest you."

"News, huh?" Moretti snarled. "So far I ain't got no *good* news from Carolina. Complications…just complications. So what's up now?"

"We're looking for a person who was spotted near the crime scene close to the time of the murder. We're getting tire prints and footprints. He was driving a motorcycle. A black Kawasaki Concourse 14."

"Kawasaki Concourse 14? He's got resources, huh?"

"Must have," said Jeff. "And the thing that's really gonna make you smile is that his license plate puts him as coming outta Pennsylvania."

"Oh for….." squawked Moretti and he let go a stream of profanity that could be heard by everyone in his office. Jeff held the phone at arms length.

When Moretti calmed down Jeff said, "We've found footprints and tire prints. We're gonna be taking pictures and pouring casts. We'll send you a present as soon as possible. Who do you know up there who can pay their hit man enough to buy a Kawasaki Concours 14?"

"Got several candidates," said Moretti. "First off we'll check with Motor Vehicles. We'll do some digging and get back with you."

"Good," said Jeff and he smiled and added, "Have a good day, Moretti." And he clicked off fast.

Next Jeff dialed a Matthew's number. Two rings and then a sleepy, gravely voice said, "Pace here."

"Pace…Jeff Sands. Sounds like I woke you up."

"Yeah," said Pace. "I was outside last night. Just catching a few. It's okay though. I was getting ready to get up. Dorie's got something cooking that smells mighty good."

Jeff filled Pace in on the latest developments. He told him about the biker on the Kawasaki Concours 14 and explained how it had been identified. Next he related the discovery of footprints and tire prints in the woods next to the Blankenship barn. He also told Pace that the bike had a license plate from Pennsylvania.

"Well, with a bike like that you can cover a lot of miles. Pennsylvania wouldn't be much of a challenge," Pace said.

"That's what I've been told," said Jeff. "In light of these new developments I want to talk to Nicey again. This guy came from Pennsylvania and so does she. Maybe what we've found out today will spark a memory."

"Want to talk to her now?"

"No, we're coming up," said Jeff.

"When?"

"Right away," said Jeff. "But don't tell Nicey about the biker. I get a lot from reactions to first-time questions."

"Right," said Pace. "Do you want her to know you're on your way here?"

"No," said Jeff. "Not even that much. Just keep it under your hat. Except you can save us some of whatever Dorie is cooking."

Pace laughed. "Right."

Chapter 24

Daylight was disappearing fast behind the magnificent cerulean mountains of western Virginia. A late fall wind tore at the remaining red and yellow leaves that still clung precariously to trembling branches. The black Kawasaki Concours 14 with a red flame painted on its side roared down I-81S. The biker wore a black helmet, protective glasses, a black water-proof polyester jacket with hoodie, and waterproof nylon rain pants. The legs of the pants were tied tightly around his ankles and tucked securely into well-worn leather biker boots. However, the weather gear did nothing to protect exposed areas. A spray of rain and fine sleet peppered his face until it was numb. Frustrated, he thought he'd seen all he'd ever wanted to see of the Blue Ridge Mountains and the Commonwealth of Virginia. He was tired and cold and hungry. Then a welcomed sign appeared out of the haze. It read Bristol, Virginia/Tennessee, the Twin Cities. He decided to stay in Bristol. He felt safe there. A city right on two state lines complicates police pursuits.

He rode around the cities until he found just the right kind of biker place. It was a real dive. Pieces of the clapboard siding were missing, the parking lot was dark and a small group of men huddled in the shadows…probably a drug buy. The lot was full of bikes, and loud music and deafening voices erupted from inside. Rusting metal signs advertised several brands of beer, grilled burgers, billiards, and rooms by the night. It was the kind of place that even law enforcement avoided.

He secured his bike, took off his helmet, and slowly sauntered toward the dive. When he opened the door, he immediately came to a halt. The room fell silent. Everyone stopped what they were doing, turned, and slowly, thoroughly scrutinized the stranger. This ritual reminded him of how a strange dog had to be sniffed by the pack before being allowed to join the group. Finally satisfied that the new-comer wasn't a threat, the customers went back to what they were doing, and the biker meandered to the bar.

"How far to Charlotte?" the biker asked.

"Charlotte? North Carolina? You got a far piece to go," said the bartender

* * *

Traffic had thinned on I-85 S. Commuters arrived home and the bleak weather forecast made them stay there. A fine, cold drizzle kept the windshield wipers in constant motion and the steady rhythm was becoming hypnotic.

Jeff had been exploring Nicey's laptop, and he found several files he didn't understand. He made a note to ask her about them. Apparently Nicey used some sort of code…another attempt to protect the confidentiality of her

311

work. He look up from the laptop and said, "Buddy, you want me to drive for awhile?"

"No, I'm okay," said Buddy. "I think we've got mixed precipitation...rain and sleet."

"We're almost to the Charlotte exit," said Jeff. "We can trade if you want to."

"I'll see," said Buddy.

But Buddy continued to drive all the way to Matthews. He worked his way back into Dorie Parsons' neighborhood of small, neatly kept, working class homes. As they turned the corner to her house they were shocked to see three elderly men clad in raincoats standing on the sidewalk engaged in serious conversation. Buddy slowed to make the turn and they abruptly stopped talking. They stared suspiciously at the occupants of the black Crown Victoria. But as it completed the turn the U.S. Marshal seal became visible and the three men lifted a friendly hand. Buddy and Jeff waved back, drove to the end of the street, and climbed out of the car. Two Marshals sent as reinforcements walked to the car.

"You guys pulled night duty, huh?"

Rain dripped from their waterproofs and they nodded somberly. One Marshal said, "I think there's sleet mixed in with this rain."

"That's what I think too. Say what's with that group of guys down on the corner?" asked Buddy.

"Neighborhood Watch," said one Marshal. "Everybody in the neighborhood feels real protective of Nicey. They've known her and Desiree since they were kids. So they thought it would be a good idea to resurrect their old Neighborhood Watch Group."

"Neighborhood Watch?" Jeff said. "Good lord! Be careful. Don't shoot some innocent neighbor."

"That's our concern too," said the other Marshall. "We talked with them and told them not to be sneaking up on us. They agreed to make a lot of noise if they came down this way. One of them...the oldest fellow...is a retired cop."

"Retired cop? Geez, that's even worse," said Jeff. And he and Buddy headed to the house.

They stepped inside and the smell of something hot and delicious greeted them. The aroma reminded them that they hadn't eaten since breakfast. Pace and Nicey were sitting on the sofa watching the local news. Of course, it included a rehash of the crime involving Nicey and Desiree Parsons, hometown girls. Another Marshal dozed in the recliner.

Nicey looked up when they entered. "Well look what the cat drug in," she said snidely.

"Hello Nicey," said Jeff. "Good to see you too."

Nicey stood hands on her hips. "If you've come to make sure I haven't been on line, just ask Pace. He's been a real pain in the ass over it...always checking up on me. I feel like a prisoner in my own home." Pace threw up his hands in a gesture of disbelief.

"No, I'm not here to make sure you haven't been on line. I trust *Pace,*" Jeff said. "I came to talk to you about something else. We've got some new information I want to run by you."

Nicey dropped onto the sofa. "Well, now that's different. New information means new material for my story. Shoot."

At that moment Dorie stuck her head out of the kitchen. "Why Marshal Sands and Marshal Turner what a surprise! It's a good thing I made a double batch of my lamb stew. Hope you're hungry."

Buddy said, "Yes, ma'am. I could eat a horse."

Dorie slapped her hands on her knees and laughed, "Sorry Marshal Turner, but I don't have no horse. Just lamb." And she continued to laugh as she walked back into the kitchen.

Jeff turned to Nicey. "What say we eat first then we can take our time going over the new information?"

Nicey frowned and shrugged. "Can't be very important then if you'd rather eat than work your case." Then she stood, walked into the kitchen and said, "Need any help, mama?"

Jeff looked first at Buddy then at Pace. "One of these days...."

Pace said, "Try being shut up with her night and day. I can't trust her for a minute. Tell the truth I'm afraid she'll slip out at night and hitch a ride to Durham or Pennsylvania or wherever. So I don't get much sleep. She's a handful!"

"Y'all come on and eat," called Dorie "so those poor Marshals outside can take their turn."

Pace kicked the sleeping Marshal's foot and said, "Hey, let's eat now...sleep later." The sleeper opened his eyes, stretched, and dragged himself toward the kitchen.

Pace, Nicey, Jeff, Buddy, and the sleepy Marshal ate in silence at the kitchen table. Jeff and Buddy were too hungry to talk. Nicey was too mad at Jeff to talk. Pace and the other Marshal were too anxious to relieve the outside

Marshals to talk. And Dorie was too busy refilling bowls and serving up hot biscuits.

After they were through with dinner, Pace and the other Marshal went outside to relieve two soaked Marshals who gratefully took their turn at the kitchen table.

Nicey was sitting on the sofa faking intense interest in the national news. "Nicey, where can we talk?" asked Jeff.

"You mean you *really* have something new for me?" Nicey said mockingly.

"Nicey..."Jeff bellowed and started across the room.

"Easy, Jeff," muttered Buddy.

Jeff stopped in front of Nicey and glared down at her. "Nicey, we can do this thing two ways. One...we can fool around and play mind games all evening and get nowhere. Or two...we can act like adults, pool our information, and hopefully uncover something that will help us solve the murder of your sister." Jeff was breathing hard. He paused then added, "So what's your pick?"

Nicey thought for a few seconds and said, "My room. The best place to talk is my room."

"Good. Let's go," Jeff said. And he and Buddy followed Nicey to her room.

Just inside the room Nicey turned and said to Jeff, "What about Pace? Shouldn't he be here?"

"Pace already knows," said Jeff.

An angry expression flashed across Nicey's face. She started to say something, then hesitated, and said calmly, "Okay, let's hear what you got."

Nicey sat in a rocking chair in the corner or the room. Jeff and Buddy sat on the twin beds. Jeff said, "We questioned people who were driving down Galatia Road about the time of the murder. More than one witness spoke of having seen a flashy motorcycle travel down the road, track across a field, and then head towards some woods. The woods eventually connect to the Blankenship barn. We got prints...footprints and tire prints. They're being sent to our lab for processing as we speak and we hope we'll come up with some leads."

Nicey was excited. "That's good. Isn't that good? Did anyone get a license plate number off the bike?"

"No number," said Jeff, "but the plates were identified as being from Pennsylvania."

"So you thought I might be able to help you by virtue of having lived in Pennsylvania?" she said with a laugh.

"That's what we hoped for," said Jeff.

Nicey rocked slowly back and forth and looked thoughtful. "Can't really think of anybody who owns a bike," she said. "What color...kind?"

"It was a black Kawasaki Concours 14 with a red flame painted down the side," said Jeff.

"Whew! People I hang with can't afford that kind of machinery," said Nicey.

Just then Jeff's phone rang. He took the call without leaving the room. "Sands," he said.

"Jeff...Dillon. The guys from the lab finished. They took lots of photographs and poured a whole bunch of casts of the tire prints and footprints. They had to let them set for quite a while before putting them in boxes. That's why it took so long for me to get back to you. They cushioned the boxes real good with newspaper, tagged and sealed each box, and they were out of here. Ain't nobody gonna open those boxes till the lab guys in Raleigh get 'em. Let me tell you...they pulled out of here with a *full* load. Real impressive to watch 'em work."

"Yeah, I've seen them. They're very meticulous. The reason they let the casts set so long was because the prints were in sand. Have to be careful working in sand. Anything else?"

"As a matter of fact, yes," said Dillon. "We've been asking the wrong question."

"What do you mean," said Jeff.

Dillon said, "We've been asking questions about a red convertible. Now that the word's gotten out about the motorcycle, I've had some more people come forward. Seems like a motorcycle turns as many heads as a red convertible. Little Sister said a couple folks over to the post office were talking about it. She gave me their names. I'll talk with them tomorrow. I stayed out at the woods all day with the scene guys."

"Great!" said Jeff. "Maybe this thing is beginning to come together." He smiled at Nicey who incredibly enough...smiled back.

"Oh, one other thing, Jeff," said Dillon. "Remember those high school kids we questioned early on in the case?"

"Yeah."

"I called the one who was the passenger...you know the one who did all the talking. I asked him if they'd seen a motorcycle that day."

"And?"

"And, yes," said Dillon. "The kid said he looked back when the red convertible pulled off of 301. The

317

motorcycle was pulling up at the stop sign not far behind her."

"So he could have followed her to Seaboard," Jeff said.

"That's how I see it," said Dillon.

"Anything else?" asked Jeff.

Dillon laughed. "Just one thing, tell Buddy he better get back here. Little Sister's sitting round moanin' over him something awful."

Jeff laughed and clicked off. He shared the phone conversation with Buddy and Nicey…except for the part about Little Sister 'moaning over' Buddy. That could wait till later.

"So where do we go from here?" asked Nicey.

"I want to talk about the exposé you were writing for *Confidential Observer*. We believe your investigation ties into the murders of Robert and Desiree. Maybe someone was trying to silence you. Trying to prevent you from printing what you uncovered. That's why Robert Ortiz was tortured and murdered. Tortured, Nicey. And believe me if they tortured Robert Ortiz, he talked. He told them everything he knew about you and your investigation."

Nicey turned pale. "You don't have to be so explicit. I read what they did to Robert."

"Nicey, you didn't read all they did to Robert. They didn't *print* all they did to Robert. They can't release stuff like that."

Suddenly Nicey dropped her face into her hands and began to sob. This was so unlike the Nicey they'd been dealing with that Jeff and Buddy were taken aback. Jeff leaned forward to comfort her but then thought better of it.

"Nicey," Jeff said, "I didn't mean to frighten you. I just wanted to warn you about the brutality of these people. They're animals, Nicey. And we don't want anything to happen to you, especially on our watch."

Nicey lifted her tear-streaked face, stared angrily at Jeff, and said, "You think I don't know how vicious these people are. You think I don't know how they torture and maim and kill. For gosh sake man, I'm a journalist. Yeah, yeah, I know you think *Confidential Observer* is just another smut rag. But take my word for it this isn't the first time I've been threatened and it won't be the last. So you don't have to lay guilt on me or try to scare the daylight out of me to get me to cooperate."

Jeff was silent. Then he back-pedaled, "Okay. Now we understand each other. I'm not trying to lay guilt on you or scare you. We just need to know what you know that might help us find Desiree's murderer. And we think your exposé has something to do with it."

"Okay then," said Nicey in a gesture of reconciliation. "What do you need to know?"

"Who or what was the subject of your exposé?" Jeff asked.

"Costanza Shipping International," Nicey said.

"We figured as much when you said Robert Ortiz was your source," Jeff said. "Tell us about it."

Nicey breathed deeply, sighed, and took a few seconds to collect her thoughts. Finally she said, "I met Robert soon after I moved to Philadelphia. He was a few years older than I but we were both trying hard to launch our careers...me in journalism and he wanted to be successful in business. I was tired of walking fish stories and such and he was tired of part-time jobs."

She paused as if those early memories were painful. Soon Buddy said, "You were both dissatisfied with your jobs...then what?"

Nicey cleared her throat. "Then one day we met for lunch at a hot dog stand. That's where we always met. Not much money you know."

Buddy and Jeff nodded their heads. "Go on. You met Robert for lunch and..." said Jeff.

"Well Robert was ecstatic. He said he'd gotten a job with Costanza Shipping International at what was a...by our standards...a great salary. He was hired as an office assistant. Oh, I'll never forget how excited he was. He saw himself as starting at the bottom and working himself up to a corner office with a view." Nicey smiled a wistful smile.

"When did he start the job with Costanza?" asked Jeff.

"Oh, I don't remember exactly, but I have it in my notes," she said and turned toward her notes.

Not wanting to disrupt the continuity of her story, Jeff said, "That's okay. You can look it up later. So how did Robert's job go?"

"Not too well," said Nicey. "He was disillusioned almost immediately. It seemed like his job as office assistant turned out to be no more than a "gofer". *Robert go for this. Robert go for that. Robert run out and get us lattés from Starbucks.*"

"What did he think of Costanza Shipping International as a business?"

"At first, he thought the company was a well-oiled machine. It appeared that things went smoothly according to schedules. The work environment was pleasant. Salaries with all the benefits were good. Other employees seemed completely satisfied with their job. But not only was Robert unhappy with his work, he felt something wasn't right. He talked about that feeling many times, but finally he told himself that since he had nothing to base his feelings on it must be his imagination."

"Did something in particular happen to make him realize his suspicions were not his imagination?" asked Buddy.

Nicey sighed and stared away vacantly as if watching the scene replay itself. "Oh yes something in particular happened. And I believe that was the beginning of the end for Robert."

Jeff said, "Tell us."

Nicey leaned back in the rocking chair and clasped her hands in her lap. She said, "We met at the hot dog stand for lunch...we continued eating there for sentimental reasons I suppose. Anyway, I could tell as soon as Robert walked up that something was wrong. We'd gotten so we could read each other like that you know."

"Yeah, I suppose," said Jeff who was determined to remain patient. "What was wrong with Robert?"

Nicey squirmed then continued. "Robert told me that earlier that morning he was sent on one of his grunt errands. That's what he called the menial stuff...grunt errands. He was sent out for lattés again for about five guys...like the office coffee wasn't upscale enough for them. Anyway, Robert went to Starbucks, got the five coffees, and balanced them in a cardboard container all the way back to the office. When he backed into the office with coffees in hand, Mr. Costanza's secretary asked him what on earth he was doing there. He explained he'd been sent out for coffee, and she said Mr. Costanza just went downstairs. She literally shooed him out of the office and told him to take the coffees downstairs. Wwww...ell, downstairs was three flights of steep steps to the basement and so much coffee had already sloshed out into the cardboard container that Robert was afraid the bottom was gonna drop out."

"Ah, Nicey," Jeff said impatiently. "Is this story going anywhere?"

Nicey looked insulted. "Of course, it's going somewhere...if I don't keep being interrupted. I was almost there."

"Go on," Jeff said and leaned against the head board, propped up his feet, and sat back for a long dull ride.

"Okay," said Nicey. "Where was I?"

"You said Robert was gonna have to take five coffees in a melting cardboard container down three flights of steep steps to the basement," said Buddy.

"Right, thank you Buddy," said Nicey. She paused. "Anyhow he started down the steps cautiously. And as he rounded the last level he saw the five men gathered around a large crate examining the contents. Standing on the steps, Robert's view was elevated and he could see inside the crate."

Nicey paused again for effect and waited for one of the Marshals to urge her to continue. One of them did. "Get on with it, girl," Jeff said testily.

This wasn't exactly the urging Nicey hoped for. Then Buddy said, "The crate, Nicey. What was in the crate?"

"Guns," she said dramatically.

With this Jeff bolted upright. "What kind of guns?"

"Big ones," said Nicey. "You know...big crates, big guns."

"Nicey did Robert give any description of the guns?" asked Buddy.

Nicey shook her head. "Nope. Just that they were big and that they weren't hunting guns."

"Would Robert have known a hunting gun if he saw one?" asked Jeff.

"Sure," said Nicey. "Robert was a deer hunter. He went hunting every year up to the mountains with his dad and uncle."

"Did any of them see Robert?" asked Jeff.

"Now that's what we don't know," Nicey said. Jeff noticed that Nicey spoke of Robert in the present tense.

"What do you mean *you don't know?*" said Jeff.

"When Robert realized what he'd seen, he immediately stepped *backwards* up the steps. When he'd got about half way up he coughed real loud and stomped hard to alert the men that he was coming down the steps. He said that when he stepped into the basement the crate was closed and setting on the conveyer belt. He apologized for the messy cups and Mr. Costanza just said forget it. Robert said Mr. Costanza could be nice like that."

"So he didn't think anyone knew he'd seen what was in the crate?" asked Jeff.

"I didn't say that," said Nicey.

"Well what the hell did you say?" asked Jeff.

"I hadn't gotten to that part yet," Nicey said.

Jeff thought he was one heartbeat away from a stroke.

"Nicey, get to it," said Buddy who was beginning to feel as frustrated as Jeff.

Nicey shook her head in bewilderment. "For U.S. Marshals it takes a lot of clarification for you to understand things. Lemme see...Robert passed out the coffee, and everyone thanked him...except for one man. Robert said *he* gave him a hard, evil look. Then Robert said all morning long he kept running into that creepy man, and every time he saw him the guy gave Robert the evil eye. Gave Robert the heeby-geebies."

Did he ever approach Robert or say anything to him?" Jeff asked.

"No, he didn't and Robert thought again that it was probably his imagination."

"Nicey now this is important. Did Robert tell you anything about the appearance of the man who gave him the evil eye?" said Jeff.

Nicey pondered the question. Then as if a light bulb went off she smiled and said, "Yes. Yes he did tell me something about his appearance. Robert said he was a real scruffy-looking type. He needed a shave...and a bath. He had on dirty jeans, a leather jacket, and get this...*biker boots* with heels that were all turned over. Robert said he wasn't the kind of guy you'd expect to see hanging out with Mr. Costanza."

Jeff and Buddy looked at each other.

Jeff said, "Did Robert tell anyone else about seeing the guns?"

"Absolutely not," said Nicey.

"How can you be sure?"

"Because this is when I decided this story was my ticket out of *Confidential Observer*." Nicey slipped to the front of her chair and leaned in toward Jeff. "You see Robert was more than just curious. He believed that something illegal could be going on and that he might be implicated just because he'd seen something he wished he'd never seen."

"I don't understand," said Buddy. "How does Robert's seeing the guns translate to being your ticket out of Confidential Observer?"

Nicey looked exasperated. "Let me give it to you simple like. Robert was going to find out all he could about the guns, feed information to me, and I'd write a big exposé giving Robert credit for said info thus exonerating him of any illegalities. Robert would be a hero, and I'd have my ticket out of *Confidential Observer*." She paused breathlessly. "Got it?"

The room fell silent. Now Jeff leaned in close to Nicey and spoke disapprovingly, "Nicey, do you have any idea how much danger you and Robert were in?"

Nicey didn't answer.

"These men are professional criminals. Professionals, Nicey. They take all kinds of risks and think nothing of killing anyone who stands in their way. There's no way to get away from them. They have access to assassins all over the world that are willing to take out *anyone*...from a president to a person as insignificant as an investigative reporter who works for a smut rag like *Confidential Observer.*"

"Don't preach, Sands," said Nicey.

"These people baffle the FBI and the ATF and the U.S. Marshals Service. They're cunning, brutal..."

"You're still preaching," said Nicey. "You said you wanted the story...the whole true story. Well, I gave it to you. What happened...happened. I can't go back and change it. Robert couldn't go back and change seeing the crate of guns. So there were a few flaws in our plan."

Jeff felt that his head would explode. "A few flaws? I gotta get out of here," he screamed and virtually fled from the room.

Jeff walked to the front door, stepped outside, took a deep breath, and exhaled loudly. "I told you she was hard to take." Pace stepped out of the shadows.

"That's an understatement," said Jeff. "If I can just get through these interviews without losing it, I'll deserve a medal."

"You'll make it," said Pace.

Jeff said, "This is another one of those times that I wish I smoked cigarettes."

"Don't do it, Jeff. It ain't worth it," said the voice of the other Marshal.

After awhile Jeff calmed down, turned, and reluctantly walked back to Nicey's bedroom. She was rocking in her chair and looked up at him impatiently. "How long's this gonna take?" she said.

Jeff spoke as calmly as he could. "I think we're just about through. Just a couple more questions. Did Robert write down information to give to you?"

"Nope," said Nicey. "His reports were always verbal. He gave me what he saw, and when and where he saw it. A sorta schedule of events."

"Did *you* write it down?"

"Sure. At least, I put it in my laptop."

He paused and said, "You've got backups?"

"Sure. I back up everything," and she dangled a couple of memory cards in the air.

"Okay, let's call it a night. Tomorrow I'll want you to explain some things to me that are on the laptop."

"Sure," said Nicey and grinned.

For the first time since Desiree was murdered, Nicey slept soundly. Recounting the events that led up to the death of her sister and Robert was somehow therapeutic. Jeff on the other had no such respite. He tossed and turned on the lumpy sofa. He pitched a pillow on the floor and tried sleeping there. It felt like every bone in his body ached.

Finally he stood, walked to the door, and went outside. The rain had stopped but there was a crisp chill in the night air. Pace was surprised to see him. Jeff said, "You go on inside and get warm. I'll do outside watch for awhile."

Chapter 25

Jeff listened to the early morning sounds. Car doors slammed. Engines coughed into the frosty air. A dog barked in the distance alerting its owner that it was morning. And down the street at the corner of the cul-de-sac Jeff saw a flashlight beam working its way up the sidewalk toward him. Jeff positioned his hand near his belted gun and walked toward a man wearing a yellow slicker.

"Good morning, Mr. Marshal," said a croaky voice. Then Jeff recognized the old man as one of the Neighborhood Watch Group.

"Good morning, sir," said Jeff. "It would be best for you not to come any closer.

The old man stopped and said, "Certainly. Just wanted to let you know we've got our eye on things too. We know everyone in this neighborhood and we'll call up to Dorie's house if we see someone that don't belong." He held up a cell phone.

"Glad to hear that you'll call. We think we're dealing with vicious people. U.S. Marshals are here to protect Dorie and Nicey until the perpetrator's caught. I hope you men aren't taking too much on yourselves. The weather is supposed to get worse before it gets better."

"Don't you go a worrying 'bout us. First off I'm a retired cop. Second, me and the two men who were here last night are seasoned Vets."

"That counts for a lot," said Jeff.

"Sure does," said the old man in the slicker. "Spent many a night in a ditch full of water in Vietnam. Weather's got to be the least of our concerns here."

"Yes, sir," said Jeff. "Just remember not to creep up on us. We don't want any accidents."

"Works both ways, don't y'all be a sneaking up on us neither. Well, 'hey' to Dorie and Nicey. Tell them the Neighborhood Watch is on duty. That'll make them feel better," and he turned and slowly walked away.

When Jeff returned to the porch Pace was standing there with a mug of coffee. "Dorie's fixed a breakfast big enough for an army. Neighborhood Watch?" asked Pace and he nodded toward the old man in the yellow slicker.

"Yeah," said Jeff. "Far as I know we've got no right to order them off their street and out of their yards. But I keep on warning them not to surprise us. Can you imagine if one of them was accidentally shot?"

"Don't want to think about it," said Pace. "Dorie says to come on in and take your turn at the table."

"Best offer I've had this morning," said Jeff and he went inside. The television was blaring, and the house smelled of bacon and buttermilk biscuits. Jeff hurried to the kitchen. Nicey and Buddy were sitting at the table. Buddy mumbled *morning* and continued to eat...Nicey just continued to eat. Dorie was filling coffee cups, serving up seconds on biscuits, and humming a hymn. Jeff couldn't remember the name of the hymn but recalled the words...*and He walks with me and He talks with me and he da, da, da, da, da, da.* This went on for five minutes as Jeff ate breakfast. Finally he couldn't take it any longer.

"Okay, Dorie," he said. "I remember the words but not the name. What's the name of the hymn?"

Dorie laughed. *"In the Garden.* Want I should sing you a few verses?"

"No. No thanks," they said. Dorie laughed.

Jeff told Dorie that the old man from the Neighborhood Watch Group wanted her to know they were on duty too. "Why yes," said Dorie. "That does make me feel safer. After all we trusted our country to those men back in the war days we can certainly trust our neighborhood to them now. Right Nicey?"

"Yeah, sure," said Nicey. Then she turned to Jeff. "What are we going to do today?"

Jeff took a swig of hot coffee and said, "The first thing I want to do is have you show me around your computer files. When I get a feel for what you have, I need to call my boss in Raleigh and then call the Marshals in Pennsylvania. Remember they've got a murder investtigation going on up there too."

"How can I forget?" Nicey moaned.

It took Nicey some time to brief Jeff and Buddy on the documents on her laptop. First she showed him a word file that explained in detail the incident wherein Robert had witnessed the crate of large firearms and how it was lifted onto the conveyor belt. Then she opened a file on notes she'd made of subsequent conversations with Robert. Another file displayed a schedule of dates, times, places of events Robert had witnessed that might be suspicious. Another file contained dates and names of dubious people who visited Costanza in his office or at the shipyard. Jeff realized that Robert had taken huge risks.

Jeff let out a whistle. "Nicey, how long did this go on?"

"About three months," said Nicey. "What do you think of my documentation?"

"Superb," said Jeff. "And dangerous. No wonder they have you in their cross hairs. This stuff's dynamite!"

"Some of this is personal, you know?" she said. "And I don't want anybody stealing my story. It's exclusive."

"I know," said Jeff. "We'll work it out. I guarantee the story is yours. But the people in Pennsylvania need this information, Nicey. They need it to help them catch Robert's killer. You want that don't you?"

"Don't be ridiculous," said Nicey. "Of course, I want that. But I want my exclusive story too."

"You got it," said Jeff.

As he reached for his phone he checked the clock. It was nine-thirty. Two rings, then a pickup.

"Arlis Bryant's office. Cathy Roberson speaking."

"Good morning, Ms. Roberson, would it be convenient for me to speak to Mr. Bryant at this time?" Jeff said in an affected voice.

"Jeff Sands!" she spit out the words with loathing. "What do you want? Mr. Bryant is terribly busy…too busy for your childishness."

Jeff continued with his dramatic drivel. "I'm sorry to be such a pain in the ass, but I've just been made privy to some startling information about the Nicey/Desiree Parsons case that is a real mind blower. Realizing that Mr. Bryant likes to be privy to anything that blows, I naturally desire to share this with him."

There was a click and then dead air. Jeff looked at Buddy bent over with laughter. Nicey just gawked at him as if he'd lost it.

Then a voice exploded from the phone. "You just won't learn will you Jeff? This time you've crossed the line."

"Bryant. Good morning to you too. Can't imagine what you're talking about," said Jeff.

"What do you want, Jeff?" Bryant said choosing to sidestep a confrontation.

"As I told Cathy...ah, Ms. Roberson...we've become privy to information that can go a long way toward solving our case and the one in Pennsylvania. Nicey Parsons has opened up all the files on her laptop to us. And it is dynamite."

"Did she do this willingly?" asked Bryant.

"Yes," said Jeff.

"Absolutely?"

"Yep. No warrants necessary," said Jeff. And for the next twenty minutes Jeff reported how Robert Ortiz stumbled onto evidence that Constanza International was shipping illegal guns. He and Nicey planned to expose Constanza International's illegal operation in an article written by Nicey. When their plans were discovered, Ortiz was murdered, and a contract taken out on Nicey. The hit man obviously followed Nicey to North Carolina to execute the kill. Instead he killed her twin in Seaboard.

When Jeff finished there was long silence on the other end of the line. Jeff waited. "Good Lord!" Bryant finally exclaimed. "No wonder they wanted Nicey Parsons dead. She's okay, right?"

"Absolutely," said Jeff.

"Have you called Pennsylvania?"

"Not yet," said Jeff. "That's my next call."

"Right," said Bryant. "We got to secure those file, Jeff."

"I know," said Jeff. "I'm on it."

"When are you coming in?"

"Tomorrow. Today I have a few more things to sort through with Nicey. Buddy and I will probably leave in the morning."

Bryant hesitated. "Jeff is she safe? I can send more men if they're needed."

"I think we're okay. We've even got a Neighborhood Watch Group."

"What?" Bryant bellowed. Jeff told him about the old men who had taken it upon themselves to protect their own.

"Holy cow!" screamed Bryant. "All we need is for three old Vets and a retired cop to be shot while helping out U.S. Marshals. Are *they* safe, Jeff, for Pete's sake?"

"I think so," said Jeff. "We've had the safety conversation several times. We stay out of their way...they stay out of ours. Besides we can't keep them from trying to defend their neighbors and neighborhood."

"Good grief," shouted Bryant. "I'll be glad when this one is over. Keep me posted."

"Right." And he clicked off.

Jeff looked at Buddy. "Holy cow, good grief, for Pete's sake, good Lord, holy cats...he'll use any cliché to avoid swearing".

Buddy laughed. "Always thought a few cuss words cleared the mind. Not good to bottle that rage up inside you."

Jeff called Pennsylvania. This time he got Salas.

"Salas here," he growled into the phone.

"Hey Salas. Jeff Sands."

"Well if it ain't our Southern connection. Hey Jeff, want to ask you a question that we've been debating 'round here for awhile."

"Sure, shoot," said Jeff knowing he was stepping into it.

"Is it true that you marry your own cousins down there?"

"Only if they're good looking," said Jeff.

Salas guffawed and Jeff heard him repeat his answer to others in the office. There was more laughter and then Salas said, "So what's going on down South?"

Jeff's conversation with Salas proceeded along the same line as his call to Bryant. Unlike Bryant, Salas did not interrupt. He listened intently to every word Jeff said.

Jeff finished his report, and Salas let loose with an impressive rant of obscenities that Jeff was sure Bryant had never even heard much less used. Finally Salas said, "We gotta have copies of those files, Jeff. This could bust our case wide open."

"I know," said Jeff. "I'm on it. We'll get you copies as soon as our techs check out the laptop thoroughly. You know things can be hidden on computers." Nicey who had been listening to Jeff's end of the conversation crinkled her nose and stuck out her tongue out at Jeff.

"Okay. When?" Salas said.

"Tomorrow. Bryant will supervise the actual transmission. Wouldn't hurt to give him a call today," Jeff said.

"Will do," said Salas. "Good work, for a Carolina boy."

"Well Raleigh knew y'all would need all help you could get up there, so they sent you the best," said Jeff, and he clicked off before they became involved in a battle of barbs.

Jeff and Buddy spent the day going through Nicey's handwritten notes and laptop documents. Once they were in the files they found they were so thorough that they needed little explanation. Nicey had included a personal photo gallery on her laptop and there were many shots of a smiling Nicey along side a handsome young man. Jeff could see the sadness wash over her as she explained when and where the pictures were taken. Dorie called them for dinner and after they'd eaten Nicey excused herself, quietly went to her room, and closed the door.

"Rough," said Buddy.

"Damn rough," said Jeff. "I get the feeling he was all she had up there."

Chapter 26

He crouched behind a thick hedge of holly bushes that lined the driveway of a small white house. With the arrival of nightfall the weather turned bone chilling and a fine rain mixed with pellets of ice stung his face and hands.

He watched the three old men standing down at the corner. They didn't seem to mind the rain and sleet. They were dressed to stay dry in yellow slickers, rain pants, and waterproof boots. The watcher, however, felt wretched. His watch cap was soaked causing his wet hair to stick to his head and forehead. The bottoms of his water repellent biker pants were tied tightly around his ankles but his biker boots were waterlogged. His worn leather jacket was zipped up to his neck, and it concealed a sheathed hunting knife fastened securely to his belt. The problem was that every time he knelt down or bent over it jabbed him in his groin.

Earlier he hid his Kawasaki Concours 14 behind a dumpster in the back of a Middle School reasoning that no one would drop by the school on such a miserable night. As added caution he climbed into the dumpster, threw out several plastic bags filled with garbage, and stacked the bags around the motorcycle.

He heard the old men at the corner laugh. How long were they going to stand on the street corner in this weather? His knees began to ache and he shifted weight from one leg to the other. He had to get to the end of the cul-de-sac. Had to reach the house where Nicey Parsons was being protected by U.S. Marshals. He smiled. Did they really think they could protect her from **him**? They knew nothing. They didn't know his history...what he was capable of.

The laughter stopped and the group of old men dispersed. The biker watched a few minutes and realized they were taking different trails in order to cover various parts of the neighborhood. Ah, the opportunity he'd waited for. As he started to stand he stepped on a limb that had fallen from a nearby oak tree. It made a loud pop. Two of the old men stopped and walked toward each other. They spoke and stared intently into the surrounding yards. Biker lay flat on his stomach on wet mulch. Then Biker gawked as one man took out night vision binoculars. Who were these old men who had night vision binoculars and were willing to stand out in freezing rain and sleet. Finally the two men went separate ways. Biker nervously waited another two minutes and then moved stealthily through backyard after backyard staying behind high shrubs and outbuildings.

Now he could clearly see the blue house at the end of the cul-de-sac and there didn't appear to be a sentry posted. He knew better. There was always a watch outside... usually two. So he waited longer. Finally he saw movement in the corner of the porch and made out the outline of a tall muscular man leaning against the wall. It was easy enough to avoid this one by just staying beyond the tree line. He noticed there were thick bushes hugging the outside walls of the house. If he could reach those, he'd have cover around the entire house. Pinpoints of light penetrated the drawn shades. He'd have to wait...wait for an opportunity to dart across the yard to the thick bushes against the wall. Finally his opportunity came. The front porch Marshal was momentarily distracted by a noise inside the house. This was the biker's chance. He made a dash across the yard and dived into the thick shrubbery.

He remained motionless for about three minutes... watching, listening. There must be another guard outside. If he had to take on one of the outside guards he'd rather it not be the man on the front porch. A fight there would certainly attract attention. Then the biker moved noiselessly toward the back of the house. He could hear a television playing softly and there were occasional intervals of laughter. When the laughter came, he moved fast. He crept toward a rear room that was illuminated by a dim light...a nightlight. The shades were too narrow and left small gaps on each side of the window that allowed a partial view of the bedroom. And there she was...Nicey Parsons. She was curled up on a twin bed. She was restless, and seemed to be frowning in her sleep. Her mouth was slightly opened and her hand tucked underneath her cheek. He watched her closely and finally decided she was asleep.

He scanned the room. Two beds. Of course, Nicey and Desiree were twins. Two rocking chairs, one dresser/clothes chest combination, and two desks. Two desks...and on one desk there was a laptop computer. Could it be he'd hit pay dirt?

The rain and sleet fell harder and immediately froze on the branches of the holly bushes creating frozen needles that scratched his injured face. He mopped his brow and eyes with his gloved hand and realized his thick eyebrows were coated with ice. He struggled as he thrust his hand into his jacket pocket and fumbled for his pocket knife.

Finally he dug it out and opened the thin, razor sharp blade. Crouching in front of the window, he began to cut the screen around the window ledge. It was a slow and cumbersome process.

* * *

Inside, Nicey stirred restlessly. She'd cried herself to sleep. This was the first time she'd wept so uncontrollably since Desiree's murder. The long session with Jeff and Buddy left her feeling drained. Then demons from her past surfaced and prodded her and she'd relived all the mistakes she'd made this last year. Nicey was zapped. She forced herself to lie still and listen to the whisper of the rain and sleet against her window screen. Finally she'd fallen into a restless sleep.

* * *

Outside, the Biker worked slowly, carefully. He disengaged the screen at the top of the window and along one side. When he cut the other side, he planned to simply lay the screen down and tackle the problem of the window which appeared to be unlocked.

At that moment he heard the crunch of heavy footsteps. So there he was. The second sentry. The Biker peered between the holly branches where thick ice-covered leaves clung. The man who approached his hiding place looked every bit as formidable as the Marshal on the front porch. Biker reached under his jacket. He caressed the handle of the hunting knife and slowly withdrew it from the scabbard. This would be awkward. Although he was well hidden behind the shrubbery, his movements were restricted. These conditions could impede his ability to execute a clean kill… the kind of kill that had earned him a deadly reputation.

He positioned himself to leap from the bushes. Then with hunting knife in hand he waited patiently until the Marshal passed exposing his back. With knife raised the Biker sprang from behind the holly hedge, rushed toward the unsuspecting Marshal, and plunged the knife deep into his back.

The blow caused the Marshal to twist around and the Biker saw his shocked expression. His cry sounded like a wounded animal that realized the terrible nature of his injury.

"A…augh! A…augh!" And he slumped onto the muddy ground. He added a barely audible, "Help!"

The Marshal on the porch opened the front door and said, "You hear that?"

Jeff and Buddy were already up and headed to the door. "Sure did. Where's Pace?"

"In the back," said the Marshal.

They tore down the porch steps, guns drawn, and headed to the back yard. As they rounded the corner of the house they saw him. The Biker knelt over Pace, knife raised, prepared to execute the coup de grace.

"Hey," Jeff shouted and the Biker looked up, stood, and dashed toward the wooded area that skirted the cul-de-sac. The second sentry rushed forward and joined Jeff and Buddy in pursuit. Nicey and Dorie appeared and raced to aid the wounded Pace.

Jeff and Buddy pursued the Biker into the woods. "Stop," shouted Jeff. Then again, "Stop...or I'll shoot." Then shots were fired and the Biker went down.

By the time he hit the ground Jeff, Buddy, and the other Marshal were there. The Biker was restrained, and searched for other weapons. They found no hunting knife only a small, razor sharp pocket knife.

"You shot me in the knees," wailed the Biker. "Both damn knees."

"Shut up," shouted Jeff. "You're lucky to be alive."

"Yeah," said Buddy. "Actually I was aiming just north of your knees if you get my drift."

"Pace," said Jeff. "Check Pace." And he turned toward the house. He saw Dorie and Nicey assisting Pace in the rain and sleet. Pace laid face down on the muddy ground.

Jeff rushed toward them. Dorie was kneeling beside Pace a bath towel pressed against his back. A dark red circle was slowly seeping through the towel. Jeff said, "Let me..."

"No," said Dorie. "He's bleeding bad. I'm keeping pressure on the wound till the ambulance gets here." Jeff stood and stepped back. He knew Dorie was doing all that could be done at that moment.

Nearby Nicey held a phone against her ear with one hand and pressed the fingers of her other hand against her ear to shut out the noise. "Yes, a man shot....she gave her address...yes, he's bleeding bad...my mama is already doing that...we need an ambulance here right now...hurry...a U.S. Marshal named Pace....P A C

341

E…that's right…yes, other Marshals…I'm Nicey Parsons…yes, *that* Nicey Parsons. "

After what seemed an eternity but was just a few minutes, sirens were heard in the distance. Dorie said, "Stay with me Pace. I hear the ambulances a-comin' now. Stay with me, boy."

It looked like every light in the neighborhood was on and a crowd quickly gathered at the corner. A Marshal was taping off the scene, and Neighborhood Watch men in their yellow slickers and rain boots held back the neighbors.

The ambulance pulled in and two attendants sprang out. "How bad?"

"Real bad," said Dorie. "He's lost a lot of blood. Got pressure right here." And she nodded toward the bloody towel.

"Okay hold it there," one attendant said. Then to Pace he said, "Sir, we're going to get you in the ambulance and get you started on some fluids. No. Don't try to roll on your back. We're going to move you face down. Okay, one, two, three." And they had Pace on a stretcher and in the ambulance in less than a minute.

The ambulance sped off and an eerie silence fell over the crowd. Suddenly a belligerent voice shouted, "What about me? I'm laying here with my knee bones laying in the mud and that ambulance just pulled out and left me."

Buddy turned and looked at the Biker with disgust. "You'll be lucky if we don't make you walk."

Then another siren was heard in the distance and a second ambulance pulled into the yard. The ambulance attendants looked warily at the plastic restraints and the gun shot wound. "Who's going to ride with this one?" an attendant asked.

Two Marshals' voices answered in unison. "I am." Jeff appointed a Marshal to go along.

When everything settled down Jeff turned to Dorie and said, "Where did you learn to handle emergencies like that?"

"Foster parenting," Dorie said simply. "All foster parent applicants have to pass a first aid course in order to qualify as a foster parent. You wouldn't believe how many times I've used different things I learned in that class…of course, I've never dealt with the likes of this before."

Jeff took out his phone to call for a crime scene unit and local backup. Just as he started to click in the number one of the elderly Neighborhood Watchman came to the edge of the yellow tape.

"Hey, Mr. Marshal," he called. "You might want to see this." And he focused a flashlight beam on a clump of dry pine needles.

Jeff walked over, looked at a shiny metal object, and pulled out a plastic bag. The object was a large hunting knife.

"He must have tossed it over here in the woods when he ran," The old man's eyes twinkled brightly. Jeff looked at him anxiously. "Don't worry. Nobody's touched it. I'm the retired cop. I might be old, but I ain't forgot how to handle evidence."

Jeff smiled. "I'm sure you haven't. Thanks for your help. Thank them to," he said as he nodded toward the corner.

343

"Don't mention it," said the retired cop. "That's what Neighborhood Watches are for." And he turned, walked to the corner, and joined his neighbors.

Chapter 27

The scene unit worked feverishly to finish the crime scene before the weather worsened. Rain and sleet blew onto the crime area in spite of the canvas tent that was raised to protect it. Jeff and Buddy watched for awhile, then turned, and went into the kitchen. They'd already updated Bryant on the situation, and Bryant said he'd take care of notifying the Pennsylvania Marshal Services.

"Good job, Jeff," said Bryant letting Jeff know that his confrontation with Cathy Roberson bore no ill feelings.

"Thanks," and Jeff clicked off.

"We're going to the hospital. Will you be okay?" Jeff asked Dorie.

"Now don't you go a-worrin' none about me. I've got everything under control," Dorie said as she reached for a canister labeled coffee. A thirty cup percolator set on the kitchen counter, and the aroma of something sweet permeated the room.

"I'm going too," said Nicey.

Jeff started to say something but Dorie stopped him. "Of course you have to go, honey," said Dorie. "Pace is our friend."

So that settled that. Jeff, Buddy, and Nicey started to the hospital. Jeff drove and it was no minor feat. Everything glistened with ice...the tree branches, the parked cars, the electric wires, and most importantly, the roads. Black ice!!!

They rode in silence and after thirty perilous minutes Jeff pulled into the hospital parking lot. They carefully picked their way to the emergency room entrance, opened the door, and welcomed the first wave of warm air.

Jeff walked to the nurses' station, identified himself, and asked to see the doctor treating the knife victim, Marshal Pace. The nurse listened carefully, asked them to take a seat, and hurried off to find the doctor. They had no sooner sat down than a bearded man dressed in hospital greens rounded the corner and walked toward them.

He extended his hand. "I'm Dr. King. Are you members of Mr. Pace's family?"

"No," said Jeff and he explained that he was a U.S. Marshal working the Nicey Parsons' case and that Pace was a member of his team. The doctor glanced at Nicey and immediately recognized her from television.

"So how is Marshal Pace?" Jeff asked anxiously.

The doctor looked grim. "Marshal Pace is in critical condition. His family has been notified and we're preparing him for surgery now. We've called in a vascular surgeon."

"Was his heart cut?" asked Nicey.

The surgeon looked at her and said, "No. If his heart had been penetrated, Marshal Pace wouldn't be here. The vascular surgeon will advise us on how to protect the heart during our surgery. Marshal Pace has serious injuries other than heart. Now I have to get back to my patient. I'll let you know how things go as soon as possible." And he turned and walked away briskly.

Buddy, Jeff, and Nicey sat down on the cold hard plastic seats in the emergency waiting room. Buddy leaned his head against the concrete wall and closed his eyes. In a few minutes he was snoring. Jeff looked at him and shook his head incredulously.

"Buddy can sleep anywhere," Jeff said to Nicey.

"He must have a clear conscience," Nicey smiled.

They sat silently for awhile and then Jeff said, "Nicey there's some things I want to tell you. I've just been waiting for the right time. I'm not sure this is the *right time* but here goes." Nicey looked at Jeff expectantly.

"Nicey, when we were searching for some connection between you and Seaboard we uncovered your mother's name...and we also learned who your father is."

Nicey sat up instantly. "Who?" was all she could say.

Jeff leaned forward, took Nicey's hands, and began to recount the saga of the Wood family that lived on Galatia Road and the Hollis family that lived in a shack across from them. He explained that the Hollises were migrant workers who worked for Myron Blankenship to harvest his tobacco crop. Jeff omitted nothing. He told Nicey about the handsome John Wood who fell in love with Katie Hollis and that Katie became pregnant. Then Jeff told her about the flu epidemic that ravaged Seaboard one winter and took John Wood's young life. Finally he explained in detail about Sara, John's ornery sister, and the pitiful twin sisters.

Nicey didn't say a word during the entire report. She listened closely, and several times her eyes welled up with tears. When Jeff finished he said, "You have a right to know, Nicey. Desiree had a right to know."

"Where is Katie Hollis buried?" asked Nicey.

"That's still a big question. We've never been able to find her grave. But Clinton Harvey, Seaboard's dogged

347

town clerk, is on it. He's in charge of the sale and maintenance of plots in the Seaboard Cemetery. Even though this happened before his tenure, he doesn't like the idea that someone is buried in the Seaboard Cemetery without his knowledge."

Nicey leaned back and shut her eyes. Jeff didn't intrude. He'd just dumped a lot on the young woman whose sister and boy friend had recently been murdered. He stood and walked to the coffee machine.

After some time the emergency room opened and the Dr. King returned. He looked tired and much older than he'd looked before the surgery. Jeff nudged Buddy's foot to wake him up and he, Nicey, and Jeff stood expectantly.

The doctor said, "Marshal Pace is in recovery. He is still in critical condition, but his chances of survival are considerably better than they were when he was brought in. We had to replace practically all the blood in his body."

"Can we see him?" asked Buddy.

"Absolutely not," said the doctor. "He is certainly in no condition to have visitors."

Jeff said, "Let me explain. Pace is part of our team. The bond between Marshals on a team is very strong. If we could just speak to him or even just wave to him. Anything to let him know we're here for him."

The doctor looked thoughtful and then said, "Okay. But just a few seconds. And I do mean seconds. Just say something to let him know you're here and then out of there. A few seconds," he repeated. And he turned, motioned for them to follow, and walked down a long sterile hallway to a room designated Recovery.

A white curtain surrounded the bed and the doctor pulled it aside. "Marshal Pace, some friends to see you." They were shocked by Pace's labored breathing and his face looked gray and gaunt.

Nicey was the first to speak. "Hang in there Pace," she said. "We're pulling for you."

Buddy was next. "Hey, Pace, it's me Buddy. You did it man. We got the bastard."

Jeff added, "Pace, we need you man. So hurry up and get outta here." Pace moved slightly and with that the doctor motioned for them to clear the room.

Chapter 28

That night Jeff and Buddy talked about the trip they'd make next day. They would transport Nicey, her laptop, and any other notes pertinent to the case to the U.S. Marshal Services Office in Raleigh. A meeting was planned for ten o'clock that morning with Jeff, Buddy, Nicey, Bryant, Ned Cosden, the Pennsylvania Marshals, and others associated with the Nicey/Desiree Parson's murder case. At this meeting Nicey would tell her story and answer questions. Then in late afternoon Nicey would meet alone with the Pennsylvania Marshals. This meeting would be to discuss Nicey's return to Pennsylvania to give evidence in the Costanza case.

It was one thirty when Jeff and Buddy stretched out to grab a few winks.

It seemed like they'd only been out for a few minutes when they heard Nicey's voice, "Better roll out guys. It's already five thirty."

The showers were quick and the clothes they threw on were crumpled and stained, but the smell of Dorie's coffee and sweet bread gave them the jump start they needed.

Jeff took a big bite of something delicious and a gulp of coffee and while attempting to chew he mumbled, "Dorie, you've got to be careful now. This guy we arrested last night isn't the only one willing to kill for profit."

"I know. I know," said Dorie. Our local police and the Neighborhood Watch have already discussed that with me. They're gonna be my guardians till this is cleared up."

"And the U.S. Marshal Service. Don't forget we're still on it."

Dorie giggled. "Never thought of myself as being so important as to need this much protection."

Dorie and Nicey said their tearful goodbyes, and at six thirty the travelers steeled themselves for the 175 mile drive to Raleigh. The neighborhood roads were treacherous. Once more they had to contend with black ice. When they reached the interstate, things were clear. They sped along in total silence. Jeff drove, Buddy slept, and Jeff occasionally peeked at Nicey in the rear-view mirror. She was silent and had a dreamy, far-away look in her eyes.

Finally Nicey said, "I have to go there, Jeff. I have to meet Sara and Mary and Rebecca."

"Okay," was all Jeff said.

* * *

At nine forty-five, Jeff pulled into the parking lot of the Terry Sanford Federal Building at 310 New Bern Avenue, Raleigh. In spite of the ice, rush hour traffic in Raleigh was heavy and the parking lot filling up quickly. Jeff pulled to the back and into a space marked *Official Use Only.*

"This is it," said Buddy as he piled out of the car and stretched broadly.

Nicey looked expressionless at the cold modernistic building. "It'll be okay," Jeff said reassuringly.

351

They walked into the building, straight to the elevator, and pushed the button beside the number five. Nicey wrapped her arms around her laptop and a paper portfolio and held them tightly to her chest. They exited the elevator and started straight for Arlis Bryant's office. Heads turned as Nicey was recognized. When they entered Arlis' office Buddy and Jeff were not surprised to see Cathy Roberson busy at her desk.

She looked up, scanned the three, and said curtly, "They're waiting for you. They've been waiting for you for half an hour."

Jeff started to say something but thought better of it. Cathy stood and started toward Arlis' private office. Jeff headed her off and opened the door himself.

"Good morning everyone," said Jeff with flair.

Cathy looked miffed at not being allowed to announce Jeff and Buddy. And she especially wanted to announce the long-awaited arrival of Nicey Parsons.

"Jeff, Buddy," Bryant boomed. "Come in. Come in. And this lovely young lady must be Nicey Parsons. Nicey, I'm Arlis Bryant and I assembled this little party." He waddled toward Nicey and held out his fat, damp hand.

Nicey shook his hand and then she took in the mob of people (all men) crowded into the office. In addition to Bryant there was Ned Cosden, two lab techs Jeff didn't know, Ernesto Salas, Miguel Moretti, the State Attorney, and an Assistant Attorney...altogether ten men. She gasped and instinctively stepped back toward Jeff and Buddy.

Bryant smiled. "Don't worry Nicey. This is going to be a rather informal meeting. Come sit." And he motioned to a chair at the head of the enormous conference table. Jeff noticed, however, that Arlis's oversized leather chair had been moved to the side for him. At each place there was a carafe of water (Cathy would not hear of using plastic bottles), a glass, yellow legal pads, and pens.

Nicey walked to the head of the table and continued to hold her laptop and portfolio tightly to her chest. She sat down.

Cathy Roberson still stood at the door. She said, "Mr. Bryant, will there be anything else?"

Arlis Bryant's did not take his eyes off Nicey as he said, "Huh? Oh...no Miss Roberson. That will be all for now."

Bryant continued, "Nicey, I'd like to introduce every one." And he went around the table calling the names of each man. "You'll also notice that we have name tags. I thought that might make it easier for you." He grinned as if name tags were a unique idea.

Bryant said, "Nicey, I would like to record our meeting. Is this alright with you?"

"Sure, I record all my interviews," she said.

Arlis clicked on the recorder. He gave the date, time, place, and names of those present at the interview. Then he said, "Since we're going to be very informal today, I thought we'd let you explain in your own words your involvement in the Costanza Shipping case and how you think it might have led to the death of your sister, Desiree, and your friend, Robert." Then Bryant sat back, folded his hands across his rotund chest, and smiled.

Nicey took a deep breath, set her laptop and portfolio on the table, and looked at each member of her audience. Then she opened her laptop and began. In her most eloquent delivery she explained how she and Robert planned to expose the illegal shipment of guns by Costanza Shipping International. Robert hoped his efforts would land him a better job, and Nicey would write an exposé that would be her ticket out of *Confidential Observer*. Then she talked about Desiree and how she had gone to Seaboard in search of their birth mother's grave. With tears in her eyes, Nicey concluded that Desiree must have been killed because she was mistaken for her. She spoke briefly about being under the protection of the U.S. Marshals of the Eastern District of North Carolina, and she expressed her appreciation for her safekeeping. Then she took a deep breath, closed her laptop and portfolio, and sat back as if to say *what now.*

Nicey's audience was sufficiently impressed. They had not expected such a well-prepared and eloquent briefing.

"Well," said Arlis. "I suppose we're ready for questions now. Anybody?"

In a technique of intimidation, Ernesto Salas leaned forward in his chair and glared at Nicey. Then he barked, "Do you expect us to believe that you put your life in jeopardy just to write a story?"

Arlis sprang forward in his chair as quickly as his heft allowed. "I apologize I should have announced a break at this time. We'll take ten." And he glared at Salas.

With relief Jeff quickly realized that Arlis Bryant was not going to allow this meeting to become a confrontational inquiry. Arlis had apparently established ground rules and expected everyone to go by them. Jeff stood, stretched, and walked over to Buddy.

"Stick close to Nicey," he whispered. Buddy nodded.

Jeff walked into the hall, found a quiet corner, and pulled out his phone. He dialed up Sophie's number.

After a couple of rings Sophie said, "Jeff?"

"None other than," Jeff said.

"Where are you? We've been worried sick. We listened to the news and heard that a U.S. Marshal was injured and in critical condition. They wouldn't give his name because they hadn't reached his family. Jeff..."

Jeff realized that he should have called. "Sophie, I'm sorry. I should have known it would be on the news. That was inconsiderate of me."

Sophie said, "Well, there are ways to make amends." He heard Gladys huff in the background.

"Make a list," he said. "Listen, I'm in Raleigh at a meeting. We're taking a break. I need to ask you...how do you feel about having a guest for a couple of nights?"

"Who? Besides you?"

"Nicey Parsons," he said.

"Nicey Parsons...here? Well, of course, she's welcome to spend the night," Sophie said. Again Jeff heard Gladys and Melvin muttering in the background. "Why Gladys can hardly wait to give her advice."

"Great. Don't know what time we'll get in tonight. This meeting could go on for hours."

"Don't worry," said Sophie. And then she added in a seductive voice. "I'll be waiting."

Jeff clicked off, smiled, and shook his head. Then he scrolled down and clicked on Dillon's number. "Jeff, that you? Thank God. We heard...."

Jeff interrupted him. "Yeah sorry about that. Should have called. Listen Dillon I only got a couple minutes. I need you to do something."

"Shoot."

"I need you to go out to Sara Wood's place. Tell her that she's gonna have a visitor tomorrow...her niece, Nicey Parsons."

"Holy Todedo! Nicey Parsons here?"

"That's right. Nicey wants to meet her family and after what she's been through...she oughta get whatever she wants."

"Nicey Parsons...I'm on it, Jeff."

"And Dillon, keep this quiet. Top secret. Press, you know."

"Gotcha."

When Jeff went back to Arlis Bryant's office Nicey was answering questions. She was completely at ease and answered every question without hesitation. At one thirty a cart was rolled into the office. It held an assortment of sandwiches, veggies and dip, deviled eggs, sweet ice tea, and coffee. A smaller cart came next with a variety of desserts. Arlis eyed the dessert cart greedily. They talked informally as they ate. Jeff and Buddy could tell that everyone was impressed by Nicey's report. Here was a woman that any District Attorney would give their eye teeth to testify for them.

In the afternoon Bryant announced that the Pennsylvania Marshals would now have an opportunity to question Nicey alone. Everyone started to stand. Nicey said in a loud voice, "Mr. Bryant, may I say something first?"

"Why, of course," said Bryant and everyone sat back down.

Nicey said, "I want to thank y'all for your consideration. Frankly, I didn't know what to expect. My laptop and portfolio contain all my notes. I hope they help you with your cases. I have made three copies of the files on my laptop. One copy to go to Pennsylvania, one for Mr. Bryant, and one for me. I've erased all my personal files such as photographs from the laptop although I know you can get them off my hard drive. I've also made three hard copies of the files in my portfolio to be distributed the same way. I have written a story about my experience under U.S. Marshal Protection which I have already sent to a newspaper in Durham. I'm leaving the actual laptop and portfolio with Mr. Bryant. I want to assure y'all that I'm willing to help in any way I can to bring the murderer of my twin sister, Desiree, and my ah...friend, Robert Ortiz to justice." Then she looked at the Pennsylvania Marshals. "Also I will willingly travel to Pennsylvania for questioning and to give testimony that will help you in your case against Cosatnza Shipping International. However, I request that I be escorted back to Pennsylvania by Jeff Sands and Buddy Taylor. All that having been said, I would like to remain in Matthews, North Carolina with my mama till that time. She needs me and I need her." Nicey choked for just a second. Then she continued. "Also, I've learned I have family in Seaboard and I want to meet them."

The men shifted uncomfortably. Finally Arlis Bryant said, "I see no problem with your staying with your mother for the time being, but as a witness you must remain under the protection on our Marshal Service." Then he turned to Jeff. "Jeff, what do you think?"

Nicey looked at Jeff imploringly. Jeff said, "Sounds like a good plan." Nicey smiled.

"Now as for these relatives in Seaboard…we need to know who they are, how long you'll be there, and who you'll be staying with," said Arlis Bryant.

Jeff spoke up, "Buddy and I can escort Nicey back to Matthews after she visits her relatives in Seaboard. Both Buddy and I will be in Seaboard with her. Nicey will be staying at Sophie Singletary's home."

Bryant shifted uncomfortably in his chair. "Well with Dillon and Stewart on site too, looks like you're covered, Nicey." Then he looked at Jeff and said, "I want to know when you move her back to Matthews." Jeff nodded.

Bryant pushed himself up and everyone stood. "Now, Nicey, these *gentlemen* from Pennsylvania would like to speak with you alone. You may use the next office." And he motioned to the door. Nicey left with Salas and Moretti.

Jeff and Buddy spent their wait time hanging out with the guys on the fifth floor and irritating Cathy Roberson. The offices slowly began to empty and Jeff and Buddy were anxious to get on the road.

"I'm tempted to knock on the door," said Buddy.

"Or better yet send Cathy in," said Jeff.

At seven o'clock the door opened and Nicey, Salas, and Moretti walked out. Nicey looked exhausted. And Salas and Moretti didn't look much better.

Jeff said, "How did it go?"

Nicey said, "Okay, I'm just bushed."

At that moment Cathy Roberson appeared out of nowhere. Didn't she ever go home? "Mr. Bryant said you had a laptop and portfolio to be left for him."

"Yes," said Nicey and she handed them to Cathy. "It's like loosing a friend."

They said goodbye to the Pennsylvania Marshals who had shifted their attentions to Cathy Roberson. Then Buddy, Jeff, and Nicey took the elevator to the first floor, crossed the empty parking lot, and piled into the car for the last leg of their trip...Seaboard.

As he pulled onto New Bern Avenue Jeff realized that Nicey was mumbling unintelligibly to herself. "Hey Nicey, you okay?"

"Okay," she murmured. "I was just trying to remember the names of my new relatives...Sara, Mary, Rebecca. Sara, Mary, Rebecca," she tired. Then she laid her head on the back of the seat and closed her eyes.

Chapter 29

When they drove into Seaboard the town was shut down. There were no cars parked along the street. Stores were dark. Town Hall was dark except for an alarm system light in back. Jeff drove down Main Street, passed the two churches and turned right onto the street where Frances lived. The only illumination in her apartment came from a strobe that bounced red and blue flashes against the closed curtain.

Jeff pulled into the driveway. Buddy bounded out, raced up the steps, and the door flew open. The last thing Jeff saw was Buddy being yanked into the apartment. Jeff shook his head. As he backed the car out of the drive he said, "Wake up, Nicey. We're there."

Jeff turned left then another left and parked in Sophie's driveway. The house was lit up like a Christmas tree, and Melvin's car was still in the back. Nicey sat up and gawked at the house. "Gggg...olly!" she exclaimed. "What's the occasion?"

"I think the occasion is you," said Jeff as he opened the door.

Nicey climbed out slowly and stared up at the tall yellow Victorian house. She reluctantly followed Jeff up the front steps and watched him take out a key. "This where your girl friend lives?"

"Yep," said Jeff as he unlocked the door.

"You planning on marrying her?"

"Yep."

"Don't blame you. She must be rich. When?"

"When are we getting married? Well, she tells me in December."

Nicey didn't have a chance to ask anymore questions. The door swung open and the most elegant lady Nicey ever met stood there wearing a satin lounging robe and a beautiful smile.

"Jeff!!! I thought you'd never get here." And the beautiful lady flew into his arms and they kissed long and hard.

Nicey was embarrassed. First of all she'd never seen Jeff express affection much less passion. For that matter she'd never thought of Jeff as having passion at all. She turned away and stared up at the clear, cold autumn sky.

Sophie slowly moved away from Jeff and looked at Nicey. She extended her hands, smiled and said, "And you must be Nicey. Welcome, Nicey. Come in out of the cold." And she pulled Nicey through the doorway into a hall that was unlike any hall Nicey had seen.

"I'm so glad you are safe, and can spend some rest time with us. Seaboard is a good place to rest. You'll see." Jeff knew that Sophie was just babbling.

"Gosh, ah, ah Sophie," said Nicey not sure what she should call her hostess. "This house looks like something out of a magazine."

Sophie laughed. "Well, it is in a way. It was featured in Southern Living Magazine last year. I understand *you're* in the magazine business."

At that moment there was a shuffling from the dining room door. "Don't be a-borin' that girl with no magazine talk. Cain't you see she's hungry?" It was Gladys with Melvin right behind.

"Nicey, this is Gladys and the man hiding behind her is Melvin. We've all been anxious to meet you."

"I ain't a-hidin' behind her," Melvin mumbled.

"Glad to make your acquaintance," said Gladys. "Now let's get you in here to the table."

Jeff took Nicey's coat and said, "Good evening to you, too Gladys."

Gladys kept walking to the kitchen. "Don't be a-smartin' off at me, Jeff Sands. Your fault if'n supper's cold." Nicey liked Gladys immediately.

Even though the dining room was elegantly set, the atmosphere was intimate and warm. The food was delicious and Nicey hadn't realized how hungry she was. She immediately felt at home as she laughed at the exchange of barbs between Jeff and Gladys. At one point Sophie leaned over to her and whispered, "They really love each other like mother and son."

When the meal was finished Gladys brought out a bottle of wine and three glasses. She set a glass in front of Nicey and poured her a generous amount. "Now this here is gonna make you sleep."

Jeff, Sophie, and Nicey sipped wine and Jeff related the events of the day. It was like sitting through a rerun of a movie, but Nicey felt detached from the script. As Jeff's voice droned on and on Nicey's eyelids became heavier and heavier.

Then Gladys walked back into the dining room and Nicey heard her say, "I'm done in the kitchen, and I'm a-goin' home. It'd bid us all well if'n we sleep late." Then as an afterthought she looked at Jeff and said, "And don't y'all go a-disturbin' Nicey tonight with your foolishness." Then Gladys was gone. Nicey look perplexed.

"Don't mind Gladys, Nicey," said Jeff. "She likes to get in the last word."

"Shall we go up?" said Sophie.

Sophie showed Nicey to a bedroom and a bathroom. She also pointed out her room and told Nicey to knock if she needed anything at all. Then she brushed Nicey's cheek with a kiss, walked out, and closed the door.

Sophie crossed the hall to her bedroom. The window was opened slightly and cold air drifted in. The curtains fluttered and three candles on the mantle flickered as the scent of vanilla filled the room. Jeff sat in a chair beside the fireplace staring thoughtfully into the fire.

Sophie crossed the room and sat on his lap. "Penny for your thoughts."

Jeff smiled. "I'm confused. I can' figure it out."

Sophie looked serious. "What Jeff? I thought you were wrapping things up nicely. Has something gone terribly wrong right here at the end?"

Jeff hugged her to him. "No, no things are actually going OK with the case. It's it's…"

"What?"

"I've always prided my self in being…well, appealing to women. But I don't understand these *young* women."

"What? What young women?"

"Frances and Nicey. They act like I'm poison."

Sophie threw back her head and laughed. Then she kissed him hard. "Jeff, Jeff, I thought Gladys and I explained this to you. Let me try again. These young women are very attracted to you. After all you're tall, dark, and have the body of a Greek God." Jeff grinned. "But you intimidate them. They'd like nothing better than to have your approval or better still your attention but they're afraid you'll …well you'll laugh at them. So in order not to lose face, they strike first. They reject you before you can reject them. Simple. See?"

Jeff thought for a moment then said, "No."

Sophie continued to laugh and Jeff continued to feign confusion. Then she stood and said, "I'm taking a shower. Join me?"

"Not now," he said and picked up a sheet of paper and began to read what was on it.

Soon Jeff heard Sophie humming in the shower and was tempted to join her but found the contents of the paper more interesting. Finally she came in with a white bath towel wrapped around her wet body.

"What 'cha got?" she said lifting an eyebrow inquisitively.

He smiled. "Your list. The one you made of ways I can make amends."

She stood in front of him and let the towel drop. "Shall we start with the first item on my list?"

Chapter 30

Sara Wood had been a nervous wreck since Dillon told her that Nicey was coming to see her next day. Sara cleaned the house, although she doubted Nicey would want to come inside. Late afternoon she raked the yard and scrubbed the porches. And through it all she'd tried to explain to Rebecca and Mary that their niece was coming to visit them. She told them how Nicey was like an angel sent by their brother John to visit them. She told them that Nicey was sweet and beautiful and how much they all loved her. Of course, Rebecca and Mary didn't understand, but they were caught up in Sara's excitement and tried to help out in their own way. Sara didn't even lose her temper when Mary spilled dirty scrub water on the clean kitchen floor and Sara had to wash it again. Sara didn't scream at Rebecca when she decided to catch a chicken for supper and let the whole flock out of the pen. Sara was determined to hold her temper and her mouth. More than anything Sara wanted Nicey to accept them. After all Nicey was John's child.

The next morning Sara bathed and took out the only decent dress she had. Of course, it was too tight, but it was clean and pressed. She scrubbed the grim from under her nails and washed her hair till her scalp was sore. Then she started on the sisters. She scrubbed them until they screamed that she was killing them. She curled their hair and dressed them in dresses she got from Goodwill in Roanoke Rapids. The dresses were lacey and covered with bows...suitable for four-year-olds. The sisters giggled and twirled round and round in front of the mirror, and Sara almost didn't hear the car drive into her yard.

But she did hear a car door slam, and she shhh-ed the sisters and sternly told them to calm down. She took each sister by the wrist and walked onto the front porch. Dillon and Jeff got out of the front seat and Dillon opened the back door. Nicey swung her feet onto the ground and stepped out of the car. Sara slowly crossed the porch holding tightly to her sisters' wrists as they clumsily made their way down the front steps. Nicey did not move. Sara's heart sank.

"She must think we look like a bunch of crazies," Sara thought. She wanted to cry. How foolish to have hoped that even a part of John could be back in her life? Sara began to tremble but forced herself to continuing walking toward the car. The sisters had sensed the change in Sara's mood. Sara was afraid. Rebecca began to whimper. Mary pulled back toward the house.

Then suddenly Nicey started walking...first slowly, then quickly toward the three sisters. As she came closer Sara saw John's eyes...John's eyes smiling. And as Nicey got closer the smile grew bigger and brighter. Nicey reached Sara and grabbed her arms.

"Aunt Sara," she cried. "Aunt Sara I'm your niece, Nicey."

Sara released the sisters' wrists and fell into Nicey's arms. Tears of joy streamed down her tired, wrinkled face. The sisters slowly moved closer to Nicey and began cooing and stroking her hair.

"Pretty," they cooed. "Nicey is nice."

Then they began repeating the mantra, "Nicey is nice. Nicey is nice." Nicey drew back from Sara and they all began to laugh.

Jeff and Dillon were reluctant to intrude, so Jeff just called out, "Ah...Nicey, we're off. Call us when you want to be picked up."

Nicey turned and smiled. "I'm okay, Jeff. I'm okay now. I'm with my Aunt Sara."

The End

21375294R10215

Made in the USA
Charleston, SC
15 August 2013